The
Story
of Jane

Catherine Cusset

SIMON & SCHUSTER
New York London Toronto Sydney Singapore

SIMON & SCHUSTER
Rockefeller Center
1230 Avenue of the Americas
New York, NY 10020

Copyright © 2001 by Catherine Cusset

Simon & Schuster and colophon are registered trademarks
of Simon & Schuster Inc.

Designed by Katy Riegel

Manufactured in the United States of America

1   3   5   7   9   10   8   6   4   2

Library of Congress Cataloging-in-Publication Data
Cusset, Catherine, date.
[Problème avec Jane. English]
The story of Jane/Catherine Cusset.
p.cm
I. Title.
PQ2663.U84 P7613 2001
843'.914—dc21   00-054737
ISBN 0-7432-0299-6

Acknowledgments

Thank you, Chuck Adams.

Thank you, Todd Schuster.

to Vlad and Claire

Some days you don't feel even the slightest sadistic joy when you open the door for the neighbor's cat and he gets drenched by the rain suddenly blowing into the foyer.

Jane let the door close and sighed. The weather didn't help. It would get even worse in fifteen minutes if she found no e-mail message from Alex at the office.

The fat gray cat was staring at her with reproachful eyes, as if the rain were her fault.

Her eyes rested on the brown package with the handwritten address; it had been there last night. Next to the package a *New York Times* in its blue plastic wrapping was lying on the floor. Maybe she would take it. A neighbor was probably out of town. In any case, her own newspaper had been stolen often enough, back when she was addicted to her morning dose of reality. This was why she had canceled her subscription.

Earl Grey turned around and faced the door to the hallway, meowing plaintively to be let out of the small foyer and back inside the house. She reintroduced her key in the lock and pushed open the heavy door for him. He disappeared into the stairwell.

Like the cat, she didn't have the courage to throw herself into this windy deluge that would turn her umbrella inside out in less than a minute. She leaned forward to see which of her neighbors hadn't picked up his package yet. She saw her name. Her eyes opened wide. Last night she had been too disturbed by the news of Xavier Duportoy's death to think of checking the name—she never received packages at home anyway. She lifted it. Solid, rectangular and rather heavy—probably a book. Her face brightened. Alex must have gotten her address somehow. After thirteen days of silence he was sending her a gift instead of an e-mail. The handwriting on the envelope, both dancing and well balanced, quick and nervous, looked just like Alex. He used a fountain pen and blue ink—so did she.

Her bad mood was gone. She struggled with the padded envelope, which was both taped and stapled. Some soft gray-brown stuffing fell from the torn paper. Inside was a plain white envelope—this was a well-protected book. She took out a yellow folder. A computer disk slipping onto the floor startled her. Inside the folder was an unbound manuscript. The first page read:

The Story of Jane
a novel

No author's name. On the second page there was a table of contents:

Bronzino, Eric: men in her past. She looked at the brown envelope: no sender's name. The package had been mailed in New York five days earlier, when Alex was still in France. It could not be Alex, of course.

Jane quickly skipped through the first pages. It was about her. About her and Bronzino. Nine years earlier. Someone well informed. Three hundred forty-eight pages. She turned to the end and read the last sentence:

"Downstairs she found the package with the manuscript." She shuddered and looked up. Nothing could be seen through the glass panel but the rain and the water-soaked pink-and-white flowers of the magnolia tree.

She would go to the office later. She had to clear up this unpleasant mystery first. The anonymous sender had chosen his day well—as if the storm, Duportoy's death and Alex's silence at a time when she needed him so badly weren't enough. She picked up the disk on the floor, unlocked the heavy door between the foyer and the hallway, and climbed the three flights of red-carpeted stairs. When she stopped in front of her door, something touched her right ankle. She jumped to the side with a scream. Earl Grey. She laughed nervously and stamped the floor with her foot to make him go away. Once inside, she double-locked her door, took off her raincoat, turned on the chandelier—at barely 1 p.m., in May, it was as dark as evening— and, still standing near the table, started reading.

I. Dinner with Bronzino

I

The windows of Provence were too high for her to peek inside. This was the best restaurant in Old Newport, where Jane saw elegant couples walk in and out on Friday and Saturday night on her way back from the Film Society. She would have liked to eat there tonight. She had almost suggested the place to Bronzino when he phoned her this morning, but it would have been too fancy for a dinner between colleagues, and she couldn't afford it anyway. As she passed the Romulus Café, a short black guy with a beard, whom she had already seen panhandling around campus, turned toward her. "Got a dime?"

She stopped, glad that she didn't have the reflex to say no, and took her wallet out of her bag.

"Actually," the small man said, "we don't need a dime but a dollar. We have ninety cents in coins," he added quickly, "could you change them against a dollar?"

A fat guy hidden in the shadow of a door moved forward, smiling, and handed her the coins in his large open palm. Some of his front teeth were missing. Jane took a bill from her wallet.

"That's fine. I can spare a dollar."

"Thanks!"

They didn't sound very surprised. They walked away. Jane laughed, guessing this was neither the first nor the last bill they got this way tonight. Maybe the first time they really needed a dime.

You should never despair: life was a constant movement of ups and downs, balancing each other in the end. For six years in Chicago she had eaten pasta and lived in dumps shared with other students, places with so little heat during the winter—six months of the year—that she had to sleep in socks and a wool stocking cap. Then came the light at the end of the tunnel, the dazzling offer from Devayne University, even though she wasn't any more intelligent than anyone else and she hadn't even completed her dissertation: a real job, with a real salary, in the best French department in the whole country, on the East Coast, one and a half hours from New York—a dream, the beginning of a glorious life, happiness. She broke up with Josh, the boyfriend she had never really loved, moved to Old Newport, Connecticut, found an elegant and well-heated apartment with high ceilings, moldings, a working fireplace and a splendid hardwood floor made of large oak boards, bought a magnificent rug, a real bed and her first sofa, and started teaching at Devayne, where she had just now spent the worst nine months of her entire life, growing lonelier and more depressed from day to day.

Until three days ago. It seemed that there was no absolute negative: the lower you fell, the higher your spirits could go when pushed by just a tiny little thing. Therefore, the dinner invitation of an older colleague had filled Jane with joy. But it wasn't just any colleague: Norman Bronzino was a very famous critic, the star of their department as well as the director of the important Kramer Center for European Studies, which he had founded. All her fellow students at Northwestern (and Josh particularly) would have been astonished to hear that she was having dinner alone with him.

She arrived in front of the Pearl of Bombay and saw her reflection in the glass door: with the mascara that made her eyes bigger, the brownish lipstick and her styled dark hair falling well on her shoulders, her triangular face had something soft and pleasant in it. An Indian waiter welcomed her with a bow.

"I'm meeting someone."

"A tall gentleman? He is here already."

In the still-empty room, Bronzino had chosen a table as far away as possible from the bay window. He stood up as she walked toward him. He was as tall and thin as her father, and she decided he must be about her father's age, but he looked younger with his thin mustache and short brown hair, which perhaps he dyed. As usual, he was wearing a perfectly ironed shirt, a bow tie, and a classic beige New England tweed jacket, as well as leather shoes with rubber soles—the only thing she didn't find elegant. His hand was warm and he held hers one second longer than necessary. She blushed and asked quickly: "Have you been waiting for long?"

"Not at all. I just got here."

He helped her take off her raincoat and gave it to the waiter, who handed them the menus. They sat down. He suggested they look at the menu first and he took out of his inner jacket pocket a pair of small rectangular glasses that made him look even more dignified.

Jane's stomach gurgled. She had eaten nothing since morning and had spent the whole afternoon cleaning her apartment. The waiter approached their table and poured water into their glasses from a crystal carafe. Jane drank a few sips of icy water and felt her empty stomach react with sharp pain. She put her glass back onto the table and stared at the menu without reading it. A sudden cramp almost made her gasp. This wasn't a hunger pang. She changed position and crossed her legs in the other direction, suddenly feeling pale and horribly tense.

Bronzino, absorbed in his reading, hadn't noticed anything. He closed the menu, took off his glasses and smiled at her. The waiter came to take the order. Jane took the first entrée on the page. It was also the cheapest, barely $7. She had $40 in her wallet but would rather spend only $10.

"Don't you want an appetizer?"

"No, thanks. I'm not very hungry."

He ordered an assortment of appetizers and an entrée of jumbo shrimps tandoori that was the most expensive dish. A man like him, of course, didn't pay attention to prices—the privilege of fame and age. Hopefully one day she too would be able to live without counting pennies. At first, her $30,000 yearly salary (after living on $700 a month for six years, and nothing in the summer) had seemed huge to her. But after taxes, her monthly expenses and the students loans that she had to continue to repay for the next ten years, there wasn't much left.

"Red or white wine? With the seafood I'd prefer white if you don't mind."

"I don't drink, thanks."

Wine on her empty stomach would make her drunk immediately. Bronzino ordered a glass of Chardonnay.

"Nice necklace."

"Thank you. It's from Israel."

"Have you traveled there?"

"No. It's a gift."

She blushed. He smiled. "So, how is your first year among us so far?"

"Wonderful. It's a pleasure to teach such intelligent students. And the library is amazing: I found an original edition of *Madame Bovary* which I could check out for the entire year!"

He nodded modestly, as if she were praising his property. "We're spoiled, that's true."

There was another noisy gurgling that couldn't have escaped Bronzino's hearing. By now Jane's stomach ached terribly.

She examined her fingers. "I should wash my hands. I was at the library, and there is so much dust on the books in the stacks. . . ."

"I think it's near the entrance."

She got up and walked at a normal pace. The door of the women's room was barely closed before she ran to a toilet and fell on the seat. Her liquefied bowels dropped noisily. She tensed, terrified that someone could hear her. She flushed the toilet. The crisis wasn't over yet. Someone else walked in. 6:15. He was probably beginning to look at his watch. This was a marvelous start for a dinner she had been looking forward to for three days—no, for nine months: her first real social outing since she arrived in Old Newport.

What had surprised her most was the absence of social life at Devayne. Professors had fifteen-minute lunches together at Bruno's Pizza, but there were no dinner parties. She expected to become friends with the two other assistant professors hired at the same time she was—Xavier Duportoy and Carrie Martins. The Parisian Duportoy sounded fun and intelligent. Twice she had asked him for coffee and twice he was too busy. In November, at a time when she felt particularly fragile, she remembered that the only way to get rid of that oppressive feeling of loneliness was to go toward other people. She had invited Carrie for dinner. Carrie, a blond and serious young woman who also complained of the lonely and cold atmosphere at Devayne—her husband was finishing a Ph.D. in California—had accepted with such enthusiasm that things had started looking up again. But by canceling at the last minute, with a profusion of apologies but no suggestion for another date, Carrie had left Jane in an even deeper abyss of despair with a veal roast and a tiramisu that could feed ten people.

It was better to spend all evenings at home, working, without any risk of a last-minute change of plans. She couldn't even call her friends in Chicago. None of them had a job yet, so complaining about her lack of social life would have been indecent. Even with Allison it wasn't easy: Allison and John, at age thirty, were starting law school after finishing Ph.D.'s in literature, so they would be able to find jobs in the same city and earn a decent living. In fact, all of her friends were depressed: could it be a generational phenomenon? Or Flaubert's fault? Maybe her father, who couldn't see the point of doing research in literature, was right: literature professors were doomed to sink with the ship. Even Bronzino was a dinosaur. This thought made her smile.

The other woman finally washed her hands and left the restroom. Jane suddenly felt such pain that she thought she was going to faint. There was sweat on her hands, as well as her forehead and above her upper lip. She started moaning and bit her right hand. A second release followed. She felt better. She put her hand inside the metal toilet paper container. It was empty.

She searched her pocket; her elegant pants were just out of the dry cleaners. Not the smallest tissue inside her bag either, and she always usually had a pack with her; just the stupid bottle of whiskey she had bought on the way in case Bronzino came in for a last drink tonight. Since the other woman had dried her hands at the automatic air dryer, the situation seemed hopeless. Tears rose to Jane's eyes; she held them back because of the mascara.

She cautiously opened the stall door and peered outside. She exclaimed with relief when she saw a metal container above the sink, with paper towels inside. It was enough to make her bless the managers of Indian restaurants.

When she returned to the dining room, people were seated at tables near the window. She had been away twenty minutes. Bronzino had been served the appetizers. She was grateful he didn't ask her if she was all right.

"It's delicious. Would you like to taste?"

"Thanks. I'm really not very hungry."

His way of looking at her made her feel ill at ease.

"How old are you?"

"Twenty-eight. Almost twenty-nine."

"So young! All your students must be in love with you."

She laughed, embarrassed, and congratulated herself for choosing the suit with pants rather than the tight black dress.

"I have always thought," Bronzino resumed, "that there is no pedagogy without eroticism. This is not something you can say nowadays in this country, but it seems to me that one learns well only from professors with whom one is in love."

Jane thought of the blond boy who stared at her three hours a week in class with adoring Bambi eyes. During spring break he had sent her a postcard from his hometown. Indeed, he was her best student. But this wasn't something she could tell Bronzino. An older memory came back to her.

"When I was fifteen I fell in love with my French teacher, and in college I took French as my major."

"You see. Did something happen?"

"Something?"

"With your teacher."

"No! She was a married woman and the mother of two children."

"Not a Simone de Beauvoir."

He smiled. She had always seen Bronzino as so cold, reserved and dignified that she had never credited the rumor about a graduate student accusing him of sexual harassment a few years earlier. She wasn't so sure anymore.

"How are you getting along with everyone in the department?" he asked in a more serious tone, while bringing to his lips a piece of vegetable somosa that he had cut delicately. He was chewing discreetly, swallowing elegantly, and never speaking with a full mouth.

"Very well, thank you. Everyone has been really nice. Of course, they are also quite busy. At Devayne it's normal."

"I know. I wanted to have lunch with you for months and it's already April. Time flies by, especially in the spring semester."

He swallowed another bite and there was a silence. Jane silently reviewed the topics she had prepared to discuss just in case. Was it the moment to let him know that she had read all his books and particularly loved *Beauty and Justice?* Such an abrupt compliment might sound artificial.

"What about your new colleagues, Carrie and Xavier?" he asked. "Are you friends with them?"

"We are friendly, but I don't know them well yet."

"Carrie was my student as an undergraduate. She's an extremely bright and sweet young woman. I hope you get to know her better."

"I hope so too. Her schedule is quite hectic right now. Her husband lives in Palo Alto and she commutes there as often as she can."

Bronzino nodded. "That's right. It would be easier if her husband lived here or at least in New York, like Xavier's girlfriend."

"Xavier has a girlfriend in New York? I didn't know that."

"That's how we got him. He had another offer from Harvard. But we're closer to New York."

It went without saying that the Devayne French department was better. Jane smiled.

"Does his girlfriend teach at New York University?"

"No. She's an actress."

"An actress!"

Jane didn't add anything. Bronzino would think she was easily impressed—or interested in Duportoy. She was actually relieved to learn that Xavier's reluctance to socialize with her was nothing personal: he just didn't have the time since he was commuting to New York. A waiter finally took Bronzino's plate away and brought the entrées. Jane was dizzy with hunger. Bronzino ordered a second glass of wine and started on his shrimp. She took a big bite of chicken curry and made a face. The sauce was much too spicy. She could only eat the rice.

"Did you find a nice apartment?" he asked.

"Oh yes. I was really lucky. The first place I saw in July. A first floor, but surprisingly bright. I signed the lease five minutes after entering the place: love at first sight."

She started describing her European-style apartment with enthusiasm, and then stopped abruptly, wondering whether she sounded like she wanted to attract Bronzino there. But he was listening with the same benevolent smile.

"Sounds like a nice place. Is it in a safe neighborhood?"

"On Linden Street, three blocks from campus."

"Good. Did you hear about what happened last Thursday?"

"I know; it's crazy."

A student's mother, visiting for only three days, had taken a bullet in the thigh as she was crossing Central Square, the small park at the center of Old Newport. At four in the afternoon she had accidentally found herself in the middle of a shooting.

"I hope you're careful, Jane."

"I lived for six years in downtown Chicago and nothing ever happened to me. I wasn't even mugged once. I never saw any weapons except at the movies."

"This is no joke, though. Last year a student was murdered on campus, right next to the president's house. Don't go out alone at night. Do you have a car?"

"No. I don't like to drive. It's a shame mostly because I love the sea and you need a car to get to the seaside."

"Yes. The coast is quite picturesque around here. Have you ever been to the national park half an hour away?"

"No."

"Someone should take you there some day."

Was this an invitation? She blushed and took her glass of water. Bronzino's hand reached for his glass at the same moment and brushed hers. His skin was so white and hairless that it was almost obscene. He had long fingers and a large golden ring on the middle finger of the right hand. She thought of asking him what the ring stood for, but the question would be much too personal. He ordered a third glass of wine. A bottle would have been cheaper, she reflected.

"You still don't want anything to drink?"

"No, thank you."

He was looking at her. Her lips and cheeks felt hot and as alive as if he were touching them. She lowered her eyes again.

"So tell me: why Flaubert?"

She looked up with relief. "Because of my father."

"Is he a literature professor too?"

"No! A dentist. He wanted me to go to law school and was furious when I started working on a Ph.D. in French."

"So?"

"I always disappointed him. He wanted a boy so he could teach him how to play baseball on Sundays. He tried with me. I could never catch the ball. He yelled at me because I closed my eyes when the ball got near. The louder he yelled, the more tightly I closed my eyes."

Bronzino smiled. Majoring in French, Jane continued, had been her way to rebel against her father, even though he didn't realize that until it was too late. He had been so strongly against her doing the Ph.D. in

French—a mere waste of time and money—that they had a terrible argument and he didn't give her a penny for six years. When she read *Madame Bovary,* she was struck by Flaubert's irony toward the hypocritical, boring and bourgeois French provinces, which reminded her of the green, conformist suburbs where she grew up and was bored to death. The pragmatic pharmacist Monsieur Homais in *Madame Bovary,* who could never have understood what Emma Bovary was longing for, and who was only trying to achieve some social success, sounded just like her father.

Norman laughed. "It's hard to be a father: children are pitiless. What are you working on exactly?"

"On Flaubert's 'muscled sentences,' on his 'virile'"—she drew quotes—"conception of style as a repression of the soft, the sentimental—of the feminine, one might say."

"Interesting. I actually don't like *Madame Bovary* much. In every sentence you can feel that Flaubert repressed himself, don't you think? Maybe the trouble with him was that he was scared of the woman inside him."

Jane, who loved *Madame Bovary* and was hearing this judgment for the first time, struggled for something to say that wouldn't sound too stupid. Bronzino relieved the pressure as he glanced at his watch.

"We can discuss it more next time; I have to go."

"Sure! I'm done."

The two hours had passed by like two minutes. Her stomach didn't hurt anymore. He had put her very much at ease.

He turned around and waved to the waiter. The room was now full.

Jane anticipated what might follow. "Just five minutes," he would say after parking in front of her house. She should have bought a better Scotch, Chivas Regal or Glenlivet. Careful: he was her hierarchical superior, and he was not married. Fortunately she had never been attracted to older men.

He was looking at something on the other side of the room. Jane turned her head and saw a woman with long, Titian-blond hair and a perfect profile.

"Nice piece," Bronzino said in a connoisseur's voice.

Jane nodded yes, a bit shocked.

"At least a century old."

Jane looked again. Behind the woman a large rug with dark red colors hung on the wall. It gave the room a warm intimacy.

"Do you like rugs?" she asked excitedly.

"I do."

"In September I bought a nineteenth-century Caucasian shirvan with an amazing combination of warm colors, all natural dyes. The purchase was totally unreasonable because I was penniless, but I couldn't resist. It has an amazing effect on me: just looking at it relaxes me."

"As you know, Freud hung Persian rugs all around the room where he listened to his patients."

The short, plump waiter put a black folder in front of Bronzino, who opened it and got hold of the receipt before Jane could say or do anything. He looked for his glasses in his inside jacket pocket and resumed: "I have a Canadian colleague who has such a passion for Persian rugs that he lives, sleeps, eats and works on rugs. So of course he is still single."

"Why?"

"As soon as a woman moves in to his place, she wants to introduce a table or a bed."

Jane laughed. He put on his glasses and started mumbling numbers. "Forty dollars and ten cents, add fifteen percent, that's about six dollars fifty, let's say seven . . ."

His way of reading numbers aloud embarrassed Jane, who wondered whether she should protest and insist on paying her own tiny part of the bill. Or was it more appropriate and more discreet to let him treat her and just to thank him? This was a professional dinner—the department would probably reimburse the bill.

Bronzino looked up and said: "Forty-eight. That's easy: twenty-four each."

Jane's cheeks turned purple. She bent to the left, picked up her handbag, took the two $20 bills out of her wallet and handed them over without looking at him.

"Give me twenty, that's enough. Are you OK?"

"Yes, why?" She forced herself to smile.

"You're red. The meal was good, but heavy. Fresh air will do us good."

The waiter put two small plates in front of them. Bronzino frowned. "We didn't order any dessert."

"On the house. Just to try. Very good."

Jane looked at the sweet milky balls swimming in honey.

"It's nice of them," Bronzino said, "but I'm not hungry anymore either."

She put on her raincoat by herself while Bronzino was counting the change. Outside, he put out his hand for her to shake. "That was very nice, Jane. Let's do it again sometime. Do you want me to drop you somewhere? I have to warn you, my car is parked pretty far."

"Thank you, but it's not necessary. I'm going back to the library."

He didn't insist. She shivered as she watched him quickly walk away. It was cooler now. 8:15: a whole evening ahead and as much desire to prepare her class as to swallow a dozen of those sweet white balls swimming in honey. She would be even lonelier among the students dozing in the library's leather armchairs, or among the truly lonely ones trying to escape their depression at the Romulus Café. She walked slowly along Central Square, on the campus side, better lit than the park side.

"Got a quarter?"

The raucous voice right next to her ear startled her. The beggar was barely visible in the dark, his face half-hidden under his black sweatshirt hood.

"I don't have any change."

She stepped off the sidewalk.

"God bless you anyway! Have a good night!"

A long, loud honk made her jump. The car was zigzagging down the street, already far away. The driver had shouted an insult at her through his open window. With her gray raincoat, she was as invisible as the beggar in the dark. Her legs were trembling when she reached the other side of the street. Suspicious shadows appeared among the trees in the park. She started running. A drop fell onto her nose. Soon another, and then many. She had forgotten her umbrella at the restaurant. Too late to turn around. And it was, of course, a new umbrella.

Jane was puzzled. Photographs snapped by a stranger that evening nine years ago wouldn't have had as much effect as this text. It was like a blow to her. Years had passed, yet she remembered as if it were yesterday that moment when she got home, even more depressed than she was soaked from the rain.

A charming image. Her, moaning with pain on a toilet seat, impressed by every word Bronzino said and obsessed with the price of the meal. Whoever wrote this clearly thought that she had an unresolved Oedipus complex as well as a sexual development arrested at the anal stage.

The author could only be Bronzino. He was in the best position to know all the details about that dinner. It wasn't too difficult to figure out what happened to Jane when she disappeared for so long at the beginning of the meal. Nor was it difficult to guess that she was furious at him for making her pay for half his dinner. He probably didn't care.

So this was why he summoned her to his office yesterday! He was simply curious whether she had received the manuscript. If he sounded so strange, warmer and more emotional than he had been in eight years, it wasn't because of the terrible news he had announced to her but because of the package awaiting her at home.

She got up and called the Center. Nobody answered. Lunchtime. It would be better to go there and confront him. His face, his eyes, would reveal what his voice on the phone could hide.

She looked through the window. The sky was darker and the rain more dense than ever. She would go a little later. She picked up the second chapter.

2

The swimming pool had made her hungry and she had cooked a healthy dinner for herself. She was now dressed in her comfortable green velvet robe and sheepskin slippers, sitting on her beige-and-white-striped sofa and reading Stendhal's *The Red and the Black* again, when the phone rang. She took a quick look at the clock on the mantelpiece: midnight exactly. Josh always waited until eleven in Chicago to get the lowest rate. She knew he would finally call.

She leaned her elbow on the sofa's arm and picked up the receiver.

"Hello?"

"It's me. Is this a good moment to talk?"

He had a dramatic voice. She guessed what he was going to say. She knew him by heart.

"It's OK. Why?"

"I met someone." He paused. "I wanted to let you know. I want to be honest with you."

The words hurt, but her irritation was greater than the pain.

"Who is she?"

"One of my former students. You don't know her. I ran into her at a gallery opening three weeks ago, the day of our last phone call."

"It has been going on for three weeks?"

"Yes. We slept together the night we met."

Jane could imagine her: a plump girl with long curly hair, large glasses and cheap silver earrings, wearing a baggy dress made in India and flat leather sandals.

"I didn't think it would last," Josh continued in an unhappy voice. "I didn't really care. I slept with her only because I was very upset with you that night—and I did it not as a revenge but as a way to get rid of the bad energy after our argument. I never thought it would get serious. But I'm getting attached to her."

Josh's devout honesty was irritating—as if the movements of his bowels (or of his soul) were of any interest to others.

"So what do you want to do now?"

"I don't know. I guess it depends on you."

"On me?"

"You know I love you. If things work out between us, I'll break up with Stephanie."

Stephanie. The name suddenly evoked another image: a thin and silly girl with blond braids, giggling at every word Josh said. Could he have made up the whole thing just to try and make her fly to Chicago? No. The drama in his voice was too real.

"I don't like this 'if' very much," she said coldly. "It sounds like blackmail to me. You know what? It's already after twelve. I'm tired and I teach tomorrow. I was going to bed just when you called. Let me sleep on it, we'll talk later."

She was very calm when she hung up. An undergraduate student who had a crush on Josh wasn't going to give her a headache. The whole thing was so clichéd.

Josh had surprised her only once: when he landed in Old Newport eleven months ago. It hadn't been easy to persuade him to come and visit her for the weekend, when Jane had called him just after her dinner with Bronzino. She hadn't talked to Josh for nine months and she had been pretty brutal when she left Chicago in July. But, as expected, he had yielded. So he had rung her doorbell at 8 P.M. on May 2 and this was when the surprise happened. He wasn't any taller; he still had the same dark frizzy hair, impossible to comb; he still wore the same wrinkled black jacket and old Hard Rock Café tee-shirt. But she had forgotten what a friend looked like. She was even more surprised at the end of dinner three hours later, when he asked her:

"What's happened to you, Jane?"

"What do you mean?"

"All you talk about is Devayne, Bronzino, your dissertation, publishing. Don't you have a life?"

She was going to retort that she certainly had more of a life than a broke student, but she burst into tears instead.

Josh slept on the sofa bed in the living room. In the morning he wanted to go to the beach. She smiled at his naïveté: there was only an industrial zone near the sea in Old Newport, beaches were miles away and you couldn't get there without a car. Two hours later they were on the beach, in Woodmont Park. A twenty-minute bus ride from downtown Old Newport and 75 cents for a ticket. In her ten months at Devayne she hadn't found out about that bus, because nobody she knew ever took the bus. Woodmont Park beach wasn't the nicest beach in the world—the gray sand looked like dust and there were no waves because of Long Island Sound—but it was the sea: big, open, blue, and sparkling with sun.

It was Josh's turn to talk: he thanked her for her tough words when she had left Chicago in July. He really needed a kick in the butt. He had spent three months working like crazy, doing copy-editing in the morning, working as a research assistant in the afternoon and delivering pizza at night. He hadn't written a single line of his dissertation and hadn't gone to the Modern Language Association Convention. In November he had left for Eastern Europe and spent three months traveling there. He landed in Berlin on the day the Berlin Wall came down: "hundreds of thousands" of people were dancing and singing in the streets and on the Wall. Jane, a precise person, smiled at his little exaggerations, but she was impressed and his enthusiasm was contagious. "History, Jane, with a capital *H.*" Something he would tell his grandchildren one day.

This trip certainly sounded like more fun than her life at Devayne. She was imagining places with exotic names. He spoke with strong indignation about Romania, at the eastern end of Europe, a country ruled by a crazy dictator and his family for over forty years. To build a palace to his glory and a huge avenue leading to his palace in the center of the capital, Bucharest, the megalomaniac tyrant had wiped out three entire neighborhoods full of houses dating back to the seventeenth and eighteenth centuries and of Orthodox churches that were little jewels. The palace was so huge that you needed more than an hour to walk around it. Everything inside was marble and gold. Elena Ceauşescu, the dictator's wife, was so ignorant that she even requested the stucco decorations to be made of marble. "Why? What are they made of usually?" Jane asked. Josh burst into laughter. "You're kidding me: of stucco!" People in Bucharest hated the palace. Josh didn't find it so ugly, but this was an opinion you couldn't express without offending the deepest feelings of Romanians.

"This guy, Ceauşescu, was King Ubu, really. But this is not literature. It cost the lives of thousands of people. The revolutionaries arrested him and his wife in December, tried them very quickly and shot both of them."

They were walking on the beach, barefoot, and sometimes dipping their toes into the still-icy water. He spoke of a Romanian woman, Dora.

"Were you in love?"

"No, but sexually it was fantastic. Women in the East do amazing things!"

"Like what?"

He laughed. "I would lie on my back and she would sit on top of me and place herself just above my cock, which she would make go in and out of her at a very fast pace. . . . It was incredibly exciting."

Jane blushed. She felt like leaving for a long trip, having a romantic affair in the Balkans in the middle of a revolution. The sensation of the cold sand between her toes and under her feet was pleasant. First, though, she had to finish her dissertation, as was stipulated in her contract with Devayne.

"You would love Prague: the city is full of yellow Baroque palaces and tiny streets paved with cobblestones. Do you know how they say 'thank you' in Czech? 'Dick'! Actually it's *diky,* as a contracted form for *děkuju,* but you pronounce it 'dick.'"

At sunset they were kissing. They spent Sunday in Manhattan, walking in Central Park with thousands of New Yorkers out on that first real spring day, and seeing an exhibit at the Museum of Modern Art. Then they walked down Fifth Avenue to Greenwich Village and Jane took him to a Chinese restaurant on Sixth Avenue. They slept through the train ride back to Old Newport. Josh was gone when Jane awoke on Monday morning—deliciously happy: a great weekend, and she was no longer alone.

In June, Josh had flown back to Old Newport with his books and his computer. They spent the summer working on their dissertations and taking the bus to Woodmont Park beach in the afternoon, when it was hot.

She didn't need to make love at the end of the long days. She would have agreed with Proust that a glass of fresh orange juice—or a swim in the sea—was more desirable on hot days than another sweating body. But she couldn't say no all the time. When they made love, she asked him not to touch her belly or her hips: it tickled her; not to suck or even lick her nipples: it hurt. Her extreme sensitivity, Josh said, was a sign of a sensuality that would blossom one day, maybe when she turned thirty-five, the peak sexual age for a woman. "Is it, really?" she had asked sarcastically.

In mid-July he started writing a novel. He had been thinking about it for a long time. He had just found the voice. He was delighted.

"What is it about?"

"A love story."

"Between a Northwestern graduate student and a Devayne professor?"

"Novelists never invent anything, you know; it's all transposition and condensation. Of course, I'm inspired by our story. But that's only the flesh. To write a great novel, you need a bone first, a great idea. I got it."

"What is it?"

"Hubris."

"What?"

"That's what the Greeks called an excess of pride and self-confidence, always punished by the goddesses of vengeance, the howling Erinyes."

"I know that. So?"

"It means that you can never be too happy in life or the Erinyes strike you. It's as if humility was a mathematical law of life. Haven't you noticed? Each time you're overconfident, it's almost a guarantee of failure. I'm writing about an enthusiastic guy who learns humility little by little."

If this law was applied to his novel, his own enthusiasm guaranteed its failure. She didn't say anything. In her view it was just another way to procrastinate and to avoid facing his responsibilities. He would do better to finish his dissertation on the sublime and look for a real job. But it was not her business. He was getting on her nerves. He systematically used the wrong bowl for his cereal or the bread knife to cut a grapefruit; he disturbed her when she was working by crossing her room to get some water in the kitchen or by whistling in the shower; even worse, he dared to use her towel.

The worst, though, was when he started psychoanalyzing her: "The trouble with you is that you don't like your body and you refuse to be a woman: that's why you've never had an orgasm. You don't know how to relax."

"That's not true at all. Just not during intercourse, that's all."

"But that's the best! You don't know what you're missing. I'm sure it's because of your father."

"What's that?"

"You told me he wanted a son, or at least that's what you think. Anyone who has a father like yours should see a shrink, anyway."

"This father of mine, by the way, took you to a very nice restaurant in Chicago and you let him pay. I don't think you should insult him."

By the end of the summer, it tickled her in anyplace he put his hand. She didn't want to kiss him either. She only tolerated his fingers on her clitoris. She would close her eyes, forget about him, and then, maybe, come. These rare times, she allowed him inside her afterward. He was so excited that he came in barely a minute.

The night before Josh's departure, she cried. She made him promise that he would never abandon her. She then calmed down and they had a serious conversation about their relationship. It was love, or they wouldn't still be together after six years, especially after breaking up once already. It was reassuring to hear this simple, logical reasoning. Maybe he was right—maybe she was critical of him only because she couldn't accept herself, because of her father. Josh told Jane that she shouldn't attach so much importance to sex: it wasn't the most meaningful thing in love; it came and went. He was frustrated with all her restrictions, but still, there was no other woman to whom he wanted to make love more. What really mattered anyway was the mental space she gave him: he could write his novel when he lived with her, which meant he could live with her all his life. He only wished that she could have more fun.

"I'm like that. It's not my fault."

"I know. I don't blame you."

That was almost seven months ago. Since then, they had seen each other only once, for Christmas, in Chicago. The department had paid for her plane ticket and hotel room because she was part of the committee hiring a twentieth-century specialist. She had spent five days locked up in a room interviewing candidates and discussing them with her colleagues; they finally chose a young woman who had written a thesis on Simone de Beauvoir's bisexuality, Natalie Hotchkiss. Josh, however, had plenty of time; he had only one interview in spite of the new additions to his curriculum vitae and his travels in Eastern Europe, which definitely made him look more interesting than all the depressed graduate students buried in their studies. She knew what the problem was: the case of a dossier that had been around for too long. After a while, everyone knew that this was someone nobody wanted to hire. The law of desire—it made him even less desirable.

Josh was furious that Jane didn't get him an interview with De-vayne—some good friend she was! She told him he had to finish his dissertation: an important factor these days. After five very tense days, he confessed to her that he had writer's block and that he was seeing a shrink once a week. Jane softened. How was the novel going? He had put it aside. They had a nice walk along the lake, the last day, enhanced by strangely warm weather. The water was a clear blue-green, the ice melting everywhere. That night they made love. They planned to see each other during spring break; he would fly to Old Newport.

He had called her in late February: he was replacing a pregnant woman at a publishing company and he couldn't come. Could she fly to Chicago instead?

That wasn't the plan. She didn't want to stay in Josh's apartment, with the roommates. She said that she had too much work.

"Make an effort. Don't be selfish."

"Selfish? Who flew to Chicago last time? I can't buy tickets all the time, I'm not that rich!"

"The department paid for you at Christmas! You earn a normal salary and you know very well I don't. I paid for the trip twice last year."

"With the American Express vouchers it's only eighty-nine dollars for a round trip. I'm not a student anymore. I pay more than three hundred dollars, and I don't earn all that much, by the way."

"You're so cheap, Jane!"

"Cheap? Who paid in the restaurant in Chicago? Did you give me any money last summer for groceries or bills?"

"You know I'm broke! That's why I need this job at the publishing house!"

"Don't say I'm cheap, then."

That had been their last conversation, before tonight. Tonight's conversation was just as petty—his blackmailing her with a twenty-year-old.

The problem, though, wasn't that girl, nor who paid what.

Working changed you. This was the actual etymological meaning of "adult": someone who had changed. She was teaching a graduate seminar for the first time. Every week before her seminar she had stomach cramps, and she repeatedly had the classic nightmare of facing the students without having anything to say. Josh would have said such fear was infantile. What was infantile, though, was his ideal of Freedom with a capital *F.*

A few days passed and Josh still hadn't called back. She wondered whether she had offended him by telling him she was going to bed as if she didn't care about his sleeping with someone else. Maybe she should call him now. But then he would think she was dependent on him. That probably was what he wanted to show her by making her jealous.

Josh was so annoyingly didactic, she reflected as she walked into Bruno's Pizza after her graduate seminar. She immediately noticed Bronzino and another professor, Edwin Sachs, at a table near the entrance. Bronzino wasn't eating pizza but a real lunch—beef and mashed potatoes with gravy. As she passed the table, he quickly looked up and smiled. Of course, he would never ask her to join them. At Devayne there was no familiarity between senior and junior professors. Since their evening together one year ago, they had only exchanged a few hellos in the corridors or at the department's cocktail parties. He was perfectly nice and reserved with her, as with everyone, which was to be expected from a man whose ambition, she heard, was to become the president of Devayne. But she knew that he was attracted to her, because she often met his eyes when she looked at him during the lectures or faculty meetings and he immediately turned his head away. He was probably too scared—of gossip, of damaging his career, and of his own desire—to go forward. Not her problem. As Allison said, there was nothing to expect from a fifty-five-year-old bachelor who was still living with his mother and who, on top of everything else, was cheap.

She ordered her pizza. While she waited at the counter, she looked around, hoping Carrie would be there. She recognized the bald head of her colleague James Copland. He was eating alone and grading papers. Xavier Duportoy was there too, at a small table in a corner farther away. The place was almost an annex to the French department. Across from

Xavier sat a woman dressed in black. Jane saw only her back—her thin waist, long neck, and pale blond hair tied in a bun. The actress? Xavier gestured energetically as he talked, his tall body leaning toward and almost over the woman. The pizza was ready. Jane paid for her slice and ordered a Coke. When she took her tray and looked for a seat, the couple had left.

"Professor Cook! Do you want to sit with us?"

The invitation came from a Korean woman who was taking Jane's graduate seminar on Flaubert. Jane was glad to join her. Miran introduced her companion, Kathryn Johns, a first-year graduate student in the department. Jane recognized the blond woman who had been sitting with Xavier just a moment earlier. Her face was as beautiful as her pale hair and long neck had promised. Kathryn immediately said that she was sorry not to be able to take Professor Cook's seminar, which, she heard, was excellent. Unfortunately, she had a scheduling conflict. Her affected politeness, perfect self-control and cold smile made Jane ill at ease. "I'm sure you've read Flaubert already," she replied in a friendly voice.

"I was just telling Kathryn," Miran said, "that I have never been so depressed in my life as I have since I got here as a graduate student. Sometimes, at night, it's so heavy that I'm paralyzed for hours."

"The same with me!" Jane exclaimed. "The worst is always at dusk. Then in the morning, I'm fine. Do you think it's because of Devayne? What about you?"

She turned toward Kathryn, who shook her head. "It never happens to me. I've not been depressed since I got married."

"You're married!"

She noticed the thin gold ring on Kathryn's left hand, with its long and perfectly oval-shaped white nails.

"But her husband lives in L.A.," Miran said. "It's not exactly next door."

"What does he do there?"

"He makes films," Kathryn replied.

"Films!"

That night, Jane couldn't fall asleep. She would close her eyes and see Kathryn Johns, her long neck, her face with its symmetrical features and her cold smile, which held something ironic and judgmental. It was obvious that she would never take Jane's seminar.

Finally, Jane got up. In the living room she turned on the light and dialed Josh's number; it was 2:15, only 1:15 in Chicago. The roommates never went to bed before 1 anyway. Someone picked up the phone. There was a sleepy sound in the receiver.

"It's me, Jane."

"Oh, hi," Josh whispered. "Anything wrong?"

"I just wanted to talk to you."

"Not now. I'll call you tomorrow."

He hung up. Stephanie now seemed very real. Jane sat there and stared at her rug without seeing it, until the phone startled her one hour later. She picked it up. "Josh?"

The line went dead. Jane waited for a few minutes. She realized she was trembling with cold. She got up and walked to the window. There was a man sitting on the steps of a brownstone right across the street. A lamppost nearby lit his white shirt and a brown paper bag from which he was drinking. His face was difficult to make out in the shadows. It was rather chilly to be wearing only a shirt. The man seemed to be looking in her direction. Hers was probably the only window lit on the whole block, and her curtains were almost transparent. She stepped backward, turned off the light and went back to bed.

It was barely 7 A.M. when she opened her eyes. At 10:30 she dialed Josh's number. Nobody home. She called the publishing company and dialed his extension. He picked up the phone and didn't sound cheerful when he recognized her voice. Maybe he had gone to the office on Saturday just to avoid her call.

"Sorry I didn't call you back yet, there was a lot of work here," he said in a tired voice. "Jane," he added hesitantly, "you can't call me at home so late."

"Was Stephanie with you?"

"Yes. I told her it was a wrong number, but she isn't stupid. We spent the whole night talking. She wants me to commit myself or she'll break up right now. It's understandable. She loves me and she's scared of getting hurt."

Jane felt like crying. As if she cared about Stephanie! Josh sighed.

"I have to give her a clear answer by tonight."

"I see. So you have to break up with me now and you didn't have the guts to call and tell me this."

"Someone just walked in. I'll call you tonight."

Could he really abandon her after six years, for a twenty-year-old with whom he'd had a three-week affair? The girl must have cried and Josh was weak. A needy girl is often attractive to an insecure man. Tonight she would promise to fly there as soon as classes ended. Maybe she could invite him to the August cruise in France; she was allowed to take her boyfriend along.

She was sitting on her beige-and-white striped sofa, biting her nails—on her knees lay an open book of which she hadn't read a single line—when the expected ringing startled her at nine.

"It's me. Sorry for this morning." Josh's voice was awfully sad.

"No problem. Do you want me to call you back?"

It was well intended but sounded once more as though she wanted to show him she had money and he didn't.

"No, that's OK."

"So, have you been thinking?" she asked in a falsely casual voice.

"I love you."

She tensed.

"I have been thinking all day long. I choose Stephanie."

"Why?" she cried.

"You can't make up your mind. I don't think you know what you want."

"Yes I do! I want to be with you. I have been thinking today too. I want you, Josh." She didn't manage to pronounce the words "I love you."—"You can't leave me; you promised. We love each other—you said so. You said that there was no other woman you liked to make love to more than me. You said that with me you could write your novel!"

She burst into tears. Josh didn't say anything.

"I'll come to Chicago this weekend."

"No, Jane. No. You have to understand: it's over."

"But I love you!"

She had never loved him so much.

She cried for a long time after hanging up, then finally fell asleep. She was running after Bronzino in downtown Chicago without stopping at traffic lights and cars were honking at her furiously when she suddenly woke up: the phone. She ran to the living room.

She was genuinely surprised—and disappointed—to recognize Josh's voice. In her semisleep, she had expected it would be Bronzino.

"Did I wake you?"

"I guess so. I was dreaming. What time is it?"

"Four. Sorry. I can't sleep: I'm thinking about you all the time," he said in the same tearful voice as seven hours before. "I love you. I can't stand the idea of your being unhappy. I thought of a solution: what if I divided myself between Stephanie and you until you're happy? Or do you want me to break up with her? I will, if you ask me to."

He would never have suspected that she could fall asleep and dream of Bronzino just after he broke up with her.

"No, Josh. Stick with your decision. It was right. It's as you said: I can't make up my mind. Don't worry about me. I'll be fine."

"Are you sure?"

"Yes. You should go to sleep."

"I'll call you tomorrow to see how you're doing."

"No. It's over, Josh. Don't call me anymore."

She hung up, turned around and looked through the window with the strange feeling that she was being watched. The same guy was there again on the steps of the house across the street, this time wearing a leather jacket. She still couldn't see his face. He suddenly made an inviting gesture at her, pointing to his cigarette. So he *was* watching her. Jane stepped back immediately. What did he want? To sell her pot? She made sure the windows were well locked and turned off the light.

She went back to bed and replayed her conversation with Josh. So that was that. A clean break. It didn't really hurt. She felt nothing but the vague fear of now being under anesthesia, only to wake up later and find out that she had been mutilated in her sleep.

Jane smiled. The author of this piece wasn't Bronzino. Petty revenge, signed "Josh." She should have thought about him at once. He had read Freud, he thought that she hadn't resolved her Oedipus complex. Thinking back, she realized he could easily have written the first chapter too, since she had told him everything about the dinner with Bronzino.

It was so much like Josh to use their relationship as material for his novel. Finally he was able to control Jane by constructing her as a character. She could picture him, hanging up after a painful conversation, crying, full of self-pity, and feverishly taking notes for The Novel. He must have been taking notes to remember tiny details such as the guy across the street who was watching Jane and who had scared her.

Poor Josh—if this was the novel he had been writing for years.

He probably hadn't had too many experiences in recent years if he could remember in such detail a relationship of which Jane had almost no memory now. Who would be interested in a flat love affair between an assistant professor and a graduate student? It might be better if he showed some humor at least, instead of taking himself so seriously.

Maybe he was hoping to achieve some success by including Bronzino's name to provoke a scandal. But who was Bronzino in the vast world?

She looked at the brown envelope on the table. The handwriting was very different from Josh's, which she remembered to be big and curly. He must have asked someone else to write the address.

The package had been mailed in New York. She got up, walked two steps toward the wooden table near the stove, and dialed the Manhattan information number. She was lucky: an operator answered at once.

"Joshua Levine," Jane said.

There was one minute of silence. Jane heard the woman typing.

"I have five Joshua Levines and six J. Levines. Do you know the address?"

"No."

"Do you want all of them?"

"No, thanks."

She stood motionless near the phone. She wasn't even sure that Josh lived in New York. If he did, it could be in the less expensive boroughs of Brooklyn or Queens. Or maybe he was just subletting a room or sharing an apartment, and wasn't listed. She had to find a faster way to get his number. Through Allison? She and Josh had been good friends in graduate school. Maybe they had stayed in touch.

It was 1:50 p.m., 10:50 a.m. in Seattle. She picked up the receiver again, opened her phone book, and dialed Allison's office number. Allison's recorded professional voice answered: "I'm either on the phone or away from my desk. Please leave a message after the tone, and I'll call you back as soon as possible."

"It's Jane. Could you call me back this morning? I'm home. Thanks."

Before sitting again and resuming her reading, she glanced through the window to the left of the stove; it was still pouring outside.

3

As she stepped out of Macy's, the sun made her squint. On a hot day like this, she would be better off swimming in Woodmont Park than shopping at Macy's. Fortunately, the store would close by the end of the week, maybe even tomorrow. There was nothing left to buy. Since the liquidation sale had reached 80 percent off the marked price—which was already a sale price—the department store looked like an army barracks in wartime. The fourth, third, and second floors had closed one after another. The leftovers had been squeezed into a space that covered only half the first floor and was surrounded by yellow tape like the kind used by police at crime scenes.

She stopped at the traffic light before crossing Main Street and suddenly saw Bronzino coming from the other side of Government Street. He was walking fast, his eyes on the ground, absorbed in his thoughts. He was wearing a long-sleeved white shirt and a blue bow tie, and carrying his jacket folded on his right arm. Jane smiled. She had known she would run into him one of these days. Just as Macy's was closing: perfect timing. There was a whole summer ahead.

In April, a few weeks after she had broken up with Josh, a visiting French professor had taken her to dinner at the elegant restaurant Amici. He had made her taste excellent wines and done most of the talking, explaining the French education system to her, how its elite schools produced brilliant people like himself and were terribly damaging for those who failed. He protested loudly when Jane took her wallet out of her bag after the maître d' brought the bill: "Please. Don't be ridiculous," he said.

Jane felt much more ridiculous fifteen minutes later when the short, bald and plump Frenchman, who was forty-two years old, but looked at least fifty, tried to kiss her on her doorstep. He was married and the father of four little children whose pictures he had shown her over dinner, and she felt so little attraction to him that she hadn't thought there was the slightest ambiguity between them.

He awkwardly tried again, before exclaiming with a strong French accent: "You must find me ridicu*lous!*"

"Not at all," Jane protested, blushing. "It's very flattering, but . . . I have a boyfriend in Chicago, I'm not available."

He walked away without a word, and never talked to Jane again during his few remaining weeks at Devayne.

This was how Jane realized that she still liked Bronzino, in spite of his absentminded way of making her pay for half his own dinner. She had started wondering whether she wasn't the one who had unconsciously kept him at a distance all this time.

He was right in front of her now, but he hadn't noticed her yet.

"Hi, Norman."

He looked up. His face brightened. "Jane! How are you?" He stopped.

She rested her heavy Macy's bags on the ground between her legs. Her arms were tired already. "Fine, thank you. Glad to be on vacation. Congratulations! I'm delighted that you'll be our chairman next year."

He nodded graciously. "Thank you. Have you been shopping?"

"Yes. It's the very last days. Macy's will close at the end of the week. Maybe even tomorrow."

"Macy's?"

"You mean you don't know? They filed for bankruptcy two months ago! There have been huge liquidation sales. Great deals. Look."

She opened one of the bags and extracted a transparent plastic envelope containing something blue and green. "A Ralph Lauren flannel comforter cover. Queen size. Used to be a hundred and ten dollars. I got it for eight."

He made an appreciative face. His eyes followed her movements as she put the comforter cover back inside the bag.

"How many did you buy?" he asked in a surprised voice.

She laughed. "Five. For gifts. At this price I couldn't resist. Plus I always have a fear of not having enough."

He smiled, then sighed. "It's so sad that Macy's is closing. This city won't look any better. More jobless people. It was such a charming place thirty years ago."

"How did this happen?" Jane asked in a serious tone.

"The recession, and a big mistake in urban planning, in the sixties: they built a highway through the city and all these horrible concrete buildings, the mall on Main Street, Macy's, parking lots. Middle-class families moved to the suburbs. It killed downtown Old Newport."

She shook her head sadly. Fortunately he didn't know that Macy's bankruptcy had been the most exciting event in her second spring at Devayne. Going there every afternoon for more than a month now had given a purpose to her days. As soon as she left her apartment, she was already smiling with anticipation. Ready for hunting. There was an extraordinary pleasure in searching through piles of clothes, buying, accumulating, and getting great deals. She had bought a fake fur coat for twenty bucks when it was 90 degrees outside, a cashmere sweater, designer suits and shirts, sport shoes and snow boots, a Donna Karan New York long evening gown in black silk embroidered with pearls that would be perfect for the cruise, satin bed linen that kept slipping unpleasantly, and all kinds of bizarre and useless objects that now filled her only closet. A lot of fun for barely $300.

"How about some coffee?" she suggested.

Her apartment was not far from there. She could even invite him home. He would help her carry her bags and then she would serve him tea or coffee on the balcony outside her bedroom, using the Royal Doulton porcelain cups she had just purchased for $3 each, with matching plates.

"I'd love to, Jane." He looked at his watch. "Unfortunately, I have lots of errands to do before five."

"What about lunch next week?"

"But I'm leaving for Paris tomorrow."

"Really! For how long?"

"A month."

"Lucky you! Will you be back here in July?"

She had made no plans for the summer except for the cruise in August.

"No, I'm going directly to Nantucket. I have a book to finish and it's more quiet there."

"Do you have a house in Nantucket?"

"A small house. My mother gave it to my brother and me. My nephews will visit, which is nice. Jane, I have to run. Have a good summer."

He was already crossing Main Street, walking fast.

"Bon voyage!" she yelled.

He didn't turn. He probably didn't hear her. She continued walking along Central Square. The bags were really heavy. Why did she buy these five flannel comforter covers? And these porcelain cups, when mugs were so much more convenient? Plus all these designer clothes she would never wear?

The handle of one of the bags broke. She grunted with anger. She could barely carry the broken bag in her arms, while the other pulled painfully on her right hand. As she crossed the street, a teenager laughed. The white courthouse glowing under the sun like a Greek temple made her feel even hotter. There were no trees or shade. She was sweating. What was the matter with her? He was her boss, twice her age, and twice now he had told her no. Wasn't that clear enough?

A week later she turned thirty. July went by quickly. Jane was busy writing her first article as well as an application for a fellowship that would allow her to spend her fourth year in Paris. She liked Old Newport best when it was empty, hot and humid. Sometimes she took the bus to Woodmont Park. By now she recognized some people on the bus: the old lady with a wooden cross pinned to her jacket, carrying heavy plastic bags filled with clothes, and the deaf old man with a cane who leaned toward her to whisper that he had been a Devayne professor before the FBI had forced him to retire. The black and Hispanic teenagers sat in the back as if there were still segregation laws. People on the bus seemed to be wondering what this well-dressed young white woman, with no visible handicap, was doing among them alone.

She bought a TV and a VCR. Evenings at home felt cozy as she sat on her comfortable sofa in front of her small Sony and her exquisite rug and watched films she had borrowed for free from the Devayne Film Center. She would never meet anyone in Old Newport. Her father, with his customary tact, had recently sent her an article saying that the chances of finding a man got more and more rare from year to year after age thirty, especially for women with Ph.D.'s. Something in her life had to change before it was too late.

"Move to New York," Allison had suggested. Susie said the same. But in New York for twice the price of her Linden Street apartment she would only get a dark hole full of cockroaches in a bad neighborhood. You had to find a lawyer to be able to afford New York, someone like Tony, her sister's boyfriend. Susie and Tony had organized a dinner party for her with two single lawyers, and the cute one had immediately mentioned a new girlfriend. Lawyers bored her anyway. Her only hope was in getting that fellowship and spending next year in Paris. She should be able to get it without too much difficulty. Carrie and Xavier had both been granted that same fellowship for the coming year. Carrie would spend the year in Palo Alto, and Xavier in Paris, with his girlfriend, the actress.

On August 4 she left for France.

A woman working for the Devayne alumni had called her in April and invited her to travel for free along with a group of alumni, to Paris for two days and to Bourgogne and Provence for ten days on a boat with a fairy-tale name, *La Comtesse de Bourgogne*. The brochure with pictures of French villages had made Jane daydream, as well as the dazzling price of the trip: $7,500, or three times her monthly salary before taxes. In exchange for the free trip, Jane only had to give three short lectures and to socialize with the alumni at lunch and dinner. It would be her first luxury trip and her first journey to France in nine years.

"Maybe you'll meet a millionaire," her father had said.

"Sure, an eighty-year-old man."

"Then you would be a rich widow."

Typical of her father. But the thought had crossed her mind after she heard of a middle-aged art history professor who, on a cruise with the Devayne alumni on the Amazon River two years earlier, had met a millionaire with a huge estate in Virginia. He had given her a helicopter as a wedding gift for her commute to Devayne, since she didn't want to stop teaching.

On August 5, Jane checked in at the Ritz Hotel on the Place Vendôme. She had never seen such a beautiful hotel. On a low marble table in her suite she found a basket with a bottle of champagne, exotic fruit and a handwritten welcome card from the hotel's director, personally addressed to her. The bathroom entirely made of gold and marble would have pleased the wife of the Romanian tyrant. There was a Jacuzzi in the bathtub. Her room overlooked the Place Vendôme, glowing under the rain. It rained uninterruptedly for two days. The second day she had to wake up at 7:30 in the morning, 1:30 at night her time, after three hours of sleep in her luxurious room at $800 a night, to give her first talk during breakfast to the old alumni, who all looked perfectly fresh and awake and assailed her with questions afterward about the French Impressionists, about whom they knew more than Jane. The third day, after a TGV train ride to Lyon, they boarded *La Comtesse de Bourgogne.* Quite a surprise: it wasn't a French boat but a German one. All the waiters and maids spoke German. It was like being in occupied France during the war, some of the alumni who had been at the landing in Normandy said with good humor. The chef was German, too. Nothing would deter the alumni—neither the tasteless sauces covering every dish with which they declared themselves enchanted, nor the tiny cabins where you could barely turn around, nor the incessant rain. They were delighted about everything and all of them were in love with Jane. They were eager to know when it would be their turn to sit at her table.

Her only escape was the boat deck, quite empty since it rained all the time. This was where she met the doctor, a blond and handsome young German who was free to sit wherever he liked in the dining room for lunch and dinner. That was where Jane had noticed him—the only young man aboard—in the company of a blond woman with rather common features. On a rainy afternoon, as they were leaning against the railing, looking at the very green trees on the embankment, he confirmed what she had suspected already: he had married the blond woman eight years before because she was pregnant, only two months after they met. In Catholic and conservative Bavaria, an abortion was out of the question. His wife, then a nineteen-year-old literature student, had dropped her studies. Now they had three children. He had given up his dream of doing an internship in a large hospital in a city like Hamburg or Berlin. He had become a generalist in his hometown, Eichstätt.

On the next-to-last day, as they were sitting on wet chairs on the deck just after a rain shower, with the sun starting to shine feebly, a bee got stuck in Jane's hair. The insect was buzzing against her ear. She froze and moaned with fear. Dieter extended his hand and delicately freed the bee. She could feel his fingers slightly trembling. She blushed. He was looking at his index finger.

"Oh no! Did you get stung?"

"It's nothing," he said with his lovely German accent.

She saw his watch. "Five past four! My lecture!"

She ran downstairs. Everyone was already waiting for her in the grand salon. The doctor's wife, seated in the last row, stared at Jane. The doctor walked in one minute later and sat next to his wife. When the talk was over, as the doctor was nowhere to be seen, Jane ran after his wife.

"Is your husband all right?"

The woman stopped. "Why?"

"He was stung by a bee that got stuck in my hair. That's why we were late."

The woman turned pale and walked away without a word before Jane could add anything. That night, before dinner, the organizer of the trip, the fifty-year-old woman who had recruited Jane, knocked at the door of her cabin.

"The doctor's wife just had a nervous breakdown."

"But I didn't do anything."

The woman smiled. "I know that. She's very sensitive. Probably since she's pregnant."

"She's pregnant?" Jane cried.

"Didn't you know? That's why she stays in her cabin all the time: she feels nauseous. You know what you could do for her? Don't talk to her husband today or tomorrow. I know it's not your fault," she added quickly since Jane was blushing again, "but it's easy to understand why she's jealous. Here you are free, successful, independent, and beautiful, while she's stuck with three kids and a fourth on the way."

The night of her return to Old Newport, Jane was thrilled to step into the brownstone house where her apartment was. Home, finally. Her place, much nicer than the tiny cabin on the boat, or even the luxurious room at the Ritz. She wouldn't keep any memories from that trip. It was nothing but a bizarre tangent without any relation to the rest of her life, an absurd waste of time. She had seen nothing of France, hadn't developed any real relationships. She had managed only to make a pregnant German woman jealous. Well, that was something. It had never occurred to her that her life could be an object of envy.

She emptied her mailbox and skipped through the bills, ads, and account statements. A lot of junk mail, but not a single postcard or letter from a friend. She hadn't written any either. She inserted her key in the upper lock and, turning it to the right, met resistance. The lock was open. Her heart started beating fast. She knew what that meant. She had heard many stories of apartments being broken into in Old Newport, mostly in August. Hers was on the first floor. In the spring, after noticing the guy who was watching her at night, she had thought of getting a better lock and insurance. Of course, it had remained a thought. She struggled nervously with the lower lock, panicking and trying to remind herself that material goods could always be replaced and that she had backup files of her work at the office. She took a deep breath and pushed the door open.

The living room looked as clean and orderly as she had left it. Her rug was still lying on the floor in front of the fireplace. The TV and VCR were still standing on the small table next to the bookshelves. She quickly walked to the bedroom. The computer and printer on her desk hadn't moved. She opened the chest of drawers. Everything was in place. She was lucky. She had probably been distracted the morning when she left.

A week later, as she was walking into Goldener Library on a sunny Sunday afternoon, she almost bumped into Norman Bronzino, who was walking out.

"Hi!" they said at the same time, with voices expressing pleasant surprise.

Sun-tanned and in a pair of Ray Bans, he looked younger—barely fifty. His light brown jacket and the blue Oxford shirt fit him well. No bow tie.

"How was your summer?" she asked.

"Good, quite busy."

He was holding the heavy wooden door for her.

"I'm not in a hurry: I don't mind walking with you, if you like," she proposed.

"Sure."

They walked down Garden Street. Bronzino had returned from Nantucket just the night before.

"Did you have a good time with your family?"

"Yes. My nephews are very entertaining. My mother loves to see them."

She wondered whether she should ask more personal questions. He seemed so relaxed and in such a good mood.

"You know what?" he asked in a voice full of pride. She was sure that he was going to announce his forthcoming wedding, but instead he said, "I wrote a novel." His eyes were sparkling.

"You did!"

"It's a Greek novel," he continued with childlike excitement. "It takes place in Athens in the second century A.D. It's about a very important moment in my life, when I was twenty-four years old and I spent a year in Paris."

"A Greek novel?"

He laughed. "Yes. Last spring Heinrich Diethof, from the classics department, gave a fantastic lecture at the Center about bilingualism in antiquity, and it gave me a great idea. The Greeks had been conquered by the Romans, and they despised them. Greek was the language of culture, of the elite; Latin, compared to Greek, was a very poor language. Exactly like French and English, and the attitude of the French toward the Americans: defeated but proud and scornful! I could transpose my own experience into that of a young Roman who spends one year in Athens. Nobody will ever recognize me, so I can say everything! And it's full of sex." He chuckled.

Jane blushed. His manner had changed. Because of writing a novel? What did all the men she knew have with the Greeks? They were at the entrance of the Kramer Center. In a minute he would be gone. She took the plunge: "Would you like to have lunch or dinner this week?"

"I would love to."

There was no "but." She breathed more easily. "When are you free?"

He didn't take the black datebook out of his pocket. "I'm completely free, since I just came back."

"Tomorrow night?"

He nodded. "Where do you want to meet?"

"Actually . . . do you mind coming to my place?"

"To your place?"

Her cheeks turned red. She was ready to backtrack.

"You sure it won't be too much of a hassle?"

"Not at all!" she said immediately. "It'll be easy."

"Where do you live?"

"Really close by"—she pointed with her finger—"204 Linden Street, at the corner of Almond."

"It's not far, indeed. What time?"

"At seven?"

"Perfect. I'll bring wine."

Jane slowly put this last page on the small stack of overturned pages to her left.

This text brought back to her memory incidents that she had entirely forgotten, like the cruise on the German boat: this useless episode had left no trace in her life—unless living consisted of getting rid of the past like a snake shedding its skins.

Only two people could know all of this: Norman and Allison.

Allison and Jane had been friends for fifteen years. They hadn't seen much of each other in the past nine years since Allison and John had moved to the West Coast and Jane to the East Coast, but they had kept a close phone and e-mail relationship. Allison knew Jane well enough to be able to write a novel entitled *The Story of Jane.*

But Allison didn't like to write. And between the three kids and her work as a lawyer, where would she have found the time to write her best friend's biography, even for the fun of serving her a warmed-over past on a silver platter?

Bronzino, then?

He probably never managed to publish his Greek novel. She'd never heard about it. Was he now trying a new genre, autofiction, using his own name at the risk of endangering his career? Professors of literature these days wouldn't hesitate to sell their souls—or their colleagues' souls—just to get a few crumbs of literary glory.

There was one ingredient from the Greek novel he described that he should have kept, though: sex. This novel definitely lacked spice, and she knew only too well wouldn't get more exciting if the next chapters contained an accurate account of their affair.

Would Bronzino, however, have enough critical distance to denounce the mediocrity of academic life? He had been living in Old Newport for more than thirty years and he didn't complain about it. He had done several of the cruises with the Devayne alumni, which had delighted him.

This last chapter wasn't about Josh at all, but something in the tone reminded her of Josh. The focus on her shopping at Macy's, at the beginning of the chapter, fitted the image Josh must have retained of her, that of a frivolous middle-class girl and of a bored-to-death academic. But where could he have got so much information about her? How could he know about the cruise, and the German doctor?

Jane got up, walked to the phone and pressed the REDIAL button. As soon as she heard the recorded voice, she dialed Allison's extension. The answering machine again. She didn't leave a message. She looked at her watch: 2:35 P.M. She called the Kramer Center. The secretary wasn't there.

Lightning flashed outside, followed immediately by a terrible explosion. She imagined fire coming through the window and burning her, and she stepped backward. She sat down again and looked at the manuscript. A new part was starting. "Eric's Way." She smiled sarcastically and, with avid curiosity, began reading.

II. Eric's Way

I

"**Life changes** our plans sometimes."

Dr. Elaine Brooks took a tissue from a box on her left and handed it over to Jane with a warm smile.

"I don't mean to influence you. Think about it this week and try to envision every possibility. You're thirty years old. There is always a slight risk of infertility involved afterward, in case of a scarring of the lining. You should be fine because it's still early, but you cannot be a hundred percent sure. It would be your first, right?"

Jane nodded.

"Personally I am pro-choice. But in our society right now, there is a lot of pressure not to abort. You may feel guilty later. You might consider adoption too. . . ."

Jane shook her head. The gynecologist took her hand.

"A baby is very abstract for a man before he holds it in his arms. What I can assure you is that keeping the baby won't destroy his love. He may thank you one day."

Couldn't she stop? This was torture.

"Again, it's your decision: I am neutral. I'm just trying to help you."

Jane lay down, knees up. The young woman introduced the speculum.

"Relax. You are very tense."

Jane tried to breathe calmly, but her body suddenly became a huge cramp. She screamed and her face turned red.

"Take deep breaths," the doctor ordered her.

Jane opened her mouth, gasping for air. The doctor extended her hand. Jane held it tightly. She managed to breathe.

"Good. Do you want an injection?"

"No. I'm sorry, I don't know what's going on with me, you didn't hurt me, I have Pap smears regularly, this is ridiculous! I'm just being hysterical."

"Don't be hard on yourself. You were only hyperventilating. It's common. Lie down here until you feel better. I'll see you in a week."

When Jane walked out of the modern building, the sun made her squint. Green Avenue deserved its name this early October morning, with its fresh lawns on both sides of the road and the green leaves on the high trees in front of the brick and stone mansions. There was very little sign yet of fall and its golden colors.

Students in tee-shirts or shirts with rolled-up sleeves were heading toward classrooms. Birds were giving a concert. A squirrel crossing the sidewalk stopped and stood up on his hind legs when Jane got close, his little eyes anxiously rolling around. She usually looked at squirrels, but didn't even notice today as this one ran away in a panic and jumped back onto the tree.

She had let out a scream of joy yesterday when the secretary at the clinic had called and confirmed the test was positive. It was impossible, since she was on the pill. But she had felt something so strange, so deep, such an opening in herself, when he was inside her that night, that she had cried. He had suspended his movement. "Am I hurting you?" "No, no!" This was the moment when she had conceived. She was sure. Their first night.

Yesterday, after an initial five minutes of ecstatic happiness, she fell back down to earth. Life was now giving and at the same time withholding what she suddenly realized she wanted more than anything.

She had immediately dialed the eleven-digit number. It was the first time she was calling him. He had phoned her twice since he left. It was 10 P.M. in Germany. He picked up the phone.

"Hallo?"

"It's Jane."

"Jane! How wonderful to hear your voice! I was just lying in bed, and here you are! It's like a dream."

How could he sound so surprised? Jane couldn't hear the phone ring without hoping immediately it was him. She was thinking of him every minute of the day.

"I have something to tell you."

"What?"

"I'm pregnant."

Silence.

"Are you sure?"

"I had a blood test."

"Didn't you tell me you were on the pill?"

"Apparently it happens."

There was a silence for a few seconds.

"I am so sorry," he said softly. "I wish I were with you now." Then he added less hesitantly: "Of course, I'll pay for anything that isn't reimbursed. Are they doing it at the Devayne Health Center?"

"It." Just enough decency not to be able to say the word.

"I don't know."

"What time is it there? Five past four? Call your doctor and I'll call you back, not right now because I'm meeting someone for a beer, but in one hour. OK?"

She had left her apartment and run to the Old Newport Cinema where she had given the cashier a $10 bill.

"Which movie? They all started already."

"Anything!"

There was no message on her answering machine when she came back. Maybe he had called but didn't know what to say.

That had been last night.

She was home. She slowly walked up the stairs and unlocked her door. 10:15. She had one hour to prepare her class. She sat at her desk and opened Benjamin Constant's *Adolphe.* Tears gushed from her eyes.

She started the class by asking the students to resume their previous discussion. The most serious student, a fat, awkward teenager named Steve, with thick glasses, who almost lay down on the table to read the text, his face right against the book, raised his arm.

"Death," he said in French, "is a source of torment in *Adolphe.*"

Jane was listening distractedly, her eyes turned toward the blue sky.

"The hero doesn't know how to tell Elleonore. . . ."

"Ellenore," she corrected mechanically.

The students kept adding that *o.* Steve nodded apologetically.

" . . . Elle-o-nore that his death for her is dead. But he . . ."

She slowly registered what she had heard.

"It's not death, it's love, for God's sake. *L'amour,* not *'l'amor.'* That sounds like *la mort.* There is a difference between death and love!"

Everyone in the class laughed.

"*Ou, o,*" Jane continued. "Don't you hear the difference? *Ou—o.* Repeat after me: *Ou.*"

Steve looked at her with earnest eyes. "*Ou,*" he said.

"*O.*"

"*O.*"

"*L'amour.*"

"*'L'amor.'*"

"*L'amour!* Don't you hear it? *L'a-mour!*"

"*'L'amor,'*" he repeated.

"Death! You keep saying 'death'! You have to go to the language center and work on your phonetics. This is a literature class; you can't waste our time like this."

The twelve students looked up at her, suddenly confused. She wasn't being very nice. Was it the fault of their classmate if the French language used almost the same sounds for love and death? None of them could hear the difference. Steve was all red and seemed to be on the verge of crying. But it was Jane who burst into tears.

At this, the students looked even more surprised. A professor crying in front of them was unheard of at Devayne.

"Professor Cook, are you OK?" a girl asked.

Jane couldn't speak. She got up and turned toward the wall. No one said a word. Steve didn't dare to look up. Jane took a tissue out of her pocket and blew her nose before turning around: "I'm sorry. I don't feel well. I'm canceling class."

"Sure, no problem," one of them said.

They all put their notebooks and books in their bags. They looked at her with sympathetic faces.

"Take care, Professor Cook."

She walked like a robot from the Neo-Gothic Kenneth-Whitman Building to the department offices, five minutes away. She climbed the stairs to the third floor.

"Is he in?" she asked Dawn, pointing to the chairman's office door.

Dawn nodded yes and added, "There's no one with him right now."

Jane knocked at the door.

"Come in!"

She pushed open the door. Norman Bronzino, from behind his large desk full of books and papers, smiled happily. "Jane! How are you?"

They had only exchanged brief hellos since she had told him three weeks ago that she needed to be alone for a while. They were seated in his car in a parking lot, facing the sea, not because it was romantic but because Bronzino didn't want to be seen in town with her. There was something wrong about the affair, she had said: she didn't feel comfortable with the age difference; she had to think it over. He had been very understanding, even though he thought that love had nothing to do with age. He had told her that it was actually better for him too if they didn't see each other for a little while—he was extremely busy with his work at the university as well as with his search for a full time aide to look after his ailing mother. Also, he didn't want his mother, who was ill and fragile, to learn right now that he was seeing someone—and a woman as young as Jane. During the three weeks of their affair, he had asked Jane not to call him at home, and he had always sneaked into her place at the end of his workday like an adulterous husband, staying barely one hour because his mother expected him for dinner at 6 P.M.

She closed the door and started crying. He walked over to her and hugged her.

"What's the matter?"

She freed herself and stepped backwards.

"I'm pregnant."

"I was going to ask you. I noticed a change in your eyes, in your skin, in your whole body recently. So I was right!" He smiled, pleased at the news or at his own instinct, perhaps both.

"I don't think it's yours."

He stared at her with wide-open eyes. Jane faced his gaze.

"I met someone else," she said. "I meant to tell you. Not like this, of course. I'm sorry. Please don't be angry. I'm in too much pain. I'm going to have an abortion."

Bent suddenly like an old man, he slowly walked back to his office armchair behind the large modern desk. He sank into the comfortable chair and started playing with a pen, pulling off the cap and putting it back on. The phone rang. He picked it up. "Yes. . . . No. I'll call him back in two minutes." He put the receiver down and looked at Jane coldly. "What do you want?"

"A leave of absence. I can't teach right now. After the abortion I would like to stay with my parents for a few days."

"And who is going to teach your classes? Me?"

She didn't answer.

"Do you think that the students pay twenty thousand dollars a year just so you can get laid here and there?"

Tears were flowing down her cheeks. She got up.

"Who is it?"

Bronzino's voice was softer. She looked at him. There was so much pain in his eyes that she stopped before reaching the door, to answer him. "Someone in the art history department. He's on sabbatical in Germany right now," she added quickly, thinking that it would make Bronzino feel better to know that her new lover wasn't around.

"What's his name?"

"Eric Blackwood."

"I know him. He was a fellow at the Center last year."

Bronzino paused. Clearly he had nothing to say. Young and handsome Eric could only win. And to be a fellow at the Kramer Center for European Studies, which admitted only the crème de la crème of academics, Eric had to be very bright too.

"So this is why you broke up with me. I should have figured this out."

"No! What I told you was true: it didn't feel right. I met Eric afterwards."

It was only a half-lie. At the time of the break she and Eric hadn't yet exchanged so much as a kiss and there was still nothing sure. But that wasn't true. It was as sure as two plus two equals four. She knew it the very night when she and Eric met. He had walked her home toward 11 P.M.

"Do you want to come in for a drink? I have some whiskey."

He had looked at his watch. "I would love to, but I should go to bed. I have an appointment at nine in New York tomorrow morning, and tomorrow night I fly to Germany."

"To Germany?"

The usual story: you meet an attractive single man and he immediately puts an ocean between you and him. Or was he single? It was what she had assumed, but she actually didn't know. Maybe he was married and not wearing a ring. Or he was engaged to a German girl. Or, in the best-case scenario, he was divorced and the father of three children.

"Why don't you come along?" he had asked suddenly, his voice inspired, his face creased with a joyful smile.

"To Germany?" she had repeated flatly.

"Lufthansa is having a special promotion right now, and the round-trip tickets are barely three hundred dollars. The conference is in a small town two hours from Munich—Eichstätt, it's called, full of Baroque buildings—and not far from the Black Forest, where we could go hiking this weekend."

"Eichstätt?"

"Do you know it?"

"I know someone who lives there."

He sounded surprised, but not as much as she did. Everything was dazzling: Eric, to start with—his looks; his going to the very place where the German doctor from the boat trip lived; their meeting just when she was wondering what was wrong with her affair with Bronzino—his asking her now, as if this were the most natural thing in the world, to fly to Europe with him, and therefore to share his hotel room in Eichstätt, when they had met only four hours earlier and hadn't even touched hands yet. To her even greater surprise, she was very close to saying yes, very close to doing the craziest thing she'd ever done in her life.

"Call from the airport and tell the secretary you're sick," Eric had suggested in a seductive voice.

But, of course, she couldn't. Not because of teaching. Something important, she had told him, without specifying what. It was the following day that she had asked Bronzino not to see or call her for a while.

The phone rang again. Bronzino picked it up.

"Yes . . . Right. Tell him to hold, please."

He looked up. "Take your two weeks' leave," he said in a tired voice. "Good-bye, Jane."

He kept the receiver in his left hand and, with his right hand, adjusted his glasses and leafed through a stack of papers on his desk, making it clear that he had more important matters than Jane to take care of. She walked toward the door and put her hand on the knob. Then she hesitated. "Thank you."

He looked up at her with sad eyes. "I guess *I* should thank you for being honest."

On October 20, she woke up early to take the pain reliever. At 8:50 A.M., she gave her name to the secretary in the Gynecology Department at the Devayne Health Center. She couldn't sit down and she paced the floor. She smiled at a cute four-year-old girl who was sitting next to her brother, a teenager reading a magazine. The little girl blushed, got up on the seat, pinched her brother, pulled his magazine and grabbed his baseball cap.

"Stop it!"

She continued, laughing and screaming in a high-pitched voice, while looking at Jane out of the corner of her eye. Jane turned her back to the child and paced the floor even more nervously. All the magazines on the table were free issues of *American Baby*. Jane walked up to the secretary.

"Is the doctor coming soon?"

"What's going on, sweetheart? Don't you feel well?"

"These children are so noisy!"

She started crying. The woman took her to one of the little examining rooms and brought her a white paper shirt. Dr. Elaine Brooks walked in five minutes later. She apologized for being late. Her warm smile was reassuring. The secretary didn't know what Jane was coming for; they were actually going to the sterile room on the fourth floor. A nurse and a midwife were waiting for her.

"You're staying, right?" Jane asked the doctor, anguish in her voice.

She did everything just as Dr. Brooks instructed. The metal supports under her bare feet felt uncomfortable. She felt almost nothing when the midwife inserted the stick. Then the vacuum cleaner was sucking out the lining of her uterus. Jane kept her eyes wide open, concentrating on her breathing and staring at her doctor, who was smiling and telling her to breathe, to inhale, to exhale; it would soon be over. The process seemed much longer than the six or seven minutes it actually took. The midwife took out the instrument and the speculum, and cleaned up the blood. Dr. Brooks congratulated Jane for being so brave and told her to rest here for a while. When Jane got up, she turned around and saw the basin under the table. Inside there was blood and a thing that looked like a tiny bloody ball. She felt like throwing up.

Jane took a cab home. Two hours later her whole stomach felt like a stone. She went to pee and there was blood in the toilet bowl. She couldn't even walk. She was folded in two. Even sitting was painful.

Every position hurt. She lay down and tried to sleep, but couldn't. It hurt too much. She had told nobody in Old Newport what she was doing. What if something had ruptured inside and she was going to die? Then again, maybe it was normal: maybe this was what Dr. Brooks meant by "sore." She had to wait until the morning.

The phone woke her up around ten that night. She walked painfully to the living room, folded in two, cursing herself for not having called the phone company yet to have them install a phone jack near her bed.

"Hi! I thought you weren't home, I had already prepared a message."

The last time they had talked was ten days earlier. Allison had been very supportive when she learned that Jane was pregnant, though it was a shock for her, and quite ironic since Allison had tried in vain for three years already to have a baby. She had offered to fly to Old Newport and stay with Jane for a week. For Allison—as for everyone else: Jane's parents, Susie, and Eric—an abortion was the only choice. Jane couldn't keep the child of a man with whom she had spent only one night, and she couldn't have a baby when she was just starting her career. She would have a child eventually, but at the right time. It was preferable to establish a solid basis first. "It would mean that Eric and you never had any time alone," Allison had said. "It would be very unhealthy for the relationship." "I don't think you understand. I don't think you can understand," Jane had replied. Allison had remained silent for a few seconds before resuming slowly, in a slightly trembling voice: "I can't understand because I've never been pregnant? Is that what you're telling me, Jane? That's not very nice."

Jane had apologized; she was tense and stressed out. Allison had softened: "But why don't you keep this baby if you want it so much? Why not, after all? Follow your guts." "Because," Jane had slowly replied, "it could be Bronzino's. I know it's not, but in terms of dates it makes more sense." "I see." There wasn't much to say. Allison knew everything. Jane had called her on September 15 just after breaking up with Bronzino. Allison had screamed at her first: "What? Already? I don't get it. You make me think of the guy who doesn't want to be part of a club that's willing to accept him as a member. It's infantile, Jane." A week later, when Jane had told her about Eric, Allison got it.

"So," Allison was now asking, "did you finally schedule the abortion?"

"Yes."

"When will it be?"

"It was this morning."

There was a silence. Allison, who rarely cried, burst into tears at the other end of the line. Something relaxed in Jane; for the first time since the morning, she cried.

She had planned to stay with her parents for a week, but she left after four days. Except for breast tenderness, she had no more pain. She wanted to be home, to wake up in her own bed, and to resume teaching.

Bronzino called her ten days later to tell her what wasn't yet official: she had been granted a fellowship and would be able to spend the following year in Paris. She didn't care much; next year, Paris, were abstract. She was glad that he wasn't resentful. As an afterthought, she wondered whether he hadn't defended her candidacy just to separate her from Eric one more year. But Bronzino couldn't be that Machiavellian. He sounded sincerely happy for her.

Eric and she were talking over the phone barely once a week, for no more than ten minutes, frequently interrupted by uneasy silences. She bought a ticket, as planned, for Thanksgiving; she would spend a week in Germany with him.

She didn't know anything about him except that he was handsome.

They had met twice. The first time had been on September 12, at the opening of the Chinese art exhibit at the Devayne Gallery, when he had walked her home afterward and made the dazzling offer: "Why don't you come along?" The second time was on September 17, the night when Eric flew back from Germany to have dinner with her.

He had rung her bell at 7 P.M. sharp. When she opened her door, she was a bit anxious: she didn't remember his face precisely; she could have been simply impressed by his elegant suit the night of the opening. There he was, on her doorstep, dressed in jeans, sneakers and a gray tee-shirt, as surreal as if he had just walked out of a fashion magazine. There was something almost too perfect about his symmetrical features and gracious smile. Eric was the kind of man who had never looked at her before. But here he was, looking at her, smiling at her, and even holding out to her a single tall, yellow rose. The same type as the only man she had ever loved passionately, Eyal, only more handsome: tall and slender, with broad shoulders, full lips that were delicately designed, straight light brown hair falling on his forehead, and this radiant smile with something tenderly ironic in it, a smile that displayed his large and regular teeth and formed little stars of wrinkles at the corners of his hazel-gray, almost blue eyes.

"May I come in?"

She was transformed into a statue by her awareness that something exceptional was happening to her.

He had taken her to a restaurant in a neighborhood she didn't know, the Little Italy of Old Newport, on the other side of the train tracks. The Scala di Milano was full of people—not of Devayne professors but of real people from town—and the food was delicious. Or so it appeared to Jane, who couldn't eat. They talked for hours, leaning toward each other, their faces lit by a candle. As soon as they stepped outside, their lips established contact. They stood motionless for a few seconds, their bodies as taut as a bowstring, before kissing madly while passersby looked at them. They continued in the car for at least one hour before he started the engine, and then at every traffic light until drivers started honking behind them. He turned off the engine in front of her house and asked with a smile, "What about that whiskey?"

At breakfast he had explained the situation to her: he had a fellowship to spend the year at the Dahlem Museum in Berlin. He had to leave that very day.

"Today?"

He had changed his original plan to go directly from Munich to Berlin, but there was a reception tomorrow that he couldn't miss.

In other words, he had chosen to spend two days in a plane just for a dinner with Jane, and in two hours he would be gone.

She had taken the limo to Kennedy with him in the afternoon, not even noticing the beautiful day. They had spent the whole ride swallowing each other's lips, tongue, and saliva. In the airport too. If only she could eat him, keep him inside her. It was mad. It was love—love like she had never experienced it.

"Eric Blackwood is expected at Gate A23 for immediate departure on Lufthansa 006 to Berlin," the speakers had announced loudly throughout the whole airport.

She had watched him running down the long corridor. He had turned around and waved before disappearing. When she walked outside, it was dark and chilly. She had cried all the way back to Old Newport.

That had been two months ago. Tomorrow she was flying to Berlin. Today, actually: it was already 12:40 A.M. She dialed Allison's number. It was convenient to have one's best friend in San Francisco when one needed to talk late at night. Allison picked up the phone after one ring.

"It's Jane. Am I disturbing you?"

"Hi! Not at all. I have to write a conclusion for a workplace discrimination suit in my civil law class, so I'll be up all night. Exciting, isn't it? How come you aren't in Berlin?"

"I'm leaving tomorrow."

"Lucky you. When will we meet the charming prince?"

"I'm scared."

"Why?"

"He says one wrong word and it's over. I'm angry."

"With him? It's not his fault."

"He didn't hesitate. Not for one minute. I don't know if I can ever forgive him that one minute."

"You weren't even sure it was his baby!"

"But he thought it was his and he didn't hesitate."

"Jane! You're so unfair! Do you think it's easy for Eric? Poor him! He must be terrified of losing you too. You can't do that to him. You can't be angry at him."

"I don't want to. But if he says one word that shows he doesn't understand, I may stop loving him immediately."

"Do me a favor," Allison said in her big-sister voice. "As soon as you land in Berlin, you let Eric know what's going on in your mind. You put him on your side against yourself. OK?"

From the moment Eric embraced her and she rested her head against his chest in the Berlin airport, there was no need for words. There was his smell. She cried. He looked sad. That first night, she said she couldn't make love.

"Would it hurt?"

"No."

Three nights later, after two hours of fondling and kissing, he penetrated her. But when he saw the expression on her face, he withdrew.

She liked Berlin. Eric lived in a bourgeois neighborhood in the western part of the city, near Savigny Platz, but he also knew lots of funky bars and underground clubs in der Mitte, which quickly became Jane's favorite part of the city. It once had been East Berlin, and now looked like a huge construction site full of ruins, holes and cranes, mostly clustered around the former Wall.

Three weeks later she flew back to Berlin for Christmas. The day after her arrival, they left for Prague, half an hour away by plane. The trip was Eric's Christmas gift to her; like Josh, he thought that she would love the city. He had reserved a room at the Hotel Pařiš, a monument of Art Nouveau architecture in the center of town. The room was disappointingly small, the food was not exactly dietetic—consisting mainly of pork, cream, potatoes and boiled bread. The Czechs looked sad and were badly dressed, the shop windows were either ugly or full of crystal of which you grew tired after a few days, the dog shit was harder to avoid there than in Paris, the sun proved unable to pierce the pollution lid, and water remained suspended in the air even when it didn't rain, making the cobblestones dangerously slippery. Night fell by 4 P.M. In one week they barely saw daylight. Because of the jet lag, she woke up late, and they rarely got out of the hotel before 3 in the afternoon. Eric never rushed her. Prague was a night city anyway, with its tiny streets barely lit by old lamps with a pale yellow glow, lights that sometimes turned themselves off, and other times on, when you got near them. The first time she said "dick" in a restaurant, Eric opened his eyes wide while the waiter nodded politely. She burst into laughter. The word had come back to her in a flash of memory.

Eric and Josh were both right: Jane did love Prague. It was impossible not to love Prague. Not only for its beauty and labyrinth of tiny cobblestone streets, which were the paradise of wandering lovers, but, like its dampness, the city's melancholy penetrated you little by little and made you feel deliciously good, as if you were high.

"Do you get high often?" Eric asked.

They were standing near the Charles bridge, leaning against the railing above the river and staring at the black water of the Vltava full of tiny white dots—sleeping birds. The huge castle above, all lit in pastel blue, pink and yellow, looked more like a wedding cake than a Kafkaesque nightmare.

"Actually, you know what? I've never been high," Jane replied. "My friends kept checking to see if I was inhaling. That stuff has no effect on me."

Eric raised his eyebrows. "Coke?"

She laughed. "Marijuana and hashish, but still."

She shivered. Eric put his arm around her shoulders and placed his warm skin against her cheek. He had a secret internal heating system, as obviously did the long-legged Czech girls who were wearing miniskirts in freezing temperatures. Jane remained silent, dazzled that this man she had met three months earlier, and who was now standing next to her in a postcard scene at the heart of Europe, was real.

In Prague they made love again. It was intense, delicate, and tender, but, unlike their first night, slightly shy and reserved. They both knew why.

"Promise me," Jane said, looking into Eric's eyes just before he penetrated her, the night of their arrival in Prague, "never again. Next time. . . ."

". . . we'll keep it, I promise."

Jane had been biting the nail of her middle finger for ten minutes already. There was a weight in her chest and a familiar sensation of nausea in her stomach. Prague, Berlin and, before this, the white room on the fourth floor of the Devayne Health Center. She breathed deeply and shivered, shaking herself like a dog coming out of the water. She wouldn't let her memory be manipulated.

It couldn't be Eric. She was sure. Not simply because she had never told him what happened between her and Bronzino. But writing a novel based on their intimate life was totally inconsistent with Eric's character.

Many of her colleagues had probably heard about her breaking down in class. This was the kind of incident people loved to gossip about. She had told the story of her romantic encounter with Eric to anyone who had wanted to hear it. She had often described the melancholy and charm of the Czech capital. But few knew that she had an abortion. And even fewer, what happened in Bronzino's office that day. Allison, and Bronzino.

It had to be Bronzino.

She was outraged by his use of her most painful and intimate memory in a novel. The whole description of the abortion was so insensitive and clichéd. It had been written by a man who couldn't put himself in her place, not even for a minute. She had never seen the basin with "a thing that looked like a tiny bloody ball." That detail was disgusting and ridiculous. Of course the hospital staff had carefully hidden everything from her. Bronzino could at least have done some research before he dared to touch such a topic.

She grabbed the pages she had just read. She suddenly felt like burning them as well as the rest of the manuscript. She got up and looked for matches, but couldn't find any. She was scared of fire anyway. She put the pages back on the table and called the Kramer Center. Again, a machine answered. She thought of going there now, but she wasn't even sure Bronzino would be in his office, and it was still pouring. She should also wait for Allison to call back. It was now 3:15 P.M.—12:15 P.M. in Seattle. Allison would probably call during her lunchtime.

Jane sat down again and resumed her reading.

2

The fast train for the airport arrived in the station just as she got to the track. Fortunate, since at this early time of day she could have waited half an hour. In twenty minutes she was at Orly. Maybe the gods who had sent her a train so quickly would also push his plane. She ran to the bathroom and then took up her post at the gate for international arrivals.

It wasn't yet 7 A.M. People were arriving one or two at a time and standing next to her, all of them freshly shaved and combed. Some were yawning, others were looking at the gate with expectant faces, others were reading newspapers. A smell of freshly ground coffee and warm croissants tickled her nostrils. The café was opening. She had wanted to bring fresh croissants to Eric, but the bakery in her street was still closed when she left. Here they would be twice as expensive and probably not as good.

The automatic gate opened. Everyone looked up. A few people emerged. Jane's heart started beating fast. The gate slid closed, and then open again. She tried to see inside. A large crowd.

"Are you arriving from New York?" she asked a man who came through the gate.

"Boston."

She looked at her watch. 7:25. He had not landed yet. Three little children next to her screamed "Papa!" and ran toward a tall man in a long gray coat; he opened his arms. The kids were dressed in the French way: shirts with tiny round white collars and cute sweaters matching their pants or Scottish skirts. A beautiful, tall, thin brunette carrying three little coats with velvet collars on one arm and a quiet blond baby on the other followed them. "Hello, you!" the man said, pinching the cheek of the moody baby, who hid his head in his mother's neck. The man quickly kissed his wife on the lips. "Did everything go well?" Jane smiled. The perfect French bourgeois family.

"Your coffee, ma'am."

A *garçon de café* in a white suit, holding a tray with a small paper cup, had stopped in front of her.

"It's not mine, sorry. I didn't order any."

"Your friend sent it. He paid for it."

"Eric?" She spun around. "Where is he?"

"He went to the toilets. He said he would be back in five minutes."

She took the cup and the waiter left. Why did Eric go to the restrooms before even kissing her, when she was dying to see him? Did he have a bad stomachache? Or did he see her, standing there with a sleepy look, and did he decide to surprise her? Yes, this could be Eric's way of doing things. She smiled. The coffee was hot and strong, delicious. Just what she needed. Eric was so thoughtful. Maybe he went to shave, so his skin would be fresh and soft. In a few minutes she would hold him in her arms. His body. His shoulders, his skin, his smell. Real.

Five, ten minutes passed. Eric didn't show up. She suddenly looked at the board. The word ARRIVED wasn't inscribed next to Eric's flight number. He hadn't landed yet. She had just drunk someone else's coffee. She smiled. It was really not her fault. The letters started moving at the same moment. TWA 602 . . . LANDED. It was there, in red letters. The plane wasn't even late. Eric was in France, on the same ground as she, ten minutes away from her. That was just the time it would take to get his suitcase, if he had checked it, and to pass customs. A long shiver ran down her spine.

"Great coat," a woman said to her.

Not the first compliment she had received about that coat. But the first time in France.

"Where did you find it?"

"In the States, two years ago. For twenty dollars on sale."

"Twenty dollars!"

But the fake fur coat was the only item she had saved from her shopping spree at Macy's. The woman reached out and lightly touched the coat.

"Is it real?"

"Real teddy bear, yes."

"Synthetic? I would never have guessed!"

She laughed. Jane felt too warm and took off her coat.

"You have taste," the woman said, looking at her long, reddish-brown, body-fitting jersey wool dress, closed from top to bottom by tiny nacre buttons.

"Oh, thanks! This one I got yesterday in Paris, at—"

"Not for me: you need to be very thin to wear this."

"But you're thin too."

The woman burst into laughter. "Sure. Are you also expecting someone from New York?"

"My boyfriend."

The gate slid open. They both looked up. A sleepy girl pulling a big suitcase and looking quite lost appeared, reminding Jane of her own arrival three and a half months ago. The gate opened again and let out several sleepy people, each pushing carts. They looked like they were from New York.

"Were you on TWA from Kennedy?" Jane asked a young black man in a leather jacket, who was carrying a large music instrument case on his right shoulder.

"New York, yeah," he answered in a strong New York accent that made her nostalgic for a Manhattan avenue full of potholes and honking yellow cabs.

The gate kept opening and closing, letting more people out. 8:45. Eric could appear at any moment. She had been waiting for almost two hours already. No: for 3 months, 10 days, and 110 minutes.

The woman who had admired her coat let out a joyful exclamation and walked up to a big, tall man with gray hair, who embraced her. Jane couldn't decide whether he was her father or her lover. They walked away and the woman waved.

"Bye! Happy New Year! Have fun with your boyfriend."

Fewer people around now. 9:10 already. Her heart was pounding as soon as the automatic door opened. None of the people who had been waiting with her one hour ago were still there. A new crowd had replaced the sleepy 7 A.M. group. The passengers getting out had darker skin: a plane had just landed from Tunisia. 9:42. Had his suitcase been lost? Then he was probably filling out forms for insurance.

She felt dizzy. She had not eaten anything this morning. She had been standing here for three hours.

9:55. The plane landed two hours ago and everyone had already left. Another exit? She had to ask at the information counter. What if he came out just now when she stepped away? She approached a middle-aged woman in a mink coat standing next to her and described Eric to her.

"I'll have to leave as soon as my friend arrives," the woman said reluctantly.

Jane ran to the information counter and cut to the front of the line. She looked so anxious that nobody protested. The cute young woman with a pointy French face behind the counter spoke into a microphone and Eric's name resounded throughout the whole airport.

Jane ran to the international arrivals gate.

"Nobody like you described," the woman said.

Jane ran back to the information counter. She was sweating. The jersey wool would soak up the bad smell.

"You should check with TWA," the girl said. "Do you see their counter? Just over there."

Jane ran across the hall to the TWA counter. She gave Eric's name and the flight number. The woman typed them into her computer.

"I don't have this name," she said flatly. "He didn't board that plane."

"That's impossible. He bought his ticket two months ago already."

The woman shrugged her shoulders.

"His name isn't in the computer: he didn't board the plane."

"But that's impossible! He had the ticket in front of him when he gave me the flight number the day before yesterday!"

There was the shadow of an ironic smile at the corner of the woman's lips. A fat forty- or fifty-year-old lady with a permanent, dyed-blond hair and long varnished nails. A monster of indifference.

"Unless he left from Boston? Maybe I didn't hear right, I don't know. Could you check, please?"

The woman sighed and impatiently typed into her computer.

"No Blackwood."

Jane ran back to the information counter.

"Nothing, sorry," the young woman said with a sympathetic smile.

Jane walked back to the gate.

10:40.

He never boarded that plane. There could be but one reason: he was dead. An accident on the way to the airport. While she was buying a $200 dress and narcissistically wondering whether Eric would undo all the tiny buttons or simply slip his hand underneath, his burned body was being extracted from his totaled car by a team of paramedics and taken in an ambulance to the hospital or directly to the morgue.

The fear hurt so much she could barely breathe. She couldn't cry.

She had to find a phone. But whom could she call? Eric's mother? She didn't have the number with her right now. It was 4:45 A.M. in Maine. Could she wake Nancy up in the middle of the night to ask whether her son was dead?

When you panic at the idea that a loved one is dead, he isn't dead. It's usually a mere projection of your own desire.

Who told her this? Sergio, in Chicago nine years ago. She had woken him up in the middle of the night: Was Eyal there? No. Then he was dead! A sleepy Sergio had told her not to worry: Eyal was certainly fine. He had given his little theory about desiring someone's death. Sergio was right, of course: Eyal had just spent the night with another girl.

She may have desired Eyal's death. But Eric's?

If Eric was dead, she could do but one thing: throw herself from her attic window onto the paved courtyard—having slashed her wrists beforehand.

She walked slowly toward the arrivals gate.

Eric didn't board that plane.

He wasn't dead. He just didn't come.

She leaned against the wall and closed her eyes.

Two days ago on the phone, did she let Eric know how madly happy she was at the thought of seeing him?

No. When he told her that he was returning to the States on January 5 instead of the originally planned January 12 because of a new seminar to prepare, she had cried. How could a seminar be more important than them? "If this is your reaction," Eric calmly replied, "then I wonder whether I should come at all." His words and voice blew like an icy wind inside her. Sheer terror. She backtracked immediately. "No. I understand, it's OK, I'm sorry, it's just that I miss you so much."

The end of the conversation was softer. Eric inquired about the weather in Paris. "See you day after tomorrow," he said. He was probably sincere. But, as he was packing, he must have thought again about that conversation, and about many conversations this semester and even last year.

All along she had known he would abandon her. She didn't deserve him. He was too handsome, too charming, too close to her little girl's exalted dream. From the moment when she landed in Paris—or, even, boarded the plane at Kennedy—she had felt depressed. A horrible three months. Unable to leave her bed and to call anyone she knew in Paris. She didn't even feel like walking around. Polluted and gray Paris stank, mostly where she lived, in the center, near the Seine. She and Eric talked on the phone twice a week, on dates fixed by Jane, for she couldn't stand to wait without being sure he would call. Most often she would remain silent or accuse him of not loving her, of not knowing what love was. Or wonder how did he manage to sleep, to eat, to teach, to get interested in the electoral debates on TV, and to have a joyful voice when he called her. He said he couldn't wait to see her: but he could wait very well, or he would have flown to Paris for Thanksgiving, as she did to Berlin last year. He woke her up after Clinton was elected, in November: he was celebrating with friends and he wanted to be the first to tell her the news. As if she cared! The tense conversations, interrupted by long silences, left her desperate. The worst had been one time in October, the day before the first anniversary of the abortion. Eric was the one calling. She just couldn't let him hang up. They had spent two hours on the phone, saying almost nothing. "Don't you see that this cannot work?" she kept asking. She had woken up in a cold sweat in the middle of the night, waited until it was 8 A.M. in Old Newport, and called him. He had not slept at all. He had been thinking. There had been such a threat in his cold, metallic voice that she had managed to control herself, managed not to cry. She had been able to apologize, to promise she wouldn't let anxiety overcome her again. She had won him back. But then he must have received the phone bill and paid a crazy amount. After that she was more careful. She had forced herself to do things so she would have something to tell him. She had dragged herself to the Musée d'Orsay, one block away, and discovered the room with the Bonnards. But this brief moment of enthusiasm couldn't make up for the rest.

He knew everything. How she had lost her virginity at age twenty-one with a drunk baseball player she had followed to his room at the end of a party. It had happened without feeling pleasure or pain, just relief at not being a virgin for the rest of her life. In the morning, she had to spend an hour—the most memorable of the whole time—reassuring the boy, who was afraid he had raped her and that his whole life would be over if she denounced him. She now remembered Eric's embarrassed smile when she told him the story after seeing a flyer about date rapes on the table at the college dining hall where they were having lunch.

Eric knew how, much like a dog, she had followed everywhere the only man she had passionately loved before him, ready to do anything for

Eyal, even to help him flirt with other women although it tore her heart; how Eyal had finally slept with her, after seven months, one night when he was really drunk, he too, quickly and brutally satisfying himself but not caring about her. How, one morning when she was doing her last-minute revisions before her qualifying exams that were taking place that very afternoon, Eyal had summoned her by phone: she had to come immediately and scrub the bathtub she had left dirty. She, who was scrupulously careful never to leave a hair in his bathroom, had gone there and scrubbed the bathtub, kneeling on the tiles, while he insulted her. Another funny story.

But she had broken up with Eyal. She had finally understood that his brutality was not a right given to him by his country's political situation and the scar left on his right thigh following his military service in South Lebanon. She had made promises to herself. One day when she had fallen from her bike during a pouring rain, twisted her ankle and forgotten to mail a letter for Eyal, he had slapped her: she had told him she was leaving him and she had left him. At night he had called her. She was desperately waiting for his call and she had burst into tears at the sound of his voice. He had ordered her to come there at once or it was over. She had swallowed three sleeping pills and, the following day, to break the vicious circle of rejection, desire and violence, she had slept with a sweet, funny, and gentle fellow student who had been ready to comfort her for a long time: Josh. Six years with Josh. Then Bronzino, three months after Josh: the only thing Eric didn't know. But he knew enough—that she was a woman scared to be alone.

He had freed himself from the ball chained to his ankle in a discreet and radical way. Eric's way.

Jane was crying silently. She had to get out of here. She walked fast toward the RER entrance. Someone hit her from behind with his cart. She gasped. The Japanese tourist apologized with a bow. She rubbed her ankle and started running: she couldn't stand to hear the speakers announcing arrivals and departures anymore. Someone grabbed her bag. Red with anger, she turned around to hit the aggressor with her free arm.

"But where are you running, Mademoiselle?"

Eric asked the question in French, with a charming accent. He was smiling at her. She screamed and collapsed into his arms. His smell. Fresh and so good even after a night flight. He held her tightly and kissed her passionately before licking the tears on her cheeks.

"I'm so sorry! I had no way of letting you know."

"What happened?"

"The TWA flight was overbooked. They put me on a Delta flight, promising it would arrive at the same time. It did, but at Roissy."

"I went to the TWA counter and a horrible woman told me you didn't board the plane: I thought you had an accident on the way to the airport."

He hugged her tenderly.

"My poor darling! These TWA people, they're going to hear from me. They better send me a free round-trip ticket to Paris—business class."

He hadn't slept at all on the plane—there was a baby crying right behind him and the plane was packed—but he didn't feel tired. He was so happy.

Everything delighted him. Jane had warned him that the calm, sunny, and charming apartment she had seen advertised in her department in April was actually a tiny attic with a low ceiling and two small skylights barely letting in any light. The maid's room reminded Eric of a painting in Munich he liked a lot, that of an old, bearded philosopher in an attic, lying on his bed with an umbrella above his head. The seven flights of steep stairs were excellent exercise. The single bed with a cheap metal frame, squeaking springs and a soft mattress, rejuvenating: like in college again, and a pleasure to sleep close to each other. The toilets three doors down: a bit inconvenient, but funny, like camping, and at least they were private. The location simply couldn't be better. If you stood in the middle of the Tuileries Gardens, five minutes from her place, you could see the axis linking the Obélisque de la Concorde, the Arc de Triomphe behind it, the Grande Arche de la Défense barely visible in the far distance, and, ahead, the small pink Arc du Carrousel, the Pyramide about which Eric wasn't so sure, and the Louvre: the most beautiful perspective in Paris.

When Eric left for Old Newport on January 5, Jane's attic room remained inhabited with his smell, his smile, and a few clothes he had left because his suitcases were packed with French and German books. Her depression was replaced with a feeling of urgency: the book that she was writing. Now she set her alarm clock every morning for 7:30. One hour later, after wrapping around her neck the huge dark rose cashmere scarf that Eric had given her for Christmas, she left for the Bibliothèque Nationale. She couldn't believe that for three months she had remained indifferent to the beauty of this walk. She crossed the Pont Royal, looking at the spacious view of dark green water, bridges, nineteenth-century buildings, and skies with quickly moving clouds, strangely smaller than in the States, entered the Tuileries Gardens, turned left under the Passage du Louvre, where there was still construction going on, and walked through the elegant and peaceful gardens of the Palais Royal to the rue des Petits Champs, which intersected the busy and polluted rue de Richelieu, where the Bibliothèque Nationale was.

Only by being early could she get a seat immediately. In the first semester, she had never gotten there before eleven or noon and always waited, sometimes for hours. She liked the old library in spite of the messy, absurd French (dis)organization. In front of the coffee machine in the hallway, she met American scholars who, like her, were spending a year or a few months in Paris. She contacted Eric's colleagues as well as a few people she had met in Paris ten years before. She was now invited for dinner parties. The friends she made at the Bibliothèque Nationale asked her to go to the theater and restaurants. Jane usually answered that she wasn't free that evening. She still had her debts to pay back, life in Paris was rather expensive, and she was saving money for the summer. She spent the evenings in her attic and sometimes went swimming at the Piscine Deligny, on a barge just across the street from her place.

In early February she used the pretext of Eric's birthday to fly to the States. In mid-March he visited her for a week with the free ticket he had gotten from TWA. Now she only needed to wait until mid-May, when Eric would join her for the summer. She had read her dissertation again: it seemed awful to her, but Eric assured her that was a normal feeling.

One morning in early April the reflection of the sun on the river, which made the water golden-green, put her in an excellent mood. After four hours of examining Flaubert's manuscripts, she closed the precious documents containing his actual handwriting, got up and left the quiet room. As she pondered Flaubert's own lunches with his mother and niece after a morning of writing at Croisset while poor Louise was desperately expecting his visit in Paris, she stepped out of the courtyard of the Bibliothèque Nationale and waited on the sidewalk to cross the busy and narrow rue de Richelieu, next to a tall young man who had walked out of the library just ahead of her. He had a Latin look, but something about his body made her think he was North American. He noticed her gaze and smiled at her. They started chatting as an uninterrupted flow of cars and stinking buses passed in front of them. He was indeed American and an assistant professor of medieval history at the University of California in Santa Cruz. When she introduced herself, she mentioned Eric almost immediately. She and Vincent ate a sandwich together at a café nearby.

They met again for lunch the following day and it soon became a regular habit. It structured the day and helped them work better. When the library closed at night, they met outside and often walked together or went for a drink. Vincent had lived in Paris for several years with a French painter: he was invited to parties almost every night. A week after they met, he asked Jane to come along to a party given by his ex-girlfriend, Rosen, who lived in a charming old house hidden in a courtyard on the rue de Charenton. Jane immediately liked Rosen, a calm and quiet woman, who was originally from a village at the western end of Brittany, Lannilis, where she invited Jane and Eric to visit her during the summer. Thanks to Vincent, Jane's life in Paris became much more fun. Seeing the apartments and studios of painters in various neighborhoods, mostly in the cheaper northern and eastern parts of Paris, fulfilled her voyeuristic instincts. Artists were interested in her as soon as they learned she was American and teaching at Devayne, where there was a famous art school. At the Bibliothèque Nationale, being American wasn't so prestigious: on the contrary, American scholars could gain the good graces of the librarians only by being especially humble and docile. Vincent was always joking and making her laugh. She couldn't believe they had met only three weeks ago. It was almost May, spring was blossoming, and Eric would be here in three weeks.

On May 1, after a party in the apartment of a painter on avenue Ledru-Rollin, since it was three in the morning and they couldn't find a single cab in the deserted streets, she accepted Vincent's offer to crash at his place in the rue du Faubourg Saint-Antoine nearby.

❧

The phone ringing startled Jane. She got up and picked up the receiver.

"Hi, it's me. What's up?"

Allison. Jane was really glad to hear from her. She now doubted that the secret writer was Bronzino. There was no way he could know all these details about her life in Paris.

"Thanks for calling back. How are you?"

"Up to my neck at the office. Lea and Nina have an ear infection. They kept us awake all night."

"The poor babies! I'm sorry to hear that. Listen. I just have a tiny question that will seem rather out of context: did you keep in touch with Josh after I broke up with him?"

"With Josh? We did. Why? I didn't let you know because it had nothing to do with you."

"No problem, don't worry. Did he ask you about me?"

"I guess so, a few times. Why?"

"Did you tell him about Bronzino?"

"I don't remember. Why?"

"What about the abortion? Did you tell him?"

"But why? Has something happened?"

Jane hesitated. "No. I was just wondering. Do you still see him?"

"He lives too far away. But we do talk on the phone once in a while."

"Where does he live?"

"In New York."

"In New York! What's he doing?"

"He works as an editor for Doubleday."

"Really! Has he published any novels?"

"Not yet. Last time I talked to him, he said he was finishing a big novel. He's been working on it for years."

Jane nodded. This was all she needed to know.

"Is he married?"

"No. At least not as of a few months ago. He broke up with Stephanie about four years ago, and since then there have been many women but nothing serious. He says he's like all forty-year-old single men: disillusioned and unable to fall in love. He remains convinced that you were the woman of his life."

"Sounds like Josh."

"But why are you asking all these questions? Come on, tell me what happened."

"Nothing, really. Well, just a little thing."

"What?"

"Did Josh visit you in San Francisco or Seattle?"

"Not in Seattle. In San Francisco, yes, a couple of times. But tell me!"

"Do you keep a diary?"

"What?"

"You know, a diary, where you write down your thoughts and the things you did today. . . ."

"I haven't kept a diary since I was a teenager! What are you talking about? What happened, Jane? Come on!"

"Nothing, really. Yesterday I cleaned the apartment and I found stacks of old photographs. I realized that I couldn't even date them. So I started to take a few notes to trace the chronology, and suddenly I felt like writing." The lie came to her instinctively. For some reason she felt that Allison shouldn't know about the manuscript—not yet.

"So this is why you're asking me about Josh?"

Allison sounded disappointed. Jane smiled. A good thing there weren't yet telephones with screens where you could see the face of the other person.

"Yes."

"So what are you writing? Your memoirs? A novel?"

"An autobiographical novel."

"Not an academic novel, I hope."

"Why?"

"Boring. Transpose it into another professional milieu."

"Lawyers, for instance?"

"That's been done already. No, find a profession about which nobody has written yet. We'll think about it. I like the idea. Finally you'll do something that you really like. But, listen, I have to go. Lawyers do work."

"Can you give me Josh's number? I'll need him to help me with my chronology."

"I have to ask him first, if you don't mind. I'll call you back."

"Sure."

Jane walked back to the table, drank some water and sat again. She smiled. She was glad she had resisted her impulse to tell everything. She resumed her reading. Where was she? Paris. Vincent. Josh was amazingly well-informed.

❖

She had drunk a little too much for her very limited capacities, and smoked some good pot that had an effect on her: she was sleepy and dizzy. She lay on a sofa in the small living room. He sat next to her. He didn't try to kiss her. He caressed her neck, her breast, and she let him do that, before he lay down alongside her, then on top of her, and they rubbed their bodies against one another. It was so incredibly exciting that she almost came. Vincent undressed her. While saying no repeatedly and telling him with anguish that she couldn't do that, that it would be terrible if she got pregnant, she let him inside her and when he touched her clitoris she came immediately. Then she pushed him out, and he came outside her, on her breasts.

He let her have his bed and slept on the sofa. When she woke up around 10 A.M., it took her a few minutes to remember where she was.

Someone slammed a door. Vincent was just back with a fresh baguette. They had breakfast together. There was no uneasiness on either side. They kissed lightly on the lips when she left.

"That was fun," Vincent said.

She couldn't disagree. Something extraordinary had happened to her: her first orgasm ever while a man was inside her. She had never managed to relax enough, not even with Eric. The more she was in love, the more she felt the pressure of being a good lover. Now she wondered whether getting drunk and rubbing her body against Eric's wouldn't produce the same miracle. She felt grateful to Vincent, who had taught her something about herself.

She would miss their lunches and the parties, but she couldn't see him anymore: too risky. He would understand. That day, he didn't show up at the Bibliothèque Nationale. In the evening, she found herself remembering all the circumstances of the night and getting increasingly excited. At 10:30, she dialed his number; he wasn't home. She didn't leave a message. She started remembering the women around him at the parties and nervously bit the tip of her pen. Jealous? Ridiculous. He could have called her, though. These Californians didn't know how to behave. She should go to bed. She had slept only four hours last night. She heard the phone ring as she was flushing the toilet; she ran and picked up the receiver, out of breath, with a quick look at the alarm clock on the night table: 11:40. She had to make it clear that he couldn't call her that late.

"Hello?"

"Have I woken you up?"

Eric.

"Oh, hi! No . . . not at all, I was in the bathroom, and . . ."

"Is something wrong?"

"No, why?"

"You sound funny. Are you sure you're fine?"

"Yes. It's just this guy I met at the Bibliothèque Nationale: he stood me up for lunch today and I thought he was calling to apologize."

She bit her lip: at this hour?

"Who's that?"

His voice was tense.

"Vincent, you know. He teaches history at the University of California in Santa Cruz."

"I don't know."

She was sweating. Great. Why not tell Eric about last night?

"I thought I told you about him."

"You didn't."

"Just some guy I met at the library. You would like him."

"Well, frankly, I'm not sure," Eric replied in a jokingly threatening voice. "Tell this Mr. Vincent that he shouldn't get too close to you if he doesn't want me to crush his balls with a baseball bat."

Jane laughed. "Come on! You aren't going to be jealous."

She was very pensive when she hung up. Awful and scary how close he was to the truth—and yet how far; he could never imagine what happened. Or he would leave her—this she knew.

She had just had enough of a warning to take some serious measures: no more going to the Bibliothèque Nationale. She tore Vincent's number from her phone book and threw it away. She did the same with Rosen's number. She wouldn't go to Brittany with Eric. Her fault. She wasn't in love with Vincent—so why couldn't she stop thinking about him? Was memory stuck like a leech to the body of the man who made love to you? Or was she simply piqued that he wasn't running after her? A clever bastard: he knew she wanted to be the one to dump him.

On May 19, she waited for Eric at home. She woke up around 8 and did some reading while drinking her coffee. As she read, she kept looking at her watch, every ten minutes. At 9:10 she recognized his step in the corridor. She opened the door before he knocked. He was wearing a gray tee-shirt and a pair of light blue jeans, carrying his black Samsonite suit bag on the right shoulder and a black carry-on on the left, and he had a tiny bouquet of yellow flowers in one hand and a white paper bag with croissants in the other. He was out of breath, and there was sweat on his forehead. He smiled broadly. "I ran. They're still warm," he said, lifting the paper bag.

Here he was, looking barely tired, and so much more handsome than

Vincent. They embraced. His own good smell mixed with that of the warm croissants. Vincent was nothing—just an epiphenomenon of her love for Eric. She had made it. There would be no more being apart.

They traveled to Italy and Greece. He wanted to show her the Istrian Peninsula, which he had discovered fourteen years ago when he was working for *Let's Go* in southern Europe, just after graduating from Harvard, but the war in Bosnia made tourism in these regions difficult and unsafe. On June 18, the day after Jane turned thirty-two, they took a train to Venice. She couldn't sleep one second in the compartment full of stinking feet and snoring people that made her wonder why she had let herself get talked into going to this tourist trap. When she walked out of Santa Lucia train station at dawn, smelled the salty air and saw the blue-green water sparkling under the already-strong sun, the stone bridges with steps, the gondolas and vaporettos bringing newspapers and fresh vegetables, and the pink Renaissance palaces with windows bordered by a line of white stone—Venice waking up on a summer morning—she started laughing, dazzled, like a little girl. As soon as you got off the tourist path, Venice, like Prague, was deserted, even at the height of summer. One night they made love against a door in a tiny street leading to a canal. She couldn't really relax, as she was scared someone would surprise them, but even so had an exuberant feeling of youth and happiness. Then they traveled down the Italian boot, going to Florence, then Rome—where it was so painfully hot that they were forced to take long siestas—on to Naples, and finally to Bari, where they boarded a boat for Crete. They got there after a night spent on the deck; they arrived all sticky with sea salt. They spent five weeks hopping from island to island.

She would forget the names of the islands. Only the sunny sound of their endings in "os" would remain, the image of a quiet room on top of a hill with an infinity of blue around, the lazy sensation of days spent swimming, sunbathing and loving each other, the smell of grilled fish at night when you are starving, the pleasure of being pretty in a white dress with tanned skin, and the exotic inflections of Eric's voice as he was trying his Berlitz-method Greek. With him everything was simple, easy and light. While Jane waited in a café with the luggage, he would find a charming, quiet and clean room in a private home in fifteen minutes. At night he had incomparable techniques for killing mosquitoes. His instinct led him to tiny isolated beaches where he convinced her to swim naked. She was scared that they would be arrested by cops in a country where women didn't even show their bellies on the beach, but Eric was right: you did believe in a natural state of man when your body, free of clothes, slid through the sea like a mermaid. Only once did she doubt his power: in Chios, where they landed by chance and discovered with horror that it was the disco island. During the two days they waited for the next boat, they rented a motorbike to escape the noise generated by the international golden youth. The bike broke down at noon on an unshaded road in the deserted countryside, under a murderous sun. While she was crying, convinced that they were going to die of dehydration, Eric, his torso and face dripping sweat, never lost his calm as he tried to start the bike a hundred times in a row. The hundred and first time, the engine yielded.

Several days later, in a fish restaurant on Delos—a name she would also remember—as their visit to this enchanted place of white sand and white houses, blue sky and blue sea, was getting close to its end, leaving them healthy, thin, and suntanned—Eric, suntanned, looked like a god—he suddenly kneeled in front of her. She screamed in fear and lifted both feet. Was it a huge cockroach, like the one in the bedroom last night, or a rat?

"Will you marry me?"

She burst into laughter, then into tears. Everyone in the restaurant noticed the scene. Violinists started playing wedding music; the waiters were dancing and the old Greek owner taught Jane and Eric the steps; soon there was a circle clapping around them.

That night she drank almost an entire bottle of white wine. Eric had to carry his drunk fiancée home and help her into the bathroom, as she desperately needed to pee but was too dizzy to sit down. Later she couldn't remember when or how he undressed her. The only clear memory would be that of their bodies rubbing against each other and moving like the rings of a muscled snake, and of the scream she let out when he was deep inside her, so loud that he put his hand over her mouth—the first time they came together.

Jane helped herself to a glass of water. Her throat was dry. She saw again the white room in Delos and the white bed linen with which she had covered Eric's naked body, still asleep, in the morning. The image actually came from a photograph where the flash hadn't worked. In the dark room with closed blinds, you could barely make out the white buttocks of Eric, as he slept on his stomach. She had thrown away the picture, but the image was still inside her mind—inside her skin. She got up, poured some water into a pot for tea and noisily put the pot on the stove.

She paced the floor in the living room, nervously playing with a spoon she had picked up from the kitchen counter. Had someone been stalking her for years? Neither Josh nor Bronzino, but a stranger so obsessed with her that he had meticulously gathered facts about her life? Had this man broken into her Linden Street apartment almost eight years ago? Was he in the Paris airport six and a half years ago, did he send her that coffee? Did such madmen—the characters of Hollywood scripts—exist in real life?

She got an idea: call a psychiatrist. A professional would identify the symptoms of madness.

She walked to the table where the phone book was and opened the yellow pages. Under "Psychiatrists" it read "see Physicians Surgeons—Medical—M.D." She turned the page and found "Psychologists." There were hundreds of names. Should she call one at random? But what would she say to him? Ask whether stalkers sometimes wrote novels about their victims? Or whether people who wrote novels about women they knew, using very intimate details, were stalkers? The psychologist would laugh: in that case most novelists qualified as stalkers.

No, this manuscript was certainly a joke. And the author was most probably Josh.

He didn't have to be in the Paris airport to know how panicked she was when Eric didn't show up at the arrival gate. She had described the scene to several people, even the incident of the coffee, because she thought it was funny. It made absolutely no sense that Eric would send her an espresso instead of running to her, but she had immediately accepted this absurd fact and found a plausible explanation for it—as if you couldn't help but fabricate meaning with whatever erroneous data you had.

Josh could also have heard from Allison the details of her trip to Greece. Josh, of course, knew about Eyal and about her past love life. He knew about her insecurity. He could guess her thoughts and feelings.

But what about Vincent? She had never told anyone about her little Parisian affair, not even Allison, who had been in San Francisco when this happened in Paris.

She tried to remember whether any of her acquaintances could have seen her with Vincent at the National Library in Paris.

What if Josh had learned about it from Vincent himself? He could have met him at a conference. They could have talked at dinner and discovered they had a friend in common. Then, it was enough from one smile for Josh to understand everything that Vincent wasn't saying explicitly and to ask a few indiscreet questions. Josh knew Jane well enough to deduce some very intimate details.

3

She got off the bus at the corner of Main and Government streets. She didn't mind the longer ride, as the Fort Hale beaches Eric had helped her discover the summer before looked much more picturesque than Woodmont Park. She decided to walk instead of waiting for the other bus; it was still sunny but no longer too hot. Lots of people were walking down Main Street toward restaurants, or crossing Central Square. Suntanned students returning after a long summer vacation. New students discovering their new town. The white and green flags in front of almost every store sporting WELCOME BACK TO DEVAYNE! in large letters created the festive atmosphere of a fair.

She turned right on Union and then left on Linden, passing her former house. As she got farther away from downtown and from the crowd, an unpleasant sensation of fear constricted her chest. She had to be strong tonight. Everything would go well. There was a humility in her fear that cautioned her against any bad surprises. The opposite of hubris.

Hubris: the excess of pride and self-confidence, always rewarded with a terrible end in Greek tragedies. The word had come back to her earlier on the beach. She wished Josh were around so she could ask him about the plot of his novel.

There had been excessive happiness. Happiness increasing from day to day and year to year like a Wall Street stock in prosperous times. Two years of separation and passion, and then the wedding, two years ago exactly, three weeks after their return from Europe. She was thinking of a nice party in the spring, no more than fifty people, when Eric had suddenly said no, scaring her: could he be reconsidering? He had a better idea: to do it right now, that weekend, just the two of them. An offer one couldn't refuse. This was Eric's way. They had to wait a week for the publication of the banns. Jane had invited the family. Allison, who was about to give birth, couldn't come. Ten minutes in the Old Newport City Hall on September 5, a lunch at Provence with Jane's parents, Susie and Tony, and Eric's mother, a trip to Fort Hale for the photographs, and that was it: she was Mrs. Blackwood. They didn't even have to buy clothes: Eric had a nice suit and the long, off-white linen summer dress she had found in Florence was perfect as a wedding dress. The golden ring on Eric's hand added a funny element of femininity to his good looks; in the voice of a moody little boy, he complained that it tickled.

She would never forget the tearing inside her when Eric said "I do," a wrenching so violent that she couldn't utter a sound when her turn came to speak. Eric's eyes were fixed upon her, not anxious at all, infinitely loving and patiently trying to extract the words from her soundless throat. The vice mayor had told them afterward that he performed this ceremony ten times a week and he had never been so moved: "You're lucky to have found each other." Lucky, yes. She kept wondering how she could deserve such luck. She and Eric would look at each other and read the same thing in each other's eyes: 100 percent certainty. They would burst into laughter. The day of the wedding, during the lunch at Provence where she was devouring her meal with a hearty appetite (whereas a bride was supposed not to be hungry on the big day), she had told herself that, whatever came, she should never forget that she had had her share of happiness.

Two days later they had moved together to the Brewer Tower. The twelfth-floor apartment Eric had found for them had less character than her Linden Street apartment, but it was brighter and more spacious, and it had a panoramic view of Old Newport's parking lots and the rocky hills of Longview Park. Their first time living together. Everyone had told them that the change from a life of separation and passion to conjugal stability would require some adaptation: they should expect a few crises. But Eric was incredibly easy to live with, always funny, charming, and discreet. How could a thirty-five-year-old man as handsome as he was never have married before? "I was waiting for you," he invariably replied. After Sonia, he only had a few affairs, he told her, and they weren't serious. Jane could not understand why Sonia, the passionate woman from Chile who had left her husband for Eric ten years earlier, had decided to return to her husband after five years. Of course, Eric wasn't entirely perfect. He had a tendency not to do his laundry and to let dirty shirts and socks fill the bottom of his closet. But he didn't want Jane to do his laundry for him. If she cooked, he would wash the dishes, and vice versa. She would vacuum and he would take care of the garbage. They never argued about housework or anything material. They could work in the same room without bothering each other—something Jane couldn't do with anyone before. They had the same rhythm. The first one forced by hunger to go to the kitchen would cook for them both whatever was in the fridge, or they would go out and eat a falafel at the small Middle Eastern place one block away. They didn't feel like seeing any friends. They could do without the entire world. They were making love all the time.

The world, however, existed. One night when Eric had stayed at the office late to prepare a lecture he was giving the following day, a noise louder than anything Jane had ever heard awoke her around 1 A.M.: something like a bomb exploding inside the elevator on her floor. She was terrified, knowing that she always forgot to lock the apartment door. The phone was in the living room. She had to gather all her courage before she was able to open the bedroom door and peer into the living room. No bleeding man there. She ran to the door and locked it. It was now as silent as if she had dreamed the noise. She ate a banana, drank some water, and went back to bed, before seeing a few minutes later through her closed eyelids and the blinds the blue and yellow flashing lights that came from the street.

A body was lying on the well-lit sidewalk twelve floors down, with his arms open and a small dark object near his right hand. The young black woman who had opened a window just next to Jane leaned outside, twisted her hands toward the sky and screamed in a desperate voice: "Oh God, God, don't let him die! Don't let him die!" In the local paper the following day, Jane saw a brief item about a twenty-six-year-old man shot in the back just outside his apartment on the twelfth floor of the Brewer Tower. He had chased his killer downstairs, where he died in the street. He left a wife seven months' pregnant and three young children. A drug-related crime.

Eric decided it was time to move. And to buy. She would never have thought about it: buying was an act only real grown-ups would undertake. But apparently they *were* grown-ups; besides, renting meant throwing money out the window. Devayne gave $8,000 to members of its faculty who bought places in Old Newport, and free mortgages before tenure. With the recession, it was a buyer's market. They would actually save money, given the return on taxes. All these new terms were amusing, but Jane liked best the driving around and the search for a place every weekend, and the indiscreet but authorized peering at other people's homes and lives. At night, in their imaginations, they would already be furnishing places they liked. She had to give up her dream of a seaside house in Fort Hale—she didn't drive and couldn't be completely dependent on Eric.

In late March, on a Sunday just after a snowstorm, they found the house. It had unspoiled snow all around and a silence hung over it like that in the heart of the wilderness. The address was 2 Peach Street, a tiny street off River Road, in the woods and yet still in Old Newport, at the edge of town, a beautiful, safe forty-five-minute walk to campus. A perfect place for two, with two large bedrooms upstairs overlooking a charming garden, one and a half bathrooms (Eric's idea of luxury), and, downstairs, a living room with a fireplace and a brand-new kitchen. The place was amazingly cheap. They had it inspected. Everything was in good shape. On May 1 they moved in, their second move in seven months. Eric once again efficiently packed boxes and rented a truck. Seeing him at the steering wheel of a truck excited Jane. That night he ached everywhere. As she was opening boxes to get a bottle of whiskey for him, she found her rug and put it on the hardwood floor in front of the fireplace. Tired as they were, there'd be no making love on the rug tonight, she thought, like there had been in September the night of moving into the Brewer Tower. Ten minutes later, though, they were making love on the rug.

The following day there was a faculty meeting. Peter McGregor had circulated several memos urging faculty members to attend the most important and last meeting of the year, and to stay until the end. Even Theodora Theodoropoulos, the department's diva, whom Jane was seeing only for the second time, was honoring them with her presence. The only professors missing were Sachs, who was on sabbatical, and Duportoy, who, as usual, had found a conference to attend in Paris just the very day after classes ended. The meeting meant three hours locked up in a hot and stinking lounge where the windows couldn't even be opened because of the noise of the construction work next door, when it was so sunny outside and she could be walking with Eric around the park near their new house instead. Well they could keep her four, five hours if they liked—she had infinite reserves of patience. She was looking at her twelve colleagues around the long wooden table and she felt like laughing. The five tenured men, three thin and two fat, looked like they had been cloned from one another despite the variation in the size of their bellies, with their identical thin lips, ugly glasses with metallic frames, short hair and sad, ageless gray suits. Next to them sat the two tenured women who cordially hated each other: the gray-haired, fat and aggressive Begum Begolu, now wearing a fluorescent-green dress in cheap synthetic fabric, whom everyone knew had grown up in an Ankara shack where she had learned how to fight at an early age, and the magnificent Theodora Theodoropoulos, born into a rich Athenian family, still extremely beautiful at nearly sixty, dressed in her elegant jogging suit, the white of which contrasted with her short and very black hair. Then came the five disposable faculty members, four relatively young women, among them Jane, and a bald young man, all sickly pale, thin and childless. They looked like scared little mice and rarely opened their mouths. Poor Carrie, because she was DUS, director of undergraduate studies, had to sit between Peter McGregor, the director of graduate studies, and the old Frenchman who was going to retire soon.

Poor them. All of them. Even those who had tenure at Devayne, this sign of highest achievement. They were like kids, arguing about trifles with terribly serious voices. So little joy on their faces. Had any one of them ever made love to someone they adored with all their soul and all their body?

It was enough just to look at them. Bronzino was living with his mother. The old Frenchman was drowning his solitude in alcohol. Peter McGregor had a pretty wife and three adorable little girls, but the face of this erudite Pascal specialist had something dry and bitter that revealed his disillusionment with a world in which the austere love of rules had no place anymore, except at a university. Old Carrington, a good grandpa with white hair who had been married for over forty years already, had just come out of the closet. Even beautiful Theodora was said to be very lonely since her girlfriend had accepted a position at the University of California in Irvine ten years earlier. And what to say of Begum Begolu, with her shark's teeth and her four tiny barking creatures which had earned her the nickname—given by a malicious graduate student—of "Two-Books-and-Four-Dogs." No wonder they were all desperately hanging on to the miserable little power left to them: torturing graduate students and refusing tenure to their young colleagues.

Jane was smiling inside herself. She knew something that the twelve mummies around the table didn't know. She felt like screaming to all of them Four Commandments:

There is but one kind of love.
Walk away if there is even the shadow of a doubt.

You have only one matching half.

Don't stop looking before you find it, or you will be buried alive.

She was amazingly lucky, but it wasn't only luck. She could have married Josh or Norman or found another Eyal. She had faced her demons and accepted being alone. Even after meeting Eric she hadn't given up. Her happiness was well deserved.

While her colleagues were discussing the old French test that the students found to be too difficult, Jane had replayed in her mind images from the night before, their bodies on the rug, Eric's beautifully designed mouth, his large chest with the thin dark blond hair, his muscular shoulders, his hollow belly button, his firm and round buttocks, his thighs, his soft brown member that was so small when it was quietly lying on his balls and then rose so big under Jane's fingers, each time giving her the sensation that she was still a virgin. Not too big, though: he didn't tear her. Just the right size. She loved everything about him. His tongue delicately licking or deeply penetrating her vagina. His member inside her mouth, even the smell of pee before the shower, and that other smell, salty and metallic like rust, of the dry and blond hair under his armpits. She loved his hair, but she was sure she would also love him bald, for his face was so pretty, and his ears too, and the shape of his head. She loved his skin—the color of his skin, the texture of his skin, the taste of his skin. His regular, large teeth, not very well taken care of, which he had agreed, as a supreme proof of his love, to have examined by Jane's father, and which he now flossed every night. His always new ways of making love to her. Last night, just as she was about to come, he had withdrawn and opened her right thigh as far as he could in order to penetrate her at a perpendicular angle. In this strange position, forming a cross, he had gone deeper into her and she had been able to feel even better his member screwed inside her body with no other point of contact between them.

All tenured professors, except for Theodoropoulos, agreed with one another. The old French test shouldn't be made easier. A Devayne Ph.D. ought to remain difficult. Jane was grinding her teeth, smiling in spite of herself. Another two hours and she would be home. Eric was waiting for her there. A shiver of desire had gone down her spine. It was a fever of joy. She had suddenly met Bronzino's eyes, cold and disapproving, and bitten her lips in an effort to extinguish the sparkle in her eyes.

She could date with precision that peak of happiness: May 2, 1994, sixteen months ago. It was just after the meeting, at 6 P.M., that she had picked up her mail downstairs and found the off-white envelope from Princeton University Press.

When she had noticed the press's letterhead, her heart had started beating fast and she had brutally plunged into the kind of reality she was contemplating from on high a moment before. The first professional comment on her work of eight years. She had immediately got the feeling that it was bad news and quickly torn the envelope open. "I am sorry. . . ." A rejection. She had read the letter and the report twice during the bus ride. Not a positive word in it except that her writing was clear and energetic. When she had gotten off the bus and seen the white dollhouse where her love was waiting for her, there was nothing left of her jubilant sense of superiority. Eric had walked downstairs to welcome her. She could only hand over the report to him without a word, in a gesture worthy of a Greek tragedy. Eric, standing next to a pile of boxes, had quickly skipped through it.

"Good."

"Good? Are you crazy?"

"There isn't a single argument against your book. The reader even contradicts himself: you are saying the opposite of what everyone says, and yet you don't have any original ideas. He, or she, is just irritated."

"So what?"

"Jealousy. It means it's a good book."

"But rejected!"

"There is one good point in the report, concerning the books and articles that you didn't quote. . . ."

"I can't quote everything; I read tons of books and articles in English, French, German, even Italian! I don't quote the ones in which there is nothing for my argument, or those written by idiots."

"Idiots have a lot of power in this world, sweetie. If you want my opinion, your reader is one of the idiots whose books he mentions here. He's furious because you wrote a good book and you didn't quote him. You know what I would do?"

She was looking at him expectantly.

"Take the last book on Flaubert in English, check the index and make sure that you quoted everybody who is alive today in the United States. Don't be so upset—there is no success story without one or two rejections, you know that."

Everything he said had the simplicity and the clarity of evidence. He was so handsome, with his light brown hair falling on his forehead, his black polo shirt and his blue jeans, bare feet. She loved his long feet with their long toes—the one in the middle longer than the second one—and always-clean nails. It was like one of those Breton skies Rosen had described to her: sun, rain, and sun again, quickly following the wind that brought the clouds and then pushed them away. Eric sitting next to her on the sofa, dropping the letter, kissing her, and whispering in her ear that it was nice, last night on the rug. Making love to her five minutes later, on the rug again.

Sixteen months ago. It could be sixteen years. It belonged to the time before Herring's death. Once upon a time, when she thought that nobody could touch that: Eric. When the worst thing that could happen to her was a rejection letter. When she didn't know this incident was just a warning sent by the Erinyes. Don't be too happy. Hubris.

She turned left. Home. So deep in thought that the forty-minute walk from the downtown bus stop barely seemed five minutes. The sun would be setting soon. The white house looked golden in the early evening summer light. She unlocked the door. The living room was sad at this hour, when it was still bright outside but you had to turn on the light inside. The answering machine was blinking. She pushed the message button. Allison: Jane should call tonight if she felt lonely. Sweet.

The shelves to the right of the fireplace were much whiter where Eric's books had been. She brought some paper towels from the kitchen. Vacuum cleaning wouldn't be a luxury either. Last time they washed the windows was for the housewarming party fifteen months ago, when they received their forty guests. The photograph of Eric and Hubert Herring that Jane had snapped that day in the garden was still on the shelf. It was significant that Eric left it behind. She dusted the top of the frame, and then the other frame on the lower shelf. Jeremy running toward the camera with vacillating steps, like a little bear, his plump hands thrust forward, and a smile that would soon turn to tears—not sure whether he liked the funny mask on his mother's face. So cute. She smiled and kissed the glass. He must have changed since the last time she saw him more than a year ago, when Allison and John spent a whole week with them in Old Newport. A dream week. Allison and John under Eric's spell, she and Eric under Jeremy's spell. They spent the days hiking and the nights talking in the garden or in the kitchen around the excellent bottles of California wine Allison and John had brought. July 1994. Two weeks before Herring's death. Jeremy would turn two in ten days. She had to remember to call.

She helped herself to a glass of filtered water in the kitchen. It was dark outside. Nine o'clock already. In the bathroom she rinsed her bathing suit and took a shower. She stayed a long time under the hot water, washing salt and sand off her body. The phone rang just as she was getting out of the tub. She grabbed a towel, ran to the bedroom, threw herself onto the bed and picked up the receiver.

"Eric?"

There was no sound on the line.

"Eric? Do you hear me? Is that you? I can't hear anything. I'll hang up, OK? Please try again from another phone!"

She hung up. The room was completely dark. She shivered. She was cold. She looked at the phone and suddenly wondered whether she had locked the front door of the house. She ran downstairs, still wet and naked. The door was locked. The phone rang again and startled her. She picked it up in the living room.

"Hi, it's me."

"Hi! How are you? Where are you?"

"In a motel outside Toledo."

"Did you try to call me just a few minutes ago?"

"No, why?"

"Someone called. I couldn't hear anything."

"A bad connection."

"I guess so. But I got scared. With no car in the driveway . . ."

"Don't worry. You're safe."

"I know. You're not too tired?"

"Dead. I drove twelve hours straight. It was a good idea to leave on Saturday: there wasn't too much traffic."

"Will you get there tomorrow?"

"Hopefully. Another twelve hours at least, though."

"Don't kill yourself. Why don't you do it in three days?"

"I'll see. I would like to get there. Don't worry, I'll be careful. What were you doing just now?"

"Taking a shower." She laughed. "I'm naked and still wet."

"Ha-ha. . . ."

Missing him so much already. Toledo. Never been there. Tomorrow even farther.

"What did you do today?" Eric asked softly.

"You can be proud of me; I didn't cry. I worked five hours on the article. I finished it."

"I'm proud of you."

"This afternoon I took the bus to Fort Hale. I saw that crazy guy again, you know, the one who scared me last time. Today I had to shake his hand. His name is Sleazy; he wanted to know everything about me. He's crazy enough to be in a mental hospital, but he's a sweet crazy guy. He speaks constantly to everyone on the bus and he calls people by their names. Nobody minds him. When we crossed West Old Newport, at a stop he suddenly leaned outside the window and he was screaming: 'This is Mrs. Jackson with her daughter! Hi, Mrs. Jackson! How are you? How is your daughter? Hi, Dorothy!' He knows absolutely everyone." She laughed. "Anyway. It put me in a good mood. Maybe to realize that this crazy man wasn't dangerous and that, after all, I could be nice to him and it wouldn't hurt."

"Not *too* nice."

She laughed.

"I swam for almost one hour and I walked home from the bus stop. I should sleep like a baby tonight."

Eric yawned. "I wish you were with me."

"So do I. How is the motel?"

"As charming as in *Psycho.* I'm dead tired anyway. My only fear is that the boxes in the car are going to tempt someone. I wasn't thinking when I took the boxes for the stereo and the VCR."

"Oh no!"

"I put a little note on the window that says BOOKS ONLY. I hope they'll believe me."

Later, as she cooked dinner, she put on a CD of Brazilian guitar music. The rhythmic, soft music filled the house with a warm presence. The following night at midnight, she was waiting for Eric's call, wondering what she would do if she hadn't heard from him by 1 A.M., when the phone rang. He had just got there. He was too tired to have any impression of the place yet.

Monday he called again. Eleven hours of sleep: he was feeling much better. The apartment was great: large, bright, conveniently furnished. There was carpeting, which Jane wouldn't like, but plenty of large windows overlooking high trees and a very blue sky.

"Is it far from the center of town?"

"Right in the center."

He had already unpacked all his books. There was only one person missing for him to feel at home.

On Tuesday, the bell rang at ten in the morning. Jane ran downstairs: a delivery of twelve red roses. Their second anniversary.

It wasn't like three years earlier in Paris. She wasn't depressed. She missed him terribly, but it was endurable. She was replacing Carrie as director of undergraduate studies. When Bronzino had asked her last spring, she was furious: it meant much more work without being paid more, yet there was no way to say no. Now she was glad: it kept her busy. She spent every afternoon in her office, her door open for the students to walk in. She had traded her small fourth-floor office for a spacious room on the third floor between the offices of the chairman and of the director of graduate studies. She was reading and underlining the Green Book of rules—so boring that she had to read a sentence four times before it made sense. She and Eric called each other regularly, but without setting the times in advance. The surprise of hearing his voice sometimes made her cry. After hanging up she often remained motionless for ten or fifteen minutes, smiling. Thanksgiving was too far away. On September 18 she bought a ticket to visit him the weekend of October 20. This way she wouldn't be alone for the fourth anniversary of the abortion. When she told Eric, his voice took on the particularly sweet intonation of desire that made her shiver.

He was thrilled with his new place. The students weren't bad at all; the colleagues, very respectable scholars and, in addition, generous people. The difference from Devayne was that everyone here had read his book and talked to him about it. There was no competition, no hostility, and a real interest in one another's work. The library was also much better than expected. Another pleasant surprise was the audiovisual center, where great films were shown every night, not only on weekends like at Devayne. There was something else Jane would like: a creative writers' workshop where novelists came from all over the world. On the phone he always sounded good. It was Eric at his best: charming, tender, making her laugh with little anecdotes.

Finally he may have been right, Jane told herself on her way to George Townsend College, where she was meeting Bronzino for lunch. The six weeks since Eric left had passed like a day, and she was flying to Iowa in two days. Yet she was so upset, in June, when Eric had impulsively accepted the last-minute offer without even consulting her. Iowa seemed so far. He still had another year at Devayne; they could have remained together. But he had said: "I know my limits, Jane. Another year like this last one would kill me. Would kill us."

Yes, she remembered. It had been a slow, sure descent into hell, from the morning of August 6, 1994, when Annette Herring woke them up at

8 A.M. and announced Hubert's death in a plane crash the day before. His own plane. Flying was his hobby.

It started as a heavy silence. Eric was busy finishing his second book and helping Annette to clean out Hubert's office. He was also taking care of Herring's students. Some would continue their doctoral research under his guidance, which was good, since he had only one doctoral student so far. In September the silence intensified when he learned that the new chairperson was Judith L. Swarns. She hated Eric, having made advances to him that he rejected. His marrying Jane destroyed her assumption that he must therefore be gay. Anyway, the favorites of one regime were never those of the next. Everyone else in the department liked Eric. They all came to the housewarming party in May. His book got excellent reviews. His teaching evaluation forms were always enthusiastic: two hundred students were taking his lecture class on European painting and many were fighting to get into his seminar, which had limited enrollment. He already had a contract for a second book. His colleagues knew that he had refused an offer from Berkeley on Herring's advice: this meant an implicit promise of tenure. Swarns wasn't the only one who would vote.

On February 9, Eric was denied tenure. He had a new wrinkle on his forehead between his eyebrows. Better to know, anyway; the worst thing had been the uncertainty. It was easy to understand why he was denied: jealousy. Tenure at Devayne would have been too much for a good-looking, thirty-eight-year-old man with two books to his credit, a charming wife, and a new house. The successful housewarming party had worked to his disadvantage. His buying a house meant he thought that he was sure to get tenure. What was a certainty before Herring's death looked like arrogance afterward. Hubris.

Eric kept saying that he wasn't worried. He didn't know of any Devayne professors who had become bums. He complained of pains in his back and his neck. Between March and June they didn't make love once. Her fault, maybe. They tried and failed once or twice in February, and again in March. Then the fear was there, and she knew that it wouldn't work. She couldn't stand it, couldn't stand his body close to her, in the same bed, in the same room, under the same roof, him with his penis always soft. No desire. Eric said this was only a temporary technical problem that had nothing to do with Jane; the trouble with her was that she always thought that he didn't desire her. Jane wanted to believe him. She was terrified that Eric loved her the way she had loved Josh: tenderly, affectionately, as a security, without passion. Not the right way.

He started to sleep alone in his study or in the living room downstairs, on the unopened beige-and-white-striped sofa. He'd fall asleep watching TV, which still would be playing in the morning when she went downstairs for breakfast, relieved that the awful night was over. She cried almost every night, wondering whether they were being punished because they had been too happy. The only person with whom she could allude to the situation was Allison.

"Give him a break," Allison said. "Poor Eric. You don't know what it is to be jobless and to be treated unfairly, Jane. It's even worse for a man. He must be so afraid of disappointing you." Allison's strongest recommendations: "Never cry in front of him; don't complain; express desire, but no frustration; be tender, calm, and reassuring; don't ask for any reassurance; give him massages; give up the idea of getting laid for a while. You two have a whole lifetime ahead to make love."

In May, after sobbing for one hour on the sidewalk simply because an adorable Chinese baby had smiled back at her while she was in line at the grocery store, Jane suddenly realized what the matter was. First the wedding, then the house. The next thing on her mental agenda was a baby. Not easy to conceive a baby when you never made love. In his own way, Eric was asking her to choose between him and a baby. Loving was also about giving up. She never cried in front of him anymore.

After he was offered the position in Iowa, Eric came back to life like an animal awakening after a long hibernation. He was completely transformed; he became his old self again—charming, funny and passionate. The good months of July and August were much needed after the terrible year.

Jane reached the college gate at 12:30 P.M. She had to wait for a student to arrive and unlock the gate. She ran across the garden of the colonial dormitory. Rock music came out of an open window. Her first lunch with Bronzino in four years; she couldn't be late. She handed over her Devayne ID to the woman at the entrance to the dining hall, and recognized Bronzino's tall figure and short frizzy hair in the line. She took a tray and said hello to him from afar. Professors could get free lunches in the colleges, but their privileges stopped there: she couldn't cut into the line. She was in no hurry to join Bronzino, who wanted to talk to her about her impending review for her promotion and the extension of her contract for another four years.

He had chosen a small table in a far corner where they wouldn't be disturbed by the noisy students. She sat in front of him. He hadn't changed except that he wasn't wearing a bow tie and a tweed jacket, but a big Irish sweater.

"You look good," she said.

He didn't react. He glanced quickly at his watch.

"I'm afraid I don't have much time. Someone is coming to my office at 1 P.M. Let's get straight down to business. Your dossier is solid, Jane. The eight articles—is that right?—published in serious academic journals will make a favorable impression. And you have taught seminars on various topics. Your being DUS now is also a positive element. But you need a book."

She tensed. "I know. I'm late because I revised my book last year, after it was rejected by Princeton University Press."

"Without a book, I can't guarantee you anything. You don't need to have the book published, but at least there should be a contract. Or some people in the department may oppose your promotion."

Who? Probably Begolu, who didn't like younger women. Bronzino put a big lettuce leaf into his mouth and licked some sauce at the corner of his lips with the tip of his tongue. He had chosen, like Jane, the rice and turkey casserole. His tray was crowded with food: a plate with lemon pie; an apple, a banana and two oranges; three English muffins; even a small box of Kellogg's All-Bran. It would be tough to eat all of this in twenty minutes.

"I'm waiting to hear from the University of Chicago Press. I have reasons to believe it will work out."

"Which are?"

"The editor was enthusiastic after reading my introduction and my summary: she called me immediately and she asked for the manuscript. I think it's a good sign."

"It is. When was that?"

"Over the summer, maybe in July, I don't remember exactly."

"That's four months ago. You haven't heard from her yet?"

"No."

"Did you give her a call?"

"Not yet."

He shook his head reproachfully. "You can't waste time like this."

She blushed. "I was very busy with the DUS work since everything is new, and it hasn't been easy for me with Eric gone. . . ."

"Your family situation isn't the university's business. You need to act more professionally. Let me know as soon as you have a contract: we'll add it to your dossier."

She shivered, suddenly realizing he would be the one opposing her promotion. It was clear that he had never forgiven her. He was just warning her; after all, she had been honest with him. He was already eating the last bite of the casserole and he made short work of the lemon pie. He looked at his watch again and got up.

"By the way, my friend Jeffrey Woodrow has a book that just came out with the University of Minnesota Press, on a topic related to yours. You should definitely look at it and you may want to write to Minnesota Press. Use my name if you like. Act quickly, Jane. You need a contract before January."

While talking to Jane, he opened his bag and put the fruit, English muffins, and Kellogg's All-Bran inside. Jane's eyes opened wide. Maybe he didn't have time to shop for his breakfast. He walked away with his tray. She had barely started her meal, but wasn't hungry anymore. Three undergraduates sat at her table. They were gossiping about one of their fellow students who had visited a certain Vicky late last night. They paid no attention to Jane. A very skinny Asian student sitting across from her was peeling a hard-boiled egg, of which she ate only the white, and then took one lettuce leaf without dressing, while the fat girl next to her was starting to work on a huge hamburger with French fries. Jane got up, completely depressed. The fact was that there was no other faculty member at her level who didn't have a contract yet. Carrie's book had just come out. Even James had a contract. Without a book, not only would she not be promoted at Devayne, but she wouldn't get a job anywhere else. Publish or perish—That was the law.

The following morning, she forced herself to dial the number of the University of Chicago Press humanities editor. She left a message.

That night, when she came back home, the red light was blinking. It wasn't Eric, who had called her at the office. Her heart was beating fast when she pressed the button. She immediately recognized the professional voice. The editor, a young woman, apologized for the delay: as everyone had left the country over the summer she had found readers only in September; she would definitely let Jane know by Thanksgiving. Jane sighed. She had done her duty. She could breathe for a week.

She woke up at 4:45 A.M. to make it to the 9:30 plane at Kennedy. Almost three hours in the Connecticut Limo bus, and then two and a half hours on the plane. She waited at O'Hare in Chicago one hour before boarding the tiny commuter plane with ten people aboard. They flew through air turbulence. Jane got sick. She spent forty-five minutes throwing up in a paper bag and moaning in pain. Someone else was throwing up behind her. The smell was awful. She swore to herself that she would never, ever board a plane again—not to mention a commuter plane. She prayed to God to make them land. They finally did. The plane reached the ground in such a bumpy way that she was white with fear, certain this was her last minute alive. Eric had been waiting for one hour. They hugged and ran outside the tiny airport in Des Moines. Half an hour was spent driving to Iowa City. Eric was in a hurry; he had to teach at 2. Jane couldn't speak in the car. She was still feeling nauseous and was scared she'd throw up again even though there was nothing left in her stomach.

"I'm sorry to leave you alone. If your plane had been on time, we could have had lunch."

"Don't worry."

He just had time to carry her bag upstairs and quickly show her the house. There was food in the fridge. He was gone.

She took a shower. Unable to find clean towels, she used Eric's, which needed to be washed—along with all the dirty laundry filling his closet. He obviously hadn't vacuumed the apartment once in two months. The kitchen sink was full of dirty dishes, the sight of which made her want to throw up again. She couldn't eat anything.

The furniture wasn't to her taste. She found it common and not simple enough. The sofa was covered with an ugly multicolored fabric. The dining table was a heavy, dark, cheap imitation of a French antique. The wall-to-wall beige-gray carpet was worn and dirty. The place looked sad in spite of the large windows, maybe because of the ugly vertical blinds that hadn't been changed since the sixties. The living room windows overlooked trees and, beyond, a flat landscape with miles of fields. Downtown was already the edge of the town, since there really was no town, as she realized when they drove through Iowa City and Eric named a few buildings for her. It was only a university, with houses around it.

She rested and read, wondering when Eric would come home. He could have canceled his office hours for her. October 20 was not just any date—he knew that. He finally arrived around 7 P.M. It had been a long week. He was tired. They had dinner and went to sleep.

When they woke on Saturday, the tension between them wasn't gone. Because of it, they didn't make love. Yet the tension was there because they didn't make love. Eric cooked breakfast. Jane wasn't feeling well yet: only cereal for her. After breakfast he suggested a walk. He showed her the university buildings, his office, the lecture room, the slide library, the library, the art gallery, the audiovisual center. She did her best to express admiration. They ran into five people he knew. He was pleased to introduce his wife. They were already invited to dine with two of these people, for brunch and for dinner tomorrow. At dinner she would meet David Clark, who had a Ph.D. from Devayne. A brilliant guy, Eric told her.

Eric asked her no questions about her life. He tensed up whenever she mentioned Devayne or Old Newport. The only thing that aroused his interest was the leak in the bathroom.

They made love on Saturday afternoon. Eric afterward was lighter, more joyful. She didn't come, but she was relieved that it didn't fail. At night they watched a film. She still felt nauseous. And sad. She was always tense and angry with Eric around that date. He knew why. He was sweet and patient. There was nothing he could do.

Most of Eric's colleagues whom she met at brunch and at dinner on Sunday were older couples with children. All they talked about was their kids and their students.

"Eric said you were teaching at Devayne," a young man said to her, the only single man there, also the only young man. He was thin and short, with bad skin, dressed in a black shirt and black jeans. He was David Clark, from the French and Italian department. "Devayne is no longer what it was at the time of the Devayne School of Criticism: just a bunch of old conservatives, right? Is there anybody left except for Theodoropoulos?"

She found herself singing the praises of Bronzino, Sachs, McGregor, even Begolu. He wanted to know what she thought of deconstruction and whether it was possible to say anything new about Flaubert. If there was one topic she didn't feel like touching, he had found it. He kept bringing his face close to hers and he had bad breath. Bad teeth too, she noticed, with a lot of tartar, plaque, and inflamed gums. Gingivitis. She knew from her father that dentists wore masks because there was more bacteria in the mouth than in the anus. She kept moving her face away from him discreetly. He kept closing in.

When they had all drunk a few beers, there were many jokes and loud laughter about people whom Jane didn't know—colleagues or secretaries. Eric sometimes turned to her and explained what was funny.

"You weren't too bored?" Eric asked as soon as they got into his car, around midnight.

"No, I was fine. They're very sweet. But the plane trip out here really upset my stomach and I'm nervous about the flight tomorrow."

"I know. My poor darling."

On Monday morning he was teaching. In the afternoon he drove her to Des Moines. It was less windy than it had been last Saturday, but she swallowed three Dramamines anyway. She was so deeply asleep when the plane landed in Chicago that they had to transfer her from plane to plane in a wheelchair.

She slept all the way back to Old Newport. She was home by midnight and went straight to bed.

On Tuesday morning there was a stack of letters and memos on her desk, some of which needed immediate answers. For some reason the students seemed to have all chosen that morning to get information about majoring in French or about going to France with the Junior Year Abroad program. She sat at her desk, trying to keep a patient smile. When she had the time to look at her watch, it was already 12:55. Her stomach was gurgling. She hadn't had any breakfast and she was starving after eating so little for four days. Her class was at 1 P.M. An undergraduate was still waiting at her door and he had been here for twenty-five minutes, so she couldn't send him away.

"Just come in and wait for me one minute."

She ran toward the secretaries' offices. Mary's door was closed; she was at lunch. Jane rushed into Dawn's office, who was on the phone. The half-eaten tuna salad sandwich in a paper on the desk made her drool.

"I know," Dawn was saying, "isn't that terrible? I would never have believed that of him. When you think that she. . . ."

She ignored Jane, who was giving signs of her presence by clearing her throat.

"Wait a sec," Dawn finally said. She turned to Jane. "What do you want?"

Jane gave her nicest smile. "Could you do me a favor?"

"What?"

"I'm awfully late, I'm teaching in five minutes, there is still a student in my office, and I'm starving. Do you mind grabbing a slice of pizza for me downstairs?"

She handed over two dollars.

"I can't," Dawn replied, turning her back on Jane. "Hi. Sorry. So this is what I think you should tell her. . . ."

Jane retreated out of the office, her cheeks red, stunned as if Dawn had just slapped her. A good thing there had been no witness to her humiliation. She knew it was her fault. Dawn, who was an excellent secretary— more efficient than Mary—had to make the limits of her responsibilities very clear or she would be overwhelmed with work. Mary was the DUS's secretary, not Dawn, who was working for the chairman and the other professors. In addition, it was probably Dawn's lunch break right now. But there was more. Dawn would have talked to no other faculty member as she had just talked to Jane. Jane's mistake again: in September, she had had a nice chat with Dawn on a Friday afternoon, as everybody had already left for the weekend and Jane was in no hurry to get home where nobody was waiting for her. She and Dawn had found out that they were the same age and got married the same year and even the same month. Dawn had looked with eager curiosity at the Fort Hale wedding picture that Jane had put on her desk, and which she was quite proud to show. There was nothing to say: Eric was dazzlingly handsome and Jane didn't look bad either, with her radiant smile. Dawn, a big woman with a flat face, could never produce such a beautiful picture. Dawn's attitude toward Jane had changed soon afterward. There was no way Jane could regain her previous authority.

When she got home that night, the red light on the answering machine was blinking. One message. She had a heart palpitation when she pushed the button. Not a day for good news; on the other hand, publishers didn't call unless it was to announce good news.

"Hi, sweetheart. . . ."

Eric. She hadn't thought about him once in the whole day. She had come back from Iowa the night before. It could have been a hundred years.

" . . . I hope that you had a good trip back and that you didn't get sick this time. I won't be able to call you tonight: there is a dinner after the lecture. By the way, you charmed absolutely everyone here. I don't know what you told David, but I have never heard him praise anyone more. It was wonderful to see you. I miss you. Don't forget the plumber."

Jane put down the page and shrugged her shoulders. No more doubt. "Hubris": a signature.

If Josh thought he could publish that . . . She would sue him and the publishing company. She needed to consult a lawyer. Allison?

How did Josh know so much? How did he find out, for instance, that she had got scared, that first night alone in the house on Peach Street, after she picked up the phone and nobody answered?

Could Josh have been the caller?

Could he have been spying on her all these years?

Was he mad? Had he turned all his frustration with the university against Jane?

Once again she thought of calling a psychiatrist. The best thing would be to talk to someone at the Devayne Health Center, where there was a department of mental hygiene. But the number was in the Devayne directory that she had left at her office.

Anyway, there was no hurry. She had nothing to fear. The man who had spent years writing this novel was certainly not sane, but he was not the kind of person to commit a crime. By sending an anonymous manuscript, Josh probably wanted to surprise her more than scare her. His goal was to show her how clever he was—how superior to her he was.

This was what she had always disliked about him: his conviction that he knew Jane better than she knew herself, and that he was superior to the rest of the world.

His arrogance was particularly striking when he described the faculty meeting or her first trip to Iowa. He imbued her with an attitude of contempt that was his own. She had never felt that she was superior to her colleagues, nor had she despised Eric's colleagues, who were very nice people, certainly nicer than Josh.

Josh didn't lend her a feeling of superiority for very long: a mere reader's report was enough to ruin her happiness.

It was true that she had shed many tears because of that academic book. But it was easy for Josh to stand as a free being: he had never managed to get into the establishment, and therefore had never had to resist the pressure from within.

Jealousy, Eric would have said.

Josh thought he could portray Eric and write about their couple! He didn't know anything about love.

She smiled scornfully and picked up the manuscript.

4

She still didn't like the taste but was getting addicted to the burning in her chest. Then a good, deep, easy sleep. Not tonight. It was hard to fall asleep with whispers reaching through the closed door.

She opened her eyes. Shadows of furniture in the dark: the long, modern white chest, with its eight drawers, four and four, along the wall; the large mirror above; the pinewood rocking chair near the bookcase; two white tables on both sides of the bed. A good, hard bed. A room furnished simply, with taste.

She turned on the light. In front of her, next to the door, stood the white bookcases with the photographs and the leather-bound books that looked like they had been bought not to be read but only to decorate the shelves. If only that door would open and Eric would appear. She would immediately apologize. But she knew he would wait until she was asleep.

Simple plastic frames, the ones that cost one or two dollars. Eric as a newborn baby in his mother's arms: 1957. Eric as an adorable toddler with an anxious smile, holding mother and father's hands. Jane was surprised when she met Nancy to discover that Eric's mother was a short and plump lady with curly brown hair; that photograph had confirmed what she could already guess, that Eric looked just like his father, a blond, slender, tall and handsome man with Paul Newman's smile. Eric as an eight-year-old in ice-hockey equipment, his left hand forming a V and his right hand holding a cup; on his face, just the right triumphant smile. Eric on the beach in Florida between Ann and Nancy, a thin pre-teen already taller than his tiny grandmother and even his mother; the same photogenic smile. The high school graduation photo: big square glasses, a horrible haircut, braces, a really bright green suit from the seventies and a large tie with orange and brown squares, which made Jane burst into laughter the first time she saw it, upsetting Eric. Even so, there was present the same photogenic and slightly anxious smile. The photo of his Princeton graduation, on a sunny day, standing next to his grandmother, now barely reaching his chest: the smile again. The official picture of the Harvard graduation: a serious, handsome young man in a purple gown, with a radiant smile. How young he looked ten years ago! Next to this last picture, and halfway behind it, was the Fort Hale wedding photograph, the only one in a mahogany frame—bought by Jane. The part with her in it disappeared behind the graduation picture, so it looked like Eric in his dark suit was tenderly smiling at himself in his Harvard gown.

She needed a tissue. She got up and walked to the rocking chair with her clothes on it. The parquet floor was warm and impeccably clean—like the rest of the apartment. From the bathroom to the kitchen, Nancy's place always smelled fresh. There were little baskets of dried petals and orange skins everywhere.

It was so hot. Probably that was why she couldn't fall asleep. Nancy kept the thermostat at 75 degrees—heating was included in the maintenance charges. Two nights ago Jane had opened the window, which was how she caught the cold. The night before, she had slipped out of the room to lower the thermostat in the living room; on the way back to the bedroom, she had let out a scream of fear when she had bumped into Nancy who, perfectly silent, looked like a ghost in her long white nightdress. Fifteen minutes later the thermostat was back at 75.

If only Nancy hadn't closed the store for a week. Christmas was a good business period for a liquor store and Nancy needed the money. She would be better off leading her normal life than gossiping with Eric from morning to night. But any suggestion on Jane's part would have been like pushing the button on a bomb.

The bomb had gone off tonight anyway.

There were a few attenuating circumstances. The fever, the loneliness. Ten days already in this one-bedroom apartment, between Nancy who was hostile to her and Eric who treated her like a stranger. After months of separation, when she and Eric really needed to be together. And it was truly her favorite sweater. Not just a way to make Eric feel more guilty. But she overreacted when she summoned Eric to the bedroom just before dinner.

"What's that?" he asked.

"My cashmere sweater. The one my mother bought for me at Barney's: you put it in the dryer!"

"Oh, I am sorry . . ."

He took it from her hands and pulled it in a vain attempt to make it bigger. She took it back from him.

"It's completely useless!"

"We'll go to Barney's and get you another."

"We'll never find the same one! I loved that one. I've never had a sweater that fit me so well."

"Sorry. I didn't notice."

"This is exactly the problem! You just don't notice me these days!"

"Do you mind speaking less loud?"

"Do you need to remind me that I'm not home?" she screamed. "Do you think I don't know that?"

"Will you shut up?"

An icy order, with nothing soft and apologetic left in his voice.

"Get out of here! Get out of this room! Get out right now!"

She yelled so loud that even the downstairs neighbors must have heard. After he left the room, she cried noisily for half an hour. When she joined Nancy and Eric at the dinner table with red and swollen eyes, mother and son continued their conversation about taxes on alcohol, and the stock market. After dinner, and the little glass of whiskey to help her fall asleep, she silently withdrew to the bedroom. She didn't offer to help with the dishes, and they didn't pay attention to her.

Not Eric's fault.

Not Eric's fault if his grandmother died on December 21, the day after Jane arrived in Iowa City. They badly needed this month together. You became strangers to each other when you were no longer living in the same place. Maybe this was why Eric, in November, had accepted so many dinner invitations. He was probably afraid to be alone with her. He said she was paranoid: what could he do if his wife was the most popular person in Iowa City? Plus it was always the same: nobody invited you when you were alone and as soon as you didn't need the companionship anymore, everyone called. He had promised Jane that Christmas would be calmer.

When he learned the news, there had been no choice but to fly to Portland immediately. Eric couldn't leave his mother alone. He was also very sad. He loved his grandmother.

There was nothing Jane could begrudge him, except his perfection. The good-son side of him. The way he gave her roses for Valentine's and on their anniversary, and always made love to her on those dates. On her birthday too. She was now wondering about his romantic attachment to rituals and the beautiful smile in all his pictures. A smile asking: do I smile well? Not Eric's fault. Just too many women around him, all expecting him to be perfect. His mother, his grandmother. What else did Jane expect from him? Eric was really nice. Even here, in Portland, he was careful to spend time alone with her, and he asked every morning what she wanted to do.

Not Eric's fault.

Not his fault if Jane couldn't stand failure.

Not his fault if there was an off-white envelope with a publisher's letterhead in her mailbox when she returned from Iowa after the Thanksgiving vacation, on November 28.

She had been so scared when she found the envelope with the University of Chicago Press letterhead that she waited until she was home to open it. At home she had spent one hour at her desk, covering pages of a notebook with feverish handwriting. Mocking and admonishing herself. She hated her fear. It reduced her to the opposite of what she wanted to be: a strong, independent and free person. A rejection wouldn't be the end of the world. She would go to the library and make lists of academic publishers to whom she would first send the summary of her book to make sure they were interested in it, instead of mailing her manuscript blindly like a shipwreck victim throwing a bottle into the ocean. All along she was entertaining a secret thought: bad things never happened when you were really scared. In high school, whenever the fear of failing an exam gave her stomach cramps, she always ended up with a good grade.

The trouble was that she couldn't completely forget about a few positive signs: the editor's enthusiastic reaction to her manuscript's introduction; her promptness in answering Jane's call in October; and, simply, Jane's awareness that the book, with all the revisions, had become quite good.

She was scared, but not utterly terrified. The result was that she tore the envelope open and the first word she saw was "sorry."

The three-page letter said that the book should be published with a few changes, particularly the addition of a chapter on feminist theory, in which the author would clarify her theoretical standpoint. Jane in her introduction had explained that she didn't touch feminist theory because it had nothing to do with her thesis, which was about writing, not about the relationship between men and women. There was no other objection, and not a single argument against her book. Yet it had decided her fate. It wasn't positive enough for the young editor to go ahead and send it to another reader: she preferred to return it, and she wished Jane good luck with finding another publisher.

In that moment, Jane knew that she would never pass the barrier of not-enthusiastic-enough readers. To be published you needed a powerful connection. Hers had been Bronzino. She had lost it by doing the most unprofessional thing: mixing her career with her private life.

She had found Eric's bottle of bourbon in a cabinet and poured herself a glass, drinking it straight. It burned her throat and she didn't like the taste. She had such a migraine afterward that she had fallen on her bed still dressed and moved her head from side to side, only wishing that the bong, bong, bong would stop.

On the phone the following day, Eric had been once again reassuring and comforting, finding the right words. It was just a matter of being patient. It had nothing to do with the quality of her work, but there was no market for literary criticism these days. Even famous scholars had difficulty getting published. The first book was the hardest.

To get well known you needed to be published. To get published you needed to be well known: how did one get out of this vicious circle?

"You will," Eric said. "Just be patient."

Life was just about being patient, again and again and again and again.

The door opened. A shadow walked in silently.

"I'm not asleep. You can turn on the light."

The light made her blink. Eric turned his back to her and took his pants off. The pair of boxers with the small red and white squares she had bought at the Gap for $4 on sale were so cute on his round, firm buttocks. Good muscles there. And the legs, covered with thin blond hair, so beautifully shaped that they could have served as a model for the statue of a Greek god. Allison had noticed them. She sighed. Not easy, when he had just buried his dear grandmother, to make love to his angry wife on his mother's bed.

"I'm sorry for tonight. I didn't mean to scream like that. I don't know what's going on with me."

He turned around and sat on the bed.

"It's not easy for you, I know. I'm sorry too. I shouldn't have talked to you like I did. Do you still have a fever?"

"Ninety-nine-point-eight."

He put his hand on her forehead. She closed her eyes. His fresh, soft skin. As he was moving away, she reached out and grasped his hand. She brought it to her lips and kissed it. He smiled. He took off his watch.

"You know . . ." she said hesitantly, in a low voice.

"What?"

"I don't think your mother likes me very much."

He raised his eyebrows. "Why do you say that?"

The relationship between Nancy and Jane had always been cordial, if not the most relaxed. Each time, in Maine or in Connecticut, they had given each other carefully chosen gifts. Jane was now wearing a cotton nightdress bought by Nancy in an elegant French lingerie store. On her jacket Nancy had pinned an antique brooch Jane had brought her. Nancy was a very discreet mother-in-law who never called them, so Jane was careful to remind Eric to call his mother, and she wrote postcards for each holiday when they were not visiting Nancy.

"Remember yesterday morning? We were chatting in the kitchen just after you woke up. Your mother walked in. She interrupted us as I was talking to ask you if you had had any breakfast, and whether you wanted her to prepare your coffee and bagel."

Eric smiled. "So?"

"The message was clear: how come your wife isn't preparing your breakfast?"

He laughed. "Sweetie, you know very well that my mother is obsessed with feeding me. It has nothing to do with you. Personally, I like it that you don't force me to eat. That's why I married you."

Jane shook her head. "No, I don't think I'm wrong. Two days ago, when you went grocery shopping in the afternoon, something else happened."

"What?" He looked at her with a tenderly ironic, but also slightly tense, smile.

"I was reading in the bedroom, as usual, and your mother was in the kitchen, watching TV. I went to the bathroom for two minutes. When I returned to the bedroom, she had turned off the light."

"And?"

"Don't you see the message she is sending me? She knew I was reading there. Turning off the light was very hostile. Or she couldn't help it. In any case, she doesn't want me in her house."

He shook his head.

"I think you're being a little paranoid. Most probably she picked up something in her room and then turned off the light without even thinking about it. It's her bedroom, don't forget. She was nice to let us have it."

He got up and stepped toward the door.

"Where are you going?" she asked with anguish.

He smiled. "To pee and brush my teeth. May I?"

"Does she tell you that I should have quit my job and moved to Iowa with you?"

It was tense, suddenly. Eric frowned and looked at her with severe eyes. "That's enough, Jane. You're being ridiculous. My mother never speaks to me about you. If she is depressed right now, I'm afraid it has nothing to do with you. Her mother just died. The world doesn't revolve around you."

The following day Jane left for Washington, D.C., as planned. When she recognized her father's tall silhouette and gray hair in the airport, she cried. The familiar kitchen in the Bethesda house had never looked so cozy and warm. At dinner she couldn't stop talking. The ten days in Portland had been a hell of loneliness and silence.

"The silence in her and around her," she told her parents, "is so heavy. This must be why Eric's father left. I'm sure the silence was there before. It's terrifying. You're always afraid to say something wrong. Like now, the topic of Eric's father: it's completely forbidden, so, of course, it fills the space."

"How old was Eric?"

"Nine years old. He talked to me about it only once, before I met his mother, so I wouldn't ask the wrong questions. He remembers very well the night they spent calling everyone: friends, family, police, hospitals. His mother mad with anxiety. And then what a cop told her a few days later. Eric was there."

"What was that?"

"That if a young woman disappeared, there was a good chance you'd find her mutilated body weeks or months later. But when a middle-aged man disappeared, if you found him again, it was usually in a nice home with a new wife and new kids: it was called midlife crisis."

"Oh my God! Poor Eric, and his mother too," Jane's mother said. "And they have never heard from him, never found out anything?"

"Nothing. Disappeared. The bank account was never touched. His body never found."

Jane's father slowly shook his head. Her mother shivered. This was something they simply couldn't imagine. It certainly explained the dark side of Eric that Jane had discovered last year: the heavy silence of which he too, like his mother, was capable. Her parents believed Jane even though they had never seen that side of Eric: their son-in-law had always been warm, talkative and absolutely charming with them. They loved him.

"Don't alienate him," her father told Jane. "He must be under a lot of pressure right now. He's the only person left in Nancy's life. And you said that his grandmother was like a second mother to him."

"And," Jane's mother added, "when your mother dies, she's still your mother, at whatever age. Nancy must be very, very sad."

Eric joined her in Old Newport before flying back to Iowa City. His first time there since he moved to Iowa four months earlier. They embraced. His smell. It was so good to have him again inside their house.

"My little one," Eric said in a voice that expressed his emotion, his love, his fear of losing her.

They talked: all of this, the tension, the struggles connecting with one another, the scenes for which Jane apologized again, was normal and already belonged to the past. They could resolve everything with one word: "difficult." They had to adapt to a new situation, to a life of commuting; they both had intense professional lives. Those ten days in Portland hadn't made things easier. Eric too found his mother quite heavy. Now it would be just fine.

After Eric left, Jane was caught in an administrative tornado. Her secretary, Mary, had retired at the end of January and was recently replaced by a charming Indian lady who didn't know any more than Jane did about what needed to be done and who was always waiting for orders. Jane was acting blindly, constantly terrified of making a mistake that could have serious consequences for the department or the life of a student. She tried to express her worry to Bronzino, who shrugged his shoulders, looking annoyed, and said that he was not the DUS. On the phone with Eric, Allison or her parents, she could talk about nothing else but the most uninteresting problems that filled her days and invaded her dreams. She had become an administrative machine. When she woke up in the morning, she was already reciting mentally the lists of things to do, and the only pleasure she got was from crossing items off her lists before falling asleep at night.

In late March she spent a week in Iowa. For once it was she who had no erotic desire. She could only think of the final version of next year's schedule that she had to bring back with her. She had to satisfy everyone's druthers or she would make enemies. Bronzino had insisted that there shouldn't be two classes scheduled at the same time. But they all wanted to teach on Tuesday and Thursday. Before leaving for Iowa, Jane had spent hours negotiating over the phone. She had to abuse the goodwill of genuinely nice people like Catherine Lehman to satisfy those who, like Xavier Duportoy, wouldn't accept any compromise. It was always the same thing: the ones sacrificed were the young women, upon whom it was easier to impose an unwanted schedule. It was depressing, but the only way to avoid more arguments and headaches.

When she walked into her office after lunch on April 26, Rose had put the Green Book's proofs on her desk, with a note asking her to read them as soon as possible. Jane sat down and rubbed her eyes.

There was already a mistake in the first page. Hotchkiss's name was spelled "Hotkiss." Some secretary had been dreaming. Jane was too tired to smile. She was correcting page ten of the galleys when someone knocked at the door.

"Come in."

A petite woman with long dark hair, a thin body and fearful eyes in a pretty face, walked in.

"Do I disturb you?"

"Hi, Christine. Not at all."

"Rose told me that I didn't have a teaching section next fall," the woman quickly said in a trembling voice, still standing between the door and the desk.

"Yes. I'm sorry. There're not enough language sections for the number of graduate students in the department. We can't give any to the eighth- and ninth-year students next fall."

Christine burst into tears and hid her face in her hands.

"What will I do? What will I do?"

Jane got up and patted her on the shoulder.

"Don't worry. I'm sure you'll find something."

Christine, in tears, ran out of the office. Jane's first impulse was to step forward and call her back. But to tell her what? An impartial priority list had been established by Bronzino and McGregor. Jane could do nothing about it, even though she looked like the one in power. She sighed, closed the door and sat back at her desk.

After correcting the proofs she leafed through her mail, putting on top of a high pile on the left of her desk all the letters from the provost and from the president's office that she didn't have the time to read but didn't dare to throw away yet. When she noticed the Stanford University Press letterhead, her heart started to beat fast. She had no illusions. You got no good news from publishers through the mail. She tore the envelope, opened the letter and immediately saw the opening sentence: "I am sorry . . ." It was not even worth reading the rest—which, anyway, was only a standard paragraph. She pulled open the right drawer of her desk and put the letter in a file labeled "Publishers" where she had, by now, a nice collection of these letters. Fifteen publishers had answered "no" after reading just her summary. Last week she received a "no" from an editor at the University of Pennsylvania Press who had asked to see her manuscript. Stanford University Press, which had published many of her colleagues, had been her strongest hope.

Her book would never be published. Nobody cared. "I am sorry," the publishers wrote to her. Just what she had told Christine. "I am sorry . . ." These words were like a knife coldly and quietly stabbing someone. Compared to Christine, she was lucky; she had Eric, who had a job. She would move to Iowa and become a housewife—occasionally teaching beginning French in the French department there.

The phone startled her. It was Rose. Professor Bronzino wanted to see Jane at once.

"Now?"

"He's waiting for you in his office."

Jane guessed that she had done something wrong. Maybe she had messed up the department's budget—a mistake that could cost thousands of dollars. If Bronzino dared to criticize her, she would tell him what she thought of him. She walked toward his office and knocked at the door.

"Come in."

He was sitting behind his desk. He looked at her over his small glasses and smiled.

"Congratulations, Jane. You have been promoted to associate professor. The reports from the outside readers were excellent: the department has decided to trust you, although you don't have a contract yet."

She stared at him, and then remembered that she was supposed to look happy and to thank him.

"You can take your promotion leave next spring if you wish. Talk to Dawn, she'll tell you what to do. If you'll excuse me, I have some urgent phone calls to make before the meeting."

She walked back to her office. The sun flooding the room through the bay window was so bright that it made her squint. She walked to the window to pull down the Venetian blinds. A tiny square of sharp green grass in the garden of the Victorian Club attracted her gaze magnetically. She never went for a walk anymore. She had not even noticed the arrival of spring.

She was promoted. She still had her job for another four years. Thanks to the promotion leave, she could be with Eric as of next January for one semester. But the good news didn't seem to sink in—didn't lift the leaden cloud over her head.

She had told everyone—particularly Eric, Allison and her parents—

how scared she was not to be promoted. But in reality, she now realized, she secretly hoped that her contract would not be renewed. This way, her fate would have been decided without her having to do anything. There would have been no choice but to move to Iowa and be with Eric.

Eric would not leave Iowa. What happened at Devayne had shaken his self-confidence. He was more vulnerable than she thought and he hated to sell himself. In Iowa they would give him tenure. Eric wanted her to move there but he would never ask her to. He was not the type of man to ask his wife to make any sacrifices.

And she was not the type of woman who could give up a prestigious job after eleven years of study and six years of teaching at Devayne. She knew that much about herself. She didn't like her job, didn't like Old Newport and, above all, didn't like to live without Eric, but she wouldn't quit. For four more years they would be thousands of miles apart. One semester together wouldn't change this reality.

Her eyes rested distractedly on the clock. It was ten past four. She jumped to her feet, grabbed her bag, slammed her door and ran toward the lounge. When she pushed open the door, they all looked up. The seat to McGregor's right was free for her. Not too many people in the room for the last meeting of the year. Only seven of them. Sad, tired faces. They were already discussing page two of the agenda: Bronzino was urging his colleagues to come up with a quick idea about how to spend the $25,000 grant from the French government before next December— otherwise they would lose the money. Hugh Carrington suggested a conference on a writer who had recently died of AIDS and whom nobody around the table seemed to know, except for Xavier Duportoy, who looked up but didn't say anything; he just yawned. There was no objection. Was it the word "AIDS," or simply the extreme fatigue? Even Begolu seemed strangely absent. She kept moving her feet in and out of her red pointed high-heeled shoes. McGregor raised another important issue, that of the decreasing enrollment in French literature seminars.

The department had shrunk like a cashmere sweater put in a dryer. Carrie, James, Hilary and Veronica, who were leaving Devayne and had skipped the meeting, wouldn't be replaced. The old Frenchman, who wasn't here either, was retiring in December. The only thing Bronzino had gotten out of the administration was permission to hire a junior professor next year, to replace the Frenchman. Jane's position would probably have been eliminated too if they hadn't promoted her.

"Jane . . ." McGregor said.

She looked up and blushed. What did McGregor ask her? She met Duportoy's eyes. A trace of a smile on his lips made her want to burst into laughter. She bit her inner lip to the point of bleeding.

" . . . will tell you," McGregor continued after clearing his throat, "that she couldn't find any sections for the eighth- and ninth-year students next fall. I suggest that we don't allow them to register after the seventh year. This is what the administration wants."

"What if they can't find a job?" Natalie Hotchkiss asked in a tense, pitched voice, which Jane found as unpleasant as Begolu's voice. Maybe antipathy started with the voice.

Hotchkiss was the only professor—with Theodora Theodoropoulos—who had signed the petition of the graduate students about starting a union. Her political activism and the fact that she dared to speak out as a lesbian in an environment as conservative as Devayne made her extremely popular among the graduate students, who barely said hello to Jane: they were fighting the administration and, for them, she *was* the administration.

"They have a Devayne Ph.D., they are on their own," McGregor replied coldly. "We are a department of French, not a charity institution."

Natalie's tough features expressed anger and scorn. Jane suddenly wondered whether she was not simply jealous of her colleague. Unlike her, Natalie Hotchkiss had courageous opinions and strong principles, and she was in control of her life.

Jane walked back to her office at 6:30, closed the door and burst into tears. Someone knocked at the door. She quickly dried her eyes. "Yes? Come in!"

McGregor's face appeared. "Are you OK?" He seemed ready to present his condolences.

"Yes. Just completely exhausted."

"Ah." He sounded surprised and closed the door again.

Jane felt ashamed. He certainly worked as much as she did but he didn't cry like a baby in his office. She calmed down and checked her e-mail. It was almost nine when she left. She was so tired that instead of walking down the stairs she walked up toward her former office. On the fourth floor, as she was waiting for the elevator, she helped herself to a cup of water from the cooler. When she straightened up, a man was standing next to her, a good-looking young man with curly dark hair, wearing a shirt with thin blue and white stripes, dark blue pants, and a well-cut green jacket. His round and open face and his warm smile inspired immediate sympathy. He put out his hand.

"Francisco Gonzalez. From the Spanish department."

He had, indeed, a Hispanic accent.

"Spanish? What are you doing on the fourth floor?"

He laughed, probably because of her inquisitive tone. She blushed.

"I'm exploring. It's the first time I've gone beyond the second floor."

"That's right. I never went to the second floor either in six years here. I had an office on the fourth floor for four years and I never talked to anyone from the Italian department, even though they were right next door."

The door of the elevator opened. He followed her inside.

"Your office is no longer on the fourth floor?"

"No, now that I am DUS, I am on the third floor."

"So what were *you* doing on the fourth floor?"

His eyes were smiling.

"Nothing. I was so tired that I walked one floor up instead of going down. We've met by pure coincidence."

"We were obviously fated to meet."

He invited her over for dinner two weeks later, when exams were over. He lived in Fort Hale and picked her up in Old Newport. He was surprised she didn't drive. He was just back from a conference in Houston. He told her how it was so sunny one afternoon that he skipped the sessions and walked around. Drivers kept stopping and asking where his car had broken down and whether they could help. When he told the cops he was just walking around the city, the expression on their face made him fear, for a few minutes, that they would put him in an asylum. Jane laughed.

"I know, it's stupid," she said. "If I learn to drive, the fear will go away—I have been told that often. But the fear is stronger than I am."

"Don't worry about it. On the contrary, maintain your difference."

As soon as she got out of Francisco's car in Fort Hale, two big dogs ran over to them, jumping and barking. Her legs turned to cotton.

"Are they nice? You won't believe it, but I'm scared of dogs too."

Francisco called them off. A woman standing on the threshold, her arms crossed over her chest, was smiling ironically.

"They only want to play."

Francisco's wife, Teresa, was a tall, sporty-looking woman with a long face. She was wearing jeans, sneakers and an old sweatshirt, while Jane had put on an elegant brown velvet shirt. Jane smiled at her apologetically.

"I know it's ridiculous. I'm sure they're very nice. I get scared when they bark. I don't know why—I was never bitten as a child. I think I'm scared because I was told that dogs smell fear and it makes them want to attack."

The woman walked back into the house, clearly thinking that there was nothing more ridiculous than being scared of her two Labradors.

Inside the house, you could see the sea from everywhere through the huge windows. Jane found it breathtaking.

Teresa relaxed when she learned that Jane was married and, later in the evening, Jane decided that Teresa was actually OK: rough on the edges and strongly opinionated, but not lacking a sense of humor. She didn't like America much, though, after one year spent in California and two years in Old Newport.

"A juicy, ripe tomato, one that has been long matured by the sun, you know, a tomato with a taste, they have no idea what it is!"

She talked as though Jane wasn't one of "them"—which was pleasant. Another couple, the Gonzalezes' neighbors, a Polish carpenter and a

Venezuelan pottery maker, joined them a little later with their dog. They had dinner outside, on the terrace that overlooked Long Island Sound. The sea was relaxing. As the sun disappeared on the other side of the house, the ocean turned from that sharp, luminous blue which can only be seen at sunset on an east-oriented sea, to a more intense blue, to dark blue. When it became chilly, Teresa lent Jane a Benetton sweater as soft as cashmere but made of artificial fabric.

"It's better; moths don't eat it."

She was flying to Iowa in three days; Francisco and Teresa, back to Madrid on the very same day. These were their last days in the seaside house. Next year Teresa would remain in Spain where she had a post-doc in a biochemistry lab, and she would keep the Labradors. Francisco would move to Manhattan, where he would sublet an apartment from an NYU professor on sabbatical, right in the heart of Greenwich Village, for only $900 a month, with parking for his car. Fort Hale, and then Manhattan: some people just knew where to live. He would come to Old Newport two or three times a week. He would be the new DUS in his department.

"Poor you!" Jane said.

He drove her home toward midnight. They wished each other a good vacation. As Jane fell asleep, she thought of Teresa's sweater, of moths, of Long Island Sound at dusk and of the injection they had to give the dogs to fly them from America to Europe.

Jane's heart was beating fast. This was definitely some kind of revenge. Someone who knew about the DUS job. Someone who knew the exact circumstances in which she had met Francisco. Someone who knew about the cashmere sweater.

She blinked. The author wasn't Josh.

Hadn't she noticed here and there some expressions that only a non-native speaker would use? The style was dry, direct, "virile": Following her own theory, revised by Bronzino, the very style of a man who didn't like the woman in himself—who had repressed the soft, sentimental, feminine part of himself.

Francisco was such a man.

Everything clicked into place like the pieces of a puzzle. If she had confided to someone, it was to him. If someone had seemed to understand her, it was him.

When she was reading the cashmere sweater scene, she couldn't help blushing, but she didn't recognize herself in this distorted reflection of her. A woman who cried because of a sweater when her husband's grandmother had just died deserved to lose her husband. This was certainly

Francisco's opinion, but he omitted one fact: she was the one who had narrated the scene to him; she was the first to judge herself.

Francisco was such a good listener. She had opened herself to him totally and even described scenes in which she played a bad part, just to see him laugh and shake his head in disapproval of her and in empathy with Eric. His laughter helped her become a better person. Never before had she trusted anyone so completely.

Here was the result. She angrily turned to the next page.

III. Not Even a Kiss

I

When she walked into the Romulus Café at 12:35 P.M., she had made up her mind not to talk about Tuesday. Francisco wasn't here yet. Hopefully he wouldn't be his usual fifteen minutes late. They didn't have much time today. The café looked empty, for most of the Devayne students had already left for Christmas holiday or were now packing. Tonight she would be in Iowa; it seemed unreal. She shivered. She still had to tell Eric about the apartment. It wouldn't be easy.

She chose a table in a corner, near the bookstore part of the café, and took off her fake fur coat. The small varnished pinewood tables and the bar in the middle reminded her of the Japanese restaurant on Tuesday night.

Francisco walked in through the bookstore. She waved, smiled at him, and got up. They kissed and hugged warmly. He took off his leather jacket.

"I like your sweater," she said. "How was the conference?"

"Thanks. The usual. Boring. But I had forgotten the smell of eucalyptus. That made the trip worth it."

He looked around for a hook on which to hang his jacket. Finding none, he folded the jacket neatly and put it on the chair's back.

"What about you? Did you have a good week? Oh, by the way, did you hear from Minnesota Press?"

"Of course not. Anyway, it never works."

"Come on. It will."

"Don't worry: it's not going to spoil my mood. It's not my fault if Flaubert is dead, white, male, tall, French and heterosexual."

"*Tall?*"

She laughed.

"Academics are short."

"I'm betting a thousand dollars that you'll get a book contract in 1997."

"Do you want to give it to me right now?"

"*You'll* give it to me. I'm not so stupid."

They opened the menus. Francisco looked tense.

"Did you talk with Teresa?" Jane asked.

"Last night. She hung up on me."

"She did!"

"I'm betraying her: Christmas, the whole family, what they'll think and so on. I'm just a coward who does everything he's told to. As if I wouldn't rather go anywhere than waste a week here and then four days locked up in a hotel suite ten hours a day with my dear hated colleagues interviewing candidates. Do you know how many applications we got? Two hundred and ten—for one job! What can I do? Do you think my chair cares about my family life? They're counting on me; I just couldn't escape."

"I know. That's the trouble with you."

"You aren't going to start this too!"

She smiled.

"You're just too reliable, too nice, and too efficient. Everyone is counting on you. I don't know anyone who works more than you. Look: you teach two new seminars; you just prepared a keynote lecture for this conference at Stanford; you are the DUS in a department that is at least twice the size of mine; you are writing an editorial column every other week for the major Spanish newspaper; you work half-time as an editor for a Spanish publishing company and every night you're trying to find an American novel that would be successful in Spain; and you are now reading two hundred job applications. Did I forget anything?"

"Two hundred and ten—and twelve, actually."

"Can't you drop something? The editorial column?"

"That's the only fun thing! I would rather drop the publishing job, but it pays well and I need the money."

"What would you like to eat today?" a Mexican waiter asked in a distinguished voice.

While Francisco was ordering his focaccia with grilled eggplant and a mineral water, Jane looked around. She was startled as she recognized Duportoy's tall figure near the shelves at the back of the store. Why wasn't he in France already? For Thanksgiving he had left Old Newport right after his Thursday class and returned ten days later just in time for his Tuesday class. She had heard him say, once, that he couldn't understand how professors could spend a single vacation day in Old Newport when they had enough money to go somewhere else.

Since Xavier never talked to her, there was little risk he would ask her in front of Francisco what she had been doing in New York on Tuesday. But he was inquisitive by nature, and he had looked quite surprised when he saw her in Grand Central's main hall just as he was running to catch the 12:03 P.M. train to Old Newport. With her fake fur coat, her black hat, her hair tied in a bun, the makeup, and her glowing eyes, she had looked pretty, like a woman walking to a date—he couldn't know this was the case, but he could have guessed. He had seemed to realize suddenly that his colleague existed.

"What are you looking at?" Francisco asked, looking over his shoulder.

"Be discreet. That guy over there, near the shelves, with the gray raincoat. It's one of my colleagues. An asshole."

"Really?"

"Oh yes. Typical French arrogance. We have been colleagues for seven years, and he barely says hi to me. He spits on Devayne, but he's a real snob: he's the only person around here I ever saw order Devayne business cards. He's supposed to be brilliant. He chose us over Harvard. He lives in New York, of course."

Francisco smiled.

"I live in New York too."

"But he's nothing like you."

"You sound like a scorned woman. Are you attracted to him?"

"To him? Are you kidding?"

Francisco looked at the back of the bookstore again.

"Well, he's tall."

"I don't like his face. And he can't talk without sweating; I find it disgusting. But it's not even that. He's just not a nice person. The perfect Devayne type, I guess. There is nobody nice around here, except for you."

The waiter brought the drinks. Francisco helped himself to mineral water, drank a few sips and sighed.

"I can't stand the way Teresa talks to me anymore. She thinks I'm having fun in New York. She won't understand that I'm working sixteen hours a day. The party you and I went to in Tribeca last Friday was the first in three months."

"I know. Don't be upset at her. It's probably not easy for a woman in her condition to be alone."

"She keeps telling me that. But she has her family, her friends, the dogs, and she's having a good time. What about me? Excuse me. I'm really not fun to be with today. I received my phone bill this morning. The *coup de grâce*."

"Poor you! I know all about transatlantic phone bills. Eric and I have done this for two years. Doesn't Teresa have e-mail at the lab?"

"She does. But she wants to hear my voice." He shrugged his shoulders.

"How many months is she now?"

"Five."

"She must be starting to get big. In October you couldn't really tell yet."

The waiter brought the sandwiches. Jane suddenly had an odd sensation. Duportoy's raincoat was passing on her right and stopped. That was it. He just couldn't resist his impulse to know. Her heart started racing.

She had to come up with a lie quickly. Her brain was paralyzed. She looked up. Xavier was shaking hands with Francisco.

"Congratulations, Francisco. I heard your lecture at Stanford was fantastic. Lunch in January, right? I have to run to catch my train. Happy New Year! Say hello to Teresa." He nodded at Jane and grinned. She couldn't help blushing. "Hi, Jane, how are you? We should get a coffee one of these days."

He walked quickly toward the exit. Jane, now furious, stared at Francisco.

"You let me talk!"

He laughed. "Sorry. You didn't leave me time to say anything."

"When did you meet him?"

"Any of your business?"

"Come on! You're upsetting me."

"At Middlebury three years ago: we were both teaching summer school."

"Are you friends with him?"

"Yes. He's not a bad person, really. What you mistook for his arrogance is rather his deep dislike of Devayne; it doesn't make him a bad guy, right? I'll organize a dinner with him and his girlfriend, Anita, in New York; you'll see."

"The actress?"

"Do you know her?"

"I heard about her. They are still together? I thought he was a womanizer."

"Gossips. His essay on de Sade, by the way, is excellent: a radical and definitive answer to all the people who say that de Sade is boring and not a good writer."

"I guess I should look at it. I could never understand why Flaubert liked de Sade so much."

Francisco looked at his watch. "What time is the limo?"

She was leaving in twenty minutes. She ate the last bite of her club sandwich. "I'm scared."

"Why?"

"Eric will be mad at me. He doesn't know yet about the apartment. He sent me ten e-mails since the beginning of the week and left three messages on my answering machine. I don't even answer the phone anymore. I'm tired in advance. Why do things have to be so complicated?"

"Don't worry. I'm sure it will be fine once you are there and you can talk to him for more than ten minutes. These long-distance phone conversations are horrible."

She took his hand on the table. "One month! I'll miss you."

"I'll miss you too."

She looked at his affectionate, witty eyes behind the round glasses. There was no one she trusted more. "I did something very wrong," she whispered.

"What did you do?" he whispered back, smiling and leaning forward as if to hear a secret.

"I'm infatuated with someone."

"With whom?" he asked in the same mysterious voice.

He didn't seem to understand. She smiled like a little girl dazzled by her own audacity. "Do you remember the Danish guy I talked to for a while at the party in Tribeca?"

Francisco's expression changed completely. "The novelist?"

"Yes. I saw him in New York on Tuesday."

"You went to New York on Tuesday? When I was in Palo Alto?"

He straightened up. Her eyes were glowing and her cheeks pink.

"You shouldn't have left me alone. He had my phone number and he called me in Old Newport. The idea was to have lunch and to visit the new galleries in Chelsea." She blushed. "We didn't see much. We spent the day kissing."

"Kissing."

She saw the movement of his Adam's apple as he was swallowing. There was something strange in his voice and eyes. He wasn't smiling. He seemed to be staring at Jane from far away, to be retreating, as though he were putting a barrier between them to protect himself. It was too late to erase what half an hour ago she had promised herself not to tell.

"It's bad, I know. At least I didn't stay there overnight. He wanted me to, but I took the last train back to Old Newport. You think it's bad anyway, right?"

Francisco didn't answer. There was a reticence in his eyes and his back was stiff.

"I don't know why I did this. I'm not in love with this guy, nothing like that. But it was truly nice. I hadn't felt like that in a long time: young, sexy, desirable. Now I can't stop thinking of him. He's much younger than me: twenty-eight. But I didn't feel like I was thirty-five: I could have been twenty-something. It was just really nice." She sighed. "Anyway, I'm leaving today and when I come back in January, he'll be back in Denmark, so, you see, I chose someone with whom there was no risk."

Francisco's hands were playing with the receipt, rolling it into a thin tube. His face was a blank mask. He took his fork, picked up a pickle on the side of his plate, and brought it to his mouth. He was avoiding looking at her. She felt her cheeks redden.

"Francisco, what are you thinking?"

"Jane?" a woman said next to her, startling her.

"Oh, hi!"

Kathryn Johns was standing next to the table. Could she have heard anything? How crazy she was to say such things in the middle of Devayne.

"Fleman's biography of Colet was checked out. I recalled it; you'll get it in January."

"Thanks."

Francisco was staring at the woman who had interrupted them. He looked relieved.

"Kathryn Johns, my assistant. Francisco Gonzalez, professor in the Spanish department. Kathryn is writing a remarkable dissertation on the figure of the black servant in nineteenth-century novels and paintings."

Kathryn nodded politely. She was wearing a tight black coat over a black turtleneck and a short black skirt.

"Are you working with Jane?"

"With Alexander Smith," Jane answered for her. "He's the specialist on colonization."

"We're all more or less colonized, don't you think so?" Francisco asked Kathryn with a smile.

"More or less," she replied coldly.

Jane looked at her watch.

"Oh! It's already one-thirty! We have to run or I'll miss the bus."

"Sorry for taking up your time," Kathryn said. "Have a good trip, Jane."

They got up, and Francisco put money on the table before Jane could take out her wallet.

"You paid last time already!" she said. "It's my turn."

"Next time."

They walked out of the Romulus Café and got into Francisco's car, parked across the street.

"She's pretty," Francisco said.

"Kathryn? Yes, very pretty."

"What year is she?"

It was clear that he didn't want to continue the conversation about the Danish novelist and would rather talk about anything else.

"Seventh. She took my Flaubert seminar five years ago. You must have shocked her when you said that we were all colonized—we don't kid about that around here."

"I was serious. I am sure she agrees with me."

"Maybe. She's smart."

"I don't doubt it. The figure of the black servant—" he added in a respectful voice, "with this she is sure to get a job, right?"

Jane laughed.

"It's not what you think. She's OK, really. Do you know what she did for me in September? She gave me an ad she had found in *Lingua Franca* about a competition organized by the University of North Carolina Press for the best manuscript in nineteenth-century studies. Of course, it didn't work out, but I thought it was really nice of her. I wrote her an excellent recommendation letter."

"In exchange?"

He parked on Main Street in front of the beautiful stone mansion in which Jane now lived. An Old Newport City Landmark brass plaque next to the entrance door indicated the construction date, 1887. Once the private home of a rich merchant, the house was now subdivided into seven apartments. Francisco went ahead of her up the stairs. When they got to her doorstep on the third floor, he leaned down and picked up something on the rug. He turned around and gave it to Jane. It was a pink rose, unwrapped. Jane raised her eyebrows. "What's that?"

"A rose."

"From whom?"

"A secret admirer, I guess."

"Did you bring it?"

"Did you see me carry a rose?"

She took the flower and looked around. There was no note.

"Probably one of my neighbors who knows I'm leaving today."

It was a plausible explanation. But in the context of her recent confidence, the rose seemed to offer more evidence of her promiscuity. There was an awkward silence while she opened her door. The living room was flooded with sun.

"It's so bright here," Francisco exclaimed.

"It's true, you've never been here this early in the day. You'll see, it's a really nice place to be alone."

She put the rose on the table, took her suitcase and her computer, and locked her door. She handed over the keys to Francisco. He carried her suitcase downstairs.

"The bed linens are clean, and the towels too. The closest grocery store is on Linden Street. But you have all the pizzerias you want on Columbus Street."

"And all the funeral homes I need on Columbus Square."

She laughed. Francisco was the one who had made her notice that there were three funeral homes around her house.

He parked the car in front of the small beige brick building with a large window and a blue sign reading CONNECTICUT LIMO. They hugged. For a shorter time and less warmly than it should have been before a long separation. For the first time, they touched with some reserve.

"Good luck," he said.

"Thanks. You too."

On the way to Kennedy and then in the plane to Chicago, she was no longer thinking about Tuesday, but about the lunch with Francisco and the final uneasiness between them.

After a good summer with Eric and two full months with him in their Peach Street home, she had moved to a smaller place, which was better for her alone and closer to campus. They had easily found tenants for their pretty house: a Devayne assistant professor of economics with his family—his nonworking wife and their two young kids. After Eric left, she was terribly sad and kept imagining what their life could have been if Herring hadn't died in the plane crash. The fourth day she had run into Francisco on the ground floor of the department building. They were extremely pleased when they recognized each other, as if the summer when they had seen nothing of each other had made them good friends. She walked him to his car. He told her Teresa was pregnant. It was a shock for Jane, who had wished all summer long that the same thing would happen to her, but she congratulated him sincerely, happy for him and amused by his Latin pride. He drove her back home and stayed for dinner. Afterward they spent virtually all their free time together. She loved to see his round face and witty eyes suddenly appear at the end of a long day of teaching and administrative duties—the only human face around the department. They were the same age and they had strikingly similar situations. Teresa wanted Francisco to move to the Spanish countryside south of Madrid, where she had inherited a house from her grandmother. Francisco felt as claustrophobic there as Jane did in Iowa City.

They had lunch or dinner three times a week in Old Newport and she spent almost every weekend in Manhattan. His apartment overlooked Washington Square. In the daytime you heard the hippie guitarists and the rap music to which black teenagers performed hip-hop dances. Every night around 11:30 the cops installed blue barriers at each entrance and cruised Washington Square, screaming through loudspeakers: "The park is now closed." Francisco would sometimes repeat the sentence in the middle of the day, imitating the mechanical voice amplified by the loudspeakers. "The park is now closed." He couldn't stand to hear that same sentence twenty or thirty times in a row every night anymore. He had even written an editorial for *El País* on the new Republican mayor, Giuliani, and on his cleaning of Manhattan's parks as the first step in his realization of a Platonic ideal of Truth and Beauty.

The first time Jane walked down Fifth Avenue from Forty-second Street to the white arch of Washington Square, she felt like an archeologist in a desert who finds a fragment of pottery indicating the close proximity of the tomb he has spent his life searching for. She loved Manhattan—loved the contrast between the noisy, crazy business district and the charming West Village streets lined with trees, stone houses and small brick buildings, which led to a wide opening of sky and water and to sunsets that she would contemplate until the red ball disappeared, leaning against the railing along the Hudson River on the path reserved for rollerbladers, joggers and bikers. She loved the smell of the sea. "Don't exaggerate," Francisco would protest, "it's just a dirty river. If you want to smell the sea, come to Spain!"

Everyone at Devayne thought they were having an affair. Eric, in October, had told her he was tired of hearing how great Francisco was. It seemed that nobody could conceive of a relationship between a man and a woman without sex involved—unless, of course, the man was gay. They had plenty of opportunities, what with all the nights Jane spent in Francisco's apartment. They saw each other in their underwear. They were like brother and sister. "Don't say that," Francisco retorted. "Why do you think Egyptian pharaohs married their sisters? The best sex is obviously between brothers and sisters." They could even joke about it. There was no taboo between them, no ambiguity of any kind.

Until today. Until she had the great idea to tell him about her "infatuation." Such a vulgar word to start with. So clichéd.

Not that he was jealous. The thought didn't even cross her mind. Not the point. Francisco was Spanish, a Catholic-raised man: a moral man.

Any man would have reacted the same way. This was exactly what a man was scared of: the Delilah that lurked in every woman, ready to cut off the hair of her sleeping husband and sell him to the enemy.

She hadn't slept with Torben, but it didn't matter. She was the one who had called him. Everything was said when a woman called a man—even with "nothing in mind." She only had to remember how carefully she had chosen her clothes on Monday night. How excited she was to board the train to New York on Tuesday morning. How proud to be seen by Duportoy in Grand Central Station. How deliciously happy when she rode the train back at night with all her memories, of the strange lips and the small teeth (too small for her taste) getting close to hers, of the strange hands slipping under her clothes in the streets of Soho, in December, of the soft palms passionately looking for her breasts under the bra, of something hard against her stomach, hard for hours, and of kisses, kisses, and kisses again, long and wet kisses. Delighted with herself, feeling young and sexy again.

The worst there was in a woman.

No. The worst was boasting about it.

Maybe she was lucky she told Francisco at lunch rather than Eric at dinner. And she was incredibly lucky that Kathryn Johns had interrupted her.

They were already landing in Chicago. Before boarding the commuter plane, she took a Dramamine. The medicine had the good effect of attenuating all sensations. Particularly that fear growing in her. In half an hour she would see Eric and maybe realize that she didn't love him anymore. Like when she saw Josh in Chicago at Christmas seven years ago, a few months before they broke up. An "infatuation" was nothing but a message you sent yourself. It would never be over. Eyal, Josh, Norman, Eric. Who would be the next? The unbearable lightness of a woman.

People were getting up around her. The plane was on the ground already and stopping its motor. She couldn't remember landing.

She didn't even go to the bathroom to brush her hair and put on some lipstick as she did usually. She recognized Eric's familiar silhouette from afar. He was walking toward her in the hallway of the small airport. Her heart was pounding with fear. He was getting closer. She shouldn't be so nervous. She dealt badly with reunions anyway. It always took them a few days to be really back together. This was normal. He was now ten feet away from her. She looked at him.

The miracle happened: this tall, slender man in a dark coat, with straight light brown hair falling on his forehead, who was smiling at her, was handsome—the most handsome man in the world. At thirty-nine he was much more handsome than the young Danish novelist. How crazy she had been to worry so much. There was nothing wrong. It had just been all these long months without him. All these tense conversations because of the apartment. She ran toward him and they embraced. He pressed her against him. He smelled so good. She breathed him in, her nose against his neck. She sucked at the warm skin like a vampire.

"Hey! You're tickling me!"

He laughed and pushed her head away. They kissed. A real kiss, full of passion. He stopped it first.

"They're going to arrest us. Did you have a good trip?"

"Yes, quite short."

He looked at her with eyes full of desire.

"You look nice. Is this a new coat?"

"Are you kidding? It's the one I got at Macy's six years ago!"

"Really? It fits you very well."

She laughed. Distracted Eric. He picked up the suitcase and they walked toward the exit.

"You're going to like it. It snowed all night, just for you; it's all white."

"Oh!"

There were mountains of dirty snow along the sidewalks. They got into his car. He started the engine.

"Did you find a tenant?" Eric asked while turning the ignition key.

"Not yet."

She blushed. They kept silent during the ride.

The days, as they followed each other, were all the same—calm and monotonous, like the flat wheat fields now covered with snow. She couldn't say what day in December it was, except for Christmas Eve, when they gave each other gifts. In the morning she worked at the dining room table she used as a desk. Every afternoon she went for a long walk in the white, unspoiled snow. At night she cooked dinner for them. They listened to the radio, the TV, commented on what they heard. He talked about an article he had just read. His book on the Vienna School was coming along well. He would probably get $4,000 to do research in Austria this summer. What about a summer in Vienna? he asked. They could go back to Prague. They could get tickets for the Salzburg Festival. They could explore the Tyrol. Or, since she liked the ocean more than mountains, they could go for a week or two to Istria or the Dalmatian coast, now that the war was over. What about Dubrovnik? All these projects were exciting—but so far away. That would be after—after what they didn't talk about: her subletting the Old Newport apartment and moving to Iowa. Normal conversation. Except for the silence inside her, growing from day to day, like a shadow watching her. She was afraid—of herself, of wrong timing, of making Eric upset, of not knowing what was going on.

There was no problem, Eric had said, except in her mind. He was tired of her habit of starting discussions about their relationship just when he was falling asleep at night. She loved drama, but there was no drama. The situation could be summarized in two sentences: she had to sublet her apartment in Old Newport for the semester; she had to pack and move out here. This had been their plan. There was nothing more to say, and it was not worth talking about it for one more minute.

With Josh she had spent days and nights dissecting every feeling and every word. She respected Eric's trust in actions rather than words.

They made love the second day. It was ovulation week and she had mentioned it the night before, as she was briefly speaking of Francisco and Teresa. It would be so nice to have a baby. Eric wanted it too.

"Suck me," he asked her rather impatiently after half an hour or more of unsuccessful attempts to get an erection.

She would have done it with pleasure, but his asking for it, and in such a rude manner, was surprising: love with Eric was usually tender, silent and modest.

"I don't think you want it right now. It's OK, don't worry; another time," she added quickly, to show that she had no hard feelings and she knew it wasn't his fault.

"Why would I ask you if I didn't want it?" he replied angrily. "How do *you* know what I want or what I don't want?"

"I can feel it. You're too focused on it right now: it won't work."

"If it doesn't work, it's because of you."

"Of me?"

"You're so passive. You always expect me to do everything. When I ask you to do something for once, you *feel* that I don't want it. Great."

He laughed scornfully.

"Do you mean," Jane slowly asked, staring at him, "that I'm always too passive?"

"Yes."

"Do you mean that we've never made love well?"

"That's exactly what I mean."

She turned red.

"How dare you say this at such a moment? You're so unfair!"

She got off the bed and quickly put on her nightdress, so he wouldn't see her naked. She was getting more upset from second to second.

"If that's true, you know what?" she screamed. "Get yourself a mistress or another wife! Pay a whore! I'm sorry I'm such a bad fuck!"

She ran out of the bedroom, sobbing, and locked herself in the bathroom. She got dressed, put on her fake fur coat, her scarf, her wool hat, and her snow boots, and left for a walk on the icy road. It was getting dark. She walked around for two hours. The more painfully the freezing cold pinched the parts of her face that weren't covered with wool, the more her anger melted. Eric must have felt something. He was unfair, but right. Maybe she expected him to be like Torben: a stranger burning with desire for her, with an erection lasting for five hours without her having to do anything. Or maybe she went to Torben only because she was scared of exactly what had just happened with Eric. Her fear might just be the cause of what happened with Eric. In other words, she was afraid that it would happen, and it happened because she was afraid.

Another of life's nice little vicious circles.

"Jane!"

She was already climbing the icy steps of their house and almost slipped when she turned around. A tiny, dark silhouette was standing under a lamppost on the white snow. He got closer: the guy with a Devayne Ph.D.

"How did you know it was me?" she asked. Her head was wrapped in many layers of wool, and he had seen her only from behind.

"At this hour it couldn't be the woman who lives on the first floor, so it had to be someone visiting Eric, and who else could it be but you?" He glanced around. "Isn't Eric with you now?"

She blushed. He was scrutinizing her. There was a light just above her and she knew her eyes were red and swollen.

"I couldn't sleep, so I went for a little walk. What about you? What are you doing outside when it's so cold and so late and everyone in this town is in bed by ten?"

"Walking the dog that is inside me." He laughed. "I always go for a walk at this hour. I write very late and if I go from my computer to my bed, I can't fall asleep." He seemed to hesitate. "Do you want to have a drink? There is actually one nice bar in this town and it's open until two."

One hour earlier she would have said yes—and maybe, who knows, ended up at his place.

"Not now, thanks. How is your writing going?" she asked politely. His eyes brightened.

"Pretty good. It's a longtime project, some kind of total book which will contain everything: philosophy, literary theory, and autobiographical fragments. My model is the patchwork quilt. My grandmother was always sewing when I was little, and I was fascinated by the fact that all these little pieces of fabric put together finally formed a whole. I see a close relation between sewing and writing. This is actually the theme of the book. My grandfather was a tailor, and my mother too."

Jane unlocked her door and said good night. He seemed ready to talk for hours. A good thing she didn't go for a drink with him. "Walking the dog there is inside me." She laughed as she walked up the stairs. He was a clever guy.

Eric was asleep in his study room. The following day he apologized. He didn't mean what he said in a moment of frustration: of course they made love wonderfully well. Jane too apologized: He had a point. She would try to be less passive.

They didn't make love anymore.

For New Year's Eve they dressed up. He was wearing a black silk shirt, and Jane, a long, dark red velvet dress she had found in a Soho open market for almost nothing. "Nice," he said after she asked how he liked it. He had bought blinis, smoked salmon, sour cream, and French champagne—everything she liked. She put a white tablecloth on the fake country antique table. She found two candlesticks with white candles. Billie Holiday singing. They sat in front of each other, chewing smoked salmon and blinis.

"I'm happy I got the Norwegian salmon," Eric said. "I hesitated because it was on sale and I wondered why. But it's excellent, no?"

She nodded. With Francisco, she could say everything passing through her mind. Why were things so simple with a friend and so complicated with a husband? Any word would sound like a criticism. Maybe it would be a criticism. Maybe women were angry with men. Some kind of primary anger.

"Eric?"

He looked up, his mouth full of blinis and smoked salmon.

"What?" An impatient note in his voice.

Many words rushed to her mind. None sounded right. One wrong word and she would upset him. He was already irritated. She was spoiling the evening. Why couldn't she just enjoy the dry Veuve Clicquot with fine bubbles and the Norwegian salmon? She looked down at the pale pink salmon on her plate: the best quality. Why was it on sale, then? She couldn't eat anymore. Her stomach was tense and blocked. She heard his jaws masticating. She took her glass and brought it to her lips. Drank a little more. Put it back on the white tablecloth. She started moving the glass on the table, her eyes fixed on it, bouncing it from side to side. Stronger and stronger. The silence was now very tense. Eric was eating, ignoring her. The only action taking place in the room, filling the space and the silence, was her bouncing the glass from side to side, farther and farther. It fell and broke. She reached for it. Blood immediately appeared on her index finger.

"I won't go through this," Eric said coldly.

He got up and left the dining room. She heard the door of the study room close—not slam.

She collected the pieces of crystal and put them on her plate. It was a beautiful Bohemian crystal glass with thin diamond-shaped engravings from an expensive pair she had bought last year in an antiques shop. The broken glass and the blood gushing from her finger reminded her of a scene in a Bergman movie she had seen with Josh long ago, in which a woman introduced a piece of broken glass into her vagina in front of her husband and, staring at him, started bleeding. Jane had disliked that scene: its hysterical violence had put her ill at ease. Now she could understand why a woman would perform such a self-destructive act. The judgmental silence of a husband made you want to scream, hurt or even kill yourself—just to see him react and lose that icy self-control. She looked at the bloodstain on the white tablecloth and poured salt on it before remembering this was the thing to do for wine, not blood. She got up and put her finger under cold water for a long time.

At midnight he didn't come out of his room. They didn't wish each other Happy New Year. It was awfully sad. She cried for a long time and finally fell asleep after finishing the champagne.

Three days later she gave up. He was too tough. She had to find a way to get to him: a matter of survival. She walked into his study in the morning. He was reading and didn't even look up.

"Eric?" she asked shyly.

"What?" His voice icy.

"Can I talk to you?"

He put a mark inside his book and looked at her with the same slightly ironic impatience in his eyes.

"Yes?"

"I don't understand why we're doing this to each other when we both want the same thing: to be together. I love you. I know you love me too. I didn't sublet my place because I was badly organized and overwhelmed with work. You were right to be upset with me. But you know how I react to pressure: I get completely paralyzed. This is why I didn't answer all your messages. It wasn't bad will or bad faith. Now, listen: I'll be back here by February 6 whether I find a tenant or not. It doesn't matter: it's not such a big expense and it's covered by renting the house, anyway."

February 6 was Eric's birthday. His resistance melted just like snow on the hottest spring day. He got up to hug her. Of course he loved her. How much he loved her. How much he loved it when she spoke in that calm and reasonable way.

They went for a long walk on the snow sparkling under the sun, transformed into ice by the cold. They would slide together and hang onto each other so as not to fall, under a sky of a pure and icy blue. After every kiss he would dry the wet skin around her lips with a tissue because of the cold. Making love in the snow? They laughed. It would freeze their buttocks, not to mention more intimate parts. They came back home and she kneeled on the carpet in the middle of the living room, unzipping his pants. Active enough? He reversed her on the floor: she shouldn't be too active. A bit soft at the last moment, he still managed to penetrate her. She wanted him so much that she came as soon as he was inside her.

They rested on the carpet for almost two hours, naked, doing baby talk. Eric was so cute. Each of his words and expressions made her laugh. A pity it wasn't the right moment: his lazy little sperm would have had all the time to venture up there and get acquainted with her shy little egg. Not very scientific, but this was how she pictured it. Even the thought of Eric's sperm inspired tenderness in her.

There was no sadness between them when he drove her to the airport on January 12. She would be back in less than a month. She would be quite busy in Old Newport. She had already made lists of all the things to do, of the books to get at the library, and of items to bring back, starting with the rug.

"Are you sure? You'll have so many things already."

"Are you kidding? It's the main thing."

She was in an excellent mood on the way back, more and more excited as the plane was getting nearer the East Coast—nearer Francisco. She would tell him everything: the silence, the terrible New Year's Eve, the broken glass, and the happy ending. Jane's hysteria would make him laugh. She hoped that Teresa would have calmed down too.

Francisco hadn't left any note on her dining table nor on her desk. The comforter cover was neatly folded on the bed, next to the towels. He had found the time to wash them but not to write a note. The apartment was even cleaner than she had left it. No dust anywhere. The stove and the sink were sparkling. She smiled. His way of thanking her. The only personal trace was in the bathroom garbage can: two blue Gillette razors. He must have forgotten his nice razor in New York.

She dialed his number. Three rings. Maybe he wasn't home yet. He picked up the phone after four rings.

"Hello?"

A sleepy voice. She quickly looked at the clock above the stove: only 9:10 P.M.

"Did I wake you up?"

"Oh, Jane. That's OK."

"I'm sorry! I didn't think of the jet lag."

"That's fine, really."

His voice had a strange sound—maybe because he was deeply asleep when the phone woke him up.

"What's up?" he asked.

That was a strange question too. She never needed a specific reason to call him.

"Nothing," she said hesitantly. "I just wanted to wish you Happy New Year."

"Right, Happy New Year. . . . So you're back?"

Wasn't that obvious?

"Yes, I just came back. Thanks for leaving the apartment so clean. Did you have a good time here?"

"Very good. Thanks again for lending your place to me, it was quite convenient, I'm very grateful to you. I left the keys with Susan as you told me."

He was talking to her as if to a stranger. Maybe he was just exhausted.

"I'll let you sleep. Are you coming to Old Newport tomorrow? Do you want to have lunch or dinner?"

"No," he said quickly. "Not tomorrow. I've too much work. I'll call you."

"How is Teresa?"

"Well, thanks."

There was a silence. She felt like crying.

"Francisco, what's going on?"

He didn't answer. Could he still remember the December lunch and the unwanted confession? This was absurd. She had to let him know that everything was well with Eric, now.

Finally he spoke, answering in an exhausted but truer voice: "Things didn't go so well with Teresa."

Jane was breathing fast. This definitely sounded like Francisco—like Francisco's caustic view on women.

She couldn't pick up a single detail that wasn't true. Francisco was the only person who knew about Torben. She had also mentioned to him her night encounter with David Clark in Iowa City. Francisco had a good memory. A selective memory, of course. He was fabricating his own little patchwork quilt. Clark was right. There was a close relationship between writing and sewing. An old image for students of literature in the age of deconstruction, who all knew that a "text" was nothing but a fabric. Jane, for the first time, could see the very process of fabrication. How every little piece would follow a design, produce a pattern. Francisco was very consistent in the image he gave of her: that of a neurotic woman who was unable to love.

Something else struck her in the construction of the text. The long flashback at the beginning of every chapter, summarizing months or years in her life, reminded her of a stitch she had learned in a sewing class in grade school: you had to pull the needle forward and then backward again to the end of the former stitch, then forward again, halfway on top of the first thread, halfway farther on the fabric, and then back. What made a seam very solid, though, produced a different effect in writing. Life summarized in the backward stitch of a flashback was rather lifeless. Francisco may have chosen this construction because he lacked facts. But his purpose may also have been to give a caricatured image of her happiness and to make it look pathetic.

She was starting to understand where all of this was leading: it wasn't a novel about her, but about him, and her love life served only as a background destined to highlight his.

She got up and walked to the window. The rain was less dense already. She saw again the huge fields covered with unspoiled snow where she had gone for so many walks. Her cheeks used to be red when she would return to the silent apartment where the only lamp lit was the one on Eric's desk. She hadn't been unhappy there—at least in the images she retained, from which time had erased the rough edges.

No regret. It was a life principle: "Don't hold." What happened happened because nothing else could happen at that point in time and space.

She sat back down again and looked at the thick pile of pages remaining, her elbow on the table, pinching her lower lip with two fingers.

2

She called Francisco four times before he finally accepted a lunch date, with a reluctance that didn't discourage her—she had to understand what was going on. When he walked into the Thai restaurant on January 20, she was shocked: He had lost about fifteen pounds. His round cheeks were now hollow. He had lifeless eyes with dark pouches under them. Surely this couldn't have anything to do with her and the December lunch.

"Francisco! What happened?"

He shrugged his shoulders and avoided looking at her. Then, without preamble, he started telling her of his trip in Spain. From the first moment that he saw Teresa at the airport in Madrid, it was hell. So much hell that she left two hours later for her parents' house in Seville. She was six months pregnant: too late for an abortion.

"An abortion! Is this what you wanted?"

This was what Teresa talked about. Every word she said was intended only to tear him apart. She was pure hatred.

"But why?"

He shrugged his shoulders again, looking helpless, and didn't answer.

"Because you weren't there for Christmas? Because she went through the pregnancy alone? Did you try to explain to her what your life was like in Old Newport? How much work, how much pressure? Does she understand that it's not bad will or bad faith? Do you want me to write to her and tell her?"

"No."

"Maybe the solution would be for her to come here and stay with you, so she understands what your life is, day by day, now that you're DUS!"

"No. She doesn't want to come because of the baby; she doesn't trust American hospitals. And she has no respect for my job anyway."

He pushed the salad to the side and played with it. Jane was telling herself that Teresa was as proud and anxious as Eric, and that Francisco just hadn't uttered enough reassuring words. She was opening her mouth to give him some sage advice when he resumed abruptly, this time looking at her.

"There is someone else. I met her in December, just before you left for Iowa. I'm in love, Jane. Head over heels."

His sad smile wasn't lacking in self-derision. Jane's eyes opened wide. "Head over heels." Francisco wasn't someone to use this kind of ready-made expression lightly. Not an infatuation. A complete upside-down of himself. She swallowed. The fork with a bite of chicken curry remained suspended at mid-distance between her plate and her mouth.

"I saw her more than ten times over ten days. Nothing happened," he said, looking her straight in the eyes. "Nothing—not even a kiss. But this is love, mutual love."

He sighed. Jane was struck by the sadness in his dark eyes. She blushed. Nothing like her little December fling. "Not even a kiss." Yet he saw this woman ten times and he was in love? How did he manage? He must be very strong. And very scared to be in love.

It wasn't just the first time since Teresa: it was the first time *ever* that he had felt something like that, such an opening in himself, such a curiosity regarding someone else.

"She's so beautiful, Jane. Her face is beautiful, her soul is beautiful. She's so close to me."

Only when he talked about this other woman did his face come alive again. His eyes burned like coal. He hadn't seen her since he came back, though he had called her the night of his return.

"She told me she had made other plans and wasn't free for the whole week. Why is she doing this to me? She has her own life, I'm not stupid. I know I can't be any good to her. I'm married and my wife is pregnant—I didn't lie to her. She is thirty-three years old; she needs to find someone who is free, who can be with her—I understand that. But why be angry at me and not see me anymore? I can't take it! It's too difficult, Jane: I need to see her! Do you think she's upset because I went to Spain? But I had no choice! She isn't punishing me, right? She isn't playing with me? That would be terrible! What do you think? You're a woman, you must know."

As he talked, he pressed his fork so hard against his plate that it bent. Jane was listening with wide-open eyes. She had never known someone to expose such a deep and open wound. He couldn't control what he said. He wasn't even thinking of Teresa and of the baby. Only of this woman.

"Maybe she needs to protect herself," she suggested softly. "If she fell in love with you, she must be scared."

"Do you think so? Do you think it's because she is in love with me and she needs to protect herself? Yes, that's what I told myself."

There was so much relief in his eyes that Jane got even more anxious.

"Who is she?"

"You don't know her. I met her at a dinner at Miguel's the night I came back from California, in December. She's his neighbor in the East Village."

"What does she do?"

"She's a jewelry designer."

"But how could this happen, Francisco? How could you make your wife pregnant and then fall in love with another woman?"

He told Jane things he had never told anyone, not even his best friend in Madrid, Pascual. He had known Teresa for fourteen years. Their relationship had never been idyllic. She was dictatorial, jealous and posses-sive. She had made him sever ties with his best friends. He had always yielded to her. She was very insecure. As soon as he resisted her, she would blackmail him with threats of divorce, affairs or suicide. His friends generally didn't like her—they thought that Francisco could do better. He had always defended her; she had a good, passionate heart. She felt strongly and instinctively about everything and everybody in life—he liked that. He was the opposite.

He was used to strong women, having grown up with his mother and his three older sisters who had always decided everything for him. It would have been too tiring to argue with four women, so he stopped hav-ing opinions. It made life easier. Teresa was older than he: thirty-nine now. He couldn't refuse her a baby. He believed he loved her.

"You never thought of leaving her? You never had an affair before?"

"No. I met Teresa when I was twenty-two, in a theater course I took because I was too shy." He smiled. "She was my first and only girl-friend—except for one little thing that happened when I was twenty-three, before things got serious with Teresa. There were opportunities, but I wasn't interested: I don't like complications and I'm the faithful type. I felt good with Teresa, you know. She's a jealous woman, but she's also very respectful and protective of my space. With her I can spend my life doing what I like—reading and writing. Three years ago she had an affair and she almost left me. I suffered so much that I could never imag-ine thinking that I wasn't in love with her. Maybe my falling in love with someone else now is just some kind of revenge."

"It's very possible."

"I don't know. All I know is I love this woman, Jane. I love her."

"Maybe you don't really love her. Maybe it's only a crisis because your wife is pregnant and you're scared to become a father and face your re-sponsibilities. This often happens to men, apparently—the fear of being trapped, you know."

Francisco's eyes brightened.

"That's what I told myself! Do you think it could be so?"

"Maybe. You know, I'm not judging you at all, I just see all the sides of your situation. I know that it won't be easy for you, whatever decision you make. Remember that I'll always be here for you. Now, if you want some advice . . ."

He looked at her with eyes full of expectation.

". . . the best thing you could do is probably to stop seeing this woman. If something must happen, it will happen no matter what. Go against it."

"You're right. You're so right. But if you knew how painful it is not to be able to talk to her. It's unbearable. Give her up? Do you think I can do that? That I am strong enough? Sometimes I think it would be much easier to jump off the Brooklyn Bridge."

"Come on. Stop saying stupid things. This is just a crisis. It will pass."

The waiter brought the receipt. Francisco's plate was still half-full, whereas Jane had cleaned hers a while ago. Francisco took his wallet out of his jacket.

"Please," Jane said, "my turn."

When she walked out of the restaurant, she was sad. Was it possible that a man, alone in New York City for five months and passionately in love with a single woman living ten blocks away and in love with him too, wouldn't see her at all? It seemed beyond human power.

She walked along the Goldener Library, a Neo-Gothic building that looked like a cathedral. Just this morning she had told herself that she had to stop by there and check out a book after the lunch with Francisco. Now she couldn't remember which book it was. She also had to xerox the ad for the apartment. There wasn't much time left until February 6. And she needed to call the travel agency and reserve her ticket. Eric had asked about it.

Poor Francisco. A clever woman, the jewelry designer. An artist. Strong and independent. Not the passive mistress type. Already making him understand that she wasn't at his disposal. Thirty-three years old— no longer the age to play around. There were so many more single women than single heterosexual men in New York that, once you got hold of a man's heart, you wouldn't drop your prey easily. Francisco would yield. It would start with an affair. Jane would bet on it. Could a

Catholic-raised Spanish man abandon his wife and newborn? Could a man truly in love for the first time give up his passion?

She loved Francisco too much to have an unhealthy curiosity about this suspenseful plot. From the bottom of her heart she hoped that he would manage to forget the other woman. How would he be able to keep any self-respect if he abandoned his child?

At least this revelation explained his strange attitude when they had lunch in December. He had met this woman the night before in New York. In telling him of her fling with the Danish writer, Jane had presented him a caricatured reflection of his own heart. Maybe Kathryn Johns's interruption hadn't been so fortunate after all: if Francisco had been able to express his fear, he might have resisted the desire to see the other woman again. Now it was too late.

The temperature today was so mild for January that someone in the Music School was rehearsing with an open window. A soprano. Schubert? Mahler? A piano was playing along. She crossed the street and the music became a distant echo. There was a slight throbbing in her head. She had forgotten her Motrin at home. A sore throat too: it felt like a cold starting. Hopefully the very spicy chicken curry she had just eaten would kill the germs. She couldn't afford a cold right now. She had the office to clean and the files to put in order for the next DUS—these were the pressing things. A vague idea kept appearing and disappearing in her mind, like the nagging feeling of inconsistency. "More than ten times over ten days." How did he manage to see this woman ten times in New York when he had to stay in Old Newport to work with the hiring committee and then fly to the MLA convention? He might have returned to New York twice or three times, but ten times?

It was possible only if this woman had come to Old Newport—and stayed with him in Jane's apartment. Maybe she even flew to the MLA meeting with him. Not implausible. He might have suggested this to her impulsively, like Eric had the night she and he met: "Why don't you come along?" It seemed to be that kind of passion between Francisco and this woman. Did Francisco lie to Jane because he was ashamed to have used her apartment to that end? Possibly. Consummating adultery in her bed, making her an unknowing accomplice. Jane smiled, imagining the wild nights. She felt sad because of Teresa and the baby, and the pain that would result from this mess. But she didn't judge him. Passion was always beautiful, more so than fidelity to the past, which was often mere cowardice.

As she passed Bruno's, the good smell of pizza tickled her nostrils. She could still smell; she wasn't that sick. She opened the door of the department's building and picked up her mail. She skipped through it while waiting for the elevator. The door opened and Bronzino stepped out, almost bumping into her. Without apologizing—or saying hi—he quickly walked away. Jane reflected that she was glad to leave this place soon and not see people like Bronzino for a while. In the elevator, she suddenly remembered something strange Allison had told her when she and John visited them in Old Newport one and a half years ago—that they found it pleasant to imagine Eric and Jane making love. Jane suddenly understood why. There was, indeed, almost a spiritual beauty in the sexual act, even for an outside viewer, when lovers felt passion for each other.

There was still something wrong. "Not even a kiss"? Why this lie? It wasn't necessary; on the contrary, "just one kiss" or "just a few kisses" would have sounded much more plausible. Still, at the moment when he uttered these words, Francisco's voice had a bitter accent of truth. "Not even a kiss"—the kind of detail you didn't invent. She got out of the elevator.

That night she called Francisco in New York.

"How are you?"

"So busy right now that I don't have the time to feel anything. It was good to talk to you today, Jane. I made up my mind: I won't see her again."

"I'm glad to hear that; it's the right decision. By the way, I would like to ask you something. It's a very silly question and please don't mind it, but it bothers me and I'll get rid of it by asking you."

"What?"

"It's not Kathryn Johns, by any chance?"

Just as she said the name, she choked. She let out an embarrassed laugh. "Excuse me, it's ridiculous, I know you told me she's living in New York and she's a jewelry maker, but I don't know why, probably because you saw her ten times, I was thinking. . . ." Her heart was pounding. "Francisco? Did you hear me?"

"Don't you hear my silence, Jane? I won't lie to you."

His voice was very sad. There was an awkward silence. It was too late to apologize for her indiscretion.

She had had more respect and compassion for him before she knew who the woman was. There was something so obvious in his falling for beautiful Kathryn. He was no different from any other man, then. Jane liked Kathryn, but she also found her cold, reserved and intimidating. Maybe Kathryn wasn't like that with Francisco. Yet her attitude after his return from Spain wasn't a good sign. Kathryn wasn't the model of a well-balanced person either. She was depressed like all the graduate students at the end of the long Ph.D. process, when there was no job. She had divorced her filmmaker husband about four years ago, two years after moving to Old Newport to start her Ph.D. at Devayne. At the time of her divorce, Kathryn had spent a week in a psychiatric hospital, and Jane had heard she had been on the verge of suicide. Yet Kathryn kept displaying her magnificent, cold smile and assuring everyone, even her best friends, that everything was perfectly fine. She had always been extremely polite and pleasant with Jane and she was a very efficient assistant. But behind the mask of the controlled smile, Jane suspected anger, violence and resentment. There was only three years' age difference between them. Proud and clever Kathryn wouldn't make things easy for Francisco. A pity she was the woman it would take such difficulty for him to forget. The attraction of opposites, obviously: she was as Nordic, blond and pale as Francisco was Latin and dark. Jane couldn't help thinking that Kathryn wasn't worth Francisco's suffering. She also felt guilty for introducing them, and in such a context. Desire was a contagious disease.

That week and the week after, she left him several messages and invited him to a party one of her neighbors was giving. He didn't call back. The night of the party, as soon as she entered the apartment, heard the music and saw the noisy crowd, she realized that she wasn't in the mood to talk to anyone. She helped herself to a glass of sangria and walked into the empty study, where she looked at the titles of medical books. A couple walked in. A short, bearded man with thick glasses told Jane he was her downstairs neighbor and added that the house was so badly soundproofed one could hear everything from one floor to the next, even messages on the answering machine. He slipped out of the room while the woman with short blond hair and a blue synthetic sweater introduced herself as another neighbor, living in the basement apartment. Her name was Lynn. She exclaimed in awe upon learning that Jane, who looked so young, was a Devayne professor. Her loud voice gave Jane a headache. Lynn invited her for a drink later that week. It would have been a pleasure, Jane said, but she wouldn't have the time, as she was now preparing for her imminent departure. This forced her to summarize her situation: she was married, her husband lived in Iowa and she had been granted a semester leave that allowed her to join him there.

"So we're meeting just before you leave! Not my luck! But I'm sure all you want is to be reunited with your husband. Listen: you'll have a lot of luggage when you leave. Why don't you give me a ring? I'll take you to the airport bus."

A welcomed offer—one couldn't count on cabs and it looked like Francisco wouldn't help her as planned. Jane thanked Lynn and got up, excusing herself.

"Already!"

"Yes. I'm going to bed. I have a sore throat."

"Poor sweetie! What you need is a hot lemon juice with aspirin. No. Even better: ginger tea. It cleans everything inside and cures you instantly. I have fresh ginger at home. Let me go and get it."

There are some well-intentioned people you just can't get rid of. Jane finally got away from Lynn and went back home, thinking that everyone in Old Newport except for Francisco was boring.

The following day Jane knocked at his door on the second floor. Nobody answered. She was depressed. She missed him. Her cold prevented her from sleeping well and sapped her energy. Eric was pestering her again. Had she posted notes around? Had she called secretaries in other departments to ask whether a visiting professor would need a place? Had she bought her ticket or made a reservation at least? Was she procrastinating on purpose? The deadline, February 6, was approaching. As if this was an official deadline and not one that she had chosen of her own free will. She had finally xeroxed the ad for subletting her place, but she kept forgetting to post it around. She remembered every day at 5:05 to call the travel agency, which closed at 5 P.M. Even though she didn't forget deliberately, the lapse was meaningful. Talking with Francisco would help her to see clearer.

She was in her office on Thursday, January 30, classifying the last drawers of DUS files, when the door opened after a light knock. Francisco. Her face lightened.

"May I?" he asked.

"Of course!"

She got up immediately. He hadn't shaved, and looked worse than ever. She smiled warmly and walked over to him. He stepped back.

"I have a cold."

"Don't worry, I do too."

She hugged him. He sat on a chair on the other side of her desk.

"I'm sorry I didn't return your calls, Jane. I wasn't doing too well."

She looked at him and waited.

"A good thing I'm loaded with work," he continued. "I didn't see Kathryn. I'll never see her again. Ever."

Jane blushed. Why was Francisco so defensive?

"It must be hard."

"Hard?" He let out a small laugh. There was such an acute pain in his eyes and the muscles of his face that Jane shivered.

"It's constant torture. A fight every second with myself. I want to rip the phone out of the wall, but I can't because of Teresa. It's exhausting. I feel completely emptied."

Someone knocked at the door. Jane made a face. She couldn't pretend she wasn't in—the student probably heard their voices.

"Come in!"

The door opened. Kathryn stepped in, avoiding Francisco, who turned pale.

"Here are the articles. Colet's biography is back; you can check it out."

Kathryn was standing very straight, head up. She was incredibly beautiful with her simple black dress that reached just above the knees, her black sweater with tiny nacre buttons, her very white skin, her bun of pale golden hair tied by a black velvet ribbon, her long neck à la Modigliani, and the pearl earrings matching the perfectly regular teeth that her cold smile revealed.

"Thanks. How was the MLA? I haven't seen you since."

Jane blushed. As if Kathryn cared about the stupid interviews, when the only person she must have been thinking about during the whole convention was Francisco. They probably had dinner every night. Both of them alone in another city. "Not even a kiss." The explosive tension now filling the room was that of burning, unfulfilled passion.

"It went well, thank you."

"Did anyone call you back yet?"

Kathryn smiled politely, but her eyes—which were brown-black and not blue, Jane suddenly noticed—betrayed some impatience.

"I have an on-campus interview scheduled with the University of Virginia in Charlottesville."

"Excellent. It's a good university. You have to visit Jefferson's house when you get there. I'll cross my fingers for you."

There was an ironic expression on Kathryn's face. Jane blushed and shut up.

"I have to go," Francisco said.

Kathryn turned toward him for the first time, with the same toughness in her face. He had to pass very close to her, brushing her shoulder. She didn't move and kept displaying the same polite, icy smile.

"You two remember each other, right?" Jane asked. "I don't need to make introductions?"

Her cheeks were purple. Kathryn looked at her coldly and didn't answer. Maybe she thought that Jane was making fun of them. Francisco left. Kathryn glanced at her watch.

"Six o'clock already! I have to run. Have a good trip if I don't see you, Jane."

Two days later her sore throat had become so severe that Jane barely managed to swallow. She pulled her scarf up around her nose. The cold air outside was burning her throat. She would have been much better off in bed, but she had nothing left in her fridge. She had never wished more than today that there was a grocery store around the corner. The closest one was on Linden Street, on the other side of the train tracks—a twenty-five-minute walk from her apartment, and she was too weak to ride her bike. When she finally got to the grocery store, she felt so feverish and her throat burned so much that she decided to stop at a coffee shop next door to get a hot tea to soothe the irritation. As she stepped in, she bumped into two people coming out: Francisco and Kathryn.

"Hi!" the three said at the same time.

There was an awkward silence, in which Francisco's oath never to see Kathryn again resonated. He kept his eyes down like a kid caught with his hand in the cookie jar. On a Saturday, he had no reason but Kathryn to be in town. They had gone to this out-of-the-way café, far from campus, Main Street and Columbus Square, to avoid one person, who was right now standing in front of them.

Jane smiled cheerfully: "Isn't it a funny January? One day warm and humid, the next day cold and sunny. I like it better when it's a sharp cold like today, but I have a terrible sore throat. I thought it would do me good to drink a hot tea before grocery shopping. How is your cold, Francisco, by the way?"

"I'm fine, thank you."

They left and Jane entered the place. If they thought she was spying on them, too bad. Not her problem. She shivered. Her hands were hot. She probably had a strong fever. She had to buy a thermometer.

A funny smell like that of burned pizza had been tickling Jane's nostrils for a while. She suddenly realized that the smell wasn't inside the manuscript but right inside her kitchen. She jumped: her tea! She ran to the electric stove two steps away and took the pot off the burner. The stainless steel was completely burned. When she turned on the tap and put the pot under the water, there was a noise like that of a giant match being lit or of a witch disappearing in a Walt Disney cartoon, followed by thick steam rising in the air.

She went to open the window. The room was much brighter; it wasn't pouring anymore, not even raining. The sky seemed to be clearing. It was 5 P.M. already. Being absorbed in her past had one positive effect so far: she stopped wondering whether Alex had sent her a message. The idea of Hawaii tomorrow seemed even more unreal than a few hours earlier. With Alex!

She would go to the office after finishing the manuscript. Better solve the mystery and put it aside before her date with Alex tomorrow night. The mystery was actually solved: not mere revenge, but Francisco's only way to get over what happened to him by way of sublimation. He was pretty good at displaying his own grief. At least he acknowledged that Jane had been sympathetic to him. He wasn't totally unfair.

She drank some more water and sat down on the wooden chair. Her back hurt after being in the same position for several hours. She hadn't had lunch yet; no wonder she had a funny sensation in her stomach. She would eat something at the end of the next chapter.

3

After the scene with Eric last night, life was a bottomless pit of darkness. But she was now boarding the train to New York in an excellent mood. She found exactly the seat she wanted, in the first car, facing forward, with another seat in front where she could stretch out her legs. She put her newspapers next to her and her bag on the seat across. It was typical late March weather, not really cold but insidiously damp. She had even taken a pair of extra shoes in case it rained tonight so she wouldn't have wet feet on her way back: truly cautious for her first real outing in two months. The car wasn't very well heated, so she didn't take off her coat or her scarf. A female voice came out of the whistling loudspeakers to announce the stations where the train would stop.

She had been gratuitously mean last night. Poor Eric. She smiled tenderly. Yet he was so proud of the little test he had invented for his students, showing them slides of which they had to guess the century, the country, even the painter if they could.

"I actually taught them something. It makes me feel pretty good. There was an eighteenth-century French painting of Diana and Acteon that could very well have been seventeenth-century Dutch, and . . . are you listening?"

"Yes."

He had antennae. Her mind, indeed, was wandering—thinking of Francisco and of her trip the next day.

"So this is how they found out: the perspective. . . ."

"To tell you the truth, I don't really care."

There was a heavy silence at the other end of the line, as if she had just struck Eric with a hammer—which she had. She was as stunned as he was by her own violence.

"You know I'm still very weak," she resumed in a softer voice, to attenuate her bluntness. "It's almost eleven and I'm usually asleep at this hour. Just the effort to concentrate and listen to you makes me dizzy. And," she added with a laugh that she wanted light and apologetic, "I am a little tired of hearing about students. It's the only topic of conversation around here."

"Good night, then," Eric replied in the icy voice she knew well, that of the little boy who would never admit he had been hurt.

She had let him hang up and hadn't called him back.

It was true that she sometimes feared that Eric would become as boring and provincial as his colleagues—nobody at a dinner party in New York would have talked with enthusiasm about pedagogical methods. But it wasn't for the sake of truth that she had interrupted him last night. She had purposefully vexed him. Not gratuitous nastiness, but, rather, instinctive Machiavellianism. She knew he would react with silence until she apologized to him; therefore he wouldn't call tonight and wouldn't find out that she wasn't home. This little argument allowed her to avoid a far more dangerous scene. Her aggression, then, had been for the sake of their relationship. Tomorrow she would call him and apologize. She wouldn't say a word about her trip to New York. For Eric would never understand that she could spend an evening in New York instead of packing and moving to Iowa immediately.

Just before the door closed, two women squeezed through. One was carrying a baby carriage and the other a child. They were exclaiming noisily, all excited to have got on just in time. "Here!" They chose the seats just across the aisle from Jane. One was fat, the other thin and younger. The big woman put the child on the seat in front of her. He started screaming in a piercing voice. The two women continued laughing as if they didn't hear him. Not a baby really, but a solid toddler dressed like a miniature grown-up with baggy jeans, Nike shoes, a fashionable Levi's sport jacket and, under it, a sweatshirt with a hood. He started hitting the fat woman, who hit him back.

"I told you, I don't want none of that! You don't hit me!"

He went on yelling. Jane regretfully got up and retreated toward the back of the car, where the toilet's smell was so strong that she decided to go to the second car. As she was pulling the heavy door, she recognized a familiar sound just behind her. Two tall young men with short reddish hair, seated in the last row before the toilets, were absorbed in an animated discussion in Hebrew. *"Ken, ken,"* one of them answered in a convinced voice. Jane stepped backward and sat across the aisle from them. There were two free seats facing each other, her luck. Ever since her affair with Eyal, she always felt moved as soon as she recognized the rough sounds of Hebrew. One of the two guys glanced at her. She smiled. He looked at the newspapers on the seat next to her and resumed his conversation without smiling back. Blushing, she realized that the *National Enquirer* was the only title visible, covering the *New York Times.* The young Israeli probably didn't have much respect for people reading tabloids.

Her mind joyfully came back to the purpose of her trip. She had to remember to reimburse Francisco for the grocery shopping he did for her in early February. She had called him at the office and almost had to beg him, as Francisco proved rather reluctant. Her strong fever and empty fridge, however, had left her no choice but to swallow her pride. A good boy who always yielded to women, Francisco had complied. It had been a shock, though, when she ran downstairs at 4 P.M. after hearing the bell, delighted to see him, and found the plastic bag with food and medicine hanging on the doorknob. Francisco had already left, making it clear that he wasn't at her disposal. She had lost a friend. She had too much of a fever at the time to really be sad. The phone had awakened her two hours later: Francisco was calling from Manhattan. He apologized profusely for acting so rudely; he had wanted to get out of Old Newport before rush hour and at this time of the day, every minute counted. "Plus your flu seems real nasty, I would rather not catch it." Jane had smiled happily. How could she have forgotten that he was her friend? The only false note in the conversation had been his abrupt declaration at the end, when Jane wasn't asking anything: "I didn't see Kathryn again."

The two Israelis got up. She looked at them as they got off the train. Westport. She would have guessed they were going to New York. They didn't look like guys spending the weekend at a rich aunt's. She dozed and woke up as the train entered Stamford Station and the female voice in the whistling loudspeakers asked the passengers to free all the seats and put their luggage on the racks since the train would be crowded. She was lucky, for still nobody sat in front of her. The child at the other end of the car kept screaming in a piercing voice and the screams were getting closer; he was running in the aisle. Something suddenly crashed into her like a race car. The boy had hurled himself against her legs stretched on the other seat. He was screaming and laughing, his nose between her knees, and dripping a warm stream of saliva. He seemed to have absolutely no awareness of the fact that she wasn't a tree branch. It was funny, but the boy was heavy. His mother was calling him and probably would hit him. Jane reached out to take the child by his jacket and put him back on his feet. A hand brutally grasped her wrist.

"Don't you dare touch him!"

Jane looked up. The mother was staring at her with eyes sparkling with hate, and she was holding her wrist so tightly that it hurt.

Jane blushed: "But I didn't. . . ."

The woman took the child in her arms and carried him away, covering him with kisses. Her thumb had left a red mark on Jane's wrist. A man with well-combed white hair and an expensive-looking green suede parka, who had got on board in Westport and was seated two rows ahead, turned around and rolled his eyes. "Amazing," he said.

She quickly smiled back but didn't answer. She didn't want his complicity. What did he know of poverty and single motherhood?

Her two months in bed, an experience of patience that had left her time to think, had made Jane aware that she too was full of preconceived notions. For instance she had realized that she had, deeply anchored in her and probably inherited from her mother, the unconscious belief that a woman couldn't survive without a man. Her mother had visited in late February after there had been no more risk of transmitting the virus to Susie's baby. It had felt good to have her mother there for her, bringing her dinner in bed, checking her temperature, resting her hand on her forehead, reading the newspapers to her. Good to be a little girl again. But in the morning there was only one topic her mother would touch. "Be careful." Jane had been amazingly lucky to meet someone like Eric at age thirty. Eric wouldn't keep his wonderful patience forever. He was a handsome, charming forty-year-old man with a good job. "All men are the same, darling. What do you think they want? A woman who sleeps in their bed, cooks for them and gives them children. You're almost thirty-six; the clock is ticking. In a marriage, one of the two sometimes needs to sacrifice professional interests." It was useless to ask which one of the two was supposed to make that sacrifice. Jane's mother couldn't conceive that a wife might not follow her husband everywhere, in space as well as in thought—as if women were only satellites orbiting around the man-sun. She herself had started working only after her younger daughter went to college, and then as her husband's assistant.

Jane was glad when her mother left. Her presence had started to make Jane anxious. The day after, she had felt like hearing Francisco's voice again. She hadn't heard from him in almost a month. She had called him in New York. "Hello?" he had answered in a normal voice, one that showed that he had a normal life in which he talked normally to people calling him.

"It's me, Jane."

"Ah, Jane." There was an awkward silence. "How is your research going?"

"My research? Fine." There was another silence. "Do you want me to hang up?" Jane asked almost angrily.

"Maybe. It's still too early."

"But I don't care if you're going out with Kathryn! It was only for you that I advised you not to see her. I don't judge you, Francisco. I miss you; I need you. You're my friend, my only friend here."

"I'm not going out with Kathryn. I haven't seen her since you ran into us. But she's with me all the time, Jane, every second of the day and night, in my heart, in my mind, before my eyes. I need to forget her. It will take time. I can't see you, because you are associated with her."

What made Jane sad was his lack of trust in her. Maybe Kathryn had asked him to lie and even not to see Jane anymore. Plausible. Francisco had once told Jane that Kathryn was scared of her. If he had broken up with Kathryn as he claimed, why would he deprive himself of the only comfort left to him, friendship? If Jane was associated with Kathryn, then everything at Devayne was associated with Kathryn, the Garden Street building to start with. Their friendship couldn't be destroyed simply because she had introduced Kathryn to him. Francisco was more intelligent, subtle, more fair than that.

In spite of her promise to be as silent as a tomb, she told the whole story—skipping the part about the Danish writer—to her neighbor Lynn who, anyway, didn't know anyone involved. Lynn entirely agreed with her: there was an affair. Lynn wasn't positive about the outcome. In spite of Jane's enthusiastic description of Francisco, she thought that a man who made his wife pregnant and then fell in love with another woman could only be a bastard. So typical of men. Typical, too, was this transfer of guilt onto Jane. "Forget about him. He's not worth much."

During the strange and confusing two months of her illness, Jane had passively let Lynn enter her life, even though they didn't have much in common. Lynn had a key to her place and came every night to cook a light meal for her. Originally from Texas, from which she had retained the accent, she was a social worker. Jane was afraid to offend her by asking her to speak less loudly. Lynn always dressed in the same pair of jeans, too tight for her big bottom, and the same synthetic sweater, as if she didn't own any other clothes. She was short and stout with large breasts, almost no neck, badly cut short blond hair and a crooked nose that gave her a British look. Jane's friends had always been good-looking. As superficial as it may seem, beauty was a component in her feeling for someone. She wasn't attracted to Lynn. But Lynn lived next door. She was a warm and generous person, and she was clearly flattered to be friends with a Devayne professor. She had become the most present person in Jane's daily life. No more Francisco. No Eric except on the phone.

During all these weeks in bed, she had thought of Eric a lot. She woke up sometimes with the sensation of Eric's hand on her thigh or her breast. She dreamed of his member and the soft brown skin on which her fingertips danced. She remembered his beautiful hands, his long toes with the clean nails, his firm and soft buttocks. She had a craving for something tender and sensual, a warm love that would be both maternal and erotic.

He called her almost every day. On the phone she only whined at him; he pretended he didn't notice her hostility. "Mmmm," he would say, as if he weren't listening. Not even worth arguing with her, a sick child.

The train stopped: 125th Street. Loud sounds at the other end of the car—the two women and the toddler were getting off. Jane looked excitedly out the windows. It was dark now. The train left, passed between the tall towers, their lit windows looking like tiny stars, and then entered a tunnel. Manhattan disappeared. She opened her bag and put on some lipstick. She pulled her wool scarf more tightly around her neck.

Ten minutes later the train was in Grand Central. All the passengers got up and rushed toward the exit. Jane walked out with the crowd. A man walked toward her, smiling. She raised her eyebrows. He hugged a young woman just behind her. She looked around her as if Eric could be here right now, waiting for her to go back together to a home in Manhattan.

She walked through the marble main hall covered with scaffolding and looked up at the ceiling painted blue like the sky. She almost had to perform dance steps to avoid bumping into the many people running across the hall in every direction. She laughed; it looked like a Charlie Chaplin movie. She passed the information booth where she had run into Duportoy in December, and then took the escalator down to the subway. The vending machine was broken, and the line to get tokens or cards was very long. Jane was proud to take out of her wallet the yellow Metrocard she had bought in December, which made her look like a real New Yorker now: the only trace of her Tuesday in Manhattan three months ago. She couldn't even remember Torben's face; just a blurred image of his thin upper lip with a tiny blond mustache and the small teeth, but any sensation left of his kisses and of his hands on her had been erased by time. So there were acts without consequences—unless Francisco had paid the consequences for her. The rush-hour crowd in the subway was even more dense than inside Grand Central. She walked down to the track and put her hands on her ears as an express train entered the station with an awful noise of metal scraping metal. When you thought about it, the very concept of a city was completely mad.

She got off at Union Square three minutes later and crossed Broadway with the crowd, dizzy with the continuous flow of cars riding down the avenue, honking. A huge man who was brushed by a car because he didn't wait for the light before leaving the sidewalk hit the trunk with his fist and yelled "motherfucker" without anybody reacting to the incident. You needed special training to live in New York. After two months in bed she had lost her defenses. After she turned left onto University Place, though, she felt at home again. A crowd of students in funny clothes was walking down the avenue; many were wearing bell-bottom pants, which must be back in fashion. She passed the News Bar, the restaurant Japonica, the supermarket, stopped at a deli to buy a bouquet of bright yellow jonquils, and turned right into Washington Mews, which she exited on Fifth Avenue. A crazy joy she had contained for months was rising in her. She couldn't help smiling happily. A man looked at her in wonder. In three minutes she would see Francisco.

When she had called him five days ago, on March 22, it wasn't so much because she missed him as to be able to catch him in the act of lying. Since it was spring break, he should be in Spain with Teresa. If he picked up the phone, then everything was clear: he was in New York, which meant with Kathryn. In the rather implausible event that Kathryn would answer the phone, Jane would hang up immediately. Francisco had picked up the phone after two rings. Jane had smiled. But, after answering in a lifeless voice that he was doing fine, Francisco had said, "Teresa is here."

"Teresa? In New York?"

"Yes. The baby is due in less than a month and the airlines don't let pregnant women fly after the eighth month."

Jane remembered that this wasn't what had been planned. Teresa had always refused to have the baby in the States, even though it would entitle their child to an American passport. She didn't trust American hospitals.

"Is she with you in the apartment right now?"

"No, she is doing some errands."

"But how are *you* doing?"

"It has been very difficult. Really difficult. But I'll forget her."

Jane blushed. He couldn't even name *her,* whereas she imagined him having a good time with Kathryn. "What have you been doing all these weeks?"

"Only working. Seeing nobody. I needed to be completely alone. I could barely stand myself."

She perceived, in his sad voice, his self-derisive smile. "How is it with Teresa?"

"Hard. But better than at Christmas. We talked a lot."

"Did you tell her about Kathryn?"

Her uttering the name seemed to startle Francisco like an electric charge.

"Of course not! She would kill me. I talked about the crisis: my fear of becoming a father, the difference between a career here and the dusty Spanish academic world. She understood. But she is still very angry. She makes me pay, quite literally: I have to take her to very expensive restaurants every night and she buys every luxury baby item she finds on Madison Avenue or at Bloomingdale's. Baby Gap wouldn't be good enough. I'm penniless, but if I say something, it will be war; I prefer the debts."

"Could I see you?" Jane asked softly.

"Maybe," he answered hesitantly. "But it would have to be with Teresa."

"Sure!"

"Let me ask her. I'll call you back."

He called her back the same night. Teresa didn't have any objection to a dinner with Jane.

She had misjudged him, as had Lynn. He was a good person. More than that. He virtually had cut his own arm off rather than escaped his responsibilities. One day the secret of his repressed love would be a sweet memory between him and Jane. One day she and Eric, with their kids, would visit Teresa, Francisco and their kids in the beautiful Andalusian countryside house with the swimming pool and the olive trees.

She entered the building on Washington Square North and gave her name to the old doorman with the thick square glasses. He smiled widely and said in a Puerto Rican accent strengthened by a speech impediment, "Long time no see you!"

She rode the familiar elevator, walked to the end of the long corridor, and rang the bell.

Francisco opened the door. She knew immediately it was terrible. There was something in his face she had never seen, not even in January, when things had been so bad. His eyes wouldn't focus. Teresa walked toward her. She was huge. Fuming anger. Jane handed the flowers to her. Teresa took them without thanking her and dropped them on a table.

"Please, sit down," Jane said.

"I'm better standing up."

"So is the baby due very soon?"

No answer. Maybe they thought it was only an observation.

Jane never imagined there could be so much bitterness in a woman eight and a half months pregnant. Allison and Susie had told her that the hormones made you as happy as a vegetable. The best period in a woman's life, they said. There wasn't an ounce of joy in Teresa: only anger directed at Francisco.

They sat down in the living room, on the sofa—a futon actually—where Jane had often slept.

"You forgot the Porto," Teresa said with hostility.

Francisco got up and brought back the bottle.

"How long have you been here?" Jane asked.

"Three weeks. I'm tired. I don't sleep well here. It's too noisy."

"New York is so noisy. It struck me when I got off the subway. Plus here you have the cops screaming every night 'The park is now closed!'"

Francisco stared at her heavily. Jane blushed. Teresa clearly didn't know that Jane had stayed here overnight.

"Francisco told me that it really bothered him, the cops repeating 'The park is now closed' every night."

"The whole apartment is horrible," Teresa said. "So you have been sick?" she added abruptly.

"Yes. I had pneumonia."

"Pneumonia!"

Teresa shifted back and looked at Francisco as if he were trying to murder her and her child by introducing fatal germs into the apartment.

"Oh, but it's over completely. The pneumonia itself has been over for a long time. What happened is that I went to the hospital because I couldn't get rid of a sore throat, and the pneumonia wasn't diagnosed immediately, so the antibiotics I was given weren't strong enough. After a week my fever had only increased: I returned to the hospital and that time they took an X-ray. It wasn't pretty: a big dark stain on the right lung. The infection had had time to spread. . . ."

Teresa's nostrils moved.

"The pizzettas! Did you leave them in the oven?"

Francisco got up again. Teresa looked impatiently at Jane, who felt forced to continue with her story as if she weren't noticing the tension.

"The doctor said I had to spit. I had to learn to spit. Excuse me, it's not very pleasant; but that was the only way to get rid of the yellow stuff inside. . . ."

Teresa made a disgusted face. It was impossible to determine whether it was addressed to Jane or to Francisco, who was returning from the kitchen with a plate full of tiny pizzettas with burned corners.

"They smell delicious," Jane said. "May I?"

"They're burned," Teresa said with the same disgusted rictus on her face. "It gives you cancer."

"In brief," Jane concluded, "after a month I didn't have a fever anymore and when I spat it was no longer yellow, but my whole body hurt so much that I could barely move. I went to the hospital again: the infection was gone, but I'd spat so much that I inflamed the muscle around the lung! It's called pleurisy. I had to spend another three weeks in bed and make all the effort I could not to cough and not spit, which was very hard."

"Did you turn off the oven?" Teresa asked rudely.

Francisco nodded yes. Neither of them seemed very interested in Jane's illness. It's true, Jane reflected, that others' illnesses are like their dreams—nothing is more boring than a detailed description. But it looked like nothing Jane could say would interest them anyway.

"So that's it: I was sick for more than two months. It's weird when you're sick for so long: you enter another time, another kind of reality—"

"Two months isn't that long," Teresa interrupted with a sarcastic face. "My cousin had leukemia which she fought for two years."

"Two years! Is she OK?"

Teresa nodded yes. Jane helped herself to another pizzetta and drank some Porto. She would have been glad to leave for Old Newport right now. There was a discussion between Francisco and Teresa about the choice of a restaurant. They should have reserved earlier, Teresa said angrily. All the decent restaurants were full at night, even during the week. It was not even worth trying the Gotham Bar and Grill or the Odeon Café.

"Do you like Japanese restaurants?" Teresa asked Jane.

"I love them."

She was relieved. A Japanese restaurant couldn't be as expensive as a fancy French place.

But this turned out to be a very fancy Japanese restaurant in the heart of Soho. They were lucky: they got the last table. Two minutes later there was a line at the door. Not a sushi or noodle place. Jane absorbed herself in the menu, barely recognizing any of the entrées. Nothing for less than $35. She had a look at the dishes on the table next to them: huge pieces of raw fish served on a wooden board and seaweed salad on the side. The couple were looking at their boards in dismay. There was a guide book on the table. Tourists. The woman cut a small piece with the wooden chopsticks, tried it, made a face, and discreetly spat the bite in her hand. There was a short discussion between them. Italians. The man put a $100 bill on the table, and they got up. It was rather funny, but Francisco and Teresa seemed too tense to notice the scene. A waiter quickly carried away the untouched plates and cleaned the table; another couple sat down immediately. Jane decided on a salmon teriyaki, the least expensive and only familiar item on the menu. Teresa chose the most expensive dishes, ordered the best sake, and a $90 bottle of wine. Francisco raised his eyebrows nervously. Teresa threw him an angry look.

"It's the only wine that goes well with eel."

The waiter nodded in approval and walked away. Teresa looked at Jane, whom she seemed to notice for the first time.

"He tells me he's broke. Why does he work all the time if he doesn't even earn any money? Do you get it?"

Jane laughed as if this were a good joke.

They couldn't remain silent for the whole dinner. Francisco, though, wouldn't start a conversation. Teresa would only tear at him. Jane tried to ease the tension by describing the amazing pressure everyone felt at Devayne and the difficulties she herself had experienced with Eric, who had already forgotten how rigorous Devayne was. She and Francisco had very similar experiences because they were both directors of undergraduate studies in addition to teaching and research.

"The first year of being DUS is hell. Devayne is always on your mind. You can never relax. Everything rests on your shoulders and you're always scared you did something wrong. These kids pay twenty thousand dollars a year for their education: you can't mislead them. Sometimes I woke up at night, sweating."

Teresa was listening. Jane had found a good topic.

"This is why Francisco and I understand each other so well," she continued.

It was the moment to clear any suspicions Teresa could have formed about their relationship.

"Such good friends," she continued, laughing, "that everyone in our departments thought we were having an affair."

The word startled Teresa and Francisco as if Jane had just hit them at the same time with a rubber bullet. Teresa turned pale. Francisco looked at Jane with intense black eyes. Jane blushed. Not a word to pronounce in front of them. Better change the subject quickly.

"Have you seen the new Woody Allen?" she asked.

They had. For once they agreed: not good.

"I'm not surprised. I'm not sure he can make a good film now that he's no longer with Mia Farrow. In December I saw *Crimes and Misdemeanors* again. That was excellent. Do you remember it?"

They hadn't seen it.

"Oh, you should rent the tape! It's about a man, a doctor, who is married, with children, and who has an affair. . . ."

She stopped and swallowed. These two people in front of her looked like they were going to explode at any moment.

"And what?" Teresa snapped.

"He meets his mistress on a plane: a stewardess played by Anjelica Huston. He wants to break up with her, she threatens to tell his wife everything, and before he really knows what's going on, his brother, who has ties with the Mafia, gets a contract on Anjelica Huston, who is killed by a professional. The question is whether the doctor will collapse and betray himself. Meanwhile there is a subplot with Woody Allen as an unsuccessful scriptwriter making a documentary about Primo Levi and falling in love with beautiful Mia Farrow, whom a well-known Hollywood director is also courting. Woody Allen hates the guy and makes fun of him with Mia Farrow, whom he thinks is on his side. In the end. . . ."

The waiter brought their plates. When he walked away, Francisco and Teresa took up their chopsticks and didn't ask what happened in the end. It was better anyway not to tell them the end if they might see the film one day. And a film put into words always sounds boring, most especially when it is described by someone enthusiastic. Jane followed their example and started eating silently.

Teresa complained almost immediately. The best Japanese restaurant in Manhattan? The fish was tasteless and not even that fresh. A table wine in Spain would be better than this $90 bottle.

This provided a new conversation topic to Jane: the cruise with the Devayne alumni six years earlier. She described everyone's surprise as they boarded a German boat on a French river. Teresa smiled. Safe territory finally.

"The chef was German too."

She managed to become witty and funny while recounting the vacation of a single, lonely thirty-year-old woman among eighty-five-year-old men who were dripping saliva around her and who had all taken the Concorde to fly to Paris because it was barely more expensive and so much more convenient than a first-class ticket in a normal plane. Two-hour-long lunches and dinners which she couldn't escape. Totally depressing. A real Fellini movie. And then, the German doctor, a handsome young man who walked straight out of a Thomas Mann novel. But even the innocent and simple pleasure of chatting with him became a problem when the doctor's wife, who was pregnant. . . .

Wife. She immediately knew the word was wrong. It had a big red flashing warning light. Pregnant: a loud siren started. Francisco was obstinately looking at the food on his plate and playing with his chopsticks. Teresa was white. It was like driving a speeding car on a mountain road and losing control after a turn. The car fell straight into the abyss when Jane courageously finished her sentence: " . . . got jealous."

Silence would have been worse afterward. She went on and told the scene in a falsely joyful voice: the bee entrapped in her hair, the doctor helping her, the bee stinging him. Walking late into the room where she was giving her lecture. The doctor's wife looking at her and collapsing that night.

"I felt really sorry for her. When nothing happened."

It sounded like a denial. In any case, neither Francisco nor Teresa seemed to be listening. Jane stopped talking. She was sweating. The waiter refilled their glasses with an elegant flourish. He asked whether everything was fine.

"They can't even get the salad right," Teresa said after he left. "Much too salty."

They finished their dinner in almost complete silence. The only one talking now was Teresa, complaining about everything. Jane didn't dare to add a word. She had met Francisco's eyes one second—icy, lifeless eyes. As soon as Teresa ate her last bite, he asked for the check. He looked at it with an expressionless face and took his credit card out of his wallet. Teresa was staring at him. Jane could see that the total was more than $300, or $350 with the tip. She had never spent so much in a restaurant.

"How much do I owe you?"

"Give me fifty bucks, that's fine. You didn't have an appetizer and barely drank a glass of wine."

"You could treat her," Teresa exclaimed with a scornful rictus. "You academics are so cheap!"

Francisco rubbed his hands against the white napkin. Jane looked at the swollen veins on his hands.

As they were standing in the hallway, waiting for Teresa, who was using the bathroom, Jane apologized for her gaffes.

"Very appropriate stories indeed," Francisco said with a constrained smile.

As soon as they stepped out of the restaurant, she took a cab for Grand Central, arriving just in time to board the 9:55 train to Old Newport. She read the *National Enquirer*, without skipping one line, the whole ride back.

Jane was staring at the last line, her cheeks red. The way Francisco made her appear responsible for everything was outrageous.

She had to get in touch with him right now. The clock on the stove indicated 5:55 P.M. Too late to call the secretary of the Spanish department. Who else would know Francisco's number? Possibly his chairman, to whom Francisco had introduced her three years earlier. She remembered his name: Alfonso Menor. She would find his home number in the Devayne Faculty Directory when she went to the office later to check her e-mail. If she got Francisco's number from Alfonso Menor, then she would call him immediately. It would be the middle of the night in Spain, but she didn't care if she woke him up, as well as his wife and baby.

If he was still married; and if he still lived in Spain. The package had been mailed from New York. Could Francisco be in New York? Or in Old Newport, waiting for her reaction?

The phone rang. She jumped and picked up the receiver.

"Hello?"

"May I speak with Professor Jane Cook, please?"

Not a trace of Hispanic accent. It was not Francisco.

"Speaking."

"Hi! David Clark."

"Who?"

"David Clark, from the Department of French and Italian at the University of Iowa in Iowa City."

"Oh, hi! How are you doing?"

"Fine, thanks. Sorry to disturb you at home, Jane. I took the liberty of asking Eric for your home number because I needed to get in touch with you quickly."

Jane was looking through the window. The sun piercing the thick clouds and projecting vertical rays reminded her of a painting by Claude Gelée—also called Le Lorrain—that Eric had shown her in the Louvre. Eric loved skies torn by light after a storm. Eric? How would he know her phone number when she had changed it last year and wasn't listed? David Clark was lying.

"We would be delighted if you would come and give a lecture at our department this fall. I need your answer as soon as possible: our chairman is meeting with the dean tomorrow to get budgetary approval and I need to give him the list of lecturers beforehand. We're not very rich, but we could give you three hundred dollars for the lecture and reimburse all travel expenses, of course. We usually have dinner after the lecture. It would be late for you to go back home afterwards: if you don't mind you could stay over at my place. I have a guest room with a private bathroom and I promise you excellent French toast for breakfast. It would be nicer than a room at the faculty club."

Jane shivered. She was cold. Or hungry.

"When would it be?"

"I was thinking of October 12."

She was probably filling in for someone who had just canceled.

"I need to think about it. Can I call you back tonight?"

"Sure. Even very late, don't hesitate, I'm a night owl."

She suddenly had a vision of the icy steps and the shadow under the streetlight.

"And before going to bed you walk the dog that is inside you."

"I beg your pardon?" He laughed. "You have a good memory."

"How is the patchwork quilt going?"

"You mean my book? Thanks for asking. I completely changed my initial project. No more patchwork."

"Why?"

"Too banal. It's the new academic fashion, this mixture of autobiographical fragments and literary criticism. I think that it's narcissistic and confusing. I went back to a much more traditional structure. Now I'm writing a Jane Austen novel: the love story of an academic. Or, rather, a Balzac novel: the rise and fall of an academic. A woman rather than a man, so nobody will recognize me. It's a novel, but with a philosophical dimension, a vision of life, you know, what the Germans call a *Weltanschauung*. Would you like to take a look at it? You would be a good reader."

She was listening distractedly. There was a question on the tip of her tongue. She counted months: only four since she had last seen David Clark at the MLA convention in December, so there could be nothing new. She wasn't going to ask him; he was clearly expecting the question. It might even be the real reason for his call. This guy always stuck his nose into other people's lives.

"By the way, don't worry," David suddenly said. "Eric is on sabbatical in the fall: he won't be around."

Jane turned pale. He saw through her. "Ah. And where is he going?" she asked in the most possible casual voice.

"To Italy, I think. He's working on a completely different project: a biography of Bronzino."

"Of Bronzino!"

He laughed. "Not your Bronzino. The sixteenth-century Italian painter."

"David, I don't think I can accept your invitation. It's very nice of you, but I'll be overwhelmed between the new job and my own work."

"Are you sure?" He sounded disappointed. "Think about it. Until tomorrow morning, really. I love your work, I would be really glad if you came. It could be in the spring, if you prefer."

When she hung up, her hands were trembling. She suddenly felt very weak, and cold. She closed the kitchen window and walked to the living room to turn the thermostat to 70°. Back in the kitchen, she opened the fridge. She didn't have the courage to cook anything.

The life of an academic. A woman. She was a good reader. He called her, just by chance, in the middle of her reading. Mentioned Eric with sadistic curiosity. And Bronzino. He invited her to phone him at any time of the night. A mere coincidence?

But why would David Clark write a novel about her? It didn't make sense. He had no motivation. And where would he have got all the details? From Eric? Eric would never talk about her, about their relationship. And Eric didn't know about Francisco's love for Kathryn.

She took out the gallon of skim milk and, from the cupboard, the box of cornflakes. She filled a bowl, swallowed four large bites quickly, put the bowl to the right of the stack of unread pages, and continued eating while turning them.

4

Better to be inside than out with that rain whipping the windows. Her most positive thought right now. She was on the sofa, reading, or, rather, replaying last night's conversation with Francisco in her mind with some kind of masochistic pleasure, when the phone rang.

She ran to the kitchen and picked up the phone on the small table near the stove.

"Did I wake you?"

"Hi! No, I was reading."

Eric. Nobody tonight she wanted to hear from more. She had left him a message in the afternoon. It was midnight already.

"Sorry I didn't call you earlier; I had dinner with David. How're you?"

"Fine. It's still pouring."

"You didn't ride your bike, I hope."

"Not today, the streets were too wet. Yesterday I did, but I dressed warmly."

"You are not reasonable."

The truth was that with this weather, her lungs still made a funny whistling sound when she breathed; she wasn't going to tell Eric. He was right, but riding her bike was simply much faster than walking.

"I got the letter from the University of Minnesota Press."

"When?"

He didn't even ask her what the letter said. He had exhausted his reserve of comforting words. She wasn't looking for comfort. The letter today was a shock, though. She knew as soon as she saw the off-white envelope, before she even read the publisher's name—she had developed a special sense by now. Her last hope. Of course, there were more important matters. Health, to start with. Still. Last night's conversation with Francisco left her with a bitter taste that everything today—the rain, the letter, the wait for Eric's call—had reinforced.

"This afternoon."

"What do they say?"

"Not much." She laughed. "Saving ink for budgetary reasons, I guess. Not even a reader's report after they kept the manuscript for five months. Just saying that it doesn't meet their editorial needs right now, and that they are very, very sorry."

"You should call and ask them why."

"I don't need to. I know why."

"So why?"

"They published a book by Jeffrey Woodrow last spring on a similar topic. That's why I wrote to them originally; at least I knew the subject interested them."

"Have you read the Woodrow?"

"Not yet."

"Jane."

She could see him shake his head: very unprofessional. Procrastinating again. That book had been out for more than a year already. She hadn't even checked it out at the library, when the first thing she had to do, as a proper marketing policy, was to position herself in relation to the last book on the same subject. She knew Eric's take on this: your value on the market was only the one you gave yourself.

"I'll check it out. I didn't have the time last fall."

A theme that rang the familiar bell: "Are you getting ready?"

She was. Even before today's letter, which had confirmed that there was no other choice for her than to become a wife in Iowa. Two days ago she called a travel agency and made a reservation. She told Eric the same night. This was also the pretext she used to call Francisco yesterday. If only she could tell Eric about this conversation. But he didn't know that she went to New York and saw Francisco. Plus, he might think that Francisco was right about her.

"Yes, I am."

She blushed: she had forgotten to call the agency today, because of the letter. Now her reservation was probably canceled. Hopefully, Eric wouldn't ask about it.

"Can you wait a sec?" he said. "I have another call."

She pulled a chair from the dining table nearby and sat down, facing the stove and the window on the left. Still pouring. Weather as sinister as Francisco's voice when he picked up the phone yesterday and recognized her: so distant, so not very pleased to hear her voice. They hadn't talked since the dinner five days earlier. It was April 1, and when she dialed his number, she wondered whether she should make a joke to lighten things up—guessing he was upset with her. Maybe she could tell him she was pregnant. It would disarm him. But when she heard his voice, the idea of a joke disappeared at once.

"How are you?" she asked almost timidly.

"Fine."

"Are you coming to Old Newport tomorrow?"

"Yes."

"Do you want to get a coffee?"

"No."

She blushed. Francisco's answer was uncharacteristically blunt, but he was probably overwhelmed with work.

"Next week? Any day before Friday; I'll leave for Iowa on Friday. I would like to say good-bye."

"I don't want to see you."

Her heart started beating fast. "Because of Thursday night?"

"I'll never forgive you for speaking of Kathryn in front of Teresa. You're wicked."

"Of Kathryn? I didn't!"

"You mentioned your excellent assistant. You asked me if I remembered her. I wish I had never met you."

Jane had completely forgotten. She had pronounced Kathryn's name by chance as they were speaking about the resources offered by Devayne. She had then added the question to Francisco just to sound casual, precisely because she immediately felt like she was walking on a rope above an abyss.

"It wasn't deliberate, Francisco! Like the stories I told at dinner. There was so much tension, I was so scared for you two, I felt so uncomfortable."

He laughed. "So you tried to make it worse."

"No. It was completely unconscious! You know how it is when you shouldn't speak about something: somehow you'll end up speaking exactly about it."

"My point. The trouble with you is your unconscious—it's wicked. You can't do anything about it. You're no good. There is something else I've noticed about you: you're so competitive that if your so-called friend's life is a mess, you feel better by comparison."

That was the end of the conversation. A judgment without appeal. She had shown in one evening what she was worth.

There was a noise in her left ear. Eric back on the line.

"Hi. Excuse me. A colleague needed some information about the final exam and then he told me that our chairman walked around all day yesterday with a paper fish stuck to his back that said 'Kiss me.' April Fools joke. I'm glad the students didn't do that to me. What were we talking about? Yes, your arrival. Friday of next week at five P.M., right? I had a dentist appointment scheduled at four, but I'll cancel it. I hope that he'll be able to take me soon. I have a cavity that hurts already."

"Don't cancel your appointment."

"Why?"

Eric's voice tensed immediately.

"I forgot to call the travel agency back today. I'll check tomorrow whether I can make the same reservation again. If it's more convenient for you, I could leave on Saturday instead."

"You didn't buy your ticket yet?" Eric asked slowly.

"I forgot. Because of this letter, I guess."

"You forgot. I see." There was a silence. "Between the two of us," he resumed in a cold voice, "I don't find your little game very funny. Either you buy your ticket tomorrow by noon, or. . . ."

"Why are you speaking to me like that? I told you I forgot!"

"You're a little too forgetful for my taste. You know very well why I talk to you like that. Today is April second, Jane. This thing started in December. I'm losing my patience."

"Don't talk to me like that. This is exactly the problem. Maybe this is why I forgot to call the agency."

"Excuse me?"

"Knowing that you would react that way. It stresses me out. If only you could be nice."

"I'm not nice?" He laughed.

"When you speak to me like that, you're not nice. You scare me."

"I scare you."

"Yes. Because I know you'll never give in."

"I'll never give in."

"Stop repeating what I say."

She felt like crying. She couldn't be weak. Not now. They were touching the heart of the matter. She had to be very brave and deal with that silence between them before she went there, and Eric considered the simple fact of her being there to be more meaningful than any words.

"When you speak to me like that, I feel . . . as if you were watching me slide into an abyss and you won't put out your hand to help me, just to prove to me that I was wrong to step to the edge when you had warned me against doing it."

He laughed again. "Illuminating. I'll try to remember next time I see you slide into an abyss."

"Stop it. Don't you see that I'm speaking seriously? Can't you just be nice?"

"I'm nice," he yelled. "I'm very nice. I am awfully nice, I'm much too nice. I should have been much less nice, much earlier!"

"I can't come as long as you speak to me like that. I can't come if you can't give in, Eric."

"This is sick. Welcome to the madhouse. 'Give in, be nice.' Is that woman Lynn enrolling you in some sect? Or is it someone else? My sweet little darling, I am begging you to come here. Is that nice enough?"

She swallowed with difficulty. There was a pain in her chest. "I'm sad."

"Listen. You have until tomorrow noon to buy your ticket. That's it."

"This is blackmail."

"I'm not sure who is blackmailing the other. 'Give in or I won't come': I don't understand a fucking word you say. At least I'm clear."

"It's not a power game, Eric. It's about us. If only you could give in. . . ."

"Don't say that once more! It makes me crazy."

"Don't scream. Be nice, I beg you."

He yelled with rage. There was the noise of something falling on the floor, and the line went dead.

She dialed his number immediately. He picked up the phone after half a ring.

"How dare you hang up on me? You're the one who should see a shrink, not me! By the way, I went to see one and this is exactly what he said. The trouble is not with me but with you, with your total inability to communicate. You're exactly like your mother. No wonder your father disappeared and Sonia left you!"

Eric laughed bitterly. "Sure."

"For months I have been trying to speak with you. You won't listen. You don't care. You didn't even come here when I had pneumonia."

"I was teaching; I couldn't leave. I called you every day."

"What about your vacation two weeks ago?"

"I had a conference. You don't cancel at the last minute unless there is a very serious reason."

Her turn to laugh. "What is a very serious reason? You mean if I had died? Maybe you would have come to the funeral?"

"You're being ridiculous."

"Shut up. I cannot allow you to use that word. I'm not ridiculous. People die of pneumonia. Do you know how sick I was? Do you think I could get up with a fever of a hundred and three and cook dinner for myself?"

"Your mother came after I called her."

"Thanks. She fulfilled her mission, don't worry. But before that, during the three weeks when I was in bed with that fever, who was supposed to take care of me? Who, if there hadn't been 'that woman Lynn'?"

"Your Spanish boyfriend, I suppose."

Jane started crying. They were silent for a few seconds.

"Eric," she said slowly, "do I need to tell you that I slept with someone else to make you listen to me?"

"You slept with someone else?" he asked in an amused voice.

"Oh my God! Oh my God! You don't hear anything I say, nothing!"

"I hear you very well: you're screaming. I've heard enough, actually."

"Yes, I fucked someone last week!"

"The Spanish idiot?"

"Duportoy, if you want to know! And yes it was nice."

She wasn't crying anymore. She was stunned like a child who fires an automatic weapon at his classmates and sees them fall around him in pools of blood. Duportoy. The name came to her lips just as she was speaking—only now did she remember that she saw Xavier in the department today after she picked up her mail. He was running out, probably toward the train station, and barely held the door for her. She couldn't choose a better name. Eric had met him a couple of times and disliked him.

He didn't say anything. After a few seconds, Jane resumed in a trembling voice: "If this is all we have to tell each other, it looks like whatever was between us is dead. We may as well get a divorce."

It felt like thrusting a sharp dagger in her stomach—or, for that matter, in Eric's stomach.

"Is this what you want?" His icy voice. Never acknowledging he was hurt. Never giving in.

"At least it would be more honest."

The line went dead. Jane felt dizzy. There was sweat on her palms. The pain in her chest was much stronger than earlier, and there was a whistling sound when she breathed. She probably had a fever. She put water on the stove for tea and rinsed her face in the bathroom. After drinking the hot chamomile, she felt calmer and dialed Eric's number again. Nobody answered, not even the answering machine. He had probably unplugged the phone and gone to bed. Wise.

She woke up at 6 A.M. and waited for a reasonable time to call him. At 9—8 for Eric, there was still no answer. She tried every ten minutes. At 10:15, the answering machine was plugged in: he must have remembered that his phone was off the hook just as he stepped out. She tried the office: he wasn't there. She left a message at home, apologizing for last night. The letter had depressed her, even though she was used to rejection. She would buy her ticket today. Could he call back?

In the afternoon she tried the office again. In the evening, home: no answering machine. She was too nervous to read. She watched TV, her eyes on the clock. At midnight she dialed Allison's number in Seattle. John picked up the phone.

"Hi, it's Jane. Is Allison around?"

"She's putting Jeremy to sleep. Can she call you back in ten minutes?"

"Sure. Please tell her to call me tonight if she can."

"Is something wrong?"

"No, no."

Half an hour later Allison hadn't called. Jane was sure John had given her the message. She poured herself a glass of whiskey and sat on the sofa. "Wicked." The value of a person showed through acts that weren't deliberate. Out-of-focus details that revealed everything. She agreed. One couldn't always be on one's guard; at some point one betrayed oneself, the true self, the one beyond control. "Competitive." She had always compared herself to others—that was so true. Since she was little, she had always looked at Susie's plate or gifts before her own. Francisco had done the most difficult thing a human being could do: give up one's love to be faithful to one's word. He trusted Jane. She had failed him. Sadistically driving a nail into his heart: "affair," "affair," "affair," "affair."

She was dozing and a bit drunk when the phone rang. She ran to the kitchen and looked at the clock above the stove: 1:05 A.M. It could only be Eric. She sighed with relief.

"Hello?"

"Hi. I didn't wake you up, I hope."

Her heart collapsed. "No."

"John said you didn't sound too cheerful and you insisted I call you back tonight. I'm sorry to do it so late; Jeremy just wouldn't fall asleep. He's so sensitive that he probably felt you were expecting my call and I had to go. One story, and as soon as I read the last word he was already asking for another! Three stories, and long ones. He left me voiceless. And I can't skip a word; he knows them by heart. Especially the words he doesn't understand—those are the ones he prefers. He is so cute. He finally fell asleep twenty minutes ago, and then we had to work."

"To work?"

Allison laughed.

"LH surge day. I can't tell you how sexy it is: now John has to give me a shot in the buttocks before acting."

"What?"

"Yes. Hormones. I'm forty-one now. It's even more difficult than when we tried for Jeremy. But I guess you didn't call to hear these sexy details. What's up?"

Jane burst into tears.

"Jane? What's going on?"

Jane told Allison about the argument on the phone the night before because of the plane ticket she had forgotten to buy. Now Eric wouldn't call her back.

"It's time you guys get together and make a kid," Allison said in a tranquil and distracted voice, as if she was doing something else at the same time, like sorting papers, which was possible, since Jeremy ate up all her time during the day when she was home. "Believe me, once you have a kid you won't have any time left for this kind of stuff. You'll be less self-centered." Jane blushed. "Buy your ticket tomorrow morning, and go," Allison concluded, and then yawned. "Sorry. I'm tired."

"But then he will think he was right to blackmail me with silence."

"Didn't you say one has to give in sometimes? Give in. You'll discuss things with him once you're there. My bet is that you won't even feel like discussing anything."

The following morning Jane bought her ticket, for that same Friday, April 11, and already felt better. She had a week to gather her books, files, and papers, clean her apartment, and pack. She left a message on Eric's answering machine at home in a tender voice. She called the secretary in his department: could she tell Eric to call back after his class? It was urgent. At 4:30 she reached the secretary again, who sounded surprised.

"He didn't call you back? I saw him after his class this morning and I told him."

"He must have left a message at home," Jane said quickly, so the secretary wouldn't smell trouble and start gossiping. Eric would have been furious. But after all, it was his fault.

She poured herself a glass of whiskey that night, unable to fall asleep. Did he mention anything like a conference? He would say again that she didn't listen. In any case, it wouldn't prevent him from checking his answering machine. She called again in the middle of the night; nobody answered and there was no answering machine, which meant that he was home and he had unplugged his phone.

When she woke up toward 7 A.M., she tried again. And again, all morning long, until there was the answering machine; he had probably just stepped out. It was almost comforting to follow his going in and out through the plugging and unplugging of the answering machine. She left a humble message: He was right to be very upset. She had crossed the line. Of course she had never slept with Duportoy nor with anyone else. She loved him. Please call back. Please.

Later she dialed Nancy's number. She let the phone ring ten or twelve times: no answering machine. Eric's mother unplugged her answering machine only when she went away on a trip. She had gone to Florida in January and she had no trip planned in April. Jane guessed that Nancy was there, in Iowa, with Eric. He must have called his mother for rescue.

Sunday was horrible. Lynn was visiting her mother, who had moved into a rented mobile home in Florida, and Allison was gone for the weekend too. Jane spent the day biting her nails and calling Eric every half hour.

On Monday morning she tried again at home and at the office.

She knew what was going on. He was truly angry. Not because of this stupid thing about Duportoy, but because of her mentioning his father and Sonia. She had hit the most sensitive, most fragile spot in Eric. Her unconscious made no mistake when it was a matter of hurting someone. "Wicked," yes. Now Eric was punishing her in Eric's way: through silence. He had probably sworn to himself that he wouldn't talk to her until she was there. She had delayed her arrival too often. For good reasons, but still. Eric believed in actions, not words.

In the afternoon she found her plane ticket in her mailbox at the university. That was real; immediately she felt better. She sent Eric an e-mail: she needed to know what kind of English-French dictionary he had at home. She called Connecticut Limo and made a reservation for the airport. She went to the library, where she xeroxed articles and checked out books, among them, finally, the Woodrow, of which she would make a Xerox copy tomorrow at the department. When she left the library, it was getting dark. As she rode her bike home, she kept thinking about Eric. Silence wasn't a good method. Lynn was right to say that silence wasn't neutral but very hostile. She had to find a way to make Eric understand this without upsetting him. From afar she saw that the Market Street traffic light was green, and she pedaled as fast as she could to cross the street before cars started moving. After crossing the bridge over the tracks, she turned right along the gray concrete boxes with tiny windows where only poor people lived. The sidewalk there wasn't well lit. Suddenly she saw herself fall. It was almost like in a film: she was flying toward the ground with her hands in front of her, while the back of her bike, like that of a kicking horse, was rising in the air.

The phone rang. Jane was startled. She got up and picked up the receiver.

"Hi! I just got home. I talked to Josh."

"How are Lea and Nina?"

"They both have high fever and Jeremy is awful. He must be getting a cold too. I don't feel too well either. I'm afraid we'll all end up sick in bed. I'm yawning and falling asleep right now as I speak. Josh said he would be pleased to hear from you. Can you write down his number? Here it is."

Jane scribbled the number.

"Did he sound surprised that I wanted to get in touch with him?"

"Not really. Apparently you have some friends in common and he knows all that happened to you. He seems to be convinced that you two will end up together. He was also in a very good mood because his novel just got accepted by an important literary agent and he's sure to find a good publisher."

"What's the novel about?"

"It's a thriller that takes place in the academic world."

"Really! Must be boring."

"Why?"

"An academic novel."

"But a thriller is OK."

"I don't like thrillers. They're too calculated, lifeless—I get bored immediately. Do you know whether I am in his novel?"

"I don't know. It's full of dead bodies at the end. Maybe he killed you off too."

"I'm sure. Which friends do we have in common?"

"Your colleague with a country name. . . ."

"Jamaica?"

"That's it."

"How did he meet her?"

"Through your Spanish friend, I think."

"Francisco? Josh knows Francisco? But how?"

"Frankly, I have no idea. Wait. Wasn't Francisco working for some Spanish publishing company? I remember now: Josh sold him the rights of an American novel he had edited at Doubleday."

"Amazing—such a small world!"

"Jeremy! Don't! No! Jane, Jeremy just broke a lamp and the twins are screaming, I have to go."

Jane sat down again. She looked at the stack of pages. She had read more than two-thirds now. So Josh knew Francisco and Jamaica, and he wanted Jane to know that, or why would he have told Allison about it? Information regarding her had been circulating. Which way? Whom should she contact first? Josh or Francisco?

She would decide at the end of this chapter. Where was she? Right, the bike fall, that terrible night.

❂

She had the time to think that rising in the air and landing on its nose was something a plane, not a bike, would do, before her body brutally hit the ground. She rolled on the concrete and stopped on her left side, with the bike on top of her. Tears gushed from her eyes.

A car stopped. A door opened, loud music came out of a radio and a young black guy stepped toward her. "Are you OK?"

"I think so."

Two men in dark suits appeared and stopped. The younger one lifted the bike and the older helped her get up, while the driver got back into his car and left. Tears were rolling down her cheeks. Her nose was running.

"Are you OK?"

"Yes."

"Where do you live?" the man with gray hair asked.

"Very close by, on Main Street."

Just where they were coming from.

"We'll walk you."

"That's very nice, but I'm OK, I can go by myself."

They didn't listen. The younger man took her bike and the older her arm. "How do you feel?"

"Fine, really. Nothing broken or I wouldn't be able to walk. Just bruises."

"You're lucky. You could have killed yourself. You should wear a helmet."

"I know. My husband told me so."

She felt like mentioning a husband.

"You're married?"

"Yes."

"Where is your husband now?"

She wasn't able to lie. "In Iowa."

"That's far."

"Yes." She was crying again.

"Well, you should tell your husband that you were extremely lucky tonight. You could have broken your skull, your spine, or your knees! And here you are, walking! Are you sure you feel OK?"

"Yes, sure."

"You're so lucky my friend and I were passing by. Without us, who knows what would have happened. This young man who stopped looked very suspicious. Don't you think so, Tom? Did you see how he drove away as soon as we got there?"

The younger man, walking on the road while pushing the bike on the sidewalk, nodded. He was as tall and thin as his companion was short and plump. They looked like Laurel and Hardy. Jane smiled through her tears.

"His intentions were quite obvious: he was ready to take advantage of your weakness. He certainly didn't look happy when he saw us. Mrs. . . . ?"

"Mrs. Blackwood."

She rarely used that name—at work she was still Jane Cook and she also published under her maiden name.

"Mrs. Blackwood, you miraculously escaped two grave dangers tonight: a broken skull and sexual attack."

The tall young man nodded again. Jane didn't remember the driver looking so suspicious. On the contrary, he had seemed nice and helpful, and he drove away simply because the two other men stopped to help her.

These two had vivid imaginations. There was something strange about them. But they were dressed like serious people and they showed real concern. She shook her head.

"Yes, I was lucky. I got so scared when I fell. I saw myself fall. Here we are. I live just here."

The two men stopped with her in front of the wrought-iron fence and looked at the beautiful building. "Do you live alone?"

"Yes," she said hesitantly, "but I'm not alone in the house: there are seven apartments."

"Are you sure you'll be OK? Don't you want us to call a doctor?"

"No, don't worry. I have a neighbor who is a good friend and she'll soon be home."

"Maybe we should wait for her with you."

Were they expecting a tip? Or a drink?

"No, really, I'm perfectly OK. Thank you. You have been very helpful."

"We'll leave you then. But take this," the older man added, handing over a few papers to her. "Read this as soon as you're home."

"Thanks."

"You were really lucky today, you know. Really lucky."

She locked her bike to the fence. She didn't have the strength to carry it inside the house and she didn't want to ask these men for help. They watched her go up the stairs and push the front door open. They waved.

"Don't forget to send a reply!" the old man said before the door closed on her.

Upstairs, her first glance was at the answering machine: not blinking. The dark, heavy thought from which the fall and the two men had distracted her filled her mind again. She still had the papers in her hand. She looked at them. A business envelope with prepaid postage. She unfolded a white form: a long list of items with two columns of prices on the right, one of which was crossed out. "Car accident, Ski accident, Motorbike accident, Bike accident, Accident in the workplace, Drowning . . ." Insurance salesmen, of course. As she read the next item, she shook her head: "Argument with husband or wife." Nowadays you could get insurance for anything. She opened her eyes wide as she went on reading: "Divorce,

Rape, Domestic violence, Death of a significant other, Mother's death, Father's death, Child's death," and then, after a blank space: "Engagement, Wedding, First child, Unexpected baby for older parents, Adoption, Work promotion, Friendship . . ." Prices ranged from $9.99 to $99.99. What was that? She looked at the name on the envelope: Father Nathan G. Allgreen. A business priest! She burst into laughter. Prayers at a discount—Eric would love it.

She was still laughing when she walked to the bathroom and looked at herself in the cabinet mirror. There were red marks above and under the right eye. By tomorrow she would look like a battered woman. The priest was right: she was lucky. Her left knee hurt and her right palm was bleeding. Someone rang the bell. It was probably Lynn. She ran to her door and stopped, her hand on the doorknob.

"Who is it?"

Nobody answered. She looked through the peephole. She couldn't see anybody. She opened the door: nobody. She realized it was the intercom: someone ringing downstairs. The priest? She ran down the stairs, without even feeling the pain in her knee.

It was a crazy hope, but she had been convinced, in the time it took to run down, that it would be Eric, surprising her in Eric's way. She was ready to believe in miracles tonight. Someone was standing in the foyer, just behind the glass-paneled door. A tall man wearing a beige trenchcoat. She opened hesitantly.

"Mrs. Cook-Blackwood?"

"That's me."

"Sheriff Adam Brownswille, from the Old Newport Courthouse."

He showed her a badge. It looked real and it said "Sheriff" even though the man wasn't dressed as a sheriff. She let out a scream. "Eric!"

Why didn't she think of it earlier? She was so self-centered! Something had happened to him. Something serious, or they wouldn't send a sheriff. She burst into tears. The man looked surprised. "I'm serving the summons, ma'am."

"What happened to Eric?"

He stepped into the hallway, probably tired of holding the heavy door with his foot. The door closed. He was a big man with a mustache, a red nose, and a smell of sweat.

"Eric? I don't know, ma'am. I'm just serving the divorce papers."

He handed over to her an envelope that she took mechanically as if she were in a dream—a nightmare.

"The divorce? What divorce? I didn't ask for a divorce, it's a mistake, I have been trying to reach him for five days, I just. . . ."

"Are you OK, ma'am? Any trouble at home?"

He was looking at her face in the well-lit hallway. She blushed.

"I fell off my bike."

"I can't answer your questions, ma'am; I'm only here to serve the divorce papers. For the rest, you must consult with the plaintiff and with your attorney."

"The plaintiff?"

"Mr. Eric Blackwood, your husband. He filed for divorce in Iowa. If the defendant, that is you, wants to respond to the summons, you or your attorney should file an appearance form before the above return date, which you see up there. You have about two weeks. Is that clear? Everything is written in here."

Jane felt dizzy. She couldn't understand a word the man was saying. He stepped away, still holding the heavy front door with his hand.

"Is that your bike locked up over there?"

"Yes."

"I wouldn't leave it outside overnight. Not in this neighborhood. Have a good night, ma'am."

She walked back up the stairs, climbing slowly. She couldn't look at the envelope. She dropped it on the dining table. She ran to the bathroom and threw up. Maybe it wouldn't be such a bad idea to call an ambulance. When she was little, one of her classmates had fallen at the ice rink, got up thinking she was fine, and collapsed two days later and died in one hour of a cerebral hemorrhage—a broken skull. Jane flushed the toilet, rinsed her mouth and brushed her teeth. Her chest was burning. She walked back to the kitchen and drank a glass of water. The envelope was still on the table. Real. Should she call Allison? Her mother? Eric?

Someone knocked at the door. She walked to the corridor like an automaton and opened the door without even looking through the peephole. Lynn, wearing a blue shirt with white dots over her jeans, her cheeks and nose red from sun exposure, was smiling at her and handing over a net bag full of huge grapefruit.

"Fresh from Florida, picked just yesterday. What happened to you?"

"I fell off my bike and Eric's divorcing me."

Lynn dropped the grapefruit and hugged her.

Blackmail, Lynn told her, a childish power game; Eric wanted to scare her. You didn't get divorced just because of one argument on the phone. Even if Jane had been really mean. Couples would always say terrible things when they argued. They would always use their knowledge of the weakest spot of the other to hurt him or her as much as they could. If you divorced just because of that, there wouldn't be a single married couple on earth. There was actually no better proof of conjugal good health: to tear each other with words, you had to love each other. Jane was drinking in Lynn's words, more reasonable and plausible than everything that had happened that night. But Lynn didn't know Eric—his pride, his power of silence. Lynn shrugged her shoulders: all men were like that. She was caressing Jane's hair, holding her hand, calling her "baby" and "sweetie," and telling her that everything would be fine. Jane was wondering what Lynn knew about men and love.

In the morning the pain was still there, like a block of concrete in her stomach. Impossible to swallow or even to drink anything. She couldn't even cry. She felt like throwing up. Her whole body felt sore. Not the fall, she was sure. She had known only one similar pain before: after the abortion. But there had been a physical cause then.

Over the next days she tried to call Eric innumerable times. She mechanically pressed REDIAL and waited for the tone, knowing he wouldn't answer. She dialed his mother's number in Maine again, just to check. Nobody there. So obvious that the enemy was in Iowa, brainwashing Eric, telling him day and night that he was a cuckold, Old Newport's laughingstock.

She could fly to Iowa City. The ticket was on her desk. She would see Eric, talk to him in that controlled voice he liked, apologize and promise that she would change. They needed to be together. She loved him. He loved her. Not the kind of love you found twice in a lifetime. Or there wouldn't be this stone in her stomach. She was sure. Even though Eric had told her once that the amazing pain she felt after an argument was in no way a proof of love. He would listen to her. She would win out over his mother.

But Eric had sent her a sheriff. For all he cared, she might as well have committed suicide that night.

April 11 passed. She threw away the ticket. She didn't consult an attorney. It took her another five days to look at the papers. Finally she opened the envelope. Plaintiff, Defendant, it was all there, typed. Eric's handwriting appeared only in his signature at the bottom of the various forms. If she wanted to answer the summons, she had to file a written "Appearance" form. She still had four days to do that. But there was nothing to object to. Their case was the most simple possible: no children. In the list of things that the Court was asked to order, Eric had checked only "A divorce (dissolution of marriage)," not "A fair division of property and debts." He had this decency at least. It would make things less ugly.

Eric called on April 22 after being informed that she hadn't filed an Appearance form and that she therefore accepted the divorce. When she recognized his voice, her whole body started trembling. She had enough dignity not to cry. Eric didn't sound hostile or even cold. His sad and soft voice revealed the suffering he had gone through.

"I'm sorry I didn't call you back. This was a decision only one of us could make, because it was against the other. We couldn't discuss it."

"But I love you," she said feebly, while silent tears, in spite of her, started flowing down her cheeks.

"I love you too," Eric answered gravely, in that voice with its warm and soft inflections that seemed to acknowledge a very sad reality about which he could do nothing. "Unfortunately there are things stronger than love. I can't give you the kind of reassurance you're asking from me, Jane."

His being sweet was more terrible than hostility. It showed a calm, unbreakable determination. After hanging up, Jane didn't cry. She sat near the phone for a long time. There was a knot in her chest. She could barely breathe. She felt nauseous for several days afterward. Eric had confirmed that his mother was there.

It was only after talking to Eric that she found the strength to call Allison, and her parents. Allison was horrified. At first, she just couldn't believe it. But she didn't cry like she had when Jane had the abortion. It seemed easier to accept.

"Maybe this is actually what you wanted," she told Jane. "Or you would be there already. A marriage cannot survive geographical distance. After a while it means you two can live without each other. I never understood how you could stand it; I could never be away from John for more than a week."

Her parents knew already: Eric, a real gentleman, had called them ten days before.

"Your father forbade me to call you," her mother told Jane apologetically. "He's very upset with you. He says he doesn't understand your self-destructive behavior."

There was Lynn.

"If your parents liked him so much, then he wasn't the right guy. Don't worry. Parents are nothing but anxiety-producing machines. You should have heard mine when I got a divorce, and then, when I told them that. . . ."

"You were married?"

"You didn't know?"

Jane thought that Lynn's love life had been limited to her two cats. She had never asked her any questions. She learned that Lynn had married her high school sweetheart when she was nineteen and divorced him eight years later. He drank and beat her. She moved to Old Newport and met Jeaudine, a Devayne graduate student in Afro-American studies who interviewed her for a sociological study of the Old Newport ghettos. Lynn waited five years before telling her parents she was a lesbian. She was thirty-seven then and involved in a stable relationship with Jeaudine. But her parents were so shocked they said they would never see her again.

"I even spared them—I didn't tell them Jeaudine was black! My father would have had a heart attack."

Jane was listening with wide-open eyes.

Lynn smiled. "You didn't know I was a lesbian either?"

"No."

"Does it bother you?"

"Not at all! Why? On the contrary. All the greatest French writers from Marcel Proust to Marguerite Yourcenar are gays. And half my department."

Jane blushed. She had spoken too fast and too warmly, like racists or anti-Semites who protest they have black or Jewish friends. It bothered her that Lynn's look and voice fit the cliché of the lesbian.

"Did your friend leave Old Newport?"

"Jeaudine? She died."

"Oh, I'm sorry." She hesitated. "In an accident?"

"AIDS."

"AIDS!"

There was so much awe in Jane's voice that Lynn raised her eyebrows and looked at her.

"You don't have any friends who have died of AIDS?"

Jane shook her head.

"Well," Lynn said, "consider yourself lucky."

Lynn was silent a few seconds before resuming: Jeaudine was from the Bedford-Stuyvesant section of Brooklyn. At sixteen she was a drug addict and worked for her uncle, a small-time dealer who made her pregnant before ending up in jail. The child was given to a foster family. At age twenty-two, Jeaudine had gotten her act together and decided to go back to school, get a job and become a mother. She got her B.A. from Brooklyn College. The child, a little girl, died of AIDS before Jeaudine could get her back.

"She could have collapsed and become an addict again. But she made it to Devayne instead. I don't know if you realize what that means for a Bedford-Stuyvesant girl."

Life caught up with her. She was finishing her dissertation when she died of AIDS, at age thirty-six. Lynn spoke simply, with no apparent emotion, while eating her chicken. Jane hadn't started to eat yet.

"I'm sorry. I had no idea."

"Eat. Don't be sorry. Or be sorry for all the living dead who live to be very old. Jeaudine and I had a few very, very good years, worth a thousand lives. And she still lives here."

She knocked on her chest where the heart is.

It was May, a new, sunny May. Jane didn't notice the change of weather. She was alive. She would wake up in the morning, drink her tea, read, take notes, think about her second project. Fiction seemed artificial, but work was a lifesaver. One night she stumbled upon a passage in Balzac's *La Duchesse de Langeais* about the difference between love and passion: one had several passions in a lifetime and passion could be extinguished by jealousy or the lack of hope. But there was only one love, serene and endless. Tears were flowing down her cheeks. She had feared that Eric had no passion for her, only a calm and tender love. It was the exact opposite. What he felt for her was passion, not love. And passion could die.

There was no way she was going to think of Eric as soon as she saw the word "love" written somewhere. Be overwhelmed by emotion when she was working. Superstitiously find her truth in a novel. As Lynn said, she couldn't let herself be destroyed. If novels made her cry, she wouldn't read novels anymore. Only books of literary criticism with which there was no risk of identifying. She suddenly remembered the Woodrow book she had left on a shelf in her bedroom after she checked it out that terrible day, a month ago. She would read that book that didn't want to be read by her and get her life under control. She got up and, clenching her teeth, brought the book with the light blue jacket out of the bedroom. She sat on the sofa with a glass of whiskey next to her, her feet on the rug, and, in front of her, on the antique chest of drawers, a beautiful bouquet of irises and roses that Lynn had brought her the night before. The reading lamp, with its golden base and a white shade she had made herself by rolling a large satin ribbon around a metal frame, projected a soft light on her.

She opened the book and looked at the table of contents. There was only one chapter on Flaubert, which she browsed. She had already read so many books on Flaubert. She got more interested, however, when she noticed that Jeffrey Woodrow, a well-known scholar teaching at Duke University, had ideas quite similar to hers. This might explain why she had so much difficulty finding a publisher: as Eric had told her, she had to position herself in relation to Woodrow, or no one would see the interest of a book that seemed to repeat what had been already written. The striking similarity of their views was pleasing, though. She had found an ally against the petty readers who criticized her take on Flaubert. Woodrow had selected the same quotes as she had in Flaubert's *Correspondance* as well as in *Madame Bovary;* he was making the same argument about the difference between the male artist observer and the sentimental woman, using Flaubert's metaphor of "muscled" sentences. As she continued reading, much more carefully than at the beginning, she got a strange feeling. She went to the end of the book and looked at the footnotes. She and Woodrow had the same references. There was a thirty-line-long footnote. As she read it, she turned pale.

This footnote recounted an incident about a misunderstanding between Louise Colet and Gustave Flaubert. As they were walking by a statue of Corneille in Paris, Louise told her lover that she would sacrifice all of Corneille's glory for Gustave's love. Flaubert got upset: how could Louise say something so stupid? Louise was so offended by this apparent rejection of her love that she transposed the scene to her novel *Lui.* How petty was a man who couldn't understand that a woman would choose love rather than literary glory, a man so ambitious and cold that he would prefer glory to love!

If Flaubert had been upset, though, it was only because Louise's words revealed a confusion between art and glory that was unbearable for a purist like Flaubert who believed in art and in style. It was precisely because he loved Louise that he had reacted so sharply. How could an artist mistake glory for art? Glory was only the exterior of art, art as seen by those who didn't know art was only a patient striving toward a perfection produced by human labor. Glory didn't count at all.

This was Jane's own analysis of an incident that had struck her. She was certain nobody else had written about it in these terms. She had added this footnote to the second version of her manuscript after reading Colet's novel. She had also written an article that had come out several months after Woodrow's book. Now it looked like she had plagiarized him without even quoting him.

How was such a coincidence possible? There could be only one explanation: he had been a reader of her circulating manuscript. So this was how the system worked. A fifty-year-old tenured professor "borrowed" the work of a young, nontenured, female colleague, which would remain unpublished thanks to the report he had written on it. He didn't take everything, of course—just a few sentences, ideas, references, and interpretations. Ten years of work.

She closed the book. So strange that she hadn't looked at it in one year, as if she knew beforehand. She got up and looked at the clock: 8:45 P.M. She impulsively took the department address list from a drawer and dialed Bronzino's number. He was also on sabbatical this semester and maybe traveling right now. But he answered after two rings.

"It's Jane. Am I disturbing you?"

"No, that's fine," he said, sounding vaguely annoyed and not asking her how she was doing. He didn't know about her pneumonia or the divorce. She told him excitedly what she just found out: Jeffrey Woodrow had stolen her work.

"Why are you calling me?"

"I thought that you probably had his phone number. I would like to call him."

"Are you sure it's a good idea?" he answered in the same annoyed voice. "He'll deny it and certainly be in good faith. Did you find your sentences word for word?"

"No, but . . ."

"You see. Maybe you two simply have the same ideas. As you know, there are no ideas anyway; there is only style. Jeffrey is very intelligent, honest and reliable. He is also the president of the Society of Nineteenth-Century Studies, don't forget. You might need him one day."

She hung up without taking Woodrow's number. She was sweating. Had she expected that Bronzino would take her side against his friend? He probably considered her to be yet another hysterical feminist. He too must have already borrowed the unpublished work of a student or a younger colleague. The rule of the game. One had to shut up or enter Hotchkiss's battlefield and launch a scandal. Jane had no desire to fight. Not for this. It was fundamentally unimportant.

She sat down again and finished her glass of whiskey. Her indignation gave way to a general nausea—for scholars, work, books, Woodrow, Bronzino, Eric, and Flaubert. Yes, Flaubert. Why couldn't he simply tell Louise that he loved her instead of showing her immediately that she understood nothing about art? Couldn't he be nice? Give in?

In late May, Eric came to Old Newport. She saw him: a tall, slender, handsome forty-year-old man, to whom, one day, she would remain indifferent. They didn't hug or shake hands, which reminded her of the first night when he walked her home almost six years ago and she knew that something would happen precisely because they had absolutely no physical contact—as if just a brushing of their skins had been the spark to light a fire. But now it was different. She had no right to touch his lips or his soft cheek. They were divorced. He wasn't wearing his wedding ring anymore. She blushed when his eyes distractedly stopped for one second on her ring. She wondered whether she should give it back to him, since he had bought the rings. That night, after a long hesitation, she threw her wedding and engagement rings away in the trash can outside instead of keeping them in a drawer. A clean break with the past. The rings Eric had chosen for her would make a bum happy.

They emptied the storage room and divided their belongings without an argument. Eric was fair play itself. He rented a truck and took Jane's things to her apartment. Lynn met him.

"Not so handsome," she told Jane the same night. "Too symmetrical and cold. He looks like a Calvin Klein model. Frankly, you can do better."

They sold the house to their tenants for the same price for which they had bought it three years ago, which was lucky since the Old Newport real estate market was even more depressed now. In five days, thanks to Eric's efficiency, there were no material ties left between them.

She never saw Eric alone. His mother was with him and followed them everywhere, standing next to him the whole time. Jane called Eric at his hotel once and his mother answered: they were sharing the same room.

"With his mommy," Jane snapped.

Lynn laughed. "He must be terrified of you."

Jane slowly put the last page on top of the pile to her left and, with the back of her hand, wiped the tears that were flooding her cheeks. The cornflakes floating in the bowl next to the manuscript were all soft. She couldn't eat any more.

She remained motionless for five minutes and then got up, like an automaton. She walked to her bedroom, where she took a small red leather box from a white shelf built into the wall. At the bottom, under the jewelry that Jane wasn't wearing much these days, she found the small piece of white paper with Scotch tape. She tore at the tape. The ring was there, of course. For a moment she had doubted her own memory. At least this was one thing that the author of the manuscript didn't know: she had thrown away the wedding ring but kept the engagement ring, whose unusual shape she liked, and which she hoped to be able to wear again one day without any emotion.

For the first time in two years she was looking at the golden ring shaped like a circumflex accent with tiny diamonds encrusted on top. Eric had given it to her in a Fort Hale restaurant six years earlier, just after they came back from Greece. They'd been eating lobster and, like babies, were wearing plastic napkins with big red lobsters tied around their necks. Eric looked so serious and emotional that Jane had had to repress her impulse to laugh.

She suddenly saw Eric in front of her as if she just had to lift her arm to touch him. She could even smell him and see the grain of his skin, the shape of his ears, the changing color of his eyes, from gray-blue to hazel-gray, the tiny wrinkles at the corner of his eyes, the intensity of his gaze in the moment of desire, and his smile, the smile that made her open herself completely. She closed her eyes and put her right arm forward. She couldn't even cry. She was empty of any sensation except for the desire to touch him—and then, abruptly, a feeling of nausea made her run to the bathroom where she leaned over the toilet and tried to throw up.

She rinsed her mouth and splashed her face with cold water, almost violently. Reading this novel was making her crazy. She hadn't been so emotional in months. She believed herself well beyond that stage now that Alex had come into her life. Of course, Alex would never be Eric. Still, it was certainly Alex's absence and the tormenting wait for a message from him that were producing such a vivid and painful memory of Eric.

There wouldn't be another love in her life like that, and she had lost it. But it wasn't because she didn't want to be just "a wife in Iowa," as the author of this text suggested. After two years of wondering why, Jane could come up with only one explanation: the black widow syndrome.

When she was a senior in college, she had given a party. In the afternoon, as she was preparing a big salad, she had opened a can of palm hearts imported from Brazil and, inside, seen a huge brown spider floating in the juice on top of the white palm hearts. She had immediately dropped the can into the sink and retreated out of the house. She had wound up in the street, trembling, with the can opener still in her right hand.

Then she had reasoned with herself: at age twenty-one, she couldn't be chased out of her place by a Brazilian spider that had been dead for months. She had forced herself to walk back into the kitchen. With eyes half-closed, she had emptied the can of its juice and of the spider. Then she had cut the palm hearts into small pieces and mixed them with the rest of the salad.

Late at night, someone came up with a horror story about an aunt in Europe who had brought back a tropical plant from Africa and, one day, heard a funny whistling sound coming from the soil. Following a neighbor's advice, she had called the firemen, who had found a nest of black widows just hatching within the soil; had they not been found, the aunt and her two little daughters would have been killed that night. This story led to another scary tale involving a spider. Jane, in turn, told hers: how, that very afternoon, she had panicked and courageously fought her fear of spiders. Everyone laughed. "It's not the palm hearts you put in the salad, I hope?" a friend asked. Jane blushed. "Are you crazy!" someone else exclaimed, laughing. "Do you think she wants to kill us?" But the first friend, who had seen Jane blush, turned to her and said seriously: "If you put those palm hearts in the salad, you have to tell us right now. We need to call an emergency toxicology center at once." There was a silence. All her guests were now looking at her. "Of course I didn't," Jane replied in a trembling voice, with a forced laugh.

That night she couldn't sleep. She kept watching the movements of her stomach and waiting for a phone call that would announce the death of one of her friends.

Jane considered herself a responsible person. If it hadn't occurred to her that she might be poisoning her guests by giving them the contents of a can in which a spider had been floating dead for months, it was because her mind and energy had been entirely focused on a single issue: fighting her fear of spiders.

It had been basically the same story with Eric. She had become so focused on her terror of losing him and on the ways to fight her terror that she hadn't even realized she was actually losing him. Throughout the months and even the years following the divorce, she had somehow remained convinced that they still would end up together—as if time didn't matter.

She walked back to the living room and poured herself a glass of water, which she drank slowly, calming down, while looking at the thick stack of pages she had already read. She had to find out who was playing with her emotions. Francisco? She wasn't so sure anymore.

Francisco could have learned all this from Jamaica, directly or via Duportoy, after he left for Spain. Jamaica knew the story of the divorce with its comic series of events—the bike fall, the sheriff, Lynn's grapefruits—as well as the incident with the academic who had stolen Jane's work. Jane hadn't said who it was, but Francisco could have easily found out. But if Jamaica was Francisco's source of information, then why didn't he know about the engagement ring? Jamaica would certainly have remembered, because she and Jane had a whole discussion about it. Jane had told Jamaica that she had lied to Lynn about keeping her ring, because Lynn would have argued that Jane was denying the reality of the divorce. Jamaica didn't agree with Lynn—there was no reason why you should get rid of a valuable piece of jewelry along with a worthless husband—and she was surprised to see Jane so afraid of Lynn's judgment. Jamaica had labeled the incident, laughing, a case of lesbian terrorism.

Like Lynn, the author of the text didn't seem to know that Jane had kept one of her rings.

Jane pinched her lower lip with her left thumb and index finger. Why had she been convinced, from the beginning, that the author was a man?

There was someone else to whom Jane had talked a lot about herself without paying much attention to what she said because this person didn't matter so much.

Lynn, of course.

Lynn was a social worker; her work, like that of a psychologist, consisted of listening to other people. It was hard to imagine Lynn writing this novel. But it had been hard to imagine her married or in love with Jeaudine. If Lynn ever wrote, her style would definitely be dry, direct and "virile." And Lynn was a feminist, with a poor opinion of marriage and of men in general: the men in the novel, so far, didn't come across much better than Jane.

Jane gasped excitedly. The package had been posted in New York five days ago, and Lynn went to Manhattan last week for a march against police violence!

No jumping to conclusions, though. So far, from chapter to chapter she kept changing suspects. Francisco and Josh weren't excluded yet. She sat back down at the dining table. A new part was starting: "Recovery." A word that certainly sounded like Lynn—unless it referred to Francisco's own recovery after he moved to Spain.

IV. Recovery

1

It was 9:30 P.M. when she walked out of the gym. She looked up at the street sign where she had locked her bike. She froze. The bike wasn't there. She had two bikes stolen in the past and knew the sensation. You couldn't believe your own senses and yet the void was there. She turned around and looked at the bike racks. Her bike wasn't among the many bikes that were all falling on one another—the reason why she never parked her bike there. She laughed, suddenly remembering that she had not taken her bike tonight because she was wearing her long, tight linen dress for the date with Jamaica.

She started walking toward Boston Avenue and crossed the intersection where the garage, the McDonald's, the Dunkin' Donuts place and the twenty-four-hour convenience store stood, and where a crowd of punks with pierced noses and lips was hanging out, smoking and drinking. She walked fast, without looking at them.

As usual, the African dance had energized her. She was glad she went to the class and didn't listen to herself at 7 P.M., when she just wanted to lie down. She had slept so little last night. Even though she had read until 1:30 A.M., the dream, once again, had awakened her at 5:15 A.M.

The same dream every morning at dawn, for a month now: Eric opening the door of his house in Iowa City and finding a cop on his threshold, who announced to him that his wife—his ex-wife—had been sexually abused and murdered near the train tracks in Old Newport.

A month earlier, on a sunny day in late September, Jane was taking a stroll around her neighborhood when she had suddenly felt a hand on her face, covering her mouth and nose from behind and barely letting her breathe, while an arm half-strangled her. A voice had snapped an inarticulate order. She hadn't resisted or screamed. With a calm that still surprised her, she had slowly extracted her wallet from inside her pocket and handed it over to the man behind her. Voices could be heard nearby, teenagers punctuating their short sentences with "fuck," "fucking" and "motherfucker." The man had grabbed the wallet and disappeared. Jane had stood there, motionless for a few seconds, before coming out of her paralysis and running toward Columbus Square only one block away. She had let herself fall onto a bench in the middle of a joyful crowd taking advantage of the last summer Saturday afternoon. Her whole body had started trembling. She had put her hand on her neck where it hurt a little. There was blood on her fingers. Not much blood. Just a few drops. The cut was probably not intentional. The man must have been scared too. She wasn't even aware that he had a knife or a razor blade. She had suddenly realized what happened—and what could have happened if kids hadn't been walking by, if she had tried to escape, if the man had pushed her into the bushes. . . . She had burst into tears.

She didn't go to the police; she hadn't seen the man, couldn't identify him. Also, she was afraid to see the expression on the cops' faces, looks almost of regret that things didn't go further. Rape stories, like the ones Jane read avidly over breakfast in the *New York Times*.

Afterward she was constantly scared and often cried during the day, for no reason, when she was reading at home or riding her bike. As soon as she heard a siren or a loud sound. She had always cried easily, but never to such an extent. One day a truck driver honked at her because she was riding too far out in the left-hand side of the road. She stopped immediately and sat on the sidewalk, sobbing. She told the story of being mugged many times—to Lynn, Jamaica, her neighbors, the secretaries, her colleagues, her parents, Allison. Lynn was enraged: this was really the trauma Jane needed, just when she was finally getting better. Everyone was horrified. In the middle of the day! Jane should definitely move to a safer location, to the right side of the train tracks.

But the worst was what she couldn't tell anyone, and certainly not Lynn. How she woke up every morning with the same little film playing inside her mind: Eric learning that she was dead and realizing, too late, what he had lost. She would turn in her bed and grunt angrily, but there was no way to get rid of these images.

Casa Blue was two blocks down the avenue. Jane walked into a room with a warm atmosphere, full of people seated in old armchairs and sofas that looked like they had been found in a grandmother's attic. She spotted Jamaica in the adjacent room, close to the stage where the musicians were playing—a bald saxophonist and two guys with long hair and electric guitars. Jamaica was wearing a tight black tee-shirt that revealed her belly button, a tiny skirt with black and brown squares, and black go-go boots with thick soles. No jewelry, no makeup. She was definitely a change from the Lehmans, Martins and Hotchkiss, and even from cold Duportoy. So pretty with her curly black hair falling on her shoulders, framing her flat face like an antique mask, with big almond-shaped eyes set quite far apart from each other, the irises of which were a mixture of brown and gold, not to mention her delicate mouth with its almost Oriental shape. Jane put her hand on Jamaica's shoulder and sat next to her.

"Here you are! How was the class?"

"Fantastic. You should really come."

"I don't like classes, even dance classes."

"It's nothing like a class. It's so much fun and relaxed. And very sensual too. You know what we do at the end? We kiss the floor in front of the drummers. They're men and we're all women. It's very symbolic."

"Mm-hm. You might as well go ahead and fuck them."

Jane laughed. A waitress stopped by. Jane ordered a Baileys on the rocks and Jamaica another beer.

"I have something to tell you," Jamaica said with a mischievous smile.

Jane leaned toward her.

"Last night I was at a party at the Drama School. This tall guy was staring at me and started dancing with me. Or rather, against me: he was hard, and I could feel his cock, behind his jeans, right here, against my skin." Jamaica pointed to her naked belly. "We danced until we realized there was no more music and nobody left except for two guys cleaning the room and taking away the stereo and the loudspeakers. We had been on the verge of orgasm for three hours. His cock was like a block of concrete, and I was completely wet. We hadn't said a word, we had never seen each other before, and you know what? I knew who he was, and he knew who I was. For him it was easier because I'm black, but still, I'm not the only black girl at Devayne."

"Who was he?"

"Xavier Duportoy."

"Duportoy!"

Jane blushed. So Xavier *was* a womanizer; it wasn't only gossip. Should she inform Jamaica that he had a girlfriend in New York? But it was never good to be the bearer of bad news. "What do you mean you don't know him? Of course you know him—he's your colleague!"

Jamaica shook her head. "I had never seen him before: we don't teach the same days, he lives in New York and he didn't show up for the first two faculty meetings. Since I arrived in Old Newport, my ears have been ringing with his name. Everyone told me I had to meet him as if something special had to happen between us. And you know what? The same with him. For a month already he has been told that he should meet me. So here we are, at 3 A.M., outside the Drama School, and he says, 'Jamaica?' and I reply, 'Xavier?' Just like in *La Princesse de Clèves*."

They were now teaching the seventeenth-century French novel for a course that Jane was chairing. Jamaica was alluding to the famous ball scene in which the married Princess of Clèves is asked by the king to dance with the Duke of Nemours even before they have been introduced to each other. After the dance the Duke of Nemours says in front of the king and the queen that he has recognized the Princess of Clèves, the most perfect person at Court; the princess, blushing, denies having guessed Nemours's identity. The queen laughs and says that she doesn't believe her and that there is even something "obliging" for Nemours in her denial.

"OK for you as the princess, but Duportoy as Nemours—I'm not so sure. And then?"

"Ha-ha, you want to know. . . . First we walked around, or rather we half made love in the street. We ended up in my place at five A.M. and we made love until I left for class at five to nine. I was reeking of sex! I came back at eleven-thirty A.M. and we started again. Xavier is convinced that there is no limit to the number of orgasms for a woman if she manages to relax completely. We tried to put the theory into practice: I came nine times."

"Nine! What about him?"

"Three or four. He made himself last."

They laughed.

"And where is your Nemours now?"

"In New York. Breaking up with his girlfriend."

"Really! After one night?"

"Oh yes. It wasn't just a night."

Jane finished her Bailey's. Jamaica closed her eyes. She had long eyelashes, and there was something so delicate in her childlike face. Twenty-six—even younger than Jane had been when she started at Devayne. Jamaica looked eighteen; she couldn't enter a bar at night without showing her driver's license. She was from Philadelphia, where her father was a lawyer and her mother an English teacher. She was the eldest of seven children. The whole family went to church every Sunday. Until recently she was still writing gospel songs as a hobby. There was only a ten-year difference between them, but Jane sometimes felt like a grandmother in front of this representative of the New Age who didn't smoke, didn't really drink, ate only macrobiotic food, practiced yoga, fucked only with condoms, spoke about sex crudely and believed in romantic and predestined love. Xavier Duportoy. In a way, they were doomed to meet each other: two stars in the Devayne sky.

A little after midnight they said good night in the street. Jamaica lived nearby.

"You don't have your bike? Do you want me to walk you home?"

"No, thanks. Then you would have to walk home alone. I'll take the shuttle."

Jane walked past the Devayne Theater and the restaurants, all closed, until she reached the shuttle stop in front of the Old Campus. Nine times! She smiled. Duportoy was not her type, but there was definitely something sexy about him: the energy in his body, and his ambiguous smile, maybe.

In any case, the affair between Jamaica and Xavier put an end to Lynn's attempt to convince Jane that there weren't two kinds of attractions and that Jane, who was clearly attracted to Jamaica, should "go for it." What Jane mistook for a lack of sexual desire for Jamaica, Lynn argued, was merely a cultural barrier that would fall with the first experience, when she would discover that sex with a woman was more delicate, more sensual, more playful, softer and more generous, and without any risk of failure.

Jane waited for more than ten minutes before remembering that after midnight one had to call the shuttle. There was a campus phone nearby, but she didn't know the number by heart. From that phone she couldn't call Jamaica. She had to look for a public phone. But she didn't have any quarters and it would be hard to make change at this hour of the night, when everything was closed. Her only alternative, then, was to walk to Jamaica's place and call the shuttle from there. From where she was now, it would have been faster to walk home. But she would have to go through the bad blocks around the train tracks. It was really irritating, sometimes, to be a woman, and not to be able to walk where you wanted. The September attack, anyway, hadn't taken place near the train tracks, nor late at night. There was as much chance of being mugged in downtown Old Newport as on her way home. In all probability, nothing would happen: those kinds of bad things seemed to occur only when one didn't expect them. She decided to overcome her fear and began walking toward the train tracks at a fast pace.

The former "Manslaughter Quarter," as it was called when Jane arrived in Old Newport eight years earlier, had gotten a facelift in the past two years. Devayne was trying to rehabilitate the district between the train station and the university to make the access to campus easier. The large, empty windows on the first floor of the new brick buildings were displaying huge FOR LEASE signs that didn't look like they would be taken down soon. Jane got to Market Street and crossed without waiting for the red light to change, as there were no cars around. Even the parking lots along the train tracks had been transformed. Asphalted and surrounded by wrought-iron fences with old-fashioned streetlamps, they looked almost elegant. She stepped onto the covered pedestrian bridge. The whistling of a train startled her. The Amtrak train passed so fast that the wooden boards trembled under her feet. The neon-lit covered bridge led to a street that was a dead end because of the construction work on a larger bridge over the tracks. The boarded-up, damaged houses weren't exactly reassuring. She turned right into a street which, for one long block, wasn't lit. There were empty beer cans, broken bottles, used condoms and syringes on the sidewalk. The street would be better lit after she crossed Union Street and she would be only two blocks from home.

She passed a former garage with walls covered with graffiti and heard a noise ahead on her right. It had come from the bushes. In the dark she couldn't see anything. It had been some kind of grunting. Probably a raccoon. She had once seen one near her home: it looked like an enormous rat with a long, thin tail. Raccoons could carry rabies. It would probably run away if she screamed. She suddenly spotted the man. He was climbing the embankment on his hands and feet, coming from the train tracks. She had a flashback memory of the September attack. She froze.

He was maybe ten yards away. He hadn't noticed her yet. If she tried to pass him running, he could stop her easily. With her long and narrow skirt, anyway, she couldn't run; and her legs already felt soft like cotton. He got up. He was tall. Behind her was the street's dead end and the covered pedestrian bridge—a perfect place for rape and murder. The man's shirt was half out of his pants. He glanced around him like someone who had just committed a crime. Fear paralyzed her. She thought about everything she might have done: called a cab from Casa Blue, walked back to Jamaica's place, gone to the Devayne police and asked for the shuttle number, or simply have the number with her. Too late. She had chosen to set a trap for herself. She couldn't say that she hadn't been warned; she knew in her own body, since September, that violence existed. Eric would learn about her death near the train tracks. But she wouldn't be around to know what effect the news would have on him. She put her hand in her jacket pocket—a few dollars, her Devayne ID and her keys. She grabbed the keys and took the longest between her right thumb and index finger. She would go for the eyes as violently as she could and, at the same time, hit his balls with her knee. In the movies it looked so easy. The man turned his head. He noticed her shadow in the dark and stopped. She saw his face.

"Chip!"

He was startled. She walked quickly toward him.

"Oh my God! You really scared me!"

"Jane!"

He looked even more puzzled than she.

"Have you lost something down there?" she asked.

She blushed, realizing that this must be one of the meeting places Chip had once mentioned to her. He laughed and winked.

"I was just taking a little walk. What about you?"

"I had a drink with Jamaica. Do you mind walking me home?"

"Not at all. Did you and Lynn go to the concert Saturday?"

"Oh yes. This music under the stars, it was fantastic. I kept sobbing for two hours. Why didn't you come?"

"Hugh had a cold. The Ninth isn't my cup of tea anyway—and my tear ducts are not as good as yours."

They got to her house. They hugged and Chip left. Jane was laughing when she walked up the stairs and entered her apartment. A funny encounter.

Among Lynn's friends, Chip was the one she liked best. She had met him in June at a picnic organized by the Gay and Lesbian Association. Charles Townsend was his name. *"Chipie pour les intimes,"* he had told Jane with the affected gesture of an old queen. "Chipie," in French, meant a naughty little girl. He was a tall, slender man with big teeth, white hair and thick white eyebrows. Witty and cultivated, he had read all of Proust twice and himself looked like a character out of a Proustian novel. He had invited Lynn and Jane for dinner a week later. Jane had been dazzled to find out that Chip lived in a beautiful mansion right next to the house of the Devayne president, and to learn that half the university's buildings had once belonged to his family. His ancestors had come to Old Newport as settlers in the early seventeenth century, and they had flourished as merchants in the seventeenth and eighteenth centuries. Most of them were buried in a crypt in the oldest church on Central Square. University buildings, fellowships, rooms and lectures bore his name—to start with, the George Townsend College where Jane was a fellow. His house, full of antiques, looked like a museum. The most beautiful pieces were actually at the Old Newport Museum, which had been founded by a Townsend.

On the way home, half-drunk, Jane had revealed to Lynn her plan to marry Chip: the perfect marriage, like in the eighteenth century, sharing a social life and an intellectual friendship, and being free of the rest. She loved Chip, she loved his house and she had loved the dinner party, where there was only one false note: the presence of boring old Hugh Carrington, whom Chip had probably invited in honor of Jane. Once they were married, she wouldn't invite her colleagues to their home anymore.

Afraid that Jane actually might propose and Chip accept, Lynn had divulged a few facts. Chip was buried in debts. Banks were waiting at his door like sharks. The last descendant of four centuries of Townsends didn't have a life of leisure as Jane thought, but was working eight hours a day in an Old Newport parking lot. Jane was laughing. Lynn also advised her not to say anything about Carrington. "Why? Chip is too clever not to find him boring too." "They're lovers." "Chip and Carrington? Impossible!"

Jane fell asleep wondering whether Hugh Carrington knew about

Chip's little walks at night. If they left each other sexual freedom, how did they manage to get rid of jealousy?

She opened her eyes. It was pitch dark. The fluorescent hands indicated 4:30 A.M. She sighed. Too early. Sleeping or not, she would remain in bed and try to get some rest.

At least, for a change, the dream that woke her was not about Eric. She remembered it precisely. In the dream, she was standing in a large room; at the other end stood Francisco, and halfway between them, Francisco's mother. Jane was talking vehemently, looking at Francisco's mother and informing her that her son was an asshole, a bastard, *una mierda*. Francisco's mother was nodding in agreement. Francisco was staring at Jane angrily but didn't dare to interrupt her, either because he knew that she was right, or because he was scared of her outburst.

Jane was puzzled. Why would she dream about Francisco, whom she hadn't seen since last March and of whom she never thought anymore? What about Francisco's mother, whom she had never met, and whom she saw so clearly in her dream (a thin lady with short, silver-gray curled hair)? How come Jane, who didn't know Spanish, used in her dream the word *mierda,* which sounded quite Spanish?

When she opened her eyes again, the sun was drawing stripes of shadow and light on the white walls through the closed blinds. She looked at the alarm clock and let out a joyful exclamation. It was 10:50 A.M. If today weren't Friday, she would have missed her class. A breeze passing through the open window caressed her forehead. She had not felt so well rested in months. The firm mattress under her back and the warm, light, goose-down comforter up to her neck filled her with a sudden belief in the possibility of a future. "Trust time," Lynn kept saying. Lynn, Chip, Jamaica, the African dance class: life was giving her gifts.

Jane ran into Lynn in the house's foyer around lunchtime and told her, laughing, about her nocturnal encounter with Chip near the train tracks. Lynn scolded Jane for wandering around the city alone at such a late hour. But when Jane described her funny dream, Lynn stepped forward and hugged her. "Congratulations."

"Congratulations? What for?"

"*Una mierda!* I love it. This is recovery, Jane. I'm so happy. I always thought you weren't angry enough. This dream is also about Eric, of course: two assholes."

As she was riding her bike to the office, Jane replayed her dream in her mind and suddenly recognized Francisco's tense and miserable expression: it was exactly the way he had looked at her that last time she saw him, in the Japanese restaurant after the dinner with Teresa. Seven months later she woke up angry. Recovery? Really?

She picked up her mail. A yellow envelope with a University of North Carolina Press letterhead made her smile, reminding her of an almost-forgotten past. Seven months ago this type of envelope still had the power to spoil her mood. Now she couldn't care less. Her book would never be published—so what? At the end of her contract with Devayne, she would teach in a high school or change jobs. In any case, these people had taken their time in answering her. She mechanically opened the envelope while walking to the elevator and threw one quick glance at the standard letter: one sheet only, no reader's report. The first words, though, weren't the expected "I am sorry," but instead a strange echo of Lynn's exclamation earlier: "Congratulations!" Jane raised her eyebrows and quickly unfolded the letter.

Dear Mrs. Cook,

Congratulations! I have the pleasure to announce that you've won the 1997 Percy K. Delaware Award for the best manuscript in nineteenth-century French studies for your book "'Madame Bovary, c'est moi': Writing and Gender in Flaubert."

I am sorry to be writing so late. Some administrative complications forced us to delay the announcement of the winning manuscript.

At the University of North Carolina Press, we all hope that your manuscript is still available. Upon hearing from you, I will forward a standard contract and, after you sign it, a five-thousand-dollar check.

A joke? It had been mailed in North Carolina. She reread it in the elevator. "Congratulations!" Her loud laughter when she walked into her fourth-floor office provoked the just-as-loud barking of Begolu's four dogs in the room next door. She sank into her office chair and laughed so much that tears gushed out of her eyes. She dialed the number at the bottom of the letter.

"Could I speak to Virginia T. Prescott, please?"

As soon as Lynn got home that night, Jane went downstairs to tell her the news. Lynn screamed with joy. "I knew it. I should have bet a thousand dollars like this *mierda de Francisco.* By the way, you're lucky he's no longer around!"

"When you think that Kathryn Johns cut out the ad for me. It's so ironic. She took away my friend and gave me a publisher."

"And five thousand dollars. You lost nothing in the trade."

"I must be the only one who's ever heard of that prize. That's probably what they mean by 'administrative complications.' Only one competitor doesn't look serious!"

"Are you kidding? You must be the only academic in America not to read *Lingua Franca.* Being published and getting five thousand dollars at a time when nobody finds a publisher for their dissertation? They must have received tens or hundreds of manuscripts in literature, history, art history and I don't know what. That's what must have delayed them. You're simply the best, Jane."

Lynn organized a dinner party to celebrate, at Jane's place because Jane was allergic to Lynn's cats. They spent the whole afternoon cooking and laughing. At dinner, Jane laughed so much that she choked and red wine came out of her nose, to the great amusement of her guests. Each of them came up with a story about being an unwelcome guest or throwing up on a boat or a plane. Nothing having to do with Devayne. Jane was looking at her guests: loyal Lynn; charming Jamaica; four months' pregnant Margaret and her wife, tall Becky, whom she had married in a religious ceremony in July; delicious Chip; boring but sweet Carrington; and even taciturn Karl, whom she had invited so he wouldn't complain about the noise. Her friends. They had but two things in common: they were genuinely nice, and none of them really knew Eric. Seven months since the divorce already. She had the feeling that she was waking up at last.

When they all raised their glasses to the glorious winner of the Percy K. Delaware Award for the best manuscript in nineteenth-century French studies, she smiled proudly. There was some humility in being happy about such a tiny success. She was a pale, nontenured Devayne professor on death row, one of those who, when terminated, would soon disappear, and who were, for that reason, surrounded by a discreet and embarrassed wall of silence. Norman Bronzino, who had recently married a young assistant professor of physics, had advised Jane to start looking for a position and not wait until the end. The end. She smiled at herself. They couldn't scare her anymore, and she was in no hurry to leave Lynn and Jamaica.

Late that night, Chip read tarot cards to the few of them who were still there. He started with Lynn and Jamaica. He knew Lynn well but not Jamaica, and what he told her was amazingly accurate. He managed to scare her when he said that death would strike someone close to her in the next two years. Jane finally sat down on the sofa next to Chip.

"You may ask a secret question of the cards," he said.

She did: would she manage to forget about Eric? The first card she took meant "don't hold."

"Don't hold what?"

"The card doesn't say."

Jane made a face: not too clear. The second card was more meaningful: a great love. She immediately thought of Eric—irritating. Then there was a card about a woman who played an important role in her life: Lynn, Jamaica? The next card announced that an event would soon happen to her and she would be the only one to recognize the sign. Jane told herself that she was too rational for this kind of obscure prediction. She pulled another card that meant male energy: another great love. She smiled, already more satisfied.

Hugh walked over to them and looked down at Chip. "Can we go? It's late and I'm tired."

"Just one more," Jane replied with the begging voice of a little girl.

She quickly took the card that would decide her fate.

"Don't protect," Chip said gravely.

"Don't protect what?"

"There is no object, just a verb. This card is surprisingly close to the first you pulled. We're obviously touching the heart of the matter; here is the answer to your secret question."

"What do you mean?"

"The trouble with you, I guess, is that you hold and protect."

"That's so true," Lynn said as she overheard.

Jane rolled her eyes and laughed.

"Thanks. That's enlightening."

Jane was biting the inside of her cheek. She got up and stretched her arms and legs. She was tired; she'd been reading for six hours in a row. It would have been more fun to know what happened to Francisco in Spain.

Francisco couldn't be the author: all of this was too far from Spain. It was certainly not Jamaica either; she wasn't interested enough in Jane's past. It was definitely someone who knew her quite well—someone who understood the symbolic meaning Jane had given to the mysterious message of the tarot cards reading, "don't hold, don't protect." It had to be Lynn.

The author was describing, step by step, a positive process of reconstruction, of "recovery." Lynn thought that the divorce was a good thing because Jane had to grow up and to learn things about life that she wouldn't have learned with Eric.

But Jane had never told Lynn that she kept dreaming of Eric every night after the attack. She had mentioned her dreams to Chip, to whom she talked easily and who, unlike Lynn, didn't judge her or give unrequested advice. Could Chip have told Lynn? Or could they have written the novel together? Chip just for the fun of it, and Lynn with a therapeutic goal: to show Jane how much she had progressed in nine years and to prove to her that her great love now was just a story belonging to the past, a fiction?

Chip had plenty of time to write while he sat in his parking lot. Sending an anonymous manuscript was more consistent with his character than with Lynn's. He liked mysteries. He was naturally curious and he had asked Jane many questions.

But she wasn't entirely convinced.

A man and a woman were speaking loudly outside, arguing. A dog barked. Someone slammed a car door and drove away. Jane went to look out the living-room window. She couldn't see anything. She walked back to the kitchen and dialed Lynn's number. Nobody answered. It was already 7:54 p.m. It was rare that Lynn wasn't home at this hour during the week. Jane hung up without leaving a message. Then she tried Chip. She let it ring about ten times. There was no answering machine.

2

Jane stepped out of the car and Lynn drove away. It was chilly, but the sky was a clear, sharp blue without a cloud—rare weather for early April. She was wearing a navy blue jacket and a dark blue suede skirt on which Jamaica and Lynn had congratulated her—which confirmed Eric's opinion that dark blue wasn't a color reserved only for blondes. She should have brought a raincoat instead of dressing like a schoolgirl preparing for her class photo. Under the arch there were two doors that said POLICE. She pushed the one indicating COMMUNICATION SERVICES. A tiny room with a window and nobody behind. A man soon arrived.

"Yes?"

"Something happened to me," Jane said hesitantly.

"Do you want to file a complaint?"

"Maybe."

"Let me call an inspector. He'll be here in five minutes."

She looked at posters on the wall. An ad in big characters warned the students that they would be fined $25 if they didn't bring back their room key when they left. Soon it would be the end of the school year. On the other wall was an information sheet about bike theft, warning to never leave a bike locked at a parking meter or a street sign. She started biting the nail of her little finger. Ten minutes already. The man behind the window had disappeared. She could hear noise from a TV or a radio in the back office. Someone pushed the door.

"Waiting for me?"

"Are you . . . the inspector?"

She was expecting a short man with an old raincoat and a clever look, not a cop dressed like those managing traffic. She followed him outside. He had white hair, broad shoulders, a rather large behind with a revolver in a small leather holster hanging from his belt, and he must believe in spring too, for he was wearing a shirt with short sleeves. He stopped under the arch and turned toward her.

"What is it about?"

"Here?"

He nodded. They were standing in the passage leading from University Street to the campus, and many students were walking by.

"I've been receiving anonymous notes."

"Do you have them with you here?"

"I left them at home."

He shook his head, his arms crossed on his large chest. "You should have brought them. How many?"

"Three."

"You have to keep them and write down the exact day and time when you received them. What do they say?"

"The first was a Valentine's card on which was written, 'You're so pretty.' It wasn't signed."

He looked at her as if he just noticed that she wasn't ugly. Hundreds of girls at Devayne probably received anonymous cards on Valentine's Day. He smiled. "Looks like you have an admirer."

"I know. I wasn't worried until I received the second."

"When?"

"I don't remember exactly, late February or early March. The other two, it's easy, because the first was Valentine's Day, and yesterday was April first. Given the choice of dates, it must be a joke."

"Looks like it. Anything threatening in the content?"

"No."

He glanced sideways at her. "Anything . . . explicit?"

"Explicit?"

"Sexual?"

"Not even. Rather childish. So you think that someone is just making fun of me and there is nothing to worry about?"

"I would have to see them."

He didn't seem worried at all. She and Lynn had probably blown out of proportion something that was just routine for a cop.

"Are you a student here?" he asked.

"I teach."

"You teach! Are you an instructor?"

"A professor."

"Professor." He stood up straighter and looked at her more respectfully. "Did you receive the notes at the university?"

"Two of them."

"What do you teach?"

"French literature."

He smiled widely. "*Paalez-vous fouançais?* I never got beyond that in French. Nice language, though. Where is the French department?"

"On Garden Street, next to Bruno's Pizza. Can I ask you something?"

"Sure."

"Do lots of people receive anonymous notes?"

"It happens. Lots of phone calls. The room numbers in the dorms are the same as the last four digits of the phone numbers, so you can imagine. And then there is the rubber guy."

"The what?"

"Some guy who calls at night and says, 'Hello, I'm the rubber guy, would you like to rub against me?'" He laughed heartily. "Nothing's ever happened. He's been doing this for a long time now; everyone knows about him, but once in a while he scares a new girl."

"I feel better now that I hear you say that. It was a good idea to come talk to you." She smiled. "You should have seen me yesterday: I really panicked. Maybe because the notes are kind of scatological, I don't know."

"Like what?"

"The one yesterday said . . ." She hesitated, then said quickly, "'Let's go number two together.'"

"Number two?" He laughed. "You mean . . . to defecate?"

Jane turned red. "So you think it's funny."

"Yeah! Someone is making fun of you. What about the other?"

She looked around. "'Let's pull down our pants,'" she said quickly, in a low voice, "'I'll show you mine, you show me yours.' You see, just what kids would say."

"Kids?" He frowned. "Hmm. That's more like what a guy says to a lady in a bar: 'I'll show you mine . . . if you show me yours!'"

He was speaking very loudly. Two students passing under the archway turned their heads and looked at them with raised eyebrows. Jane couldn't face him anymore.

"I shouldn't have disturbed you for nothing."

"For nothing? I wouldn't say so. I don't like the content of that note. I don't like it at all. And in that context I don't like the other one either, the number-two one. I don't know yet if there is any threat here, but it's definitely explicit. My opinion, lady, is that you should file a complaint."

"Do you think so?"

"Absolutely. Maybe it's nothing, just a bad joke. But it's better to have a complaint filed. It's the only way to find out whether other people have received the same kind of notes."

She sighed deeply. She felt immensely relieved, like a hypochondriac who has taken all the possible tests and to whom nobody listens anymore—until a specialist finds he has a rare, real illness, which can be cured. If this cop, who didn't seem to be the anxious type, saw grounds for a complaint in what happened to her, then she wasn't crazy to have been so scared yesterday.

He put out his hand to her. "I'm Inspector John Merriman. What's your name?"

"Jane Cook."

She followed him to the office on the other side of the arch, where a woman with black hair introduced herself as Inspector Hilary Tait. She typed Jane's answers to the inspector's questions into the computer. Jane reported everything in detail. How she found the heart-shaped card on February 14 with the words "you're so pretty" written in a childish, disguised handwriting, and immediately thought of her young colleague Jamaica. That night she had called Jamaica in New York, who had told her in detail about a quarrel with her boyfriend the night before. When Jane mentioned the card, Jamaica bitterly said that Jane was lucky someone had thought of her for Valentine's. After hanging up, Jane wondered whether the card could have come from her husband.

"You're married?"

"Divorced."

The inspectors exchanged a glance.

"How long have you been divorced?"

"A year."

"What terms are you on with your former husband?"

"Oh, very good. Well, we haven't spoken since we got divorced, but it was a mutual divorce. My husband lives in Iowa; there is no way he could have dropped the card in my box."

"He could have someone else drop it."

"No, I really don't see whom, and it doesn't make sense. I guess I thought of him because I wished it had come from him, that's all."

Yes, this had been her wish. In December she had decided to send a friendly, upbeat, and neutral Happy New Year card to Eric. She had written dozens of drafts and finally given up. For weeks she couldn't open her mailbox without hoping to find a card from Eric. This she didn't tell the inspectors.

"But the Valentine's card wasn't the one that worried me."

She told them that she had had the same thought as the inspector at first—that she had a secret admirer, probably a shy student. There was also a less flattering alternative: a malicious student responding to a challenge. In which case her students would be watching her. So she decided not to talk about the card to anyone, not even to the secretaries. The inspector nodded in approval.

She really wasn't anxious until that day in late February or early March when she found a folded piece of paper in her mailbox at the university, half of a white sheet of lined paper torn from a student's notebook. It was the one that read, *"Let's pull down our pants: I'll show you mine and you show me yours."* The same childish, awkward and disguised handwriting as the Valentine card, as if a right-handed person had used his left hand. She rode her bike home, and when she got there, she locked her door and even turned the dead bolt. This was how she realized that she was scared. She read the note again and cried. Her strong reaction could be explained by the fact that she had been mugged in September and something worse could have happened if people hadn't been walking by.

"Where did you file a complaint?"

"I didn't."

The two inspectors looked at each other. If she hadn't been a Devayne professor, they wouldn't have taken her seriously. She explained that she hadn't seen her attacker.

"You don't make our work easy. That's more serious than anonymous notes. The place, the time, everything counts and it's important for statistics."

She hadn't thrown away that second note but couldn't find it anymore. In spite of her fear, she hadn't mentioned it to anyone. The only rationale she could see was a student's joke: the same person who had written "you're so pretty" was disappointed by her lack of reaction and was now trying something stronger. The best thing was not to react at all. She had gone over in her mind all the students to whom she had given bad grades. But it could be a student from another year or an eighth- or ninth-year jobless graduate student. Graduate students, though, were too mature for this type of joke. Besides, she wasn't the one to sign the final version of the teaching schedule last year.

"Apart from the students, do you know anyone who would want revenge? Someone in love with you, maybe?"

"Nobody, really."

She couldn't look at her students anymore without wondering whether it could be this one or that one, which made teaching painful. She was sure that there would be another note soon and felt nervous each time she picked up her mail. She almost wished she would find a folded piece of paper in her box after class; the worst was the nerve-racking anticipation.

"This makes me think," Inspector Merriman said, "of the guy who wakes up every night when his neighbor comes home drunk and drops his shoes on the floor. Do you know the story?"

Inspector Tait leaned against the back of her chair and stretched her fingers.

"He finally complains to the neighbor, who promises to be careful. That night the drunkard comes home, drops one boot and remembers his neighbor. So he takes off the other boot very cautiously and puts it silently next to the first. One hour later someone rings his bell and wakes him up. He opens the door and finds his downstairs neighbor, totally exhausted, who begs him to drop his other boot!"

The inspector laughed out loud. Jane smiled.

"I guess that's how I felt. But then there was spring break and no note, which seemed to confirm that it was a student, and I relaxed. I told myself that it had been a good idea not to speak about it and not to react at all. Until yesterday."

"Yesterday was the 'number two' note?"

"Yes."

Inspector Tait raised her eyebrows. Jane dictated to her the content of the note.

"What time did you pick up your mail?"

"I got home around six P.M. I don't know if I told you that I found the third note in my mailbox at home, not at the university."

"Really! Where do you live?"

"Five eighty-two Main Street, near Columbus Square."

"That's off-campus. You'll have to file two complaints at the Market Street precinct: one for the attack and one for the note. But since you got two at the university, I'll take all the information."

"It came from the same type of notebook and was written in the same handwriting. I didn't see it at first; it was stuck between two bills. I discovered it when I was already in my apartment. Otherwise, I think I would have been too scared to go upstairs. I completely panicked after I found the note. I was convinced there was someone in the bathroom. I can't tell you how scared I was when I pulled the shower curtain aside. I had brought a big knife with me from the kitchen."

She smiled. But it hadn't been fun at all, she said. She had asked her friend and neighbor, Lynn, to sleep over. Lynn was the one who convinced her to go to the police first thing in the morning.

"She was right. What's her full name?"

"Lynn Oberfield."

Jane saw the clock on the wall—10:30 A.M. "My class! I have to run."

They made an appointment for 3 P.M., after her afternoon class. Inspector Tait reminded Jane to bring the lists of her students for the past three years. She handed her a business card. "This afternoon I'll give you phone numbers and addresses of trauma centers. Some are totally anonymous."

Inspector Merriman walked her to the door. He patted her on the shoulder and told her not to worry; this was slightly more serious than he had thought at first, but probably just a student's joke that wasn't related to the September attack. He gave her his business card too. Jane felt much better as she ran to class.

When she returned to the office at three, she perceived a change in the inspector's tone. He looked at her lists and asked a few questions, but quickly; he didn't seem to be interested in them anymore. He too had lists that he wanted to show her. As she went through them, she recognized the names of Lynn's friends, all members of the Gay and Lesbian Association. Lynn's name was there too, of course. The questions now were quite different. She was being interrogated. Inspector Merriman was curious about her extracurricular activities. Easy to answer: none, except for the class of African dance, and going to the seaside once in a while. She mentioned Sleazy. He knew the man: slightly retarded and crazy, but not dangerous. He was more interested in the African dance class. Jane tried to remain calm as she described the wonderful, relaxed, noncompetitive atmosphere of a class in which many women brought their children along, even the teacher, Sheila, a warm and radiant African-American woman whose seven-year-old daughter Tamara danced like a little angel fallen from heaven. Inspector Tait kept typing as if Jane were delivering useful information.

"Sounds like fun," she said.

"It really is. You should come."

Inspector Merriman moved to another line of questioning. He wanted to know when Jane met Lynn.

"About one and a half years ago."

"This is when you started a relationship?"

"What do you mean?"

"When you started sleeping together."

"But we don't!"

"You said earlier that she slept with you last night."

"No, that she stayed overnight because I was scared!"

Inspector Merriman exposed his new theory: not a student but, rather, either an antilesbian crime or an act of jealousy from someone who was in love with Lynn or with Jane.

"But I'm not a lesbian!"

She sounded defensive. This morning inspector Merriman had been rather gallant. Now he was condescending.

Around five he drove her to the police precinct in her neighborhood. She walked up the stairs at Merriman's side as if the police had arrested her, while young people hanging around the steps looked at her. Inside, she had to repeat everything, every detail about the attack and the notes. The cops' faces reflected exactly the kind of interest she had anticipated and feared. When Lynn's name came up, they smiled.

Lynn picked her up at seven in front of the police station. Jane quickly climbed into the car. She was scared that some cops would see Lynn and it would confirm their dirty prejudices about lesbians. She burst into tears and told Lynn how humiliating it had been. Lynn laughed.

"Poor baby. Sorry I forgot to warn you. I'm so used to this kind of crap that I don't pay attention to it anymore. The cops know me because I was involved in a lot of activism after Jeaudine's death."

"But they're crazy! They were ready to accuse Sheila! Why not Tamara? I told them about Sleazy—not that I think it's him, but he's the weirdest person I know in Old Newport. They weren't interested in him. But why? Because he's white? And a man?"

"It makes them feel better to think that it's an African-American or a lesbian. As long as they don't fabricate evidence, we're fine. We need them, Jane. They'll find out who it is; you're a Devayne professor."

Jane ran into Jamaica outside her office the following day. They hugged. They saw each other rarely now that Jamaica spent most of her time in New York and ran to the train station immediately after class three days a week. She was wearing a very short black skirt, her go-go boots, and a tight stretch shirt with a black and white tiger pattern, which fit her very thin waist and the top buttons of which were undone, revealing the deep line between her breast and a fragment of a white lace bra.

"Nice bra."

"Thanks. It's French. A gift from Xavier. He bought me a whole collection. He loves lingerie."

Jane smiled. She bought her own underwear for $1 apiece: in cotton, simple and comfortable, nothing sexy. Nobody saw them anyway except for Lynn occasionally, who was nothing of a fetishist, herself wearing huge nylon underwear and inelegant brassieres for her big breasts.

"You look tired. What you need isn't a vacation, though," Jamaica said with a charming smile, "it's a lover. You aren't going to find one among Lynn's friends. Why don't you come to New York this weekend? There's a cocktail party at the French consulate Friday night, and the whole French Who's Who of New York will be there. We could go clubbing afterwards and you could stay with us overnight."

"Thanks, but I have too much work. Another time. How are you?"

"Exhausted. The commuting is killing me. Xavier is lucky: he comes here only twice a week thanks to you. It's a pity you're no longer DUS; you could have done the same for me. Whoa! 5:36. I'm going to miss my train. Do you mind walking with me for five minutes?"

Jamaica grabbed her bag and a funky plush jacket in her office. They ran down the stairs and left the building together.

"Do you think," Jamaica suddenly asked, "that two people in love should tell each other everything?"

"It depends." Jane thought of Vincent and Torben. "Actually no, I don't think so. The ideal of transparency doesn't take jealousy into account. Why? Is there something you want to hide from Xavier?"

"No. But Xavier wants to tell me everything on his mind, even when I don't want to know about it. He thinks I'm too prudish because of my education. For instance, we're walking down Broadway and he's commenting on the ass of the woman walking in front of us. He thinks that it should excite me or at least that I shouldn't mind because this is what he feels like telling me at that moment. I can't stand it. Do you think I'm wrong?"

"Certainly not!"

"And now his new idea is to make love with me and another woman. He only talks about that. But I don't want to. I can't stand the idea of seeing him inside another woman."

"I understand you. Who is she?"

"Nobody definite yet. Apparently he has several friends to whom he could propose this. Are you interested?"

"Me? Are you crazy!"

"Just kidding. It's a pity, though—with you I wouldn't be jealous. Anyhow, if he doesn't change, I'm not sure this relationship can last. Xavier says that a relationship in which one has to repress one's desires can't last anyway."

"Sounds infantile."

"I wish you could tell him! I have to run or I'll miss my train. He doesn't like it when I'm late. Bye, Jane!"

She started running. Jane turned around and walked back to Garden Street, where she had left her bike. Jamaica looked tired too, like everyone at the end of the school year. There was something else: her youthful radiance was gone. Because of Devayne or of Duportoy? Jane stopped to pick up her mail. She didn't feel nervous when she opened the box. It had been a wise move, finally, to go to the police.

Allison called that night to announce the news: she was pregnant. Twins.

"Twins! Four and a half months! Why didn't you tell me sooner?"

"Sorry. I'm superstitious. I wanted to do the amniocentesis first."

There would be almost five years of difference with Jeremy, who was delighted to have two baby sisters.

"But he's quite ambivalent too. This morning he asks me whether he can touch the babies and then, abruptly, with a wonderful smile, whether he can crush my belly. I've started reading books on psychology. I don't want him to be traumatized. But it's sad to be an only child."

"Yes. Eric said so. He wanted us to have at least two kids."

There was a silence. Jane knew what Allison thought: Jane mentioning Eric meant she wasn't over it yet.

"So when are you visiting us?" Allison asked. "Jeremy is asking for Auntie Jane."

Three children. Somewhere in the world life was going on normally. Duportoy would lose Jamaica and cry. Allison was right when she said that building a relationship was real work. That work was about repressing things: a fleeting desire, an impatience, an angry word. A simple and solid relationship like that of Allison and John, about which there was nothing to say, was the result of constant vigilance. For Duportoy, it was probably mediocrity embodied. But mediocrity might be the hardest balance to reach.

As Jane walked into the Garden Street building the following day, she kept thinking about her conversation with Allison. She hadn't visited John and Allison once since they moved to Seattle and started working there as lawyers; she knew nothing of their life. Her sister lived in New York and Jane had only seen her new niece once. She hadn't visited her parents since the divorce. They had sounded extremely concerned when she told them about the attack in September. Obviously they loved her.

They were aging. She was now living five hours away by train. Her next job might be at the other end of the United States, and it would be less easy to visit them.

When you didn't see your friends and your family, you lost your ties with them. Any relationship, not only love, demanded time and effort. This was what was so wonderful about Lynn and her friends—the time they gave each other. They formed a community, aware of being a minority who needed each other in a prejudiced society. At Devayne nobody had the time. They were all saving every minute like greedy old misers hoarding their treasure. Saving time for what? Why did they spend their life at a desk with their noses in books, barricaded against others and convincing themselves they didn't have any time?

As she inserted the key into her mailbox's lock, she had an epiphany. "Don't protect, don't hold." What? Time. Giving one's time was giving oneself; the essence of the self was time. The trouble with her was that she had always been scared to waste her time. Now she finally knew how to change things and redeem herself. She would start by visiting her parents this weekend, and then John and Allison as soon as classes ended. She took out the mail. A tiny piece of paper slipped onto the floor. A white piece of paper folded twice, lined, torn from a student's notebook. She turned pale. It was too soon after the last anonymous note and didn't fit the pattern the inspector was trying to establish. She picked it up and unfolded it with some difficulty, still holding her mail in one hand and her keys in the other. Her fingers were trembling and her heart pounding.

"Daddy isn't home tonight: wanna play with me?"

She swallowed, staring at the childish handwriting. *Tonight.* That was now, this evening. He was waiting for her in her apartment. She would listen to the messages on her answering machine, and there would be his recorded voice telling her that he was just behind her and she was going to die. And, immediately, his hand covering her mouth and her nose. She let out a moan of fear. She had seen the scene in a TV movie twenty years earlier and never forgotten it: terror itself. This time he wouldn't miss her. He would tie her up and tape her mouth. She could always beg him with her eyes or, if she could talk, promise that she would never tell anyone. It would be safer to kill her. And more exciting. He would cut her lightly with a knife, hurt her horribly, and slash her throat at the climax.

She leaned against the wall. She couldn't move her legs. She felt dizzy; she wanted to throw up. It wasn't a joke. The piece of paper was there, in her hand. The fourth one. Three days after the third, and two days after she went to the police. Maybe he had followed her and he knew she went to the police. Maybe it excited him—a real challenge. Not a student. She was sure. She wouldn't feel this terror. Someone who knew her address and who enjoyed her fear. Who was playing with her. Who might be watching her right now. She looked around in a panic. The building was quiet, typically quite empty at this hour. She stepped outside.

It was six already. She had left at home, on a table near the telephone, the business cards the two inspectors had given her. She ran to the Devayne police station. Inspector Tait's office was closed already. She pushed open the door of the Communication Services office, open twenty-four hours a day. A cop showed up.

"I need to see Inspector Merriman."

He looked at his watch. "Come back tomorrow morning."

"It's urgent. I need to see him."

She burst into tears. The cop scratched his head.

"What's your name?"

"Jane Cook. I'm a professor here. He knows me."

"Wait a moment."

He went to the back office and returned two minutes later. "Inspector Merriman will be here in five to ten minutes."

She was really happy to see him. He looked at the note and shook his head. They went to Inspector Tait's office, which he unlocked with one of the many keys on the ring attached to his belt. He typed up the new information. He drove her home. A Devayne police car would pass by the house every half hour. There shouldn't be any problem. If she was scared, she shouldn't hesitate to phone him at home.

Lynn spent the night in her place. Merriman called Jane in the morning to ask her if she knew Charles Edward Townsend.

"He's a friend. Why?"

"Just checking."

He also informed her that the Devayne police had installed a tiny, invisible camera on the wall across from her mailbox. Now they just needed to wait for the next note, and it would be the end of the series. If she found it at the university and not at home, Jane thought; if the police caught the guy before anything happened. Inspector Merriman had told her that someone writing anonymous notes wasn't the kind of person to act, but he must be worried, though, to have installed a camera at the university.

"They asked about Chip. You see, they're crazy," Jane told Lynn that evening.

Lynn smiled. "I was surprised that they hadn't asked yet."

"Why? What did he do?"

"He was arrested last year on Central Square with a Devayne student, a student in your department, I think: David Tin . . ."

"Tinderman? I can't believe it! A big baby. Oh, I remember! I was in the department the day when Tinderman arrived, looking traumatized, and said he had spent the night in the police station—he had been arrested as he was just giving street information to someone. He was terrified the cops would tell his parents."

"Chip was giving him a blow job. The poor kid must have been traumatized; cops are awful with queers. And they love Chip. Have you heard about the murder of a Devayne student on campus, about ten years ago?"

"Yes. What does it have to with Chip?"

"The body was found in the bushes under his windows."

"No!"

"The student probably surprised someone burglarizing Chip's house. Chip wasn't home that night, but his alibi was gay. The cops gave him a hard time."

A week later, as Jane was unlocking her bike in the ground floor of her house around ten in the morning, she heard a noise in the basement. Her heart started palpitating. She wanted to run outside, but her legs wouldn't obey her anymore, like in the worst nightmare. She leaned against the wall. The noise became louder. Someone was closing a door downstairs and walking up the narrow wooden staircase. The house was always empty at this hour. She couldn't scream anyway: she had lost her voice too.

"Who's there?" she asked in a faint voice.

The steps got closer and nobody answered. She closed her eyes. When she opened them, she saw a foot step onto the red carpet—a foot inside a big red slipper. It was followed by a plastic laundry basket held by hairy arms on which the sleeves were rolled up. Karl. The short and stout man nodded to her as he passed by. Not very talkative, as usual.

"You aren't working today?" she asked him.

"I have a cold. This way I can do my laundry; for once the machine is free."

Now she felt so nervous that there was a sharp pain in her fingertips every night when she introduced the key into the lock of her mailbox at the university and then at home. Whoever climbed the steps of the house behind her or even walked by on the other side of the garden fence made her tremble with fear. When she was entering her front door and a stranger was waiting out in front, she would ask, "Whom are you visiting?" Day and night, she kept asking herself the same questions: Who was torturing her and why? What had she done that could inspire such a desire to persecute her?

Lynn was infuriated. "It has nothing to do with you. There're crazy people; you can't do anything about it. The bastard will be caught and he'll pay for what he did to you. Trust me."

Lynn was sure it was a man. Without her support, there were times when Jane would have swallowed a box of sleeping pills just to stop the fear.

The bastard was in hiding. Did he know the police were watching? Had he noticed the camera that was nothing but a tiny dot in a corner of the wall? The last note had been on April 5. It was now April 24. She had lost her sense of time. She was unable to make any plans for the future and to buy a plane ticket to visit John and Allison this summer. Day after day, she was waiting. Nothing. He was probably waiting for her to be off-guard. This guy was an excellent psychologist. He would strike when she wasn't thinking about it anymore. During the summer? When she came back from a trip? She wished with all her heart that there would be another note. It was the only way to catch him. On the radio one morning, she heard about a shoot-out that had taken place in front of the courthouse the day before, followed by a speedy chase through Old Newport, like in a movie. It was around the same time that she had been riding her bike to campus, passing by the courthouse. She hadn't noticed anything and didn't even remember hearing sirens. The guy who was shot was a witness in a drug-trafficking trial and was wearing a bulletproof jacket; he knew he was a target. Real stuff. Old Newport cops were probably laughing at Jane's poo-poo notes.

She was entering the Garden Street building a few days later when she ran into a young student from the École Normale Supérieure in Paris who was spending the year at Devayne as an instructor of French.

"Good morning, madame," Hélène said. "How are you?"

Jane had asked her to call her by name, but in vain. The girl seemed to find Jane too old for such familiarity.

"Very well, thanks. Such a beautiful day."

Hélène sighed. "It's the day of oral exams for language courses; I'll be locked up in an office all day. Today is Labor Day in France: nobody works!"

"Right. May first. Are you going back to France soon?"

"I'll travel in the States and Canada for a month with my sister. First, I'm trying to find someone to sublet my sister's apartment in Paris. Do you know anyone interested, by any chance? It's a very charming place in Montmartre."

"Did you tell Dawn and Rose?"

"Yes. And I just posted an ad."

"The last charming apartment I rented in Paris, there were seven very steep flights of stairs to get to it. Your sister has an elevator?"

"No, but she lives on the third floor. She renovated an old apartment; it's very pretty. And the neighborhood is wonderful, so lively, full of shops and fashionable bars and clubs."

"It must be noisy."

"Her bedroom overlooks a sunny, quiet courtyard."

"Sounds nice. Good luck. I'm sure you'll find someone."

Hélène held the door for her and Jane stepped in. Why did she ask all these questions about an apartment where she would never live? She suddenly realized that she missed Paris. She hadn't been there in five years. She passed the mailboxes. She had picked up her mail last night, and it was too early for Dawn to have distributed the mail already. Still, she turned back and inserted her key in the lock, while shrugging her shoulders. Was she going to check her mail four times a day now?

Inside the empty pinewood box was a tiny, white, folded piece of paper. She froze. She had expected this note for so long, and here it was, just in the moment when she wasn't really thinking about it, even though a weird instinct had made her open the box. She was almost solemn as she took out the note, the one that would allow the police finally to catch him. Close to the end. He had left the note at the university—he hadn't seen the camera, he had betrayed himself. She slowly unfolded it, increasingly excited. Someone pushed open the building's door. Jane quickly closed her hand around the note and hid it behind her back. She thought it was Hélène, but Jamaica stepped in. For the first time, Jane wasn't pleased to see her.

"What are you doing here so early?"

"I'm wondering myself." Jamaica sighed. "I still teach language, as you know; we have oral exams all day long."

Her black sweater wasn't buttoned straight. She looked sleepy. Her long curly hair was a mess. She yawned. "Gee! It's fucking hot."

She rested her paper cup on the edge of the water fountain.

"How is Xavier?" Jane asked.

"Great. Leaving for France next week."

"Are you joining him there?"

"In June. If I find a ticket, with this fucking World Cup."

"World Cup?"

"Hey, Jane, wake up, drop your books. The soccer World Cup is in France this year, didn't you know?"

Jamaica picked up her mail. Her box was full: she didn't come often since classes were over. They took the elevator together. Jamaica got out at the third floor. As soon as the elevator started moving again, Jane unfolded the wrinkled piece of paper in her right hand. The same childish, disguised handwriting.

"You're going to like it, I swear."

There was a convulsion in her body. In one flash everything came back: the hand on her mouth, the arm on her neck, the man behind her, the knife, the blood, the terror. She suddenly felt the man inside her. The elevator stopped and the door opened. She ran down the corridor and unlocked her office. Begolu was sitting inside her office, right next to Jane's, with her door open, and her back turned to Jane, typing on her computer. No barking—the dogs weren't there. Jane slammed her door behind her, dropped her bag and dialed Merriman's number.

"It's me, Jane Cook," she said in a low voice, so Begolu wouldn't hear. "That's it—a new note. Yes, at the university."

There was a febrile excitement in her voice. Almost joy. Merriman sounded quite satisfied too. "Is the note threatening?"

"Very explicit."

"Are you scared?"

"Not here. There're many people around."

He made an appointment for forty minutes later.

Inspector Merriman and Jane sat on chairs in front of the small TV in the office of Inspector Tait, who pushed the start button. The three of them stared at the screen. Dawn, first, distributing mail; she wasn't a suspect. Then someone else stopped in front of Jane's box. A man. She held her breath. She recognized the profile and the white hair.

"Hugh Carrington!"

Merriman stopped the film and asked Jane to spell out the name. Her mouth was dry. Carrington? But why? Could he be jealous because Jane was friends with Chip? Did Chip or Lynn tell him that Jane found him boring? Or was it the prize? He had seemed impressed in November when he came to the dinner party. He had published nothing but a few articles since he got tenure at Devayne twenty years earlier. But he had always been nice to her. Hypocrisy? Did he need to express a hatred for women that he had repressed for over forty years?

Merriman asked Inspector Tait to rewind the scene and they looked at Carrington again. He was raising his arm but not touching Jane's box, not putting any paper inside.

"I know: his mailbox is just above mine!" Jane exclaimed.

They watched further. Someone else. The back of a dark blue or black jacket. Someone very tall, so his head was actually above the camera, and they saw only his back, his arm, his shoulder, and his neck. They were all watching carefully. The silence inside the office was intense; they knew he was the man. His bent arm, indeed, dropped something inside Jane's box. The three of them exhaled at the same time.

A name instinctively came to Jane's lips: "Duportoy."

"Who?"

Tait stopped the film. Merriman wrote down the name. Jane shook her head. "It can't be him. I guess I thought of him because he's tall and I just saw his girlfriend."

"Who is he?"

"One of my colleagues."

"Does he have any reason to be upset with you?"

"None."

"Is he attracted to you?"

"Not at all. He was never interested in me."

Tait rewound the film and they went through the scene again. Jane wasn't sure anymore. This fragment of a jacket could belong to anyone. There was nothing to confirm her first impression: no hair, no partial view of a face, of a profile. Now the movement of the shoulder didn't remind her of Duportoy or anyone else. Today was Friday. He never came to Old Newport on Friday. Plus, classes had ended, so he didn't come to Old Newport at all. He lived in New York.

"The date on the film is Thursday," Merriman said. "Seven twenty-eight P.M. It will be easy to find out whether this Duportoy was in Old Newport yesterday."

He would have left at that time to catch the 7:52 train to New York. But, if it was him, there was another, very simple explanation: someone else inside or outside the building could have asked him to drop the note in Jane's mailbox.

"It's possible, indeed. In that case Duportoy will be able to describe the suspect. Maybe he knows him. In any case, you can sleep soundly. The mystery is almost resolved."

Inspector Merriman reached Duportoy in New York that evening and asked him to come to Old Newport the following day for a matter that couldn't be discussed over the phone. At first, Duportoy denied everything, laughed and told the cops they watched too many Hollywood movies. He barely knew Jane Cook. He had just heard from his girlfriend, Jamaica Locke, and from another friend who was teaching here before, Francisco Gonzalez, that this woman had a fixation on him.

"He said that?"

His arrogant attitude lasted only until the cops told him they had him on tape, dropping a note inside the box of his colleague who had identified him. There was a change in his face. He didn't collapse. He smiled: it was him, OK, but it was only a joke, nothing to take seriously. He confessed everything before he saw the film and realized that he couldn't be recognized on it.

Jane was bewildered. Lynn too.

Jamaica called Jane on Sunday night. Duportoy had told her everything when he came back from Old Newport the night before.

"I'm so sorry. I can't believe it myself. Maybe now you see what I have to deal with."

"Did you break up with him?"

Jamaica sounded surprised. Of course not. Xavier had to change. He was so infantile sometimes, so irresponsible. The police interrogation had scared him a lot, and he was quite shaken—a good thing. He needed a shock, a confrontation with reality. Things had just been too easy for him, and he was bored, so that was why he came up with these funny ideas, making love with two women or leaving poo-poo notes to a colleague. He had a great intellectual maturity, but he was very immature emotionally.

Jane wasn't interested in Duportoy's psychological development. "Why are you calling?"

"I wanted to talk to you, to know how you're doing. I think of you all the time. It must have been awful. I'm mad at him. What are you going to do now?"

"What do you mean?"

"With the complaint."

Xavier must have asked her to call.

"I don't know yet, frankly. I haven't had the time to think about it. It's out of my hands now, anyway. The police are dealing with it."

"But it's your complaint."

"So what?"

"You could withdraw it."

Jane snorted and almost hung up. "Tell him he shouldn't worry. Devayne doesn't like scandals: the matter won't go beyond Devayne's walls."

"Look how you talk! Jane, you can't take things so seriously. I'm not calling because Xavier asked me too, but only because I know both of you. Let me explain to you."

"What?"

"Xavier likes you. He never had anything against you."

Jane laughed. "I'm glad to hear that."

"Stop that attitude. Listen to me. He says that you have always been very nice to him. Last fall you gave him exactly the schedule he wanted. You were very accommodating and he was grateful to you. He says that you're not like the others: you aren't thirsty for power and that's why you are nice."

"Really."

"He never intended to terrorize you. By the way, he didn't know you were mugged in September or he would never have done this. It started completely by chance, on February 14, when he saw a big red heart-shaped card at the newsstand in the Old Newport train station. He bought it for me because I like kitsch, and he wanted to make up for our argument the night before. But then he saw you in the department that day, and you looked sad. Xavier hates Valentine's Day and the fuss Americans make about it. The result, he says, is that single people feel extremely lonely that day. He wrote the card for you so you would believe somebody was thinking about you. You know, I never told you, but he finds you very pretty."

Jane rolled her eyes. Compliments now. "The Valentine's card wasn't the problem."

"I know, but I wanted to tell you how it started. This is what gave him the idea of the joke. Just a stupid joke. Xavier also thinks that your life in Old Newport is very sad and that you're wasting your best years."

Jane smiled sarcastically as she imagined Xavier and Jamaica together at night discussing the case of poor Jane.

"We often thought of men we could introduce you to," Jamaica continued. "I invited you to New York, but, look, you never came. Xavier said it was because Devayne had got you already. This place makes you dry up inside like an old parchment and you lose your imagination and your senses. Not you especially, but anyone here. You and I have often talked about that. Even if you never become like Begolu, because you're much nicer, one day you may buy one or two dogs too, and never leave Old Newport anymore except for the MLA convention. Just like McGregor and Carrington: dead inside. We don't want this to happen to you."

"First, I would need to get tenure at Devayne."

"Devayne or somewhere else. It will be the same. Devayne is a syndrome. I hope that you understand: Xavier just wanted to stimulate your imagination, to make you think about something other than Devayne."

"He succeeded."

"He believes in the power of words. He wanted to awaken your fantasy so you would find a lover this summer."

They spent one hour on the phone.

Lynn was furious. "You can't talk to Jamaica. Don't you understand? She's on the other side."

Jamaica's defense of Xavier was only natural. What made Jane sad was that Jamaica was so condescending—and so unaware of it. Jamaica probably agreed with Duportoy that the notes could only be good for the poor, middle-aged, divorced woman who had to be rescued from the lesbians. What Duportoy had to say on the topic, which Jane could easily guess, inspired in her a feeling closer to hate than she had ever experienced.

The disciplinary hearing took place on May 25, when fresh lawns were planted everywhere for the imminent graduation, tents with large green and white stripes were erected in the middle of campus, and the whole place looked festive. The spacious oak-paneled room with green carpet in one of the university's oldest buildings was quite impressive. They sat on chairs with very high backs around a long, antique table made of dark wood, with a Persian rug under their feet. The disciplinary committee consisted of seven faculty members from various schools and departments in the university. Jamaica accompanied Duportoy. He was wearing a green suit—Devayne's color—a white shirt and a blue and yellow tie. Jamaica and Jane, dressed in long black skirts and white shirts, looked like students from the same high school. They didn't even say hi to each other. Lynn also had chosen her best clothes, a dark blue pleated skirt and a red silk blouse Jane had recently gotten her for her birthday—perhaps a little too bright for this occasion.

The first to speak was Jane. She talked calmly about her increasing fear, the continual suspicion that made teaching unbearable, her terror when she got the first note at home and started living with the conviction someone was stalking her, and the feeling of having lost control over her life, which had begun to seem like a cheap TV series. Then it was Duportoy's turn. He spoke English with French intonations, filtered through the very proper British accent he had learned in French schools. He accused himself of acting very stupid, foolish and childish, but he also insisted on the fact that he never had anything against Jane. If the joke got out of control, it wasn't his fault but the result of unfortunate circumstances of which he was unaware. Without the September attack, Jane would never have thought that a serial killer was after her just because she had received three scatological notes that weren't threatening at all. His hands were moving in every direction and there were drops of sweat on his forehead. The committee members didn't seem to be seduced by his rhetorical talent. Duportoy was serious and looked rather humble, but he didn't appear intimidated or scared. He couldn't completely erase the ironical smile at the corner of his lips, as if all of this were just a big masquerade. Jane took a side glance at Lynn. She was clenching her teeth. Anger and hatred were burning in her eyes. Duportoy was lucky not to be in Lynn's hands; she would have emasculated him with her teeth.

The hearing lasted more than three hours. The seven professors withdrew to another room to deliberate. They came back fifteen minutes later with a unanimous decision: Duportoy was fired.

"He should have been deported," Lynn told Jane later that day. "This is so unfair to all the people for whom America was a dream and who are deported every day for no reason other than that they have no money. It's unfair to you too. You should have been able to sue him. The damage he did to you is huge: months of mental torture! He should pay for this. I'm sure his parents have money."

For a professor to be fired in the middle of his contract was exceptional. This was the most serious sanction possible. Jane couldn't help wondering what Duportoy would do next year. She remembered Jamaica's eyes and she felt guilty. Should she have dropped the complaint? But the prospect of sitting next to Duportoy at a faculty meeting and running into him in the halls was unbearable.

The news exploded a few days later: Duportoy had been hired by the New School in Manhattan. The procedure had been kept secret because, for budgetary reasons, nothing was certain until he signed the contract; a tenure-track position, in one of the most interesting schools, in Greenwich Village, in Manhattan.

Lynn was enraged. Duportoy had a file at Devayne indicating that he had been fired and this file was publicly accessible, but who cared? A purely symbolic punishment. Duportoy had probably already forgotten about the humiliating disciplinary hearing. Right now he must be celebrating, drinking French champagne. Soon he would be boasting about terrorizing stupid Devayne professors who needed a good fuck. It was just too easy.

Jane shrugged her shoulders. "It's OK, I don't care. I just don't want to see him anymore."

Three nights later Lynn knocked at Jane's door. There was a sparkle of excitement in her eyes. "Do you have a moment?"

Jane followed her into the living room. Lynn sat on the sofa, and Jane on the armchair.

Lynn smiled happily and looked about the room. "Each time I see this rug I think that you were really inspired to buy it. It gives a soul to this room. Can you make me a gin and tonic?"

She was building up the suspense on purpose. Jane came back with two gin and tonics.

"What's going on?"

It didn't have to be about Duportoy. There were other things going on in the world. Last night Lynn had talked about a woman she was now counseling. This woman had adopted a baby boy fourteen years ago after trying to have a child for ten years, and she had brought him up alone after her husband had left her. Two years earlier she had found out that her constantly sick child had AIDS. It had been a terribly difficult decision to sue the adoption agency, which had known about the baby's condition and hadn't told her. The message she risked sending to her son, the only love in her life, was that, had she known, she wouldn't have adopted him. But the boy was bright and courageous: he understood, and he stood close by his mother.

"I remembered you saying that he taught at Smith before coming here, and I have a friend whose partner is teaching there."

He. So this was about Duportoy. Jane leaned forward.

"I just heard an interesting story," Lynn continued. She drank some of her gin and tonic. "Did you know that Duportoy was fired there too?"

"Fired? No; he just accepted an offer from Devayne."

"Yes. He was a little more cautious there than he has been here. Indeed, he waited until he had signed his contract with Devayne before playing his little joke."

"His little joke?"

"Anonymous phone calls," Lynn said in a calmly triumphant voice.

"To a first-year undergraduate student—a fat, shy eighteen-year-old girl with eating disorders. She got completely terrified."

Jane gasped. Lynn drank more gin and tonic.

"Her name is Amber Martin," she resumed. "She had taken his class in the first semester. Apparently she had a crush on him. That's how he reciprocated. The police got him after they tapped the girl's phone. He obviously never called from home, nor from his office, but from a public phone."

Jane shook her head in disbelief.

"Duportoy had a gorgeous girlfriend at the time," Lynn continued, "an actress from New York, who visited him often. And this is what he did at night for fun: called a poor, terrorized fat girl, and breathed heavily into the phone. Do you see a pattern here? I don't mean a pattern in the choice of victims; there's nothing in common between this girl and you. But a pattern in the type of game. No? This is someone who likes jokes!"

She laughed. Jane was staring at her. "What are you going to do?"

"Let it be known."

"To whom?"

"The dean of the New School."

It took barely a week. On June 5, Lynn walked triumphantly into Jane's apartment. She was wearing her jeans and the red silk blouse. Jane was getting tired of the bright red and thought that she should have bought a softer color since Lynn never thought of changing clothes. She just washed her blouse at night and wore it again in the morning.

"They canceled his contract."

"They did!"

"A friend of mine, who teaches in the women's studies department, talked to the old guy who hired Duportoy, William Robinson. Last year her department wanted to hire a specialist in queer theory and a report from the same Robinson prevented them from doing it; she was delighted to have the opportunity to reciprocate. Robinson called the deans at Devayne and Smith. Then he had no choice but to talk to his own dean, who was categorical: impossible to hire Duportoy. Much too risky in the current climate. If anything happened, it would cost them millions; their liability could be proved. Mr. Robinson had to make a very sad phone call to our friend, who rushed to his office, offered to sign anything they would ask him to and to walk barefoot down Fifth Avenue with a wooden board around his neck reading SHAME ON SEXUAL HARASSERS, recited a hundred mea culpas, swore that he would never do such a thing in New York since it had only been because of the boredom he felt at Devayne and Smith, promised he would see a shrink three times a week, begged Robinson and, as a final dramatic act, cried. A Greek tragedy."

Jane didn't feel like laughing. She could see the scene. It made her uneasy. "How do you know all of this?"

"Secretaries."

Lynn helped herself to a glass of sherry and sat down at the dining-room table. Jane was standing at the kitchen counter, slicing zucchini. "What's going to happen to him now?"

Lynn smiled. "Do we care?"

"It must be terrible for him. It was the dream of his life. In one week he got the job and lost it: he must be desperate."

Lynn frowned. "Jane, you'll make me think that there really is something wrong with you. You mean you feel compassion for him? For *him?* My God! Have you already forgotten the moment when you wondered whether a serial killer was hiding in your bathtub?"

"I didn't know it was only a joke then. I was scared because of the attack in September. Duportoy didn't know. Now I'm fine. But what we're doing to Duportoy isn't a joke."

Lynn paced the floor between the living room and the kitchen space where Jane was cutting her third zucchini. She finished her glass of sherry. She sighed. Then she stopped and faced Jane. "Jane."

Jane turned toward her and blushed. Lynn was looking at her with angry eyes; her voice wasn't friendly either.

"What do you call a joke, exactly?" she said slowly, in a calm and severe voice. "Terrorizing a fat girl for the rest of her life—that's a joke, OK. What about threatening a woman with a knife in her neck? After all, that guy didn't really do anything to you either. Does it stop being a joke only when the girl commits suicide or the woman is raped and murdered?"

Jane was biting her inner lip. Maybe Lynn was right. But she was so sure of being right.

"You know what?" Lynn continued. "Use your imagination. Try to realize how you would feel right now if they hadn't caught Duportoy, instead of telling me that I shouldn't have found out about his first joke and that it would be perfectly fine if he got away with the whole thing."

"I never said that."

Jane went on slicing the zucchini, in silence. Lynn put her glass on the table and walked toward the door.

So that was it. Another chapter in her life was over. She and Lynn were just too different. Their friendship could last only as long as Jane needed help. A few weeks ago Lynn had taken Jane to a lecture about sexual harassment in the workplace at the Devayne Law School, a speech given by a famous feminist, an activist, not an intellectual—a hot topic since the president's affair with a White House intern filled the front pages of the newspapers. When Jane heard the feminist describe the hardship of beaten, raped, and tortured women all over the world, in a broken voice constantly on the verge of tears, she felt terribly guilty for not having enough imagination or compassion to devote her life to the victims of injustice in the world. As she walked out, though, she couldn't help thinking that the charismatic speaker was also a dangerous fanatic and that a world in which there was no place for jokes and subtle colors was terrifying. "She's fantastic, isn't she?" Lynn was saying. More and more often, Jane was lying to Lynn by her silence. Now, thanks to Duportoy, everything was clear. Lynn would despise her. They would never talk again. They would run into each other in the foyer and ignore each other, like Jane and Jamaica in the department's corridors. Why did Jane lose all her friends, one after another? Was the trouble with her or with her choice of friends? Lynn had her hand on the doorknob already.

"Are you going?" Jane asked with anguish, looking up, the knife in her hand.

"The cats are waiting for their dinner."

Lynn walked back to the kitchen and softly pinched Jane's cheek while shaking her head with a smile. "You!"

There wasn't a trace of anger in her voice.

She called the following night. "I have good news for you, sweetheart: your little friend has more than one trick up his sleeve. He was also granted an NEH fellowship for next year. No strings attached to it and a lot of money. He won't starve. You don't have to worry."

As Jane put this last page on top of the thick stack to her left, she shivered.

Lynn could have written this chapter: she had all the facts. But Jane knew it wasn't Lynn, or Chip, or Josh. She was staring ahead, pale. She picked up the brown envelope on the other side of the dining table and looked at the handwritten address. She had seen the scrawl before—in a postcard Jamaica had shown to her. She looked at the words "Old Newport." She remembered his peculiar *d* with its straight line ending with a curve to the left. Now she could even see some resemblance with the disguised handwriting of the anonymous notes.

A scratching noise startled her. Someone was trying to open her apartment door. She got up and walked silently into the corridor. The bolt was pushed. She looked through the peephole. She couldn't see anyone, but there was a presence behind the door, she was sure. Her heart was pounding. Impossible. He was dead. Or was his suicide a joke too?

"Meoow!"

She laughed nervously.

Even though his love of jokes and anonymous letters made Xavier Duportoy an obvious suspect, she hadn't considered him earlier, simply because he was never a friend and couldn't know anything about her—at least directly. Earlier she had told herself that Francisco could have learned what happened to her from Jamaica via Duportoy, even after he left for Spain. She simply had to reverse the proposition.

From Francisco, Duportoy had gotten precise information about Bronzino, Josh, Eric, and Francisco himself. There were incidents like her little fling with Torben, for instance, that she had told nobody but Francisco. From Jamaica, Duportoy had learned all that concerned Allison, Lynn and Chip. If he had met Josh in New York, he had certainly made him talk too. And there was nobody in a better position than Duportoy to write the whole chapter she had just read.

So he could have gathered all the facts. But how did he guess her most intimate thoughts? In the beginning, she sometimes felt as if she were reading about a stranger, although the facts were accurate. But the more she advanced in the book, the more she recognized herself in the mirror that was presented to her: these were her words, her thoughts, her feelings. This resemblance was eerie. She felt that the anonymous writer had stolen her soul, dispossessed her of herself. If Xavier was the author—and she had no doubt he was—then he knew her better than any of her friends or lovers ever had.

Could Duportoy have hacked into her e-mail account and read her correspondence with Alex?

Jane had a funny sensation. It wasn't hunger. She was breathing fast. There was a weight in her stomach. She felt like throwing up. It was fear. For seven hours now she had been reading a posthumous letter. Duportoy had spent the year writing this manuscript, and he had sent it to her just before killing himself a few days ago. Why?

She looked at the remaining pages—a very small pile now, which probably contained the answer.

If only Alex were back. She had to tell him everything: he would find the right words to reassure her.

3

Jane got to the corner of the rue des Abbesses and stopped, dazzled: the whole street was dancing. A spontaneous ball. Four black men with South African hats, seated at the café just across the street from her building, were playing drums. The street was so crowded that no car could get through. Screams and laughter rose from the crowd. *"Et un! Et deux! Et trois! Zéro!"* *"On aaaa ga-gné!"* *"Zizou!"* *"Allez Zizou!"* *"Zi-zou président!"* Jane recognized the nickname of the Arab player who had made France the world soccer champion by scoring two goals with his head. She had never seen such a public display of joy. Men and women, Arabs and French, cops and illegal immigrants—all were hugging and kissing. Earlier on TV the whole nation had seen the cold and distinguished French president, overwhelmed with emotion, climb onto a wall and kiss the bald head of the goalie.

Jane had felt too tired to follow Rosen, Vincent and Mylène to the Champs-Élysées, where there would be a national celebration party tonight. Anyway, the real party was here, in her street. The music was fantastic. She couldn't help moving her hips and her legs as she pushed the buttons on the keypad to the side of her building door. Before she had opened the door, a man took her hand and dragged her along. All the rhythms she had learned this year in the African dance class instinctively came back to her. Men around her were brushing her skin, touching her breasts, rubbing themselves against her and she didn't mind. She felt completely safe in this lively neighborhood.

It was almost 3 A.M. The waiters were putting tables and chairs inside the cafés, cleaning terraces and sweeping the sidewalks. The crowd started to disperse, leaving by foot, car, bike or motorcycle. Jane kept dancing. She suddenly spotted a young man leaning against a tree; a baseball cap hid his forehead, and large white clothes floated on his thin body. He wasn't tall and his hair was rather long. An artist, she thought. He smiled at her. He had sweet eyes. She put out a hand. *"Vous dansez?"*

He didn't seem to understand.

"Do you dance?"

She took his hand and he yielded gracefully, break dancing in front of her, his body articulated like a puppet's, spinning around, pointing his fingers up and down, as flexible as rubber, just like a teenager earning his living to the sound of a rap tape on Washington Square. She felt dizzy. Out of breath, she leaned against the same tree while he danced for her, looking at her, then taking her hand and making her dance with him again, more softly. When he smiled, his velvet eyes were smiling too. They danced, slowly, body against body and lips against lips, until the musicians stopped playing. It was dawn, the sky brightening. They sat on a bench on the Place des Abbesses and chatted. He was from Israel. "Israel!" she exclaimed excitedly. He had arrived from Ireland the night before to see the final in France, and he was leaving this morning for Tel Aviv. He had been traveling in Europe for a month already with three friends whom he had lost earlier in the crowd. Did four guys traveling together meet lots of women on the road? she asked with a smile. He had nothing against the idea. He had broken up with his girlfriend—they had met in the army three years earlier—just a few weeks before leaving on that trip. He hoped that he would meet a beautiful Norwegian girl, have some fun and forget about his love sorrow. But it had not happened.

He was twenty-two years old. A student in engineering. He didn't ask her how old she was. Kisses often interrupted their conversation. She told him she was renting an apartment just two minutes away. He looked at his watch.

"I must leave for the airport in half an hour. Are you inviting me in for a coffee?"

He had the full lips of a very young boy. She blushed.

"I don't want to make love," she said. "Is this OK with you?"

"Perfectly fine."

Inside her apartment, they started kissing again. They fell on the sofa in the living room. Jane suggested they go to the bedroom. They undressed. His skin was amazingly soft, his chest hairless. His gestures had a tenderness and slowness unexpected from such a quick and energetic hip-hop dancer. She moaned when his fingers touched the upper part of her thighs. She leaned over him and took his hard, circumcised penis in her mouth. There was a drop at the tip of the penis's pink head. He reversed her suddenly, almost brutally, got on top of her and quickly penetrated her. She gasped. She was like a virgin after all this time. A foreign body inside, forcing the entry, was a dazzling sensation. It hurt. His big, almond-shaped eyes with long eyelashes and soft black pupils were fixed upon her face with an almost sadistic intensity of desire. She suddenly relaxed and let him invade her. He closed his eyes for one second and opened them again, slowly moving sideways inside her.

"Can I come inside you?" he whispered.

No, she thought. Too dangerous. AIDS, ovulation. It could be just the right moment. Maybe he lied to her about having no affair since he broke up with his longtime girlfriend. Yet she trusted him. His velvet eyes. She closed hers without answering. With a gasp, he tore himself away from her and spat his white semen on her belly. She caressed his hair, softly.

"You didn't come," he said.

"I'm fine."

He lay beside her and gently caressed her. He seemed to know exactly the movements and the contact she liked. She pulled her legs more open. He slipped between her thighs. His soft hair was tickling her skin as his tongue was probing her. She came, closing her thighs tightly around his head.

He had to leave. No time for a coffee. He had spent one hour instead of half an hour in the apartment. He hoped that his friends would have thought of taking his backpack from the hotel. She showed him a map, explained to him how to get to the airport with the express train, and, still naked, walked him to the door. He kissed her lips. She looked from very close at his eyes, full of softness and gravity. Israeli eyes. With his baseball cap back on his head, he looked barely eighteen.

"Thanks for letting me come to your place. It's the first Parisian apartment I've seen."

He ran down the stairs. Still naked, she walked to her living-room window and leaned against the wrought-iron balcony. She saw him run away toward the Pigalle subway entrance. She didn't even know his name. A dog barking ferociously on the sidewalk across the street broke the perfect stillness of the early morning. The cafés weren't open yet and most shops remained closed on Monday. In front of the threatening dog, a young man was slowly getting on his knees while looking at the dog and trying, with slow gestures, to unlock his bike parked against the wall. The Doberman belonged to a homeless man who slept every night in front of the Arab grocery store and who was now deeply asleep, not disturbed at all by the furious barking of his dog, which seemed ready to bite the young man. The courageous cyclist managed to get up, sit on his bike and glide down the street while the dog ran after him, barking. Jane closed her window and went to sleep without taking a shower. When she woke up around noon, the sperm on her belly had formed a translucent crust that pulled the tiny, invisible hairs on her skin. Silent couples with sunglasses were eating croissants on the terrace of the café across the street. She took her teacup and her grilled bread to the living room and sat at the window. An old lady was singing Edith Piaf songs in a broken and derailed voice. Jane thought of Duportoy and felt almost grateful. Not for the prescription to get laid—even though the treatment was quite pleasant—but rather because a huge fear was still the best way to stop a painful hiccup, meaning the recurrent memory of Eric that had obsessed her and prevented her from seeing the world around her for more than a year.

When she came home after six weeks in Paris, she felt like a stranger in her own country. Everywhere there was but one topic of conversation: whether the president of the United States would fall because of a blow job. Americans had never before been so interested in politics. It was an absurd and amazing waste of time and money. Clinton made her think of Duportoy: two brilliant and smooth talkers who, at the peak of success, committed self-destructive acts that made them strangely likable.

In October she wrote nine job letters. By late December six of the nine universities had called her to schedule an interview at the MLA convention; she had targeted well. The convention would take place in San Francisco, and she got a room in the hotel she wanted, the Marriott near the Marina. She loved that city. She would fly to Seattle, spend New Year's Eve with Allison and John and meet Jeremy's little sisters.

The interviews went well. She gave a paper, "Blindness and Insight in *La Princesse de Clèves*," which was a success and was followed by a storm of questions. She went to the cocktail party organized by Devayne the following night and was congratulated by many people there. Some of the interviewers were now courting her—an enviable position. A short, thin man walked up to her.

"Jane, your talk was fantastic."

"Thanks."

His face looked familiar, but she couldn't put a name to it. She had seen so many interviewers in the last three days. A short guy with a high forehead going bald, and glasses—nothing to distinguish him from many others in the profession.

"In spite of the title, it didn't sound like a revival of the Devayne School of new criticism. What you do is closer to Gadamer's hermeneutics, right?"

Irritating not to be able to identify him. As he talked, he brought his face near hers. She didn't like his breath, a mixture of coffee, cigarettes, old books and stomach acidity. She saw the bad teeth and then she knew: he was the guy with a Devayne Ph.D., David.

"How is Eric doing?" she asked, to show that she had recognized him.

"Great. A good year for him. His book on the Vienna School came out this fall. He just got tenure, and he's expecting a child."

"Expecting a child?" she repeated as if she didn't understand.

"Well, his girlfriend, Catherine. It's still very recent."

"Cat. . . ."

Jane turned white. She couldn't say a word. She was staring at him with dilated pupils.

"Oh my God, you didn't know? Jane, I'm sorry, I'm so indiscreet! I understood you were the one who left Eric—this is what Catherine told me, she's my colleague. I'm really sorry, excuse me. . . ."

Catherine. He had pronounced it in the French way, with the stress on the last syllable: "Katrin." He was looking at her with the voyeuristic compassion of someone witnessing a fatal accident. He reached out and touched her arm in an awkward gesture. She stepped backward. She bit the inside of her lip and in an amazing effort she managed to force herself to smile. Her cheeks were hot.

"Of course I knew. I mean about Catherine. I didn't know yet she was pregnant, but it's not surprising at all. What could be more normal?"

She laughed too loud. David was still looking at her with the same mixture of sadistic interest and pity.

"Catherine is French, right?"

"Yes."

"From Paris?"

"Yes. Do you want something to drink? I'm sorry to have been so indiscreet. I'm really confused. I was convinced. . . ."

"Excuse me," Jane could barely utter before running out of the crowded room.

She found the toilets at the end of the corridor. She locked herself into one and burst into tears. She couldn't believe it. That Eric was expecting a baby. That she had just reacted with a violence that revealed her naked heart to herself first, and then to a curious, malevolent and indiscreet stranger who was delighted he had had such a powerful effect on her and would now gossip about it, reporting everything to Eric and his new companion. Was she crazy? Eric going out with another woman was perfectly normal. They had been divorced for almost two years and they hadn't talked in all that time. It was over. She knew it. She had a great time in Paris, and she returned to Old Newport with fresh energy, ready to start a new life. How could she be so weak? The baby? Everyone had babies, it was the most banal thing in the world, Eric would have plenty of them and enjoy a banal life with his wife and kids in boring Iowa. She slapped herself hard. Two women walked into the bathroom, chatting, forcing her to stop her sobbing and self-punishment. She left the toilets, washed her face at the sink and slipped out of the Hilton, giving up her original plan to meet at the Devayne cocktail party faculty members of the universities from which she wished to receive job offers.

Back in Old Newport, she was busy teaching and transforming her MLA talk into a chapter for her new book, immersing herself in her work to stop thinking of Eric and his new family. In mid-January she found an e-mail message entitled "Fan" from a certain Alex Letterman who introduced himself as an assistant professor of French literature at the University of California in San Diego. He had attended her talk at the MLA convention but hadn't dared to approach her afterward, as there were many people surrounding her. He had never heard anything as inspiring since he chose this profession nine years ago. She had reminded him why he wanted to be a professor of literature. He was impressed both with her personal involvement in the questions she asked and her rigorous linguistic analysis of every instance of the words "to know oneself," "knowledge," "insight," and "awareness" in *La Princesse de Clèves*. Did she use the ARTFL research program? Finally, he hoped that he would soon have the pleasure to read that text in an article or in a book.

That was a pleasant message. Jane took down the program of the MLA convention in San Francisco from a shelf and looked at the alphabetical list of participants at the end. No Letterman. Which merely meant that he didn't give a paper or chair a session. She got up and walked down to Dawn's office. "Dawn, do you have the MLA directory?"

The secretary picked up the light-blue book on the shelf behind her. She handed it over to Jane and pointed a threatening index finger at her. "I want it back."

"I just need to check something. I can do it right here."

Letterman, Alex. His name was there, with his affiliation: University of California at San Diego. Followed by his e-mail address. She closed the directory and gave it back to Dawn.

It wasn't paranoia. Letterman was such an appropriate name that it sounded almost like a joke, and you heard horrible stories of men meeting women online, getting their address and then raping and killing them. She smiled. Just slightly paranoid. Back in her office she did something else, out of curiosity this time. She checked Letterman's name in the library's online catalogue. Nothing. Then she opened the online MLA bibliography. There was one title: an article on humor in Chrétien de Troyes's *Lancelot*. He was a medievalist, probably just starting his career. She answered his message and thanked him; this talk was indeed part of a work in progress but still at an early stage; she hadn't used ARTFL: she preferred the archaic and slow method that consisted of reading the novel ten times and collecting words in their context.

The following day there was a new message from Alex Letterman. Re: Flaubert. He had found all her articles at the library and just finished the one on the argument between Flaubert and Colet around the Corneille statue and the word "glory." He agreed with Flaubert's conception of art but thought that his treatment of poor Louise wasn't the most gentle. It was well known that all geniuses were awful people to live with. He was highly interested in Jane's work on Flaubert, as he had written his dissertation on misogyny in the Middle Ages. Jane replied immediately and mentioned she had a book coming out soon.

She would have been curious to read his article, but she really didn't have the time. This was the last message between them anyway. E-mail proved to be an amazing waste of time: many graduate students who complained about having no time to finish their dissertations spent two or three hours on e-mail every day, corresponding with their friends throughout the States. It took Jane one hour every afternoon to read and answer her professional mail, mostly messages from Dawn and Rose. People didn't talk anymore. She would run into Rose in the corridor, go back to her office and find a message from Rose reminding her about some form.

Five of the universities that had interviewed her at the MLA convention had called and invited her to visit their campus. She was now preparing her trips. A few days later there was a new message from Letterman about another of her articles. She was pleased to see his name and to read his message. She sent him a brief reply: she was on the point of leaving for a series of on-campus interviews and she was extremely busy—a nonoffensive way of saying that she wouldn't answer anymore in case he wrote again. He did write again, in the very next minute, which meant that he was also facing his screen at this very moment at the other end of the country. Only 7:30 A.M. in San Diego; the man got up early. Did he turn on his computer before drinking his coffee? Did he leave his computer on all night? In any case, he certainly had e-mail at home, unlike Jane, who wanted to protect her mornings at home from electronic invasion. His was a brief message: since she would spend time on the plane, he recommended *Paulina 1880* by Pierre-Jean Jouve.

That night she went to Goldener Library to check out the French novel. She started it the following day, not on the plane but in her overheated room at the faculty club in Madison, Wisconsin. She put it down only after she had read the last words at five in the morning. Totally unreasonable, when she needed all her energy for a day of interviews that started at 7 A.M. At dinner that day, she couldn't help talking with enthusiasm about that love story, as sensual as it was spiritual, taking place in Florence in the nineteenth century. The chairman, who knew the novel, sounded very pleased that Jane had literary interests outside her field. When she came back from that first trip, she wrote a message to Alex: not only did she love the novel but it also proved useful professionally.

"I knew you would love it," he wrote back immediately. "Have you read *Childhood*, by Nathalie Sarraute?"

A few years back she had tried another novel by the famous French writer and got bored after fifty pages. Jane, who had been a victim of the terrorism of "good" literature when she was going out with Josh, who thought she was stupid because she could never read *Ulysses* in its entirety, didn't like novels that were too "intelligent" or reading advice that could become dictatorial. She didn't write this to Alex Letterman, though. She had no intention of starting a discussion on literature with him; her arguments would certainly be weaker than his, but her opinion would not be changed by his superior rhetoric. She borrowed *Childhood* from the library, but she didn't read it during her next trip. Back in Old Newport she found a message from Alex inquiring about the on-campus interview without mentioning Nathalie Sarraute. His discretion was the reason why she opened the book the same night.

Not a book to swallow in one night like *Paulina 1880*. You savored *Childhood* more slowly. Jane would read a fragment, stop, think about it and read it again, paying attention to the precision of every word—the same perfection as Flaubert: muscled sentences; a child was rising, alive, between the lines; words resurrecting life instead of betraying it. Jane was bewildered, not only that she loved the book but also that there was someone out there who knew exactly the kind of book she would love. Someone who had the same sensibility—no, that word was too vague, too romantic. Someone who had the same expectation of words, the same love of truth, if one could call "truth" the exact rendition of the movements of a human mind, which were so subtle and delicate that words could only give an approximate caricature of them.

The Princess of Clèves was also one of Alex's favorite novels. He was interested in the way desire circulated in the novel, and he thought that the queen, in love with the Duke of Nemours and jealous of the Princess of Clèves, played a perverse role between the two lovers. Jane disagreed. They had an argument during the course of several messages, using quotes from the novel as evidence.

"Nemours's indifference to her doesn't hurt the queen," Jane wrote, "she can't love him!"

It was strange to have such a heated debate about the feelings of characters in a seventeenth-century novel. Jane remembered what Eric had said about the possibility of an intellectual exchange outside Devayne. She was so surprised and proud of her correspondence that she couldn't help mentioning it once, just after sending her daily message to Alex, as she was standing next to Edwin Sachs in the Xerox room. It suddenly occurred to her that Sachs was a medievalist too. Did he know Alex Letterman? she asked.

"Letterman? Yes. I remember. He read an excellent paper on *Lancelot* at the annual medievalist convention in Minneapolis last spring."

"Really?" Jane exclaimed, all excited, without daring to ask what Alex looked like.

"Have you read *The Lover,* by Marguerite Duras?" Alex asked in mid-February. She had, a long time ago. "Read it again." He had something to tell her.

She reread it in two days: another good surprise, since she'd thought she was tired of Duras's novels, which she had to teach so many times in French classes. Alex had just heard a talk at his university by a certain Natalie Hotchkiss whom Jane probably knew since she was her colleague. When Jane saw the name of Hotchkiss, she had an uneasy feeling—of jealousy, maybe. She read the message with even more vivid interest. Hotchkiss, Alex wrote, argued that Marguerite Duras had become a writer in order to overcome the trauma she had experienced as a child when her family had sold her to a rich Chinese man who had raped her repeatedly. Alex had never heard anything so stupid. American feminists should be barred from interpreting French novels. Jane laughed, delighted.

"From the first moment Duras is the one deciding," Alex wrote. "She is fifteen, she's never slept with a man yet, but she knows 'that.' The moment when she knows exactly, before even experiencing it, the nature of sexual relationship, the moment when her awareness of her own power magnetically attracts the Chinese man toward her, this is when she becomes a writer. It's not a trauma at all."

They only wrote each other about novels or films. She knew nothing about Alex Letterman's life and she didn't ask. From message to message they became closer simply because their constant agreement confirmed their affinities. The correspondence structured their days. Having some-one to address gave a new dimension to everything she did. As she was flying back to Old Newport at the end of her ten-day trip to New Or-leans, Salt Lake City, and Tucson, Arizona, on March 3, she was thinking of the message waiting for her at the office. Instead of preparing her re-placement classes for the following day, she was mentally composing sen-tences that would give him the most accurate and funny image of her adventures in the Midwest.

She had to wake up early on Thursday morning to prepare her three classes at the last minute. She barely had time to swallow cornflakes be-fore running downstairs at 12:57 P.M. and pedaling as fast as she could toward the university. An old lady was crossing Market Street one tiny step after another, leaning on an empty grocery cart that helped her keep her fragile balance. The light turned green before she had reached the middle of the street. Drivers waited patiently. Her brown wig wasn't straight on her head. Jane smiled. If she felt so good, it wasn't because of the bright sun and crisp air, certainly not because of the five hours of teaching ahead, and not even because in all likelihood she would get a job offer. But the day, like this old lady, was slowly and surely moving to-ward the moment when she would turn on her computer and see Alex's name appear among others.

When she finished teaching, at six, she was so exhausted she decided to go swimming. It was torture to immerse herself in the cold water, but she had the pool to herself, a luxury. She swam for half a mile. It was dark when she walked out, all dry, warm and relaxed. She rode her bike to the office and picked up her mail downstairs. In about three minutes she would find Alex's message. She was in no hurry even though her jubila-tion increased as the goal of her day was getting closer from second to second. She smiled, remembering her father's trick when she was little and didn't want to clean her plate: "Divide your food into two portions; first you eat the one you don't want, then the rest." She leafed through the stack of mail as she was waiting for the elevator and put aside three envelopes that looked more personal than the messages from the admin-istration or the colorful advertisements she wouldn't even open. A letter from her publisher, and two where her name and address were written by hand, one with a letterhead from the University of Miami at Coral Gables and the other, a plain envelope without letterhead, which had been mailed in New York.

In the elevator she opened the letter from Florida: an invitation to be the keynote speaker at the annual convention of the Society of Francophone Studies that was taking place in Hawaii in late May. The organizer of the conference had heard her talk at the MLA convention and loved it. This was Jane's first invitation of the kind. Only well-known professors were invited to give keynote lectures and her book wasn't even out yet. This must be the beginning of fame. All expenses paid and a fee of $500. A free trip to Hawaii. She opened the letter from New York. A two-page typed letter that started with the words "Dear Jane." She turned to the second page to look at the signature. Xavier Duportoy. She was startled. She had completely forgotten about him. She quickly read the letter as she walked from the elevator to her office.

He apologized again for the harm he had done to her. He felt deeply sorry. It had been a stupid and evil joke, and even more. He was seeing a shrink twice a week and he now understood that there was something wrong with him.

I lost the one job I wanted, in Manhattan. I blame nobody but myself. I wanted that job so badly that the day when I was supposed to go there for an interview, last February, I was hospitalized with a fever of 106, for which the doctors found no cause. I'm sure that the cause was only my terror of not being good enough to get the position at the New School. That's how much I wanted that job. There won't be another one like that. I lost my chance to live in New York and to have a fascinating job. My fault, I know. This is just to tell you that you got your revenge. Many days I wake up and cry. I still can't believe what happened. Every day I curse myself. Only myself, believe me.

Now I'm just asking for the right to live. This may sound very dramatic. But if I don't find an academic job, I won't survive next year. There is nothing else I know how to do, and nothing else I feel like doing. I love teaching, I love reading, I love literature. I don't care about money, I don't care about a career. I just would like to be able to do what I care about.

I applied for many jobs this year and I got many interviews at the MLA convention. . . .

Jane shivered. He was at the MLA meeting? She was lucky not to have run into him.

. . . then I was invited for several on-campus interviews. But secretaries in all six places called me again a few days later and canceled the invitation. I tried vainly to reach the chairperson in each of these places. What happened is clear: someone warned them against me. Gossip spreads: soon everyone will know and I will never be able to get a job anywhere.

Maybe you think that I should go back to France. But I can't get a job there either. I never passed the entrance exams of the French elite schools, and I don't even hold a master's degree from a French university. I published an essay on de Sade with a good publisher, but this doesn't help at all inside the French system. I couldn't even teach in a French high school.

I beg you, Jane: please, let me get a job and survive. I will stay in a remote corner of the United States and you won't ever hear about me again. I swear to you. Take pity on me. Stop the phone calls.

This didn't sound like Duportoy at all. It sounded sincere. Jane was no longer in the mood to check her e-mail. It was 8 P.M. She rode her bike home and rang Lynn's bell in her basement apartment.

"Hi, Jane! Did you have a good trip?"

The big gray cat immediately came to rub itself against Jane's leg. She walked into the messy living room and handed over the letter to Lynn, who read it quickly and gave it back to Jane.

"Don't you think it's enough now?" Jane asked.

Lynn shook her head and smiled. "Back at square one. He should hire you as his lawyer—after committing a crime."

The cat jumped onto an armchair in order to be closer to Jane's jacket.

"There is something right about his claim," Jane said. "He has been really punished. You can't prevent him from getting a job. You don't strike a man on his knees who begs you for his life."

She sneezed and pushed the cat away.

"It's funny how this cat always sticks to you," Lynn said. "Usually he doesn't want to come near anyone. He's extremely independent, even more than Lara. He must sense your resistance. Do you want something to drink? Orange juice or sherry?"

"No."

Jane sat on the old sofa, which was covered with a plaid blanket full of cat hair, and sneezed again. Earl Grey jumped up on her knees, took up a comfortable position and closed his eyes. He was fat and heavy. Jane pushed him away. Lynn sat down on the arm of the chair in front of Jane. She was higher up than Jane this way and looked down at her. She cleared her throat.

"Nothing you'll say can change my position, Jane. Maybe the experience you lack in order to understand what I'm talking about is that of mourning."

Jane made a sarcastic face.

"One single incident," Lynn resumed, "would have been different. But we're speaking of two incidents. I read this letter and, frankly, I don't think this guy understands the problem at all. He's very sorry to have lost his job in New York, I can see that. I'm sorry for him too, but, as he says himself, he has nobody to blame but himself. I don't mean his conscious self, but that weird thing in his quite deranged self that pushes him to play jokes and terrorize girls. I don't think he'll stop, and I don't want to risk it. I wouldn't be surprised if something happened in France too—why else did he stop his studies there? It's like pedophiles: they can be awfully sorry and aware of their wrongdoing, but they can't help it, it's stronger than themselves and society has to protect its children from them."

"I'm not a child, as far as I know. And he didn't do anything, I mean to the body of anyone."

"It's only a matter of time. I don't want to risk it. The proof that there is something wrong and disturbing about Duportoy is that you let any chairman know about his little jokes, and immediately this chairman loses any desire to hire him."

"Of course! Since—"

"Why?" Lynn interrupted her, raising her voice. "Because they see a pattern and they think of the young students they have to protect. I have nothing against Duportoy personally. As long as he doesn't teach undergraduates who might have a crush on him and inspire in him the desire to play a joke on them, whatever he does is fine with me. He could study law, become a literary agent, a pizza seller or a stock broker, make tons of money in real estate—I don't give a damn. By the way, I was just heating up some leftover four-cheese pizza. Do you want a slice?"

A closed matter. Jane declined the invitation. Upstairs she put the letter aside. The following afternoon, at the office, she turned on her computer and found a long message from Alex. Witty, funny, charming. He made her laugh. She didn't know him, yet he had become the closest person to her. She enjoyed a message from Alex infinitely more than a conversation with Lynn. If this correspondence stopped, there would be a huge hole in her life. She couldn't conceive of her life anymore without this exchange they had built from message to message over seven weeks and which rested on fragile ground. Writing masked, more than it revealed, the self; it showed only the part that was under control. If Jane saw Alex, she might lose at once any desire to speak to him. What if he was short and stout like Karl? Or bald, or chinless? What if she just didn't like his face, his smile or the expression in his eyes, even though he had all the right characteristics—fair hair, clear eyes, a chin of just the right size? Then all the words he wrote to her would lose their magic spell. She was actually addressing nobody but a narcissistic double. What she liked about Alex was his admiration for her. Sooner or later, and probably very soon, as soon as his shape became more precise, the correspondence that had enlightened her daily life for the past seven weeks would stop. It wasn't pessimism. Only realism. It made her sad.

This was exactly what she told Alex on the first day of spring break, after spending the weekend writing drafts. Alex hadn't sent a new message, following the implicit rule that the correspondence would stop as soon as one of them didn't feel like answering. No dependency, no duty. It was fun only as long as it remained free—as long as they had the desire to address each other. It went without saying that she would be the first one to lose this desire. The dynamic of the exchange: he had started it, he was the one interested in her, she was the one responding.

She felt hugely relieved when she clicked on SEND after spending one hour typing. She had told him everything that was on her mind, in terms as accurate and precise as the ones used by Nathalie Sarraute writing about her childhood. It was the most important and personal message she had ever sent him. Now it all depended on his reaction. She trusted him. He would understand her fear of seeing the correspondence end, and he would find a way to reassure her.

She went to the office on Tuesday, Wednesday, and Thursday, just to check her e-mail. No reply. Maybe he was thinking about it, as she had the previous week. Sad, these vacation days without hearing from him. She was getting nervous. What if he didn't like her message, precisely when she was more herself? Everything would be clear. On Wednesday she received an offer from the University of Utah in Salt Lake City. She wished she could let Alex know. He would laugh. She had already told him about her audience of serious blond men and women who were barely twenty-three years old and already married with three kids. Thanks, but no way she would bury herself among Mormons. This offer was useful, however, in making things move. She let the other universities know and, on Thursday, received a much more desirable call from the University of Wisconsin at Madison. She told the chairman of the French department at Louisiana State University in Baton Rouge: he called her back on Friday. A third offer. It was going very well. Still no message from Alex. She had to stop thinking about him and, instead, to concentrate on a choice that would decide her life. Louisiana or Wisconsin? She was talking with Lynn. Louisiana would be more of a real change. She had been charmed by the place, the food, the weather. But in Madison she had found her potential colleagues more interesting.

On Saturday around noon she went to the office. All of the doors were closed and all of the corridors empty. Even Begolu wasn't in her office. Alex's name appeared on her screen. Jane's heart jumped. She clicked on the name.

He had to confess that he was puzzled by her long message. The tone was so different from the former ones, so whiny and melancholy. What had happened to her? Didn't she enjoy their correspondence as it was? Why did she need to cry on its grave already? It would end when it would end. This "sic transit" and "memento mori" meditation about the inevitable end of best things in this world was irritating. Sorry if he didn't please her, but he liked the other Jane better, the one who proposed a fascinating reading of *The Princess of Clèves*. If her message simply meant that she was already tired of their correspondence, there was no need for a long eulogy, they could just stop it. Then he moved to another topic: how was the job search going?

Jane clicked on the next message, from Allison.

She was very sad. Alex understood nothing. She had credited him with too much sensitivity. He allowed her only one mood: funny, witty, in control. The rest he called "whining." He found her boring. It reminded her of Eric saying that there was no problem at all when she felt there was a problem, and affirming that it was only in her mind. Alex too was a man, with all the defects and defenses of one. To start with, he didn't listen.

She could live without him. And actually he might be right—this correspondence had started to feel heavy, like any dependency. Because of him, she had been neglecting all her friends. She hadn't even answered the woman who had invited her to Hawaii. It was time to get control again over her life.

She had to make her choice. It seemed to her that she would prefer Madison. She was originally from the Northeast and she enjoyed winter and the other seasons. The university there was rich enough intellectually to make up for the absence of a real city. New Orleans was the kingdom of jazz, but Jane had no passion for jazz. And New Orleans, by the way, was one hour away from Baton Rouge, which was rather inconvenient if you didn't drive. She would be more isolated in Louisiana, farther from the East Coast than in Wisconsin. The trouble with Madison was that it was too close to Iowa City. The trip from New York to Madison was about the same distance as the trip to Iowa City. She had also changed planes in Chicago. She was sick to her stomach when she got off the plane in Madison; she knew why.

"Go to Louisiana," Lynn said without hesitation. "You don't want to be that close to Eric, you're still too fragile. Your preferring Madison is actually suspicious."

Allison said the same thing: it wasn't healthy to be too close to Eric when she hadn't forgotten about him yet.

The deadline for calling back Madison was getting closer every day. She had chosen Baton Rouge, but she would wake up in the middle of the night sweating. Any choice was anxiety-provoking anyway. This was an important choice, since it decided where she would live for many years, maybe even for the rest of her life. If only she could go back to each of the places and check how she felt. The visits had been too quick—two days here and two days there. Swimming would have helped her to see clearer, but the pool was closed over spring break. Jane had to call Madison back on Friday. On Wednesday afternoon she took the bus to Fort Hale. On this foggy day, when water remained suspended in the air, the sky and the sea merged into a single soft gray color into which she walked as if entering a land from which she would never return. She found it soothing to look at the sea. She walked for two hours and breathed the salt air. It suddenly struck her that Alex was right. Why start envisioning the end? And if she couldn't help it, why let him know? Alex couldn't do anything about it. She had been piqued like a spoiled little girl to find he didn't admire every word coming out of her mouth. When she had sent her long message, she believed she would impress him with her lucidity. He hadn't been impressed—only surprised. He hadn't rebuffed her. Instead, he had expressed his surprise in a gentle way.

When she got off the bus at the corner of Main and Government, she walked straight to her office building. She wrote to Alex. Not about his reply. About the choice she had to make and her indecision. The following day there was an answer from him. He was asking her to describe as precisely as she could the moment when she got off the plane and her first conversation with the person who picked her up at the airport. She did.

In the evening there was a new message from Alex: "I don't understand: it's obvious you want to go to Madison."

The problem was Eric, whom she had not mentioned yet. Her next message was very long. She told everything: Eric, a whole chapter of her life, the fear that it wasn't closed in her mind yet, even though it was closed in fact. In Madison she had been trembling for two days, as if there was a chance she would run into Eric and his pregnant girlfriend. She feared that her desire to go to Madison was unconsciously motivated by Eric's geographical proximity. Everyone who knew her agreed that there was something self-destructive and masochistic about her.

"You're a big girl," Alex replied. "Iowa is adjacent to Wisconsin—so what? Don't listen to your fear; ghosts will turn into dust. You're not going to bury yourself in the Louisiana bayous simply because you're sure you won't run into your ex-husband there!"

Jane smiled. This was what she wanted to hear. Yes, she wanted to move to Wisconsin. In spite of Eric. Independently of Eric. To free herself from the past. She suddenly felt much lighter. When she called the chairman of the Madison French department two hours later, she didn't have even a shadow of a doubt.

It was April. The correspondence with Alex had changed radically. They were now writing about their personal lives. Jane talked about the men who had played a role in her life: Eyal, Josh, Bronzino (whom she didn't name), and Eric. She told him how meeting Eric had convinced her that love had to be based on physical desire, and how the failure of their love story had shaken all her convictions.

Alex didn't have many convictions either, and even fewer women in his past. He was twenty-four the first time he experienced sex. This was probably why he didn't become a writer like Marguerite Duras: he didn't know "that." He didn't even know whether he was attracted to men or to women. He had had two short affairs almost at the same time, one with a man, and one with a woman. Then, at a party, when he was twenty-six, he met a young Italian man named Luciano, as handsome as an angel with his short black hair, huge black eyes and long eyelashes. He fell in love at first sight. They started an affair that night and he found out that Luciano was a Luciana: the body of a boy, no hips, no breasts, but the sex of a woman. They were together for five years, until Luciana betrayed him with his best friend. He found out about it in an unpleasant way, as he had just come back from the job market and was looking for a nail cutter in Luciana's toiletry bag. The tube of spermicide cream that was still full the last time they made love three weeks earlier was now empty. Six months later he moved to San Diego. No affair in two years; Luciana had left him with a bitter taste in his mouth. He too was recovering. He was living in a small house on the seaside, with an adorable little dog, a creamy-white fox terrier that a woman friend had asked him to feed for three days just before leaving on a trip to Mexico from which she chose not to return.

"If I write a story one day, it will be about an old maid with her tiny dog or an old, silent peasant with his cat that follows him everywhere."

Jane thought of Begolu and her four dogs, of Lynn and her cats. The story was already written, she said: Felicité and her parrot in Flaubert's "A Simple Heart."

It was spring. Birds eating crumbs on the wet earth, grass growing, tender green leaves shyly appearing on naked branches, the first pink flowers on the magnolia tree next to her house, cherry blossoms forming a magnificent white lace arch on Columbus Square. Jane woke up smiling, kept addressing Alex all day long and read his message every night with an increasing joy. Spring fever? There was no spring in San Diego. He lived right on the beach. She had a dream in which she saw his second-floor study with a view of the sea from his desk. The house had only one floor, he replied. There was one major difference between them: he hated water and never went swimming.

He was thirty-three years old. She was an old lady by comparison, almost thirty-eight. He laughed at her. There was another important difference between them: he had seen her. He had fallen in love with her as soon as he saw her behind the table at the MLA meeting. If only she had seen him too. "I was sitting in the third row, last chair to the right, the closest to the door, in order to slip out discreetly if the session was boring. I'm tall. I was wearing a light blue shirt and a pair of jeans. I have a rather long face and short reddish-blond hair with sideburns."

Jane tried to remember. She had a vague memory of a rather handsome young man with whom she had made eye contact. But she was so nervous when she gave a talk that she never really looked at her audience.

"Well, it seems like I didn't catch your eye," Alex concluded. He wasn't worried. First, the room was very crowded. Second, what she called physical attraction wasn't merely physical or she would fall in love with any man who had the characteristics she liked. One fell in love with a body, with a face, yes, but a body in movement and a face looking at you, smiling at you. One fell in love with the spirit and energy that passed through the eyes or the smile and which were the essence of the self. The same spirit animated style. Maybe writing was controlled, but it was also the most personal thing there was in someone. After more than three months of corresponding almost every day, they couldn't say that they didn't like each other's writing. He wasn't trying to convince her that she would fall in love with him; of course they had to see each other. But he had trust. And if the magic spark didn't happen, he wouldn't mind. The best way to find out if she was attracted to him physically would probably be if he flew to Old Newport and met her without saying who he was.

Jane replied immediately; he had to promise never to surprise her that way or it was over. If she couldn't trust him on that, every day would be a nightmare. Each time she saw a young man she would wonder whether it was him and whether she had failed the test of passion. She hesitated to tell him about Duportoy, but decided not to betray the secret of a man whom Alex might meet one day. Two minutes later the computer beeped to signal a new message. Alex promised he would never fly to Old Newport without her agreement. Passion, by the way, wasn't a test, he added with a smile that she could see on the screen, so there was no risk of failure.

They were speaking about passion, about physical love, without ever having met. There was so much excitement in their messages now, so much desire to make love, so much exhausting tension, that Jane's teeth almost hurt when she turned on her computer. They never talked about sex. It wasn't that. Sometimes she wished there would be no computer and no e-mail. This expectation and the happiness each time she read a message from him were too intense. She was scared.

"I'm so exposed now," she wrote, "you have awakened in me such a huge desire to love and to be loved."

They had to meet—to face reality, to see if there was anything possible. Maybe one glance at him would destroy everything. They would remain friends then. Or nothing. It would be quite an experience anyway.

Where, when? Visiting each other was too risky. Alex suggested the conference in Hawaii. His university would reimburse his trip even if he didn't read a paper. Hawaii—an exotic, neutral, professional and romantic place. They were laughing. May 17 to 21. That was soon. He reserved his plane ticket and a hotel room, not in the same hotel as Jane because it was too expensive, but not far away. When Jane turned on her computer on May 6, she clicked on Alex's name after reading the other messages, as usual, for she always kept the best for last. His message was shorter than ever: "Hav to leave in emegrency. No access ot email for a littel wihle. Love."

Five spelling mistakes in two brief sentences. He must have typed this message very quickly, standing up, with his bag on his shoulder, while the cab for the airport was waiting outside. The word "emegrency" sounded dramatic. Did an accident happen to someone in his family? She had talked to him about her father but knew nothing about his family.

When she checked her e-mail over the next days, she was slightly disappointed but not surprised not to see his name on the list of message senders. She was thinking about him, wondering what happened and selfishly hoping that it wasn't something so serious that it would prevent him from coming to Hawaii. There would be other opportunities, but Hawaii was perfect. After five days of silence she grew more impatient. There was less than a week left before the trip to Hawaii. Maybe he didn't have a laptop, but you could rent a computer anywhere. Six days. Maybe he had to be with his mother every minute of the day and take care of his father's business. Maybe he couldn't leave the isolated house in the countryside even for one hour. If only she had thought of giving him her phone number: she wasn't listed anymore since the Duportoy incident. Maybe he didn't have one second to think about her right now—knowing, anyway, that they would be together in a few days to talk at leisure. Had she made it clear how much he counted for her independently from his physical appearance? Had she expressed too much fear at the idea of seeing him and realizing he wasn't her type? Could she have scared him?

She didn't send any message. She was afraid to betray her insecurity. She wasn't going to repeat the mistake she had made with Eric. She had to trust Alex and herself. If he wanted to stop the correspondence, he wouldn't have sent the last message. She had to accept what she could neither understand, nor control, nor even imagine. "Don't protect." In four days he would explain everything. Meanwhile she should read her paper again and make sure it was good. Alex would be in the audience.

She got so anxious that she finally looked for his department's number in the MLA directory on May 14. Her fingers were trembling when she dialed the number. She introduced herself as a Devayne professor trying to get in touch with Professor Alex Letterman. Devayne's name always impressed secretaries favorably.

"I'm sorry, but Professor Letterman isn't back from France yet," the woman said amiably. "He should return by the middle of next week. Do you want to leave a message?"

Jane sighed with relief when she hung up. He was in France, maybe in a small village where he really had no access to e-mail. Maybe he had a French friend there, dying of AIDS. That wasn't implausible. "By the middle of next week" meant after the trip to Hawaii. He had probably planned to fly to Hawaii directly after returning from France.

She was leaving early in the morning of the day after tomorrow. Here it was raining, but in Hawaii it would be sunny. She had to take out and iron her summer dresses. And she needed a new one-piece swimming suit. No way would she show Alex the belly of a thirty-eight-year-old woman. She passed Dawn's office.

"Jane, you're still here! Professor Bronzino was trying to get in touch with you. He would like to see you as soon as possible. He's at the Kramer Center until six."

It was already 5:25 P.M. and the stores closed at 6. She would buy the bathing suit tomorrow. She rode her bike down Garden Street, through the rain, and parked in front of the Kramer Center for European Studies, where she knocked at Bronzino's door.

"Come in."

She pushed open the door. His office here was smaller than the chairman's office in the department's new building, but it had an elegant European look with its wood-paneled walls, antique furniture and windows made of small squares of colored glass, like in a church. Bronzino was standing in front of his dark wooden shelves, sorting out books to make some space for the piles on his desk. He stepped forward and unexpectedly hugged her.

"Congratulations, Jane. I heard that you accepted an offer from Madison. It's a very good place. Maybe one day you'll be back here—if you wish. In any case, we'll miss you. I'll miss you."

The first personal words he had said to her in eight years. He seemed sincere, even though he certainly hadn't done anything to keep her at Devayne.

"I'll miss this good old town—and you too, for sure."

He took off his glasses and put them on the desk. He had completely changed his look. He now wore dark Calvin Klein suits and gray shirts without ties. No more countryside shoes with rubber soles, but a nice pair of Churches.

"Do you know that I'm going to be a father?"

"Really! Congratulations! When?"

So this was what he wanted to announce to her: revenge for what happened eight years earlier.

"The due date is mid-September. Poor Liz will have to go through the summer with a big belly. But we're excited."

She suddenly noticed that he had aged. His wrinkled skin looked almost yellow, his cheeks were hollow and he had bags under his eyes. Sixty-six years old—not so young to father a baby. His new wife must have insisted. A baby, a young woman to satisfy, teaching, writing books, directing the Center—and she had recently seen in the *Devayne Daily News* that he would be the dean of the Graduate School next year. The man was killing himself.

She was opening her mouth to congratulate him on the new nomination when Bronzino asked in a falsely casual voice: "Have you heard the news about Xavier Duportoy?"

She tensed. "No. What?"

"The poor fellow committed suicide."

"Suicide! Oh my God! When?"

Tears filled her eyes. Bronzino shook his head. "About a week ago."

"But why?"

"Why. . . . As you're in a good position to know, he wasn't exactly well balanced. Apparently his girlfriend, Jamaica Locke, broke up with him, and he also had some professional difficulties. It's really sad. Such a brilliant young man. He was barely thirty-five."

As she rode her bike home, Jane kept thinking about Duportoy. It sounded unbelievable that he had killed himself. So unlike the Duportoy she had known—who was looking at the world with an arrogant distance and ironic smile. But hadn't she been struck by the difference of tone in the letter he had sent her? The memory of the unanswered letter lying somewhere among her papers stabbed her with shame. She had just put the letter aside. Not her problem. She had enough to fill her life: the choice of a position, her correspondence with Alex. Duportoy was begging her; his life was at stake, he had said. She hadn't listened, hadn't answered—because she was a coward. She didn't agree with Lynn's radical methods but wasn't ready to confront her and lose a friend she still might need. Why was it that she had never talked to Alex about Duportoy? It wasn't discretion but guilt. Now he was dead. Not because of Jamaica. Because of two stupid little jokes that had become his fate.

She rang Lynn's bell and threw the news at her. "Duportoy killed himself."

She stood on the threshold in her raincoat dripping water and looked aggressively at Lynn.

"I'm sorry to hear that," Lynn said calmly. "I know what you think, Jane. But this only confirms what I thought: the man was capable of extreme acts. We can be grateful to him for turning his violence against himself."

"He wasn't even thirty-five years old."

The age at which Jeaudine had died too. Maybe Lynn thought it was only fair: an eye for an eye and a tooth for a tooth. Jane bit her lip in order not to add anything nasty.

She woke up late the following day, in an awfully bad mood, and heard the rain whipping the windows. She missed Alex terribly. There was a chance he had returned from Europe the night before and immediately sent her a message. She got dressed and took her bike key. As she closed the apartment door and walked down the stairs, her mood was darker than the black sky outside. What if there was no message? What if Alex had simply lost interest? What if he had met a woman ten days ago and followed her to France? A Frenchwoman. Damn all Frenchwomen—except for Rosen. She was crazy to be so anxious about someone she would meet tomorrow night for the first time and maybe not like.

Downstairs she found the package with the manuscript.

Jane was white and breathing with difficulty.

Duportoy was wrong about only one detail: she didn't take her bike key this morning because the streets were like swimming pools. He could have predicted the rain—if not the storm—by checking the weather forecast. But how could he have known, five days in advance, that Jane would be waiting for a message from Alex with increasing anxiety, deciding to buy a bathing suit for the trip to Hawaii, and, after hearing that he was dead, feeling terribly guilty for not answering his letter? Maybe she was totally predictable, but how could he have known that Bronzino would be the one to tell her about his suicide?

She put the final page on top of the thick stack of detached pages and saw, on the other side, a line written by hand. Blue ink, the same handwriting as her name and address on the envelope. She brought the page closer to her tired eyes: *"There is no copy of this text other than the one you have."* His handwriting and the direct address to her made his presence so real that she shivered, as if he were in front of her and he had touched her arm. She got up and put the manuscript in the drawer of her phone table near the stove.

It was almost 10 P.M. She placed two phone calls. The first to Bronzino, who confirmed what she suspected: two days earlier he had received a brief note from Duportoy asking him to personally let Jane know about his death. Norman apologized for respecting the last will of a dead man; he had seen nothing offensive to Jane in it and just thought that it was a delicate attention on the part of Duportoy, who had anticipated that his suicide would be a shock for her. Norman gave her details regarding the sorrow of Xavier's parents and the transport of the body to France that made it impossible to doubt the reality of his suicide. She learned something else: Duportoy had committed suicide in New York, but he had done some research in Los Angeles during the winter. Norman knew this from his colleague Peter Kolb, director of the Clark Library, who praised Duportoy highly and thought it was a real shame Devayne had let go of such a talented young man.

The second phone call was to Edwin Sachs. She apologized for calling so late and explained her situation: she was staying with friends in New York and leaving early tomorrow for a conference in Hawaii, which Alex Letterman was attending too. She had an urgent message to send him and didn't have his e-mail address with her. Did Edwin know it by any chance? By an extraordinary coincidence, Sachs had received a letter just that day from Jane's young protégé, inviting him to participate in an issue of *Stanford French Studies.* The e-mail address was on the letter. It was simple: Alex.Letterman@compuserve.com.

Jane had never sent a single message to that address. She shook her head and swallowed, with the feeling that her stomach was brutally emptying itself. But she must have known already. Otherwise she wouldn't have called Sachs to check Alex's address.

"Why not his university account?" she asked with an effort to repress the trembling of her voice.

"I think he didn't use his university account this year because it was slower to access from Lyon than a CompuServe account. As you know, he spent his whole sabbatical year in Lyon, for his research."

"That's right. I wasn't thinking."

After hanging up, she collapsed. Karl heard her scream. He alerted Lynn, who ran upstairs and tried unsuccessfully to open the door with her key—the bolt was shut.

Finally she threatened Jane, "If you don't open up, I'll call the police."

When Lynn learned who Alex Letterman was, she was so horrified that she wanted to exhume Duportoy to check whether it was really his cadaver. Jane had been going to meet "Alex" in Hawaii—to throw herself between the tiger's paws. Lynn was convinced she had saved Jane from a horrible death by pressuring Duportoy to the point where he felt completely trapped and committed suicide.

This was a man who had terrified a colleague and, one year later, borrowed someone else's identity to keep playing with this same woman. Duportoy had learned somehow that Letterman wasn't using his university account. He had easily gotten the password. Then it had been fun to rape Jane's soul a little more every day. A game that wasn't boring at all. Indeed, what could be more exciting than having his victim become love-obsessed with him, and ready to give herself passionately to him?

Even more exciting, he could watch the shock on his victim's face in the moment when she arrived in a taxicab at the deserted house on the cliff where he had set the meeting, rang the bell, and recognized him. Too late. He had already closed and locked the door behind her.

When he killed himself, they were a week away from acting out that scenario.

At first, Jane felt outrage, a burning rage against a man who had totally manipulated her and gotten control over every corner of her life and her soul. However, the more that Lynn expressed her fury and her satisfaction at having saved Jane, the more Jane's rage and humiliation melted. What was left was the anger at having been abandoned by a lover who had killed himself.

For it was love. The proof was there, between her hands: the manuscript. He knew everything about her, the kind of knowledge only love could give. Alex loved, if not Jane herself, at least that character he had created and which was amazingly close to her, as if he had somehow managed to inhabit her skin. Alex hadn't killed himself because Jamaica had left him, because he couldn't find a job for the next year or because he was mentally deranged. He had done it because there was no alternative: they couldn't meet in Hawaii nor anywhere else because it was impossible—because he was Xavier Duportoy.

She moved to Madison in July, rented an apartment flooded with light, with a view of the lake, and started teaching there in September. She bought a creamy-white fox terrier puppy, a playful and sensual creature begging for caresses on her soft belly. She named her Pauline. Her book on Flaubert discreetly came out in October. She had been told that it was an amazing experience, seeing your name on a book cover for the first time. When she received a copy of the book by mail, though, it didn't do anything to her.

She reread the manuscript, changed a few names, and wrote a beginning and an ending as well as passages describing her reaction to the reading. It came very naturally. The words were flowing. She could see Alex smiling over her shoulder. Alex-Xavier. Alexavier. He wanted her to do that, or why would he have sent the manuscript to her, with the disk and the little note saying that there was no other copy of the text? It was their novel. Their child together. His writing, his idea, his structure, his style, but her story—the flesh, the plot, details, everything came from their e-mail correspondence or from her own confidences to Francisco and Jamaica, which Xavier had gotten indirectly. She found out that he had met Josh in New York and they had become friends. She also learned, from Rosen, that Vincent knew Xavier. When she wrote the last word and then printed the whole thing with her name as the author, she burst into laughter. It was fun playing a joke and tricking the whole boring, serious world. Nobody would know. This was the secret she shared with Alexavier, who lived right here in her heart—knock-knock-knock.

In December she sent her manuscript to an agent whose name Josh gave her. She spent New Year's Eve in bed with the flu and a cup of ginger tea. It was sweet to spend a quiet evening at home, alone, while the entire world was celebrating the beginning of the new millennium. On February 21, 2000, she flew to New York and signed her contract with Simon & Schuster. They gave her $60,000. The agent promised he would get more next time. Jane laughed. The money she had received as a price for her academic book—$5,000—had seemed a huge sum.

The Story of Jane came out one year later. It took several years for academic books. Another world.

Whenever Jane typed her name on the library's online catalogue, under "Cook, Jane Elisabeth, 1961—," two titles now popped up.

The novel was reasonably successful. Jane's favorite review was that of a famous *New York Times* literary critic who concluded that the author's exquisitely feminine style contradicted the premises of the plot: there was no way to believe that this novel had been written by a man.

In October she received an enthusiastic message from David Clark. He was organizing a session on the contemporary American novel at the MLA convention in December and he wished to invite Jane as a guest of honor. She thanked him. A lingering curiosity made her ask him whether Eric's child was a boy or a girl and what was his or her name. David wrote back that Catherine had had a miscarriage and she and Eric were no longer together. He added that Eric, who had read *The Story of Jane* and liked it a lot, had asked David to give Jane his new phone number.

This last part of the message pleased Jane without moving her particularly. She was over him, finally. She was no longer angry. She felt something like compassion. Poor Eric had no luck. Yet his ambition, to start a family, wasn't excessive.

It was 6:10 p.m.—at this hour she had a chance to reach him at home. Why not now. Silence was not an ending; they needed to have a conversation at last.

She dialed his number. The ring made her wonder whether she would leave a message or not, and which one. Unable to decide, she was going to hang up when Eric answered. His voice shook her.

"It's me," she said.

"It's you."